A FUTURE ARRIVED

ALSO BY PHILLIP ROCK

The Extraordinary Seaman

The Dead in Guanajuato

Flickers

The Passing Bells

Circles of Time

A FUTURE ARRIVED

Phillip Rock

wm

WILLIAM MORROW

An Imprint of HarperCollins*Publishers*

This book is a work of fiction. References to real people, events, establishments, organizations, or locales are intended only to provide a sense of authenticity, and are used fictitiously. All other characters, and all incidents and dialogue, are drawn from the author's imagination and are not to be construed as real.

HarperCollins books may be purchased for educational, business, or sales promotional use. For information please write: Special Markets Department, HarperCollins Publishers, 10 East 53rd Street, New York, NY 10022.

This book was originally published in 1985 by Seaview/Putnam.

FIRST WILLIAM MORROW PAPERBACK PUBLISHED 2013

Library of Congress Cataloging-in-Publication Data has been applied for.

ISBN 978-0-06-222935-9

13 14 15 16 17 OV/RRD 10 9 8 7 6 5 4 3

To Bettye
for her love and courage

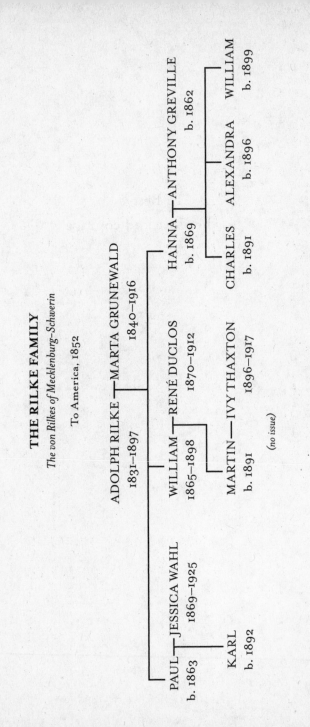

THE RILKE FAMILY

The von Rilkes of Mecklenburg-Schwerin

To America, 1852

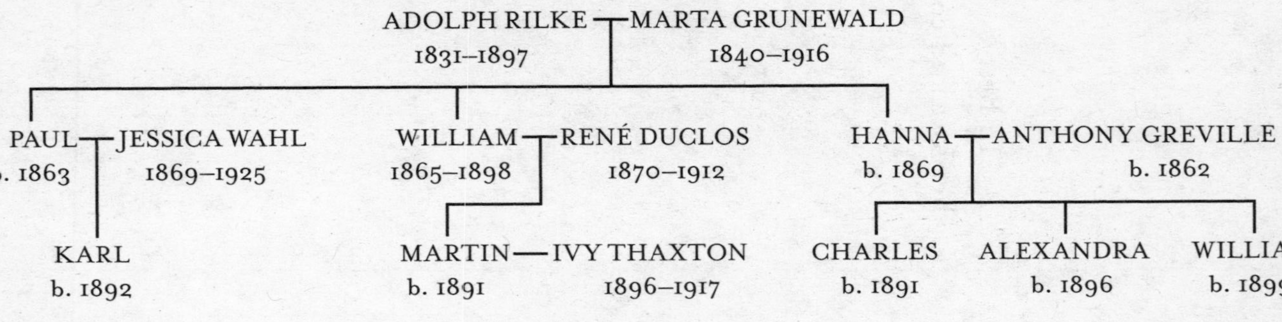

THE GREVILLE FAMILY

Spring 1930

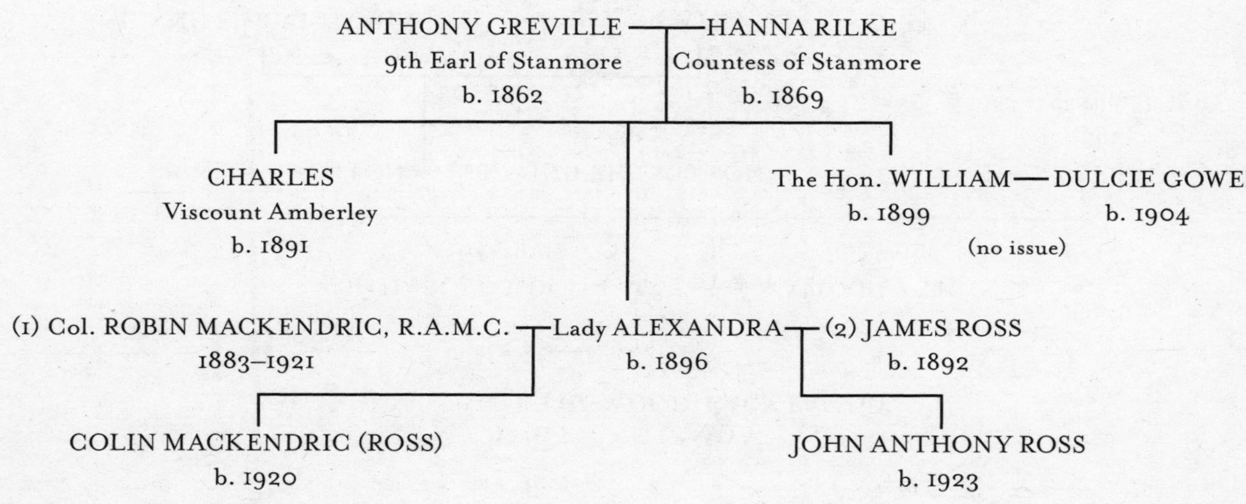

ANTHONY GREVILLE
9th Earl of Stanmore
b. 1862
HANNA RILKE
Countess of Stanmore
b. 1869
CHARLES
Viscount Amberley
b. 1891
The Hon. WILLIAM
b. 1899
DULCIE GOWER
b. 1904
(no issue)
(1) Col. ROBIN MACKENDRIC, R.A.M.C.
1883–1921
Lady ALEXANDRA
b. 1896
(2) JAMES ROSS
b. 1892
COLIN MACKENDRIC (ROSS)
b. 1920
JOHN ANTHONY ROSS
b. 1923

THE WOOD-LACY FAMILY

Spring 1930

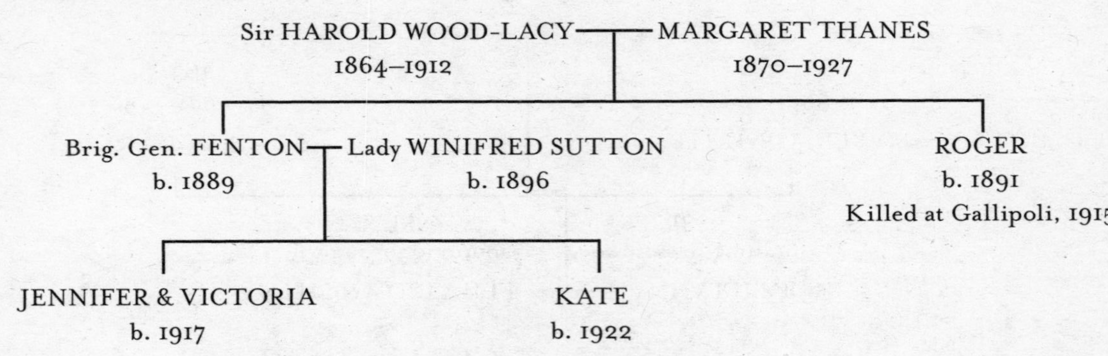

Book One

A PAST FORGOTTEN

1930

An April Morning

Spring came at last after a winter of snow and icy winds that had sent trees crashing in the tangled depths of Leith Wood and had blocked the narrow country roads with drifts. Some of the more isolated villages in the Weald had been cut off for days at a time, causing farmers and their wives to pen furious letters to those county councillors responsible for maintenance of the king's highway. Their children, kept from going to school in Abingdon by the appalling condition of the roads, had been less choleric about the matter. But all the troubles of January and February disappeared by the end of March. A west wind brought patchy blue skies, fleecy cumulus, and gentle, intermittent rains that melted the snow and set once placid streams tumbling with white water toward the rivers and the sea. There would be further discomfort—mud and sodden fields—but what was that after so gray a winter? One could tolerate a bit of flooding here and there if it meant crocus and daffodil, budding elm and beech. If it meant spring and the joyous promise of summer.

Anthony Greville, Earl of Stanmore, was up at first light, as he had been every morning since the weather broke. There were a thousand things that required his attention and not enough hours in the day to supervise them all. There were stone walls that had tumbled in the frost, paddock fences that sagged and drooped, gravel paths and driveways that were rutted or scoured away by wind-drifted ice and snow, roofs that needed new slate, windows to be reglazed, walls painted, stables repaired—all the myriad tasks that accumulated in so large an estate as Abingdon Pryory during a long, hard English winter. His valet, stifling yawns, drew the earl's bath and laid out his clothes for the day—moleskin trousers, a flannel shirt of tattersall check, a well-used tweed jacket, and a pair of sturdy half boots waterproofed with neat's-foot oil. Bathed and dressed, he awaited his tea and toast—four slices, extra crisp, the tea strong, amber brown Ceylon.

The rapid knock on his sitting-room door was too loud and insistent to be the maid with her tray of teapot, toast slices, and jam jars. The sound was startling and he opened the door himself. Gardway, the head groom, stood in the shadowed corridor, his usually cheerful, ruddy face turned pale and solemn.

"What on earth . . . ?"

Gardway, who had at one time been a steeplechase jockey of note, turned his cloth cap in his small, restive hands. "Begging Your Lordship's pardon, but Mr. Coatsworth has done and gone."

"Gone?"

"Dead, sir. Poor old gentleman." He shielded his mouth

with his cap and coughed nervously. "I . . . I thought you'd be wanting to know right off."

Lord Stanmore stared down at the man. "Coatsworth dead?" His tone reflected his incomprehension. "That's difficult to believe. You're quite sure, of course?"

"I am that, sir. I went by the cottage on my way to the stables. Saw a light burnin' and popped in. He was sittin' up in bed. I . . . did the courtesy of closin' his eyes. God rest his soul."

"Thank you, Samuel. That was most kind."

"I'll miss the old chap, I'll say that."

"Yes. We all will. Does anyone else know?"

The groom shook his head and tightened his grip on his cap. "No, m'lord. I reckoned you'd be wanting to tell the staff."

"Quite so." He turned away from the door and stared across at the telephone. "I'd best call Dr. Morton . . . and make arrangements." The sky was the palest blue. A cloud hovered above Burgate Hill, framed in the tall windows of the room. Cloud and hill tinged rose with dawn. It would be a lovely day and Coatsworth would not see it. "I thought him eternal," he said to no one.

There was a chill to the wind as he left the house. He turned up his coat collar and walked briskly along the flagstone terrace and down the broad, stone steps into the sunken garden with its marble statuary and rose shrubs still tied in their winter coverings of burlap. One covering had rotted away into windblown strips. He paused for a moment and plucked a desiccated pod from the bush and crumbled it to powder between his fingers.

He could sense death as he entered the cottage. Felt its presence in the gentle ticking of a mantel clock and the dust floating in a solitary shaft of sunlight. A comfortable, ordered room that said much for the man who had lived in it. Nothing extraneous. No bric-a-brac or mementos. A sofa, Morris chair, desk and straight-back chair. A bookcase with some well-used leather-covered volumes of Dickens and Shakespeare. A painting that he had given to Coatsworth one Christmas in the distant past. *A View of Leith Hill as Seen from Wotton Common*—by Thomas Piggott, R. A. Signed and dated 1891.

He felt loath to enter the small bedroom but did so. The bedside lamp still burned, casting its glow on the motionless figure propped against pillows. Gardway had touched nothing. Just the closing of the eyes. He stood close to the bed, reached out, and touched the once imposing head that seemed so shrunken now, so fragile in death.

He spoke in the servants' hall before breakfast. Only a few of the twenty-five cooks, maids, footmen, gardeners, and grooms that he employed had known Mr. Coatsworth when he had been butler. Those few mourned openly. The others retained a respectful solemnity to fit the occasion. To them he had been simply an ancient retainer living in retirement in one of the cottages. The earl's declaration of a half holiday on the day of the funeral drew a greater response than his pronouncement of Coatsworth's demise.

The doctor arrived at nine o'clock, followed shortly by a hearse from a mortuary in Abingdon. After Coatsworth's body had been driven away the earl escorted Dr. Morton into the library and poured two stiff whiskies from a crystal decanter.

"Painful business, this."

"Death usually is," the doctor said. He set his bag on a table, opened it, and removed a printed form. "Although, if you ask me, it's the mechanics of it all that causes the most distress.

Death certificates and funeral arrangements, wills and probates, all the bookkeeping of passing on. *Requiescat in pace* is all very well for the deceased, but hardly applicable to the living."

The earl handed him a glass of whisky. "To John Harum Coatsworth, God bless his soul."

"Yes, to Mr. Coatsworth." He took a swallow, set the glass on the table, and drew up a chair. "Well, let's get on with it." He sat down and removed a fountain pen from his pocket. "Did he have a certificate of birth?"

"No. A family Bible. He was born on tenth October, eighteen forty-one . . . in Lavenham, Suffolk."

"Let's see, that would have made him eighty-nine next birthday. Eighty-eight for the record. A goodly span of years."

"He came to work for me in eighteen eighty-two. The first servant I hired after my father passed away. The first servant I'd *ever* hired, if it comes to that. I was twenty. Forty-eight years ago. Good Lord."

The doctor glanced up at the earl's stricken face and then turned back to the certificate. "Did he leave a will, by the way?"

"My solicitor drew one up for him some time back. He had no heirs. Bequeathed his savings to various charities."

"Cause of death. Let's see . . . Congestive heart failure. Bit of a catch-all for dying of old age." He signed the certificate, recapped his pen, and took another sip of whisky. "And that's that. Not taking this too hard are you, Anthony?"

"Why do you ask that?"

"Because you have a face that is most easily read. It's a sad day, my friend. A loss to all of us who knew him, but at eighty-eight it can hardly be considered a tragedy."

The earl finished his whisky and splashed another dollop

into his glass. "It's not that, dash it all. He led a good life . . . the life he chose to lead, anyway. It's just that . . . well, so much seems to be slipping away."

"Time, dear chap. Only time."

Blast! He couldn't explain. The words would not come. He could be quite inarticulate at times, a heritage from his days at school where terseness had been considered a virtue and the mark of a gentleman. He watched the doctor's car move off down the driveway and then strode to the stables where he found Gardway, in hacking jacket and shiny leather gaiters, overseeing the exercise of a chestnut hunter.

"Saddle Launcelot for me, will you, Samuel? I feel like taking a ride."

"Very well, m'lord. But I'd avoid Bigham. Tom Dundas told me it's a sea of muck."

"Tipley's Green. Stop off at Burgate House first and see my son. Be a shock to him. Knew Coatsworth all his life."

He felt better on a horse, the great life-filled body cantering down the gravel road. He bent forward and patted the strong neck. The stallion broke into a gallop, glad to be out of the stable and stretching his muscles. Sniffing spring and frisky as the devil. He reined him in slightly and jumped a low gate at the end of the lane, taking it cleanly with feet to spare, then slowed the big horse to a steady trot along the high meadows bordering Leith Wood. Sheep bleated out of the way, their thick coats dirty gray and ragged after the bitter winter. He paused for a few minutes amid the fringes of a beech grove to let the horse graze in a patch of new grass. Lighting a cigarette, he sat stiffly in the saddle and gazed off across the Vale of Abingdon.

How much it had changed. Only one who had known the view from a perspective of well over half a century could possibly understand his feeling of regret. How crowded it all was. The pastoral vistas of his youth encroached and spoiled by row upon distant row of red brick villas. The environs of Abingdon; suburbs of what had once been no more than a village sleeping in the gentle folds of the Surrey hills. Crown lands and his own acres surrounding the Pryory kept the brick at bay, but there it lay along the near horizon, street upon street waiting to lurch forward if given half a chance and cover meadow and wood with more mock-Tudor houses and country clubs. Golf courses. "Garden" cities. By-pass highways from London. Town centers and cinemas—the hideous conglomeration of modern times.

The hypocrisy of his thoughts was not lost on him. A good many of those now despised houses had been built on his land. He had aided in the expansion of Abingdon in 1924 by subdividing a hundred and fifty acres near the village. He had then formed, and headed, the Abingdon Planning Commission. Middle-class housing had been built for the new breed of London commuters and for the executives and engineers of the sprawling Blackworth aircraft plant only eight miles away. Damn good houses had been constructed, even if they did have a sameness about them. Nicely ordered communities surrounded by parks and trees. And yet now, with painfully sharp memories of a time long past thrusting vivid images upon him, he wished that some giant hand would crush brick and plaster and sweep it all away.

It was a darkly brooding man who rode across the fields and dismounted in the driveway of Burgate House School. He tied his horse to a railing and stood for a moment gazing at the building. A symphony in ugliness. Gothic spires and Romanesque arches in a graceless blending of limestone and brick, Palladian windows and stained glass. A house built by a duke during the reign of Queen Anne as a memorial for his dead son. Part palace and part tomb. An unorthodox building to say the least and, for the past seven years, a most unorthodox school of which his eldest son, Charles Greville, Viscount Amberley, was now headmaster.

Three boys, in a diverse assortment of clothing, bolted around a corner of the building and raced down the drive, closely pursued by an untidy-looking girl who was throwing green horse chestnuts at them. The boys, shrieking with laughter, vaulted a low stone wall and ran off into the muddy field beyond. The girl, no more than nine years old, hurled her remaining seeds and shouted something that the earl could not hear. Burgate House was not his idea of a school and never would be. He shook his head and turned toward the massive front doors.

He walked briskly down a long, barren corridor pierced by a row of lancet windows, a stone corridor that led to what had once been a chapel but was now his son's study. The carved wood door was ajar and he entered the room without knocking. Charles was already rising from behind his desk in greeting.

"No mistaking the ring of *your* boots, Father."

The earl nodded. His son's smiling face was disconcerting.

"Coatsworth is dead," he said bluntly.

"I'm sorry," Charles said with quiet sympathy. "Did he go in his sleep?"

"I assume he did."

"Good. A gentle death for a fine man."

"He had been in my service for forty-eight years."

"Yes, I know."

"My butler for seven before I even met your mother."

"A very long time. Difficult to think of the Pryory without him."

"Your mother's still in London. I haven't told her yet."

"You can ring her from here if you'd like." He studied his father's face with concern. He looked pale and his eyes had a faraway opacity about them. "Would you like me to call?"

The earl shook his head, walked over to the windows, and stood looking out at a small, formal garden. "Lovely. I don't suppose you allow the children to play there."

"They *work* there on Saturday mornings. The garden is their responsibility. They may walk or study in it, but not rag about. That's their rule, not mine."

"Three boys and a girl were 'ragging about' in front. Like street urchins."

"New arrivals," Charles said, as though he had explained that kind of behavior many times before. "They're often like that when they first come here. Not used to the freedom. They tend to be a bit wild until they discover that freedom ultimately becomes boring. Then they join the others and settle into the school routine."

"Not quite like Eton, is it?"

"No. Not exactly."

"Odd to think of this house as a school. It was empty when I was a boy. Only a caretaker lived here . . . and two gardeners. It was that way for many years. Lord Marshland owned the property. He never came near it and I can't say that I blame him. Depressing place. After he died his heirs tried to sell it, but, needless to say, they had the devil of a time finding a buyer. It wasn't until eighteen ninety that Archie Fox came along and they could get rid of it. Just the sort of place a millionaire cockney would want to live in."

Charles frowned and walked around from behind his desk. "Do you feel all right, Father?"

He ignored the question. "I telephoned the vicar this morning. Arranged the funeral for Saturday afternoon. There will be a great deal of work to do before then, I'm afraid. All of the carriages will need sprucing up . . . saddle soap the leather . . . grease wheels . . . polish lamps . . . clean all the harness."

"Carriages?" His mouth felt dry. "What carriages?"

"Ours, of course. The phaetons and victorias . . . the four surreys. And then there are black plumes that must be purchased for the horses. And black crepe for draping. Black silk rosettes for the coachmen to wear. A thousand and one things to be done."

"Are you being serious? Those carriages have been stored in a shed since before the war. Surely you don't intend to—"

"He was a Victorian," the earl said with steely emphasis. "A man from a far more gracious and civilized time. He was born a Victorian and he shall be buried as one."

Charles cleared his throat discreetly. "He will be buried with dignity, Father, by those who admired him. Draped carriages and plumed horses on a Saturday afternoon in Abingdon High Street would be a spectacle—and a rather theatrical one at that. I think you should reconsider your plans."

Lord Stanmore scowled and stepped away from the window. His face, Charles noted uneasily, had taken on a grayish pallor. "It seems quite proper to *me.*"

"I'm sure it does," Charles said gently. "I suppose it's how one looks at things. I know how fond you were of him and what a blow this must be to you." He placed a hand on his father's arm. "Perhaps it would be a comfort to sit down and talk about him. I can remember a story or two."

"Yes, Charlie, I'm sure you can." His eyes were fixed on some distant space. "My father died when I was nineteen. His wish was to be buried in Abingdon, although I can't understand why. He hated the place so. He thought the village a dung heap of yokels and the Pryory merely a warren of old brick and timber with a misspelled name. It was an elaborate funeral. Even the Prince of Wales attended. But in all the many hundreds of people who lined the High Street leading to the church or walked so solemnly behind the casket I doubt if there was one, no, not *one* heartfelt feeling of remorse at his passing. A more disliked man never lived in England. The funeral was a duty . . . a custom . . . and if that type of funeral could be held for a man I despised, then, by George, it can be held for a man I respected and loved for nearly half a century."

There was a rumbling sound above them as a hundred chairs were pushed back from a hundred desks, and then the muted thunder of a hundred pairs of feet racing along the corridors toward the main stairs.

"Lunch," Charles said. "Why don't you join me and then we can telephone Mother."

The earl shook his head. "I want to ride over to Tipley's Green. I'll take lunch with Braxton-Gill, but thank you all the same."

"A drink before you go, then. You look pale."

"Do I? Well, it's been a bit of a shock, you know. I'll miss dropping in on the old fellow for tea and a game of draughts.

He always looked forward to it. A brandy. Just a smahan to keep the blood moving."

The four children who had been running about, tossing things, and bolting over the wall were standing in front of Launcelot and stroking his nose in unison. He was about to tell them sternly to keep away, but thought better of it. They appeared to be awed and gentle and the horse certainly was content enough. They moved away as he approached and untied the animal from the railing.

"Is that *your* horse?" one of the boys asked.

"Yes," he replied. "My horse."

"Your very own?" asked the girl.

"My very own."

"I had a pony when I lived with Father. I named her Angelica. Don't you think that's a nice name?"

"I bet you didn't," one of the boys said. "I think you made that up."

The girl's face turned crimson. "And I think you're horrid."

"Now, now," he said as he swung up into the saddle. "No bickering. Lunch is being served. You'd best go *in* before they run *out*."

They followed his suggestion and raced one another to the door. He tapped his heels against Launcelot's flanks and trotted down the long, curved drive.

He slowed the horse to a walk when he reached the road and allowed him to amble along. Odd sort of place, he thought. Those children. Muddy and tattered from running about in the fields and brambles. As dirty as urchins in the streets of Stepney or Canning Town, and just as liable to be the children of dukes as the offspring of dustmen. The famous—or infamous—Burgate House School. And Charlie was head of it. Difficult to believe.

"You mark my words, m'lord, young Lord Amberley will be prime minister one day."

He remembered Coatsworth saying that as clearly as if it had been yesterday. Charles down from Eton for the holidays and discussing British blundering in the struggle against the Boers. Charles no more than nine years old. Coatsworth had been impressed, if wrongly prophetic. Still, the lad was functioning. The war had almost, but not quite, destroyed him. Headmaster of Burgate House. He had found a niche in life and more power to him. Hardly a *lad,* of course. Nearing forty.

A cloud crossed the sun and a splattering of rain hit the road and slapped against the black branches of the bordering oaks. He glanced at the sky, but the rain would pass in a minute or two. A fresh wind, blowing toward the west. Clouds scudding across the hills. Sunshine and drifting shadow on the fields.

"And do you agree, Coatsworth?"

"I do indeed, Master Charles. We seem to make a habit of bungling about in wars. I was twelve when my father went off to the Crimea, servant to Colonel Wilkinson of the Twenty-third Foot. My father never came back—dead at Inkerman. Oh, I agree with you heartily."

A conversation overheard in a corridor over thirty years ago, and yet he could hear those two voices as though the wind had borne them across the meadows with the rain. Odd. Very odd indeed. He felt light-headed and there was a peculiar buzzing in his ears. Tipley's Green was only three miles away, but it seemed suddenly to be infinitely farther than that and impossible to reach. He turned the horse around in the middle of the narrow road to head back toward Abingdon.

The bright green Talbot two-seater rounded the bend at high speed, the driver seeing horse and rider directly in front of him and hitting the brakes and twisting the wheel at the same time. The low-slung, powerful car went into a tire-smoking, screeching slide that missed Lord Stanmore and Launcelot by no more than a foot and spun to a halt thirty yards down the road and facing the way it had just come. The driver, white-faced with fear and anger, half rose in his seat and waved a fist in the air with the rapidity of a piston.

"Damn you, sir! Could have been *killed!* Keep—*bloody horse*—out of—bloody—*road!"*

And then he was gunning the car to a throaty roar, shifting gears in a fury, backing up and spinning around and thundering off down the road to leave Lord Stanmore shaken and perplexed.

"Sorry," he said, watching the car fade rapidly to a dot of green, water from the rain-slick asphalt sprayed to mist by the tires. Launcelot was in terror and only the earl's instinctive skills of a lifetime of horsemanship kept the stallion from bolting. He calmed down the animal, his hands aching from keeping the reins taut as wire.

"Good fellow . . . good chap." He patted the neck vigorously and then dismounted and led him to the side of the road, where the animal stood trembling and sweating in a shallow ditch. "Good old boy . . . good old boy . . . there, there . . ." He patted and stroked the quivering, foam-sheened hide as the rain became heavier, slapping into the dead leaves that choked the ditch, only to move on as suddenly as it had come. Watery sunlight filtered down through the gaunt limbs of the oak trees.

"Let's go home, boy . . . let's go home."

He had one foot in the stirrup when the pain struck, a crushing pain in the center of his chest that radiated quickly to his left armpit and down the arm to his wrist. The pain drove the breath from his body and for a moment he felt paralyzed. Terror swept him and he fought it back, hands clenched in Launcelot's thick mane. He must get onto the horse or he would die in the ditch. Die by the side of the road . . . and he was damned if he would. Determination replaced fear and he managed to claw his way onto the saddle. The pain was so intense now that he could do nothing but slump forward against the powerful neck, clinging desperately to it as Launcelot stepped nimbly out of the ditch and began to canter toward stable and home.

1

Martin Rilke awoke a few minutes before the alarm clock would have shattered sleep and nerves. Reaching out from under the covers he groped for the clock on the nightstand and depressed the alarm button. He fought the urge to sink back into the bliss of morning slumber and sat up with a groan. Six thirty. He wasn't used to getting up so early, but he had promised Albert he would take him to King's Cross. The 8:05 train to Peterborough. Plenty of time. He swung his legs out of bed and winced at the cold creeping along the floor. *For Let. Fully furnished. Elegant small house in Knightsbridge with fine view of Kensington Gardens and Hyde Park.* There had been no mention of drafts in the advertisement. He stood up with a sharp intake of breath as though plunging into a cold pool. His heavy wool bathrobe was draped over a chair and he padded across to put it on. His carpet slippers were nowhere to be seen. Under the bed probably, but he didn't feel like groping for them.

A pale yellow light filtered through drawn curtains and

he walked over to the windows in his bare feet and pulled the cord. A clear sky again, thank God. Perhaps winter was over at last. He stood for a moment gazing out across Kensington Road at the park. A thin, patchy mist drifted through the trees and clung to the ground. Emerging from it in blocks of dark gray came ordered ranks of horsemen, row after row at the trot along Carriage Road; the Horse Guards on an early morning exercise. It was the kind of enchanting sight that made London worth living in. Martin watched until the cavalcade passed Rutland Gate and then he turned away and hurried into the bathroom to bathe and shave.

He was thirty-nine, a man of medium height and stocky build. His body, viewed naked in the full-length mirror streaked with steam, was compact and sturdy, the chest large and the stomach reasonably flat. Rilke males were inclined to stoutness and Martin fought the proclivity by watching his diet and playing furious games of squash three afternoons a week at a club in St. James's Street. He gave his middle an approving slap and then stepped across to the washbasin. He sharpened and honed a Rolls razor in its silver-plated box and then whipped lather in a bowl with a badger-hair brush. The face in the mirror was youthful and unlined with a thin, high-bridged nose, wide mouth, and pale blue eyes. The hair, parted in the center, was thick and flaxen. It was a face that women thought of as "nice looking" rather than handsome.

Martin paid no attention to his face other than to shave it and pat his cheeks with cologne. When he went back into the bedroom, Mary, the young Welsh maid, had lit the fire in the grate—the coals spreading a meager warmth into the room. He thought of his apartment in New York, the good old Yankee know-how of double-glazed windows and central heating. A lot to be said for it, but he had never seen cavalry riding through the morning mist on West 64th Street.

He looked into the spare bedroom before going downstairs. The bed was made and his brother-in-law's small suitcase was packed and strapped and set on the floor. Albert, he assumed, was used to getting up at ungodly hours.

"Good morning, sir."

Albert Edward Thaxton stepped out of the dining room into the hall as Martin was coming down the stairs. He was a tall, dark-haired boy of sixteen dressed in gray flannels and a school blazer.

"Good morning, Albert," Martin said cheerfully. "Sleep well?"

The boy smiled, a smile that was so reminiscent of his sister's that Martin could not witness it without feeling a tug of the heart.

"Oh, yes, sir. They don't have beds like that at Morborne."

"Hard, angry little cots, eh?"

"Well, not quite that bad, but jolly close to it."

"Have your breakfast yet?"

"Rashers and eggs, fried bread and tomatoes. Super grub."

Martin glanced at his wristwatch. "I'll just have some toast and coffee and then we'll grab a taxi and get you to the station."

"May I sit with you and read the newspaper, sir?"

"Of course. And please stop calling me *sir.*"

"Yes, sir."

It was pointless, Martin supposed. English boardingschool courtesy, drilled into the young like a multiplication table. He was a fine boy and he certainly could not fault him for being polite. Ivy would have been proud. She had only seen him when he was a babe in arms and now he was nearly six feet tall, captain of his school's cricket team—of the "eleven" as he called it—and had just completed the interviews and tests that would ensure him a scholarship at Oxford.

Mrs. Bromley, his cook-housekeeper, brought coffee, toast, and the newspapers. He gave Albert the sporting section of the *Daily Post* which he scanned eagerly.

"Oh, blast!"

"Anything the matter, Albert?"

"Rangers, sir. They lost to United . . . three to two. That's knocked them out of cup play."

"Sorry to hear it." He had no interest in English soccer—or any other English sport for that matter. He sipped his coffee and read the leaders. The London Naval Conference winding down with a few concessions being made. Some limits on submarines and new battleship construction. Tonnage and gun calibers. All meaningless. Ramsay MacDonald to pay a visit to slump-devastated Yorkshire—to do no more, he felt certain, than show his handsome, kindly face to the unemployed. He put the paper aside and opened the Paris edition of the New York *Tribune*—which he received every morning, if a day late. He searched for the baseball scores.

"Bob Giffrow retired. Never thought I'd see the day."

"A friend of yours, sir?"

"In a manner of speaking. He was a pitcher for the Chicago Cubs for eighteen seasons."

That thought made him wince and feel old. He had seen the man's debut . . . Cubs versus Giants . . . the spring of 1912. Now he was stepping from the mound, his wicked, twisting "slew bobber" to confound batters no more. The Cubs still had Hack Wilson, who could slam them out of the park. And they had taken the pennant last year even if they had lost to Philadelphia in the series. But it had been Giffrow who had gotten them there, pitching with pain, his mighty arm like a gnarled and twisted oak. The great "Dutchman" walking away forever into the long shadows of a Chicago summer day. It didn't seem possible. He folded the newspaper with a sigh and shoved it behind the coffee pot.

"Now there's a game for you."

"What game is that, sir?"

"Baseball."

"Rather like our rounders, I believe."

"No, Albert," he said patiently, "it isn't anything at all like rounders."

"It's played with a round bat and a ball, sir."

"The similarity ends there. Believe me." Not that he could explain the difference. How could he describe to the uninitiated the poetry of Jimmie Foxx? Tinker to Evers to Chance? Rogers Hornsby batting .424 for the 1924 season? The Babe . . . Lefty Grove . . . Walter "Big Train" Johnson . . . Ty Cobb sliding into second with his spikes glinting through the dust as deadly as a tiger's fangs? Impossible. "I'll take you to a baseball game one day."

"Where, sir?"

"Why, in the States of course. Next summer when you leave school."

"To America, sir? Do you mean it?"

"Sure I do."

"Oh, I say, how super!"

"It'll be a good experience for you before you go on to Oxford."

Albert's ecstatic expression paled. "I'm trying not to think about Oxford actually."

"Oh? Why not?"

"The scholarship and all that."

"I wouldn't worry about it. It's more than a year away. Plenty of time to get used to the idea." He looked at his watch. "Better get your bag while I whistle down a taxi."

Albert said nothing in the taxi until they rounded Hyde Park Corner and headed toward Oxford Street.

"My going to university means a great deal to Ned. That's natural, I suppose. I mean to say, he wants the best for his baby brother . . . all the things he didn't have."

"He wants what's best for *you*," Martin said. "As do I."

"Balliol will be horribly expensive even with the scholarship, and you've given so much already."

"I can afford it."

"Perhaps. I'm rather wondering if I can."

"I don't follow you."

"What I mean is . . . well, some of the chaps at school look at things the way I do. This slump. Your American stock-market crash. A worldwide financial collapse. Did you know that thirty percent of the men in Birmingham are unemployed?"

"I'm aware of it," he said dryly.

"Yes, of course. I mean, after all, as a journalist . . ."

"What are you trying to say, Albert?"

"That I don't want to study for a First in Greats. It seems so . . . pointless and esoteric somehow. Fiddling while Rome burns. Nothing practical. I could earn a degree and then do nothing more with it than teach Greek or Latin at some place like Morborne. I want more out of life than that." He turned on the seat to face Martin. "I'd like to live the way you do. Travel about the world . . . witness and write about important happenings. I speak French . . . my German's coming along nicely . . . I seem to have a good ear for languages. I *know* I can write. I'm always top boy in school at composition."

Martin smiled ruefully. "A newspaper man. Heaven help you."

"It's made you rich and famous—although it's not money I'm thinking about. It's doing something worthwhile . . . something *important.*"

"I would say you've given a good deal of thought to this."

"Yes, I have. I could go to the University of London . . . and I could get a job. Copyboy or something like that . . . on the *Daily Post,* say. Mr. Golden would hire me if you asked him. Don't you think?"

"Jacob would hire you if *you* asked him. He was very fond of Ivy. Best man at our wedding."

"Work . . . take a few classes . . . share digs with a couple of chaps. I could do it on my own."

"I'm sure you could, at that." He gave Albert's knee a pat. "But let's not discuss it now. You still have a year to go at Morborne. If you feel the same way then . . ."

"Oh, I will, sir . . . I know I will."

". . . I'll talk to Jacob. I'm sure he can do better for you than a copyboy job. Perhaps a cub reporter . . . on sports. You probably know more about cricket and soccer than any kid alive."

It was the decision Ivy would have made, he thought as he watched Albert hurry down the platform toward his train. It was uncanny how much he resembled his sister. Not just in looks, the black hair and almost violet eyes, but in his zest for life. Ivy's education had been limited, but she had read everything she could get her hands on. Geography had been her passion. She had wanted to visit every dot on the globe. There were so many exotic lands and yet she was to see only France and a tiny, shell-torn strip of Flanders before she died.

The taxi had waited for him, meter ticking, the driver reading a paper and ignoring swarms of commuters anxious to hop in the back and be taken to their offices. Martin ran a gauntlet of dark-clothed men bearing tightly furled umbrellas and clenched briefcases, turned a deaf ear to pleas to share the ride and climbed into the cab. The driver folded his newspaper and placed it behind the meter.

"Where to, guv'nor?"

"Forty-seven Russell Street."

He sat back and lit a cigar as the taxi clattered away from the station and along Euston Road. Turning down Gower Street he could see the soot-grimed buildings of London University looming over the tree-shaded streets and squares of Bloomsbury. A fine, no-nonsense school. If Albert was sincere about wanting to become a journalist he could not choose a better place to learn. But it was not Balliol, with all the prestige an Oxford education implied. His not going up to Oxford would disappoint his brother. No doubt of that. Ned Thaxton, fifteen years older than Albert, had set his heart on it. Ned had been bright enough as a boy to have won a scholarship—had he been kept in school long enough to try for one. The poverty of his family had ruled against that. He had left school at fourteen to work in a Norwich shoe factory as an oiler of stitching machines. A self-taught man, studying at night, he had become at eighteen a junior clerk in a solicitor's office. Eventually, with Martin's financial help, he had become a lawyer and was now a partner in a Birmingham firm.

He drew thoughtfully on his cigar. It was impossible to tell if Albert really wanted to be a newspaperman or was just momentarily dazzled by the profession. He knew so little about the boy. He had only seen him two or three times over the years and then only briefly. This was the first time they had spent any time together and had gotten to know each other—in a tentative sort of way. Difficult, he imagined, for Albert to think of him as a brother-in-law and not some sort of distant uncle. Thus the *sir* all the time and not *Martin.* And no doubt he had impressed the lad a bit too much. He had told him about his time as a foreign correspondent for A. P. and European bureau chief of the International News Agency . . . and then of his six years in America as a radio commentator. All exciting stuff to a sixteen-year-old schoolboy. And he had taken him to lunch at Whipple's, that haunt of Fleet Street journalists for over a century. They had been joined at the table by Jacob Golden and a man who had just come back from China, covering the Far East for the *Daily Post.* His stories of Chinese warlords, gunfights in Shanghai between Kuomintang secret police and communist agents had kept Albert open-mouthed. Gathering news might not always be exciting, but it was certainly more so than teaching Latin or Greek.

There was no question that he had influenced Albert, but then his impact on the Thaxton family as a whole had been profound. He had never met any of them until long after Ivy's death in 1917. It had been the summer of 1921 when he had finally managed to get back to England and had driven to the village near Norwich where his wife had been born, the eldest of John and Rose Thaxton's six children. It had been a painfully formal meeting. Almost incomprehensible to the elder Thaxtons that "their Ivy" had married a rich American. All that they had known of it had been contained in a letter from Ivy dated December 1916, informing them that she had married a war correspondent from Chicago, Illinois, U.S.A. Not a church wedding, either. In front of the mayor of a French town called St. Germain-en-Laye. That in itself had seemed peculiar to them and they had worried over the legality of it. The whole world gone topsy-turvy and no mistake. Their firstborn off at the age of seventeen to be a housemaid and ending up in a foreign country, an army nurse, marrying a Yank. A queer sort of business, John Thaxton had remarked.

After Ivy had been killed near Ypres, they had never expected to hear from her husband (they could not think of him as their son-in-law and would refer to him as "Mr. Rilke" until they died, within three months of each other in 1927) and had been surprised when they had received a letter, on Associated Press letterhead, three weeks after their daughter's death. The letter had come from Paris and had contained, along with Martin Rilke's condolences, a check for two hundred pounds—more money at one time than they had ever seen in their lives. Their welfare, he had written, had always been uppermost in Ivy's thoughts. That letter had been followed in December 1919, by one from a firm of lawyers in London informing them that a trust fund had been established by Martin Rilke, Esq., with monies derived from the rental of a house at No. 23 rue de Bois-Preau, St. Germain-en-Laye, France, for *their com-*

fort and support, and the comfort and support of their children, Ned, Tom, Cissy, and Mary Thaxton and for the future education of their youngest child, Albert Edward Thaxton, in the current amount of five hundred pounds per annum. The dispensation of said sum to be at the discretion of Hiram Galesworth and Sons, Solicitors, of 14 Tooks Court, Cursitor Street, London, E.C.4.

The enormity of the amount had stunned John Thaxton. Two pounds a week had been the most he had ever made even at the best of times. His only regret had been that the money did not go directly to him for dispensation at *his* discretion, but his wife had silently blessed that provision of the trust, knowing only too well how much brass would have gone to the publican and the bookmaker.

Tom and Ned Thaxton, both in their early twenties, had heard of Martin Rilke and had looked forward on that bright summer day in 1921 to meeting him for the first time. They had read his syndicated articles in the Norfolk *Weekly Examiner* for years and had known that he had been awarded a Pulitzer prize for his coverage of the Versailles Treaty. Even seven-year-old Albert Edward had known where Chicago, Illinois, was located. Their parents had known nothing. Simple people, they had felt uncomfortable in the presence of their benefactor and had only half listened as he had explained to them about the house in France. How he had bought it cheaply in 1914 because the owner had believed the German army would win the war in a matter of days. And of how he had given the house to Ivy, if not legally at least spiritually, on their wedding night there. Now the house was rented by the Brazilian ambassador to France.

A house in France? A spiritual wedding gift to their Ivy? A Brazilian ambassador laying out five hundred quid a year in rent? It was all too incomprehensible to grasp. They had been grateful for the money, but this man, this Martin Rilke from Chicago, Illinois, lived in a world too alien to their own. A stranger to them now and forever. After that one brief visit Martin had never seen them again.

There were FLAT FOR LET signs on some of the old houses flanking the street. Albert would have no trouble finding a place. A flat to share, or a room of his own in one of the many boardinghouses scattered throughout Bloomsbury and St. Pancras. He had to admire the lad's resolve. The noble art of journalism! He smiled ruefully and tapped cigar ash at his feet. He would find out soon enough that it was not all honors and riches, Pulitzer awards and by-lines, travels to China and whisky-sodas in the mellow atmosphere of Whipple's bar. A summer job as a copyboy might not be such a bad idea. Running his legs off for twelve hours a day in the racketing chaos of a Fleet Street editorial room would soon strip away the glamor of a profession that was, in the words of a long dead editor of the Chicago *Herald*, second only to whoring in age and respect.

The offices of Calthorpe & Crofts were on the third floor of a building facing Bloomsbury Square. They were small but respected publishers of avant-garde novels and poetry, left-wing criticisms of bourgeois mores, and other esoterica of dubious commercial worth. Arnold Calthorpe had been severely wounded during the war while serving as an infantry officer. He was now a passionate exponent of world peace and was president of the United Kingdom branch of the No More War International Society. A great many of the books he now published were on pacifist themes, both fiction and nonfiction. A current title in the latter category was *An End to Castles* by Martin Rilke.

Mrs. James was boiling water for tea on an electric hot plate and Arnold Calthorpe was sorting through the mail when Martin entered the office. Calthorpe, a look of disgust on his heavily scarred face, tossed the stack of envelopes back into the wire basket on his secretary's desk.

"Bills and more bills. How comforting it would be to bring out a book that at least paid its own way."

"Sorry," Martin said.

"Not your fault, dear chap." He peered at Martin over his horn-rimmed eyeglasses. "Up with the lark this morning, are we?"

"I had to take my brother-in-law to King's Cross."

"Ah, yes. Young Albert. How did it go?"

"Very well. He's bound to get a scholarship, but it seems he doesn't want one. He'd like to learn a trade—journalism of all things."

"Jolly good for him. The streets are chock-a-block with unemployed, and unemployable, graduates of the hallowed halls of Oxbridge. I told my nephew just the other day to forget about learning to translate Tacitus and take up plumbing instead."

"Would you like a cup of tea, Mr. Rilke?" Mrs. James said.

"I would. Thank you."

"Bring it into my office, that's the dear," Calthorpe said. "And put a tot of rum in mine."

Calthorpe's office was a small, cluttered room with piles of books, manuscripts, and proof sheets taking up most of the available space. The editor searched through a pile of material on his desk and withdrew a square of art board covered with a sheet of tissue paper.

"The cover—as promised." He folded the tissue back and held up the board for Martin to see. "Well? What do you think?"

Martin studied the artwork. It was an allegorical painting of cannon turning into factory smokestacks and a medieval castle transformed into a Bauhaus-style apartment building. The colors were vivid orange and red with the title of the book in black.

"It looks like a Comintern poster."

"Precisely! We seek eye-appeal at the factory gate, as it were. We won't sell many copies in the House of Lords, you know. A good proletarian book cover, if you ask me."

"A bit . . . garish."

"The whole point, my dear Rilke. We want the book to fairly scream out to be purchased by those poor souls who bore the brunt of the last war and will no doubt bear the brunt of the next." He beamed with delight. "We'll sell out the first printing, never fear. I have the highest of hopes for this one, old boy."

"I hope you're right, Arnold. Is there any way I can help?"

Calthorpe propped the drawing against the side of the desk. "A speaking tour would do no harm. I was hoping to have you interviewed by John Mugg on the BBC, but he would have none of that. Refused to give you a forum—his word—a *forum* for disarmament philosophies. Willing to have you on the air if you would promise to confine yourself to a discussion of American wireless news commentators vis-à-vis British news readers. That sort of twaddle. Turned him down flat. A total waste of your valuable time."

It was nice to know that his time was valuable, as he certainly had enough of it on his hands. He sat in the office until nearly noon discussing one thing or another with Calthorpe and Jeremy Crofts, and then he went with Calthorpe to drop off the cover drawing at a lithography shop near Covent Garden and then on to lunch at Whipple's.

It was only two thirty as he headed home, the taxi crawling through the traffic on Piccadilly. A long day stretching ahead. Albert would be back at school by now. He would, he suddenly realized, miss him.

"Oh, I'm so glad you're here, Mr. Rilke," the housekeeper said, meeting him in the hall as he closed the front door. "Lady Stanmore just rang up. Desperate anxious to talk to you she was. I couldn't understand half she was telling me . . . but I wrote it down." She squinted at a scrap of paper in her hand. "Something about the three-twenty for Waterloo . . . or . . . call her if you come in before three—Marylebone seven-nine-eight-six, I think she said."

The elderly woman was flustered and Martin calmed her down with a pat on the arm.

"That's all right, Mrs. Bromley. I know the number. I'll call her right away."

"Oh, yes, sir, please do. She seemed in such a state."

He had never called Lady Stanmore's house without having a servant answer and intone "Stanmore residence," but it was she who picked up the phone on the first ring with a quavering, "Yes?"

"It's Martin, Aunt Hanna. Is there anything wrong?"

THE TRAIN CLATTERED through the gray fringe of London—on trestle and embankment through Battersea, Clapham, and Wandsworth: Rows of slate-roofed houses and serpentine streets. The occasional green patch of a playing field, gas works' small factories, refuse dumps and scrapped cars, and then the city fading into strings of red-brick townlets and open space. Railway cuttings thick with wildflowers, hedgerowed meadows, soft hills, and distant woods, the tower of a Norman church rising above a frieze of elm—Surrey, the most English of England's counties sweeping past the windows of the train.

"Almost there," Martin said. "It won't be long now."

Hanna Rilke Greville, Countess of Stanmore, said nothing. She stared blindly through the window in a stupor of dread. Her gloved hands rested in her lap, fingers twisting a handkerchief of Belgian lace. She was still a beauty at sixty-one. Her golden hair had grayed and her once voluptuous figure had thickened, but, looking at her radiant skin and vivid blue eyes, it was not difficult to understand how this Chicago heiress had taken London society by storm at nineteen and captured Anthony Greville's heart. That heart may have stopped forever as far as she knew. The telephone call from Abingdon had been clear enough, but the words had thrown her into such a panic that they had become hopelessly jumbled in her mind—a sudden death . . . a collapse on a horse . . . pain . . . doctors. A litany of tragedies. She was grateful that Martin had called the Pryory and spoken to Charles, and that Martin sat beside her now, but his reassurances and comforts could not still her feeling of impending doom.

"Abingdon station next, Aunt Hanna." He touched her

restless hands. "You must stop tormenting yourself. I'm sure Anthony will be fine."

"He could be dead."

"No . . . no. Some sort of spell or seizure. He's at home, in his own bed, Charles said. If it had been anything terribly serious they would have taken him to the hospital in Guildford. Now, you know that."

"There's death in that house," she whispered.

He squeezed her hands. "Mr. Coatsworth died. A very old man."

"Yes . . . dear Coatsworth . . . and now my Tony." She raised her eyes to heaven and cried in anguish: *"Wo bist du, Gott?"*

She spoke German only when under great stress, the comforting language of her childhood. She had been ten years old before her father had permitted English to be spoken in the house.

Martin answered her in German, holding her tightly. God, he said with quiet emphasis, is always with us. He never deserts anyone. He is with her and Anthony. He was with Mr. Coatsworth when he died . . . bringing the death that is no more than the natural end of life's phase. As Heine said in a poem . . . Men will arise and depart. Only one thing is immortal: The love that is in my heart. "Hold on to that love, Aunt Hanna," he said in English. "It will sustain you."

She began to cry softly, pressing the twisted handkerchief against her eyes. When the train pulled into Abingdon she had composed herself and stepped onto the platform dry-eyed and steeled for the worst.

Charles was there to meet them, looking gaunt and pale. She scanned his face, searching for signs.

"Is he . . . still alive?"

Charles embraced her. "Of course he is, Mother. A fortnight in bed and he'll be good as new."

"What did the doctor say?" Martin asked.

"Angina pectoris."

Hanna gasped. "His heart! I knew it!"

"It sounds worse than it is," Charles assured her. "More frightening than fatal. He responded instantly to a nitroglycerin tablet. But he must stay in bed. You'll have to be very firm with him."

"If I have to tie him down with ropes!"

A chauffeur took Martin's small pigskin valise, containing just a few items of clothing and shaving gear, and led the way to the venerable Rolls-Royce parked in front of the station.

Charles smiled wryly at his cousin. "It takes a crisis to get you down here for a few days. You will stay through Saturday, won't you?"

"If you want me to."

"I'd appreciate it." He lowered his voice. "Coatsworth's funeral. I welcome your moral support."

The chauffeur held the car door open for them and a few moments later the gleaming Silver Ghost was pulling away, as smoothly as a bolt of silk swept along the road.

A village no more, Martin observed as they drove up the High Street. He had first seen Abingdon in the early spring of 1914, a day such as this with great fleecy clouds drifting over the hills and the soft smell of rain on the wind. A quiet place. A cobblestoned main street with one or two automobiles and dozens of horse-drawn carts and wagons. Sheep and cattle being driven in for market day to the pens where the railway station now stood. The nearest station in those days had been Godalming, twelve miles away. Suburbia now. F. W. Woolworth; a Marks & Spencer; an Odeon cinema palace with a garish marquee. And beyond the town, rows of neat little villas with rose bushes, laburnum, greenhouses, and birdbaths.

The houses ended at the edge of Leith Common with its rolling meadows and tangled undergrowth. There were still herds of deer in Leith Wood—King's deer protected by the Crown—and foxes that were hunted in the winter. The road skirted the common and Abingdon Pryory came into view, its myriad brick and stone chimneys seen above the beeches and evergreens that screened the house. The chauffeur slowed the car in front of ornamental iron gates as one of the groundkeepers swung them open. Beyond the gates, a mile-long gravel drive meandering to the house.

Well, Martin thought, some things did not change: the Pryory in all its stunning magnificence, its limestone façade mellow in the afternoon sun. An oasis of richness and stability in a world reeling into chaos. Only serenity here among formal gardens and clipped lawns, broad stone terraces and gently swaying trees.

Hanna and Charles went upstairs to see Anthony and talk to the doctor. Martin trailed the butler into the library where a drink was offered and not refused.

He slumped into a leather chair, sipped a gin and bitters, and stared morosely at the dusk-tinged windows. He associated the room with Anthony Greville. The silver riding trophies . . . the decanters of whisky and gin . . . the myriad leather-bound books, few of which his uncle had ever read . . . *"No time for it, dear lad . . . no ruddy time for it."* A strong, vital, sporting man. Impossible to think of him struck low.

"Martin Rilke, is it?"

A slender, gray-haired man entered the room carrying a medical bag which he set on a table by the door.

"Yes," Martin said, half rising from his chair.

"Don't get up," the man said, advancing across the room. "Is that pink gin you're drinking?"

"It is."

"Any more about?"

Martin gestured toward a sideboard. "Any number of bottles over there."

"Of course there are. I was a fool to ask. Gin's the perfect sundown drink, wouldn't you say? Sharpens the appetite for dinner." He crossed to the sideboard, poured gin into a glass, and added a few drops of Angostura. He then leaned back against the heavy oak table and smiled at Martin. "You wouldn't remember me, of course. Lord no, but I remember you. Nineteen fourteen . . . a few months before the war. A supper party to welcome you to England."

"I remember," Martin said.

"Perhaps, but not *me.* Most unlikely. One face in the crowd. The name's Morton . . . David Morton, physician and surgeon. *Sir* David, blowin' me own horn. County coroner and former M.P. for Crawley. Best slow bowler Surrey ever fielded in 'eighty-eight. Captain of the eleven when his nibs and I were at school."

"You've known Anthony that long?"

"Lord, yes. Same age to the month. 'Course I look older.

Only natural. Led a harder life." He swirled the gin and bitters in his glass. "I'm a bloody good doctor in spite of playing cricket and going off to Parliament. Might have snagged a peerage if I hadn't opposed the war so vocally. But did me duty, though, to put it mildly; cut, sew, and amputate for four bloody years as chief of surgery at Number Seven General Boulogne. Bellowed me rage every second of the time." He fixed his hard, pale eyes on Martin's face. "Still bellowing, if it comes to that. Past president of No More War International, Surrey and Sussex chapter, and represented *all* England at the Brussels conference two years ago. Your books are bibles to me." He raised his glass. "So this is to you, for your arguments for sanity, past and future, and to your new book."

"How did you know there's a new book?"

The doctor swallowed his drink and set the glass on the table.

"I'm on Calthorpe and Crofts mailing list. *An End to Castles,* is that right? Due out in June. Half a crown. Sent my order in right away for a dozen copies, though I dare say I'll be purchasing more than that. Pass 'em out like ruddy pills." He drew a silver watch from his waistcoat and scowled at it. "Must be off. Anthony and his angina have played havoc with my rounds."

"Will he be all right?"

"Lord, yes. Tough as brass, that man. Went into a temporary emotional turmoil and his coronary arteries sent him a message to get his feet back on the ground. Always keep a level head, young man, and you'll keep a steady heart." He started for the door as Martin stood up. "Charles told the gaffer you were here. He'd like to see you. Slipped him a stiff sedative so he might not be too coherent. Gave her ladyship one as well and packed her off to bed." He gripped Martin's hand and shook it vigorously. "Damn glad to meet you again, Rilke. As we say in the movement—peace on earth!"

Charles was on the upper landing of the south wing, smoking a cigarette and gazing at the portrait of an ancestor on the wall.

"Which Greville is that?" Martin asked as he came up to him.

"The third earl—also a Charles. Chancellor of the exchequer in William and Mary's time. Made a fortune out of the job, or so legend has it. I was trying to find a resemblance."

"Same nose."

"Weak chin—mean little eyes."

"Well, all the good Chicago and Milwaukee blood changed that. Nothing like being half American to strengthen the face."

"I daresay." He took an awkward puff on the cigarette, not inhaling, and flicked ash on the carpet. "I had a few terrible moments today, Martin. Thought I might become the tenth earl."

"Not much chance of that, if Dr. Morton is any judge."

"I hope to God he's right. He's a first-rate man, but on the old-fashioned side. I'd like to get Father up to London . . . to Guy's Hospital where they have a bit more in the way of equipment than a stethoscope and a pocket watch."

"I'm sure you can arrange it without much trouble."

Charles scowled and puffed furiously. "I thought you knew his nibs better than that. He's lying in the bed he was born in and it would take death itself to get him out of it."

"Perhaps I could put in a word on behalf of modern medical science."

"I wish you would. He has a high respect for your opinions." He buried the smoldering butt of his cigarette in the moist earth of a potted fern. "I have to get back to the school for a while, but perhaps we can have a few games of snooker later and crack a bottle or two."

"Fine. I'd like that."

"So would I." He touched Martin awkwardly on the shoulder. "I'm glad you're here. You always make things right, somehow."

Martin grinned. "I just bumble through."

"No." His long, gentle face was solemn. "You have life by the throat. I truly envy you, Martin."

He watched Charles walk away toward the stairs; tall, long-legged, dressed in baggy tweeds. His dark, curly hair had receded from the high dome of his forehead. He looked older than thirty-nine. Not the thinning hairline and the stooped shoulders, but an attitude, a middle-aged aura of weary acceptance.

There was an elderly nurse in the earl's room and she rose from a chair as Martin entered, an admonishing finger pressed to her lips.

"He's been given a sedative," she whispered. "I really don't think you—"

"I'm not asleep," came a muffled voice from the bed. "Go downstairs and have your dinner."

"I'm not to leave the room, Your Lordship. Doctor's orders."

"Damn the doctor. This is my house, Sister. Kindly do as you're told."

Martin whispered to her: "I'll only be a few minutes. Why don't you wait in the sitting room?"

Her face reflected her disapproval, but she left.

"Well, now," Martin said as he drew a chair to the bedside. "What sort of nonsense have you been up to?"

The earl rolled over and drew himself up onto one elbow. "The old heart hit me for six this morning, Martin. It quite betrayed me."

"Angina. Not as bad as all that."

"No, I suppose not."

"Still, a heart is a heart. Charles would like to have you at Guy's—for a complete checkup."

"Would he? I don't much like the idea. Bloody bunch of medicos pawing all over me and clucking their tongues. God alone knows what a group of bright young chaps might find abhorrent in a sixty-eight-year-old body. I won't have it. I refuse to be a candidate for collective predissection." His head slumped to the pillow. "Oh, Lord, they gave me something fizzy in a glass. I feel quite odd."

"A sedative. To make you sleep."

"Yes. A sedative. I sleep well. A few whiskies and a glass of port. Sleep like a log. No more of that, I suppose."

"A whisky a day won't do you any harm. Cut out the cigarettes, though."

"Yes. That will please Hanna. Filthy habit anyway." He struggled against sleep and managed to sit up. "Good of you to come, Martin. Pleased Hanna . . . and me. Oddest thing, old boy . . . truly the oddest thing. Ever happen to you?"

"What?"

"Rather like going to a moving-picture show. Everything so uncannily vivid . . . scenes . . . voices . . . Charlie down from Eton talking to Coatsworth in the pantry. And I was playing tennis on the lawn with Raymond Halliburton the summer

Coatsworth arrived in a dogcart with all his luggage. Big man with muttonchop whiskers. Back straight as a gun. Hired him away from Lord Chelmsford. He soon set the house straight. Sacked half the servants for incompetence. Oh, I don't know, Martin. Queer sort of day with the past crowding in on me like that. Do you ever recall events with such awful clarity?"

"There were times when I was obsessed by memory."

"The war, you mean? Yes. Like Charlie counting the faces of the dead. Quite understandable though, isn't it? I mean to say . . . memories of the Somme . . . Gallipoli. There was nothing ghastly in my thoughts today. Only . . . how can I put it? A terrible sadness. Something lost, you see. That old man dead and so much dying with him."

"I understand."

"Knew you would . . . if anybody . . ."

"I'd get some sleep now."

"Quite so . . . quite so." He sank back to the pillows. "Very queer day indeed . . . but . . . all things . . . pass."

2

MARTIN ATE DINNER alone in a room lined with oak paneling and carved stone, two servants in livery standing motionless behind him against the wall. He poked at the superbly roasted beef and drank a red Burgundy, Hospices de Beaune, 1921, and, for some reason, felt immeasurably depressed. When the servants brought coffee, cognac, and cigars, the tall, diamond-paned windows began to rattle as a wind-borne rain slashed against them.

"Looks like the weather's changed for the worst," he said, as much to hear a human voice as for any other reason.

"Indeed it does, sir," one of the servants replied—and left the room.

He followed the ritual of preparing and lighting a fine Cuban panatella, sipped cognac, and blew smoke down the table, watching it drift past the empty chairs. He had just finished his first glass when the door opened and Charles came into the room, rubbing his hands and scowling.

"Christ! It's blowing a gale. The side curtains on the car don't fit and I was damn near soaked."

"Side curtains on a Rolls?"

"*My* car, old chap—a rustic Austin."

"Have you eaten?"

"Yes. School grub."

"Messing with the inmates, eh?"

"We try to eat together as often as possible. Makes for a family atmosphere."

"How is it?"

"The finest school meals in England—which isn't exactly saying much. But we try our best. A bit heavy on lamb stew and shepherd's pie." He took a glass from the sideboard and poured himself a stiff brandy. "Care for a game?"

They took the decanter into the billiard room and Charles racked the balls in a desultory fashion, his mind not on the task.

"Did you have a good talk with Father?"

Martin chalked his stick. "Short. The sedative was taking effect. He balked at the idea of going to a hospital, but I think he can be persuaded."

"I hope so. Was he still dwelling on the past?"

"Yes."

Charles frowned and rolled the cue ball from hand to hand. "That was all he talked about with me. He felt certain he was following Coatsworth to the grave and a lot of his disappointments in life came pouring out. His *bitterness* is a better word, perhaps. The world that used to be. Regrets for an altered landscape—and altered lives. Mine in particular, probably—although he left that unsaid."

"You turned out okay."

"I daresay he's thankful that I survived, but, still . . . a schoolmaster . . ." He rolled the white ivory ball to the end of the table. "Care to break?"

"All right." He sighted along his stick. "Warped—this stick and your views. Is that all you think he is, thankful? You're proof to him that miracles exist. You should have been fifty times dead . . . or still hidden away in Wales with the shell-shocked and the basket cases. You're a lucky man, Charles, so please keep the undertone of self-pity out of the conversation."

"Sorry. This has been a crisis to warp anyone's viewpoint. Father's not the only one who's been dwelling in the past. My entire life passed in formal review. Charles Greville marching toward forty—though *slinking* would be the more apt term . . . and if that be self-pity, make the most of it."

Martin laughed and placed his stick back in the wall rack.

"The colly-wobbles of middle age. I know all the signs."

"You? Nonsense. Height of your powers. Premier news wallah. The world's your oyster. I'm curled up in the bloody shell."

"You don't really believe that, do you?"

"Not usually. I've been content the past few years. But it's a day for questioning, isn't it? Death hovers and thoughts soar. The things one did not do seem to loom with exaggerated regret."

Martin turned to the table where the decanter rested and refilled the glasses.

"Why don't we forget snooker and get pie-eyed?"

Brandy became heavy on the tongue and Charles sent the butler for a couple of bottles of Pommery. The champagne, pleasantly iced, had a sobering effect on Martin, clearing his head while imparting a mellow glow. It seemed the perfect drink to have while seated in front of a fire while rain slapped against the windowpanes and wind moaned across the chimney opening far above. Charles, who rarely drank more than a sherry before dinner and a glass of port afterward, began to feel the effects. He slouched in his chair, legs stretched out toward the fire, staring at the flames.

"Roger couldn't drink. You remember Roger Wood-Lacy, don't you?"

"Of course," Martin said.

"Couldn't drink at all. One drop of alcohol made him ill. I recall a night at Cambridge . . . May Week. Roger and I . . . and two girls whose names I can't remember . . . in a boat on the river, Japanese lanterns swaying in Rectory Meadows. I possessed a small silver flask filled with cherry brandy. Roger took a sip and the girls had to paddle us ashore while I tried to keep his face out of the water." He drained his glass and refilled it. "Couldn't keep his face out of the water at Sedd el Bahr, I'm afraid."

"I wouldn't think about that," Martin said quietly.

"I think about it, but never *dwell* upon it. V Beach and Gallipoli seem a thousand years in the past. So does Contalmaison and Delville Wood. Even the Royal Windsor Fusiliers have disappeared from the army list, done in by the budget. All flags cased. All dead noted and filed away—but difficult to forget. Although I do try, Martin. Try very hard. I suppose that's the main reason I like Burgate. There's something womblike about being a schoolmaster. A safe haven."

"There's a difference between a safe haven and a hideout."

"A point well made. Let's just say that I'm aware of it."

"Ever start that book on your English civil war?"

Charles held his glass to the light and squinted at the stream of rising bubbles. "The two-volume history? Actually, no. Although I did write an article which was published in the Guildford *Gazette.* Some ass felt there should be a monument raised to commemorate the Battle of Abingdon. I pointed out that there had been merely a skirmish here, in what is now our orchard, between a Roundhead patrol and a troop of Prince Rupert's horse. July, sixteen forty-two. A brave encounter but hardly worthy of a sixty-loot granite column supporting a bronze Cavalier. I squelched that ludicrous plan quickly enough, so my writing is not without worth."

"Everything you do has worth. They've even heard of Burgate House back in the States. A sterling example of the progressive-school movement, the *New York Sun* called it."

"Did they? Nothing quite so grand here, let me tell you. *Radical* and *Bolshevik* are the terms most used to describe us. A nest of little wild-eyed anarchists festering amid the Surrey hills!" He popped the cork of the second bottle. "Not that I pay much attention to critics. It's results that count. Our bunch may not conform to the public-school mold, no 'old boys' or school ties, but we do turn out children who can think for themselves, are self-reliant and emotionally solid."

He drained his glass. "You should see the state of some of those kids when we first get them. Out-of-control little savages . . . or beaten down into a stupor. Just flailing about, trying to make some sense out of their lives. Not unlike myself when the Mastwicks took me on as a teacher. Groping for something solid to cling to." He refilled Martin's glass and his own. "I have been very . . . content there, Martin. I know Father would have preferred I . . . well, why go into that? Not important, is it?"

"No."

"A good life, really. Productive and challenging. I've been . . . happy. All things . . . considered."

It was the second bottle of champagne that finished Charles. He struggled to stay awake and required Martin's help to get up the stairs to his room. His room, kept intact by Hanna for the rare times that he slept in it. The walls were lined with bookcases—books of his childhood, books from Eton and Cambridge. A tennis racket on the wall. A cricket bat. Amber-tinted photographs of boys in straw skimmers with a background of willows and the river at Windsor. An Edwardian room preserved. Martin made sure that Charles got into the bed and not under it and then turned out the light.

Hanna maintained special rooms for special people in the forty-bedroom house. There were rooms for her children. Charles's room, William's and Alexandra's. William lived on his horse farm in Derbyshire when he wasn't on the racing circuit. Alexandra lived in La Jolla, California. The rooms stood waiting, dusted and polished. There was a room for Martin, although he might not use it from one year to the next. Hanna's idea of sentimentality in giving it to him. The room he had stayed in when first coming to England in June 1914. And Ivy Thaxton had brought a vase of flowers and set it on a table. Slender and dark haired. Uptilted nose and violet eyes. Her maid's uniform so heavily starched she rustled when she walked. Seventeen years old and as lovely as summer twilight.

Christ!

He wasn't a champagne drinker, and God knows he wasn't a cognac-*and*-champagne drinker, and he was feeling the effects of the mixture. He removed his shoes, curled up on the bed, and drew the eiderdown comforter around him. The lamp still burned but he lacked the energy to get up and turn it off. The wind was dying and the rain had stopped. Water dripped from the trees outside the window, plip-plopping to the ground as melancholy as tears.

BRIGADIER FENTON WOOD-LACY had bitter thoughts.

"Twenty-two years in service to king and country is time enough for any man."

Major General Sir John Towerside had made that observation with pointed casualness at first light, over tea and biscuits at the conclusion of a night exercise on Salisbury Plain. *"Long and fruitful years, Hawk,"* the general had continued. *"If I were you, I'd pack it in now while you're still a young man, take a directorship with Vickers."*

"Silly old bugger," Fenton muttered, slumped on the back seat of his car.

The civilian beside him nodded in agreement. "Yes, but it wasn't the worst advice in the world. Most men would jump at the chance of retiring at forty."

"The man's a bloody fool, Jacob."

Jacob Golden, owner and publisher of the London *Daily Post,* tugged the brim of his fedora low over his pale, slender face and gazed out the side window at a straggling column of rain-blackened cavalry. The rain had stopped and morning mist clung to the ground, obscuring the more distant shapes of tanks lumbering off across the plain, nose to tail like so many weary elephants. "Oil and water, Fenton. It's as simple as that. Water for horses, oil for tanks. The good Sir John can't get them to mix."

Fenton swore under his breath and leaned forward to roll up the glass partition, insulating them from the soldier-driver.

"Who the hell can? Towerside's stupidity is that he insists on trying. He claims it's for the good of the service. The perpetuation of the useless bloody cavalry, he means. The fool's been around horses too much—not the brightest animals in the world, I might add."

"May I quote you on that? Brigadier makes un-English comment, says horses are stupid. Good heavens, you'll be disparaging dogs next."

The brigadier fished a battered box of cigarettes from one of the many pockets in his oil-splattered black canvas coveralls. The black beret and his own dark, hawklike face gave him a satanic look. "You believe he's right, don't you? Chucking it in, I mean."

Jacob stifled a yawn. "You know my views by now. Why bother to ask?"

"It would make Winnie happy. And the girls. Pillar to post. No proper home. Odd sort of life for them."

"Army brats, as the Yanks say."

"Do you really think Vickers would offer me a directorship?"

"Of course. They love having old soldiers at board meetings. All that talk about the glorious past over cakes and port."

"Twenty-two years." He lit a cigarette with a brass lighter of primitive design. Engraved on one side of it were the words *To "The Hawk" in gratitude. The Officers and Men. 8th Btl. The Green Howards. 1/4/19.* An irreverent lot, he recalled dimly. *The Hawk,* indeed! Saucy bastards. But he had been secretly pleased by the sobriquet at the time. Now everyone in the army called him that, except the men of course—at least not to his face. "I've been around a bit in twenty-two years, Jacob."

"We all have, dear chap."

"The Coldstreams. Those were the good years. Playing at soldiering. Palace guard . . . the Marlborough Club . . . parties every night . . . bedding Mayfair debutantes right and left. A shame the war came along and mucked it all up."

"Yes. A pity. But that's the Germans for you. Always ruining a chap's social life."

"You facetious bastard." He blew smoke through his nostrils. "If I gave it up now I'm afraid the Tank Corps would suffer the loss. Not that any one man is indispensable, mind you."

Jacob yawned openly and drew his Burberry closer around his thin body. "You are . . . at this particular time. They may dread the sight of you at the War Office, but they have to respect your views. And certainly the readers of the *Daily Post* respect them. A fully mechanized army means jobs from Bristol to Leeds. No one derives a living from the cavalry except harness makers. As your oldest friend, I would have liked seeing you out of the service years ago. As a newspaper publisher with the largest daily readership in the world to keep entertained, I find you indispensable in your current role."

Fenton, Jacob knew, would do what he wanted without any advice from him. What he wanted, of course, was to stay in the army, in his precious Tank Corps, to run it and mold it without interference from mossback generals who did not share his visions. The interference would continue because new concepts had always been resisted—an army tradition—and Fenton would grit his teeth and hang on to fight for his convictions. His intractability was apparent in every line of his handsome, weather-worn face.

Jacob's smile was knowing as he looked at his friend, the tall, whip-lean body now slumped forward with fatigue, head nodding toward his chest. He reached out and took the smoldering cigarette from between the brigadier's fingers and tossed it out of the window.

A long friendship and an unlikely one, he was thinking. They had first met as boys at a preparatory school as renowned for its excellence as it was infamous for its snobbery. Fenton the son of Queen Victoria's favorite architect, and he the son of a Jewish press lord. That his father was the confidant of kings and the savior or destroyer of prime ministers had meant nothing to the boys of that school. He had simply been dismissed as "a detestable little Jew" whose father owned "that common rag, the *Post,*" and every effort had been made to make him feel unwanted. But Fenton, the tallest and strongest boy in the school, had befriended him, though not entirely out of his fierce sense of fair play. The elder Wood-Lacy, who had designed the *Daily Post* building in London, had asked him to do so. It had hardly been a friendship made in heaven, their views on almost all matters being too disparate for that, but Fenton had offered his hand and, over the course of those school years, a bond had been forged. Time had done nothing to diminish it. They had followed widely different paths, but that long ago handshake remained as firm as ever.

Jennifer Wood-Lacy spotted the car as it turned off the Andover road and up the narrow lane leading to the house. She whistled for the dogs who were chasing rabbits through the brambles and began to run across the muddy field, oblivious to the petulant cries of her twin.

"Oh, wait for me, can't you!" Victoria was shouting, burdened by a pair of rubber boots too large for her feet. "Do slow up! Oh, don't be beastly!"

Jennifer ran on unheeding, a tall thirteen-year-old, leggy as a colt. Both she and her wailing counterpart had their father's looks . . . the dark, aquiline features, the black hair, but she was more daughter to the man than her sister. Was, she had always liked to think, the brigadier's son, riding by his right side into battle. Budding breasts had shattered the dream. Victoria was in ecstasy over hers. Simply drooling at her femininity. It was enough to make one physically sick. She ran faster, leaving her sister far behind, vaulted a low hedge and reached the lane just as the car turned the bend. The driver slowed to a halt as she jumped the ditch and stood in the center of the road waving her arms.

"Good morning, Lance Corporal Ryan," she called out cheerfully.

"Good morning, Miss . . . Jennifer?"

"Of course Jennifer," she snapped. It was irritating to be confused with Victoria. Identical twins, but she would never have it so. She thought of her sister in the bathroom that morning, reverentially massaging her tiny mammary glands with some dreadful cold cream she had bought at Boots. Her fury almost choked her, but dissipated instantly as she opened the side door.

"Good morning, Daddy . . . Uncle Jacob." She climbed into the car and sprawled onto the seat between them, closing the door as she did so. The two muddy Airedales started barking and running up and down the road. "Drive on, Lance Corporal Ryan!"

"The window's up," her father said. "And besides, I give the orders here. We'll wait for Vicky."

"She *wants* to walk," she said hurriedly. "She *insists* on walking *five* miles every day. She's quite dotty about it."

Jacob could see the girl far off across the field, stumbling, waving her arms. "She doesn't walk very well, does she?"

"She couldn't find her Wellingtons this morning so she had to wear Mother's."

Fenton scowled. "I wonder how that happened." He tapped on the glass partition and the driver put the car in gear. "This childish behavior toward your sister has to cease at once. You were always the best of pals. I won't scold you in front of Vicky, so let this be the final word on the subject."

"Yes, Daddy. I shall love her as dearly as I love Kate. You'll see." She snuggled against him, eyes closed, breathing in his essence, the manly odors of tobacco, petrol, and motor oil, luxuriating in his presence as the car swept on up the lane toward the house a half mile away.

"You smell more than usual like an armored car," Winifred said as she came into the bedroom in her robe, her long brown hair still damp from her bath. She was thirty-four, six years younger than her husband, tall and full bosomed with a roses-and-cream skin that had never known makeup paints or powders.

Fenton grunted as he took off his coveralls and tossed them into a corner. Even his long underwear was oil stained and he peeled that off also.

"Not an armored car, Winnie, a bloody abomination of an

experimental command tank . . . the Hercules Mark Two. Oil and petrol lines leaky as sieves. A wonder we didn't go up like a ruddy bomb. The exercise, needless to say, was another comedy of errors. Dragoons floundering about . . . bolting in front of the tanks. Came damn close to squashing half the king's horses. I'm not in a human mood just now."

"Sorry. You look human enough to me. The basic model of a naked male—Mark One."

Fenton strode to the closet and wrapped himself in a frayed silk dressing gown. "Not a total loss, though, I suppose. At least it gave Jacob a good look at the folly of trying to wed cavalry to tanks. He's planning an editorial on the subject to coincide with the War Office budget meetings next month." He sat on the edge of the bed and glared at his toes. "Not that it'll do much good. Whitehall is gaga over horse soldiers. Regimental elite . . . high social tone. Christ, they believe the charge of the Light Brigade was a glorious British victory! Bad form to get drunk before noon, I suppose."

"What you need is sleep." She sat beside him and rubbed his shoulder. "Hanna telephoned this morning. Coatsworth passed away yesterday . . . and Anthony had a minor attack."

He looked at her in concern. "What kind of attack?"

"Angina. Nothing serious, but they're sending him up to London this afternoon for tests at Guy's. He'll be there a week or so."

"He won't like that, poor chap."

"No, I don't imagine he will. Coatsworth's funeral is Saturday. Hanna would like us to come."

"Of course." He shook his head, smiling with faint sadness. "Coatsworth dead. Hardly seems possible. I was ten when I first met him. *Ten!* Good Lord."

"He must have been close to ninety, I imagine."

"Easily, an elderly man even then. Roger and I had been invited to the Pryory to spend the summer. Father had been engaged to remodel the house and the east wing was covered with scaffolding. He warned us to stay off it, but it was too irresistible. Roger was eight, the same age as Charles. They looked to me for leadership and oh! did I lead them! Up those rickety towers and along narrow catwalks, climbing about like ruddy apes. Coatsworth would bellow at us to come down before we broke our necks."

She rubbed his back, kneading the taut muscles. "And did you obey the poor man?"

"Of course, but we took our sweet time doing so. A noble gentleman, Coatsworth. He never told my father or the earl what we were up to."

"Hanna would like us to stay over for a week and keep her company. That is if the army can spare you."

His laugh was sardonic. "If I ask General bloody Towerside for a week's leave he'd urge me to take a few *years!* You can call Hanna and tell her she has house guests." He turned to her, parting her robe and resting the side of his face against her breasts. "God, you smell wonderful."

"Lavender soap."

"No. Inner loveliness. The perfume of the soul. I'd make love to you, my sweet, but I feel like a corpse."

She kissed the top of his head. "You're making love to me now."

He rolled over on the bed and was asleep instantly. Like a cat, Winifred was thinking as she covered him with a blanket. He would snap awake in three or four hours, springing up as refreshed as though he had enjoyed a full night's rest.

She dressed and went downstairs. She could hear the twins shouting at one another in the back of the house, Victoria's voice a high-pitched note of aggrievement . . .

"You're beastly! *Beastly!* . . ." and Jennifer sounding pained and affronted . . . "Me? *Me? Never!* . . ."

It was not an argument that she cared to referee at the moment and so she continued on through the old, rambling house to the drawing room.

Jacob Golden sat on a sofa drinking a cup of coffee. Eight-year-old Kate Wood-Lacy sat beside him showing off her collection of flowers that she had pressed and dried between the pages of a thick, unwieldy book.

"And this is a primrose," she said, turning the pages with her small hands.

"A primrose by the river's brim . . ." Jacob said. "Wordsworth."

"I plucked it from the *garden.*" She turned the pages. "And this is a jonquil."

"I can't think of any poem with a jonquil in it." He smiled at Winifred as she walked across the room toward them. "Can you, Winnie? Daffodils, but not jonquils."

"No jonquils." She sat on the sofa beside her daughter and brushed a strand of soft brown hair from the girl's forehead. They looked alike. The hair, the oval face, the same cream-and-blush complexion. "I saw Nanny on the landing. She said you didn't tidy up your room as told."

"I will."

"Indeed you will—or you stay here with Nanny when we go to the Pryory on Friday."

The little girl closed the book with a snap. "I'll tidy up . . . you'll see. Will Uncle Anthony let me ride the pony again?"

"Uncle Anthony is in the hospital, dear. He's not feeling very well, but I'm sure Mr. Gardway will take you for a ride."

"The earl's ill?" Jacob asked.

"Angina. I'm sure he'll be all right. His old butler died and I suppose it was a shock to him. He'd been with him for ages."

Kate got off the sofa, cradling the heavy book with both arms. "I'll go to my room now, Mummy. Do you mind not seeing all the flowers, Uncle Jacob?"

"I don't mind, Kate. You can show them to me the next time I come." He watched her leave the room. "A delightful child."

Winifred smiled ruefully. "Thank God I have one calm and collected girl. Jenny continues to be a hellion and Vicky, heaven help us all, has just discovered womanhood! She's a confused mixture of Janet Gaynor and Joan of Arc."

"Just a phase."

"Oh, Lord, I suppose so."

"Where's his nibs?"

"In bed. I must say you look terribly alert."

"Spent most of the night asleep in the back of a staff car. Saw all I needed . . . watery moonlight and total confusion."

"Care to stay over and dine with us?"

"I'd like nothing better, but I must get back to London for a board meeting." He stood up and held out his hands to her. "Come on, walk with me to my car."

They strolled slowly side by side through a large, overgrown garden toward the garages.

"Towerside suggested that your loving husband retire . . . take a job with Vickers, perhaps."

"What nonsense."

"The cavalry generals would love to be rid of him, you know. Prophets are without honor in this country, especially in the army. Fenton is viewed with some alarm. Too unorthodox . . . too much the zealot. He considered Towerside's suggestion for a moment. Felt it would make you happy. Would it?"

She paused and looked at him. "No. I pray the day will come when soldiers no longer exist, but in the meantime, I happen to love one. Can you even conceive of Fenton not being in the army?"

"Difficult to imagine."

"And if he were nudged out I think he'd disintegrate into a brooding, bitter man. I couldn't bear to witness it." There was a wood bench under a grape arbor and she sat down. "I don't mind living in rented houses, trailing around like a camp follower . . . Egypt, India . . . tutors for the girls, training new servants every couple of years . . . don't mind any of that as long as he's reasonably content in his job. And soldiering *is* his job. I made my peace with that fact years ago. I wish he had left the service after the war, but he didn't."

"Stubborn pride . . . not wanting to live off your money while he looked about for another career."

"It goes deeper than that, Jacob. Heavens, we live off my money now. A brigadier's wages don't stretch far these days. No. He's obsessed with the idea of remodeling the British army to his own specific vision. It's not a vision that many share, so naturally he's resented . . . even feared. The army is like the civil service, everyone jealously protecting their own little place in it. They look on Fenton as a threat."

"Yes, and not without reason. At least in this country." He sat on the bench beside her. "Would you find a few years in India too abhorrent?"

She watched swallows dart in slender blurs over the wild, unpruned garden. "Why do you ask?"

"I'll come to that."

"It's not Hampshire, but I've always liked the country . . . Simla especially. Even Quetta during the cooler months."

"Don't for God's sake say anything, but some of my gray lads have come up with something."

"Your what lads?"

"Gray lads. A host of petty clerks . . . Whitehall drones . . . faceless, meek little creatures who pass on information to me for a quid or two. I have a network of them. Even have a gray lad at Buckingham Palace."

She laughed and squeezed his arm. "Oh, Jacob, it's a good thing they no longer hang, draw, and quarter people on Tower Hill!"

"I can think of some people in Britain who would relish a revival of the practice—for the exclusive chastisement of labor leaders and Jewish newspaper owners. Anyway, one of my inquisitive little spies informs me that a move is afoot in Delhi to start modernizing the Indian army. The plan is for a completely mechanized brigade—including the dehorsing of two cavalry regiments and placing the bewildered chaps in armored cars. Fenton's gospel to the letter. Our lad would be the obvious choice to train and lead such a group, but politics being what they are, there's no guarantee he would be chosen. I will have to go to work on it with my usual quiet diplomacy and Byzantine intriguing. It's all extremely hush-hush at the moment. If Fenton got wind of it he'd go smashing his way through the War Office cliques like a bull in a china shop ruffling feathers and stomping on toes. So mum's the word, please."

She gave his hand a quick squeeze. He was about the same age as her husband, and yet he looked years younger. A fine-boned, delicate face that would have been pretty had it not been for the sardonic twist to the mouth and the vulpine eyes. "You always look out for him."

He turned to her and kissed her softly on the cheek. "And you, Winnie."

THEY BURIED John Harum Coatsworth on Saturday morning, a cloudless day, the High Street thronged with shoppers. It was a simple ceremony—as Coatsworth would have wished—and Charles's eulogy was brief, if heartfelt. The vicar, mindful of the fact that many of those in attendance were servants from the Pryory, wished to read the passage from Matthew that began with . . . *"Well done, thou good and faithful servant . . ."* but Hanna dissuaded him and he chose a selection from Isaiah instead. The last of Coatsworth's three favorite hymns was sung and then the casket was carried into the churchyard.

Massive oaks shaded lush, damp grass and old gravestones. The vicar intoned a prayer.

"In the midst of life we are in death . . ."

The younger parlormaids, dressed in their best frocks, fidgeted at the back of the crowd, casting anxious glances toward the bustle of the High Street. They had been given a holiday until five that afternoon and they yearned to make the most of it.

". . . of the Resurrection unto eternal life. Amen."

The mourners dispersed, the servants hurrying—without appearing too eager—toward the excitements of the town: the F. W. Woolworth's, the tea shops, and the pubs.

Winifred, holding a fidgeting Kate firmly by the hand, and trailed by the twins, both wearing expressions of almost theatrical somberness, walked over to where her husband stood talking with Martin and Charles and William Greville. The Hon. William, seven years younger than his brother, was a giant of a man who could easily have shouldered the casket to the grave without the aid of his fellow pallbearers—could have, that is, if his right knee, shattered by a bullet in 1917, had been up to the strain.

"We're all expected at the vicarage for sherry," Winifred said.

Charles shook his head. "Tea. Glynis Masefield made cress sandwiches and a Madeira cake."

William, his knee aching from kneeling at prayers, rubbed it vigorously and scowled. "Oh, bugger that. I'm for a pint or two at the Rose and Crown."

"So am I," Charles said, "but I'd best attend. It would embarrass Mother and disappoint Glynis terribly. You chaps sneak away. You won't be missed."

The three men took him at his word and trailed the crowd moving along the gravel path toward the street. William cast a final glance over his shoulder at the grave.

"Poor old codger. I was the bane of his life. God, how he dreaded my coming down from Eton on hols, usually with two or three of my friends—rowdies all. We were always trying to find some way of breaking into the wine cellar. He managed to foil all our schemes, but it left him a nervous wreck. Oh, well, *de mortuis* and all that. He was a decent old soul."

"Your father will miss him," Fenton said.

"Lord, yes. That was all he talked of when I telephoned him from Dublin yesterday—that and the uncivilized food. Poor Father. Never been ill a day in his life. He finds the whole hospital routine quite beyond his understanding. Dulcie just left one in Leicester. She called him to sympathize and promised to send a Yorkshire ham."

"Dulcie ill?" Fenton asked.

"Had the tubes tied—thank God and about time, too. That last miscarriage nearly did her in. No heirs from us and that's certain."

"Who is Glynis, by the way?" Martin asked.

William laughed. "The vicar's niece. A pallid, mousy little thing. Mother finds her attractive only because she's remained unmarried, and impregnably virgin I daresay, to the age of thirty. Any unattached female of acceptable social background is fair game for Mother's artful nets."

"I have the impression Charles isn't interested in women at the moment."

"Quite so. He wants only to be left alone in the sanctuary of Burgate House School. Wouldn't you agree, Fenton?"

"I'm afraid so, yes."

William shook his leonine head. "Christ! Talk about a lost generation. If all the people *ruined* by the war had their names carved on stone shafts there wouldn't be quarries enough to mine them!"

They were in the shadow of the war memorial at the top of the High Street . . .

FOR KING AND COUNTRY
1914–1918

. . . chiseled into the pale marble. Martin avoided looking at it. He knew only one of the names carved below the inscription—Ivy Thaxton Rilke of Queen Alexandra's Imperial Military Nursing Service—but that one was enough.

"How was Ireland?" he asked as they crossed the street.

"Wet. But successful. I bought a super colt in Kilkenny. A real Derby prospect."

"For yourself?"

"Yes. The old Biscuit Tin Stables. I've stopped training for others, although it was fun while it lasted—especially in the States. Saratoga . . . Belmont. I'll miss all that . . . and the bloody marvelous parties Jock Haynes used to toss at East Hampton. Poor old Jock. I understand he lost everything in the crash."

They turned off the busy street and down a short, cobblestoned alley that led to the Rose and Crown, Abingdon's oldest public house. William ducked through the low doorway of a tobacconist to buy a box of cigarettes while Fenton and Martin continued walking slowly toward the pub.

"Hesitate to ask, old boy," Fenton drawled, "but how did Mistress Wall Street treat you?"

"With a kiss on the brow. I was advised to sell out a few months before the deluge. The only shares I owned were CBC radio. Bought them at twelve dollars and sold at three hundred and five. They're down to eighteen today. I made a fortune and someone got burned. Feel a bit guilty about it, to tell the truth."

"No need to feel that. A fundamental economic law. For every winner on the stock exchange there are ten who lose their shirts."

To step inside the Rose and Crown was to step back in time. It could have been 1913 in the murky, dark oak interior, or 1813 for that matter. No American-style cocktails were served. Beer in oak barrels from the Kentish Weald. Scotch whisky in stone crocks. Good English gin—not blasphemed by French vermouth. The only concession to the times was ice for the gin and tonics—but then only on request and grudgingly, and sparingly, slipped into the glass from a teaspoon. Fenton ordered three pints of bitter. When William entered the crowded bar he was quickly surrounded by a boisterous group of men all sporting cloth caps, checked tweed jackets, and riding boots. He introduced them as friends from the racing circuit and members of the Abingdon Hunt Club. The ensuing conversation regarding steeplechasing as compared to flat racing was too esoteric for Martin and Fenton, who slipped away with their beers and went outside to sit on a bench beside a whitewashed wall.

"Horses!" Fenton muttered in disgust. "Whoever it was who said that England was hell for horses and heaven for women didn't know what he was talking about. The average Englishman would much prefer to make love to a horse."

"Difficult."

"Where there's a will, and all that." He took a sip of his beer. "I read your book, by the way. *An End to Castles.*"

"How did you manage? It's not out yet."

"Arnold Calthorpe sent Winnie a galley proof. Thick as thieves, those two. Winnie's money helps keep his presses churning out pamphlets for No More War International."

Martin set his glass on the bench and took a leather cigar case from his coat pocket. "A pacifist wife. How does that go down with the brass hats?"

He shrugged and accepted one of Martin's cigars. "The eccentricities of military wives has been an accepted toleration since Marlborough's day." He passed the cigar under his nose. "Perfect. Cuba?"

"Tampa, Florida."

"Ah, America. The best of all worlds under one roof. I must go there one day. Perhaps when I retire."

"Not thinking of doing that, are you?"

"Well, *I'm* not, but one or two others have suggested it." He lit his cigar and blew smoke from the corner of his mouth. "I liked your book, Martin . . . at least parts of it. You were bang on regarding the French fortress line. That defense minister . . . Maginot . . . allocating billions of francs for a bloody concrete trench! 'Verdun with air-conditioning' . . . as you so succinctly put it."

"He was wounded at Verdun and swore that French soldiers would never have to endure that kind of slaughter again."

"His motive was noble. It's his tactics that are wrong. Dangerous, in fact. A lulling sense of security that paralyzes the initiative of the army to achieve mechanized mobility—but for God's sake don't let me get started on *that* subject."

Martin grinned at his old friend. "No shop talk in the mess—as you used to say."

"I still do, but I don't mind exchanging a view or two with a chap in civvy street. Your motive is as noble as Monsieur Maginot's, and just as wrong. For a man who has seen as much war as you have, I can understand your passionate hatred of it. But the solution for peace which you propose in your book rests on a dream."

"An ideal. A goal worth seeking. No more than that."

"We share the same goal, dear chap. We have different approaches to the problem. God knows I want peace eternal. If Maginot remembers Verdun, I remember the Somme and Passchendaele. No more massacres of poor bloody infantry for a few yards of stinking, bloody ground . . . *ever!* As most *professional* soldiers, I'm as belligerent as a nun, but I do want England to have the best army in the world. A small cadre of forces second to none . . . modern, innovative, daringly imaginative . . . so no nation would risk drawing a sword against her. Peace through power. How does that strike you painted across a banner?"

"I prefer—the power of peace."

Fenton laughed and leaned back against the wall, tilting his face to the sun. "One might hear that phrase uttered at the League of Nations . . . in a speech expressing moral indignation at what the Italians are doing in North Africa. Do you think Mussolini gives a damn if some Swedish pastor is morally dismayed? He wants his new Roman empire and he'll get it if he has to shoot every Arab in Libya. To believe otherwise is naïve, wishful thinking, and you're hardly a naïve man."

"No, but I am a hopeful one. Total world disarmament of heavy weapons and bombing planes is the only certain answer. And it's possible to attain."

The brigadier scowled and took a reflective puff on his cigar. "Perhaps. But that disarmament commission at the League hasn't come up with anything positive on the subject in four years."

"It's not for lack of trying, and you know it. Whenever they make a recommendation one nation or another raises an objection. They're meeting again next month. I might go to Geneva and observe the conference. Their problems would make an interesting article, perhaps even a book."

"There's only *one* problem, dear fellow, and that is which nation will have the courage to be the *first* to toss its guns into the sea and stand naked to its enemies. Do you remember when Jacob came back from the Balkans after that bugger of an archduke got scuppered at Sarajevo?"

"Yes."

"Well, I've never forgotten what he told us . . . that there was an awesome amount of hate festering beyond our bucolic horizons. It seems to me there still is." He drained his beer and stood up. "But there's nothing we can do about that, is there?"

"Not much, I'm afraid."

"Except have another pint." He raised his glass as though brandishing a sword. "Come three-quarters of the world in arms and we shall shock them! If God . . . and the budget . . . be willing."

THE DINNER WAS not up to the Countess of Stanmore's epicurean standards. The half holiday had played havoc with the kitchen staff, the chef and his helpers having raised too many pints to Coatsworth's memory in the pubs of Abingdon. Still, if the saddle of lamb was a bit overdone and the roast potatoes verged on the raw, no one else appeared to notice or care. Hanna took a sip of wine and looked down the long table at her guests. So many of the people she loved most in the world seated before her. It lacked only the presence of her daughter and grandsons, and Anthony home from the hospital, for her contentment to be complete.

"Did I tell you that Alex is coming over this summer?" she said to Winifred.

"No. How wonderful."

"And bringing Colin and young John with her. I shall have a nice, noisy house for a change."

There was a sudden blare of dance music from the direction of the ballroom. Winifred smiled wryly. "You have a noisy house now."

"The girls tuned in the wireless set, bless them."

Winifred half rose from her seat. "I'll tell them to turn down the volume."

Hanna waved her back. "No, dear. I enjoy music."

"Jack Hylton's band by the sound of it," William said. " 'The Syncopation Hour from Savoy Hill.' "

Hanna reached out and touched Winifred's hand. "Remember when Alex used to play her gramophone in the ballroom and taught you all the latest steps?"

"*Tried* to teach me, you mean. The Texas Tommy and the Castle Walk. I was hopeless."

"Only charmingly out of step," Fenton remarked. "I quite fell in love with you. Your interpretation of the Bunny Hug was my undoing."

The girls were dancing by themselves, whirling across the large room in the spangled light from the chandeliers, dipping and swaying to the throbbing tones emanating from a large super-heterodyne radio receiver on the bandstand. When the adults entered with their coffees and brandies, Jennifer ran to her father and begged him to dance with her while Victoria, unconsciously playing the coquette, led Charles playfully onto the floor as the band swung into a foxtrot.

The girls were sent to bed at nine thirty—despite the protests of the twins that they be allowed to stay up until ten. Hanna and Winifred retired shortly after that and the men sought the billiard room. It was past midnight when Fenton went to his suite in the south wing of the huge house, strolling down the long, dimly lit corridors smoking a cigar and humming softly to himself. He felt mellow with brandy and the triumph of having, finally, beaten Martin at a game of snooker. He was surprised to find Winifred awake, sitting up in bed in the dark, the window drapes open and moonlight flooding the room. He put out his cigar, loosened his tie, and sat on the bed beside her. "Can't sleep?"

"I haven't tried. I've been letting my thoughts roam."

He bent to her and kissed her brow. "Over hill and dale?"

"This house. So many undertones."

"Undertones of what?"

"Sadness. Did you notice Hanna's expression while Charles was dancing with Vicky?"

"No. I had a galloping colt of a girl to manage."

"She had such a *pensive* look on her face."

"Not surprising. It's been that sort of a day."

"It had nothing to do with the funeral if that's what you

mean. When we were going upstairs to bed she insisted I come to her sitting room for a glass of sherry and to look at some photographs."

"What photographs?"

"Oh, nineteen fourteen . . . the spring before the war . . . when mother brought me here practically every weekend . . . in *expectation,* as she so bluntly put it."

He grunted and bent down to unlace his shoes. "You and Charlie posed formally in the rose garden."

"Yes."

"The prints suitable for reproduction in the *Court Circular* . . . The Marquess and Marchioness of Dexford announce the engagement of their daughter . . ."

"It was the *way* she showed them. Such a wistful return to the past . . . dragging me along with her . . . knowing I've seen the pictures before . . . also knowing those were not happy times for *me.*"

"Or Charles, for that matter."

"He thought of me as a younger sister in those days. Hanna was certainly aware of his feelings—and mine."

He stroked the petal softness of her arm. "Don't let it upset you. She was just being nostalgic. A world that might have been."

"I suppose you're right. We have so much, you and I. And Charles has so little."

He took hold of her and pressed her gently against his chest. "Hanna may wish he had more, but he has what he wants most at the moment . . . inner contentment and peace. God knows he went through enough hell to achieve it."

He tightened his arms about her, feeling the warmth of her

body through his shirt, the beat of her heart. He was thinking of the High Street and the cold cenotaph. The names of the war dead cut forever into marble. So many other names left uncarved—Charles Greville's among them. Not enough quarries in the world to mine the stones.

3

MAY BROUGHT A warm wind out of the southwest that set the windows of Burgate House rattling and whipped the great elms into frenzy. Deep banks of dried leaves, dormant since winter, swirled across the grounds in a blizzard of browns and reds.

Charles Greville stood in front of the tall windows in the common room and looked out on the rose garden and the wildly thrashing bushes. A freakish wind, he was thinking, almost tropical in its warmth and intensity. It would dry out the sodden ground, which would be a blessing, but play merry hell with hay ricks and hop poles throughout the Weald.

"The tea's ready . . . and there's hot scones."

Charles turned his back to the tumult in the garden and smiled at old Mrs. Mahon as she wheeled in the tea urn.

"Lovely. Did you make the scones?"

"No, Mr. Greville. Not this morning. I let Millie try her hand at it. My recipe, of course. Ballyconneely scones right enough."

"The ones your mother used to bake?"

"And her mother before that, let me tell you."

The scones were heaped on a platter and covered with a white napkin. Charles took one, hot from the oven, and bit into it, scorning butter or jam.

"Delicious."

"Yes, I thought as much meself. Young Millie has a natural talent for baking. I'll show her how to make a porter cake. Guinness, brown sugar . . . walnuts and cherries . . . lemon peel and sultanas, eggs and flour . . . keep for a week before eating. Oh, it's a lovely cake it is."

At seventy-eight, Mrs. Mahon was more likely to talk about cooking than actually to do any. Millie was in charge of the kitchen staff now. She was a young woman from Somerset, strong as an ox, with a West Country accent few could fathom.

Charles reached for another scone as Mrs. Mahon poured him a cup of tea. "I'm glad I was the first one down."

"Oh, Mr. Simpson was up at the crack of dawn, thunderin' out into the wind he was with never so much as a sip or a bite to sustain him. I saw him from the kitchen windows runnin' toward the playin' fields like the devil was chasin' after him."

"I'll go and see what he's up to. You might fill a vacuum bottle with tea and I'll take it out to him."

"I'll do that. Be the cricket ground. He's been mutterin' about it since Christmas."

Charles, vacuum bottle in hand and a pocket filled with scones, braced his body against the gale and walked into the teeth of it. A dying oak at the bottom of the lane was down, sprawled in all its leafless magnificence across the gravel road and two fences. He skirted the tangle of limbs and branches and cut across the field that the boys used for football and the girls for hockey. He could see the tall, stooped figure of George Simpson beyond the low hedge in the adjoining field. He was staring down at the ruined pitch and even at fifty yards Charles could see that his expression was grim. Winter snow and frost followed by the rains had scarred the billiard-table smoothness of the cricket ground, cutting miniature ravines and covering the once velvet grass with a layer of mud—mud that was fast drying in the wind.

"I brought you some tea, George," Charles said as he came up to the big man.

"Bless you," he said with a weary sigh. "I hope you put a large glass of whisky in it."

"Sorry. Sugar and milk."

"It'll have to do, I suppose. But I could go for a painkiller." He took the thermos, turned his back to the wind, and unscrewed the cap with his almost fingerless right hand. "Have you ever seen such an unholy mess? The pitch is ruined. The rain was bad enough, but now this blasted sirocco has to pop out of nowhere and compound the bloody problem. A frightfully un-English wind, if you ask me."

"I daresay it will blow itself out by end of day."

"Rolled in from Spain no doubt . . . or North Africa. One can almost smell the red dust and oranges." He filled the cap with tea and slurped it down.

Charles reached into his pocket. "Care for some scones?"

"Oh, Lord yes. A full belly makes for a happy man." He took a scone and devoured it in two bites. "Or at least reasonably happy. Cricket will be a farce this summer."

"It's always a farce. No one is quite up to it."

"I held hopes of altering that this year. Thursby major shows promise of being a cracking good slow bowler and I've finally convinced Manderson that there can be great joy in slapping a hard red ball with a white bat. All for naught now."

"And I always thought that Royal Engineer officers were impervious to despair. Have another scone."

Simpson took one and munched it slowly, his gloomy eyes roving the field. "The muck's hardening as a shell of clay. Need a tractor to shave the ground, grade it smooth. Turn the earth. Reseed it. Cut and roll. Bloody big job, Greville. Far beyond our capacities."

"There's a firm of landscape gardeners in Guildford that can build entire city parks. I'm quite sure they're capable of fixing this meager expanse of earth."

"Yes, I daresay they are—at a not very *meager* price. Several hundred pounds could be better spent elsewhere."

"Perhaps. And yet, sports have their place. We'll never field teams that could punish Charterhouse or Eton, but we could beat a few schools with some luck and a honing of skills. Be most uplifting for the chaps. A few hundred quid isn't too steep a price to pay."

"I doubt if we could find any decent school that would play us."

"Then we'll find an indecent one. I must say, George, you're being excessively dour this morning."

"I am, yes, what with this damn wind and lying awake most of the night thinking of the science lab."

"Oh? What's the matter with the lab?"

"Bloody nothing. Up to the minute. As good a facility for its size as one would find at Cambridge. And all of it out of your pocket. It doesn't seem right somehow. You're not a bottomless pit of pounds, shillings, and pence. It seems to me that the school should pay its own way. Not entirely out of tuitions, of course, but at least from contributions. There are hordes of wealthy people who are interested in progressive education. Old Mastwick knew how to tap that source. You ignore it and reach for your checkbook instead."

"I'm not John Mastwick. I don't have his powers of persuasion and I can't shuttle about the country giving speeches and passing the hat. I would find that impossible. I'm sure you understand if anyone does."

Simpson placed his war-ruined hand on Charles's shoulder. "Of course I do, dear fellow. I know what a struggle it's been for you over the years and . . . well, damn it man, I admire your courage. You're a smashing headmaster in all ways. I just hate to see you pay for bloody everything the school needs."

"I can afford it. And besides, there's little else I care to spend money on."

Nothing, in fact. His clothing was good, serviceable, and decidedly out of date. His little Austin car looked shabby and claptrap compared to the gleaming machines that glided along the road past the school on their way to the new country club, but it remained functional thanks to Simpson and some of the sixth-form boys who were wizards at mechanics. As for a social life, it was practically nonexistent. He was an honorary member of the country club—it had been built on Stanmore property—and occasionally went there to play a round of golf. He was a scratch player and would sometimes join a foursome, although he preferred to go at odd hours and play a lone round. He rarely went to the clubhouse after a game. He had little in common with the other members and found their boisterous conversations unnerving and virtually incomprehensible. He stood apart from them in manner and dress. He liked to play in old corduroy trousers and a worn Shetland sweater. The others dressed in the current style, plus-fours and Argyles, even kilts and tam-o-shanters. His drabness among such gaudy plumage was taken for eccentricity. But these wealthy, middle-class businessmen vied to play with him for the sheer snobbish pleasure of letting drop at their city clubs that they had played a round that weekend with "Viscount Amberley, you know."

He gave with pleasure to the school because the school was the center of his life. He felt secure and content within its boundaries. There was an order and a logic to the place not apparent to outsiders. His father saw only chaos and undisciplined tatterdemalions, but then he could only compare Burgate House with his own school days at Winchester, the uniformed boys and robed masters, the strict Wykehamist traditions of centuries. There were traditions at Burgate House, such as the student soviet, but they were not easily understood by the public-school mind.

The wind died in the early afternoon, leaving a balmy stillness and cloudless skies. The school went out of doors after lunch, the older boys and girls to help the caretaker and the two gardeners attack the storm damage, mainly the fallen oak, the others attending impromptu classes on the lawns or in the battered rose garden.

Charles completed correcting some sixth-form English essays in his study and then went for a walk around the grounds. Passing the old stables at the rear of the house he spotted Marian Halliday and a small group of her students seated in the shade of the apple orchard. Marian, a strikingly pretty redhead in her early thirties, lived in Abingdon and taught drawing and watercoloring three or four times a week. Once a costume designer for the Old Vic, she had been married for several stormy years to Gerald Halliday, matinee idol and rising star of British films. Their sensationally titillating divorce proceedings had been reported with such relish by the popular press that she had fled London after receiving her decree *nisi,* to escape from the notoriety of it all in the leafy glades of the country. Boredom, and an awareness that Burgate House had a reputation for being a sanctuary of sorts, had brought her to the school where her talents had been greatly appreciated for the past two years and no questions had ever been asked.

Charles waved to her and she moved her hand in a casual come-hither gesture, stood up and walked slowly toward him. He met her halfway.

"Anything the matter, Marian?"

"Don't look, but there's a boy skulking among the trees. I've been noticing him for the past ten minutes or so."

"Not one of ours, I take it."

"Definitely not one of ours. Elevenish, I would judge. Fat and untidy. School cap and blazer a little the worse for wear. Not very adept at hiding. A sort of if-I-can't-see-you, you-can't-see-me approach to concealment. He looks rather pathetic—and hungry. I didn't wish to scare him away by any overt reaction to his presence."

"Yes. Well. I see that Hawkins and Manderson are in your group. Tell them what's up and that I'd like to see the boy in my study. They'll know how to manage it."

"Another runaway, I imagine."

"No doubt of it. Probably cost us a telephone call and a railroad ticket."

"*And* lunch."

"I don't begrudge a bit of food, but I do feel that our fellow schools should have the common decency to reimburse us for the return of their own."

She stifled a laugh and pressed her long, slender fingers into his arm. "Oh, my dear Greville. What a dreamer you are! Fellow schools, indeed! We're dogsbody here. Odd man out. Our *fellow* schools probably resent getting their flotsam back."

"This makes the sixth so far this year. Quite an epidemic." He spotted a slight movement among the trees, a round, white face peeking out from behind a gnarled trunk. He looked away. "Remind the lads that gently does it."

Boys and girls ran away from boarding schools for a variety of reasons, the most common being simple homesickness. Those who ran away for that reason went home, to be returned to their schools by annoyed parents. Those who ran away and showed up at Burgate House were drawn by the school itself, by what they had heard or read of it—usually heard through the grapevine and so highly embroidered as to bear little resemblance to reality. A paradise, it was said, where there were no rules or regulations, no codes, no bells, no study, no Latin or Greek verbs to cram, no prefects, fagging, bullying, or caning. A wonderland of freedom and play. It was usually the lazy and the malcontent who came knocking at the door—to be sent away promptly and firmly, much to their chagrin.

The boy that Hawkins and Manderson half pushed, half dragged into his study was plump, untidy, and dirty. He was also sniveling and had, judging by the dark stain spreading on his short gray flannels, peed in his pants. The badge on his jacket, an embroidered emblem of a griffin holding a sword in one paw and a Celtic cross in the other, proclaimed him to be a boy from Archdean, an old and honorable public school in Wiltshire.

"Gave us an awful time, sir," Manderson said with a note of apology in his voice. "But we didn't hurt him."

"There's blood on his knees."

"Yes, sir," Hawkins said. "We came up behind him and he bolted. Tripped over a root. Mrs. Halliday's gone for the first aid kit."

"You might hop along and see if you can find a pair of gym shorts. On the large side. Fitzwilliam's, perhaps."

"He pissed. Keeps saying he's sorry. Told him it didn't matter to *us,* but it made him blubber something fierce."

"*Something fierce* is slang English."

Hawkins, a tall, strong boy of thirteen, grinned and then patted the runaway on the top of his head. "Sorry, sir, but he blubbered all the same . . . poor blighter."

"Be off with you. You, too, Manderson."

They left hurriedly and the boy from Archdean, released from their grasp, sagged to the floor in a sodden lump of misery. Sobs, barely repressed, shook him as a fever.

"You can get up," Charles said quietly, "and sit on that chair in front of the desk."

"I . . . I . . . can't . . ."

"Of course you can. Anyone can sit in a chair. There's nothing to it. Now kindly do as you're told."

The boy, eyes screwed shut against the tears streaming down his fat cheeks, groped blindly for the chair and pulled himself onto it, curling his body into the concave leather back.

"That's more like it. Are your knees terribly painful?"

"N-n-no, sir," the boy whispered to the chair.

"I'm sure they must sting a bit. We'll fix that as soon as Mrs. Halliday arrives. Mrs. Halliday's brother is 'Scorcher' O'Hara, captain of the Charlton Athletic, so she's quite familiar with banged-up knees. You ran away from Archdean. Feel up to telling me why?"

He did not. The mention of his school drove him into a shuddering silence that appeared close to catatonia.

"I didn't get anything out of him," Charles said quietly as Marian hurried into the study carrying the first aid box.

"No wonder." There was an edge to her voice. "Those two larrikins pounced on the poor fellow like two wolves on a rabbit. Scared him out of his wits. Oh, dear," she murmured as she knelt on the carpet in front of the chair. "Fresh underpants are in order, I'm afraid."

"Yes—and a bath. I'll get hold of Matron, and perhaps Gowers and Wilson can be of some help. They head the runaway committee this term. Maybe they can coax information out of him. I certainly can't."

Marian touched the boy on the cheek. "What school are you from, dear?"

The boy squeezed his eyes tighter and shook his head.

"That much I know," Charles whispered to her. "Archdean . . . near Chippenham."

"You could give them a ring, I suppose."

"I'd prefer to give them a name rather than a description. He's not a lost dog."

"No," she said, dabbing cotton wool on the boy's knees, "he most certainly is not!"

There was nothing for Charles to do. Word of the runaway's arrival had spread through the school from the moment he had been caught in the orchard. It had not been necessary for Charles to send for Gowers and Wilson, nor to inform the seven members of the soviet. Mrs. Halliday's scattering class had seen to that before the unknown boy had been dragged into the study.

Charles had been waiting a little less than half an hour, when he heard footsteps coming along the corridor. There was a respectful knock on the half-open door and Gowers and Wilson entered the study. They were both seventeen and in the upper sixth form. Wilson was a strapping six footer and the school's best athlete. Gowers was a hunchback.

"Well?" Charles said.

"He's in the tub," Gowers said. "Matron's doing the honors."

"Has the lad said anything?"

Gowers and Wilson exchanged glances. "Not really necessary, sir."

"No," Wilson said. "It's quite evident why he took French leave. His poor old bum looks like a bruised apple."

"Someone thrashed him good and proper."

A FAT, DIRTY, untidy boy. A *scug* in other words, Charles thought, remembering his Eton slang. Scugs had been treated without mercy at Eton, as they no doubt had been treated at other schools, and presumably still were. Singled out by their very grossness of appearance or habits by every bully or cane-wielding prefect and fag master. He remembered a boy named

Thorne who shirked all games and was of uncouth appearance. A disgrace to the house and the college. A dozen members of Pop had come to the dormitory one wintry night and dragged Thorne shrieking from his bed, stripped him, whipped him with a birch cane, and then had carried him out into the sleeting night and tossed him into the freezing river. Thorne had left Eton a few days later and had been hooted all the way to the train station. *A fat, dirty, untidy boy.*

The winter of 1904. He had been thirteen, a year younger than poor Thorne. He had done nothing to save him. Had watched silently as he had been carried away and had felt no outrage toward Pop, had in fact heartfully accepted his election into that most ancient of Eton societies a year or two later. He had learned a great deal about human pain and suffering since then. It was far too late to cry out against Thorne's terror so long ago, but he felt a sense of shame and outrage now.

"Why were you beaten?"

The boy shifted uncomfortably on the seat in Charles's study. He was wearing gym shorts and a pullover too large for him. He looked better now that he had been bathed and fed, but his eyes were still swollen from weeping and he shifted them everywhere to avoid looking at the tall man seated behind the oak desk.

"There's little point in your remaining silent. Quite rude, in fact, considering how decently you've been treated here—Master *Ramsay* . . . Ramsay, *D.*" The boy drew in his breath sharply. "No need to be surprised. There was a name tag inside your jacket. What does the *D* stand for? David?"

"Derek . . . sir," the boy whispered.

"Derek Ramsay. Nice name. I shall venture a guess. You

may correct me if I'm wrong. You were probably called *Dirt-ee Ram-see* at Archdean."

He cowered back in his seat and looked wildly about him as though expecting to see his tormentors. "They didn't have to tell you that. They needn't—"

"No one has told me anything, Ramsay. I haven't phoned your school yet. Some things never change. When I was at Eton we had a boy by the name of Allenby who was always getting ink on his cuffs and collar. We called him *Dirt-ee Allen-bee* . . . with some affection, I might add. There are some names that lend themselves to taunting rhyme. You were not called *Dirt-ee* with any affection whatever, judging by the condition of your backside. I want to know who thrashed you and I want to know why it was done."

"I can't tell you. I *can't!*"

Charles stood up and walked around his desk. He regretted his height, towering over the cringing boy. He lowered his voice to a gentle murmur in compensation.

"I can understand how difficult it must be for you to confide in a headmaster. But then you don't know very much about us, do you? You must have heard something though, or you wouldn't have come here."

"There's no . . . caning here," he whispered.

"That's correct. No corporal punishment at all. But that's only part of the story. This is a school run, to a very great extent, by the pupils themselves through various elected committees. The highest committee is the governing body, or soviet. They wish to talk to you, Ramsay. If you hold any hope of attending Burgate House in the future, I would advise you to answer all of their questions with the utmost candor. Lying, even half truth, is simply not tolerated here. Do you understand?"

"I . . . I think so, sir."

"And that's not my ruling. The soviet sets all standards for admission *and* expulsion." He reached down and touched the boy on the head, the thick brown hair still damp from the bath. "Come along now, they're waiting for you."

The high drama attending the arrival of Derek Ramsay had effectively destroyed the school routine for the rest of the day. When Charles went into the common room he found most of the teachers sitting about in varied attitudes of leisure.

"I say," Simpson remarked, lowering his newspaper, "they're taking rather a long time."

"I imagine they have a good deal to talk about," Charles said. "You know how some of these runaways are. Can't get two words out of them at first and then one can't shut them up once they get started."

"Poor little blighter."

Charles glanced at his wristwatch. "Been nearly two hours."

Simpson glanced at his own. "Almost time for tea. They'll break in a minute or two. No fools, the soviet."

He was correct. There was the sound of footsteps hurrying along the corridor and then an elfin face peered around the doorpost, that of a girl elected to be one of the soviet messengers.

"Please, Mr. Greville, sir, but the soviet would like to see you in chambers."

"Thank you, Valerie. I'll be right up."

The girl ran off and Charles could hear her footsteps clattering up the stairs to the first-floor landing as he followed slowly, dreading the tale he was certain to hear.

The seven members comprising the soviet were elected each term by the entire school from pupils in the upper sixth form. It was composed this term of five boys and two girls, ranging in age from sixteen to eighteen and in background from the son of a fish shop owner in Ramsgate to the granddaughter of a viceroy. A small, sunny room that had once been a nursery had been turned into the soviet's council chamber. It contained a few pieces of furniture, although the council, by tradition, conducted its business seated or sprawled on a threadbare Oriental carpet which was believed—falsely—to have belonged to Lenin during his exile in Switzerland.

The council began to get to its feet as Charles entered the room, but he waved them down again. Young Ramsay, he noted, was sprawled among them amid a scattering of toffee wrappers. The soviet knew how to make someone feel at home.

"Conclusion reached, I take it."

"Yes, sir," one of the boys said. "We've delegated Jameson as spokesman and we're all in agreement."

"Good. Tea's about ready. Why don't you take Ramsay down while I talk with Kevin in private."

Kevin Jameson, a tall, gangly boy of seventeen, closed the door after the others were gone. Charles sat in the least battered of the few chairs.

"Any trouble getting him to talk?"

"A bit, sir. In a blue funk the first half hour. Then he opened up to us. Nasty story, I must say."

"I can imagine."

"A classic case of the wrong boy at the wrong school. I have a cousin who went to Archdean. He enjoyed the school immensely, won all sorts of colors and prizes . . . captained the eleven . . . led them over Harrow at Lord's three years ago. That sort of thing. He was the type, you see. A perfect fit. This little fellow simply rubbed Archdean the wrong way from the start. Overweight, sloppy dresser . . . clumsy, hopeless at games . . . untidy. A complete twerp. And homesick. He was terribly, chronically homesick. Blubbered half the night in the dorm and then, most disgusting of all to his house prefects, began wetting his bed. Their cure for that was to thrash him every morning in his wet pajamas. Only made the situation worse, needless to say. After a few weeks of being thrashed all the time he ran away. His grandfather brought him back. From what we can gather, his parents died years ago. He lives with his grandfather and some old biddy of a housekeeper . . . ex-nanny I suppose. Anyway, he was returned to the school. Running away was the worst possible crime he could commit. An insult to the entire school. He became a target for everyone's scorn and abuse. Life became a living hell and he finally responded to it the only way he knew how—by running away again."

"Probably to be sent back again had he gone home."

Jameson nodded vigorously. "Oh, no doubt of that, sir. It seems that the old gentleman went there . . . and his father—that is, young Ramsay's father. The must-keep-up-the-tradition nonsense. I faced the same sort of thing when my father packed me off to St. Gregory's in a burst of Catholic fervor which I thought rather odd for a man with two divorces and contemplating a third. Fortunately he came to his senses after my first term and allowed me to come here. I have the feeling that this chap's granddad won't be as accommodating."

"Probably not." He stood up and slowly paced the room. "*If* he were permitted to come here would the soviet accept him?"

"I believe so, sir. He's not without faults. Bit of a glutton and chews his fingernails to the quick. Bed pisser and all that. But those are anxiety symptoms, aren't they? Placed in a more tranquil atmosphere I'm certain he'd be quite changed. I mean to say, if I knew I'd be bummed with a bloody stick for pissing my mattress, I'd never stop bloody pissing."

"Not so much of the *bloody,* if you don't mind."

"Sorry, sir."

Charles gazed thoughtfully at the wallpaper. A child's room. Rabbits in eighteenth-century costumes dancing a quadrille. "One thrashing too many and he ran away."

"More to it than that, sir. Meaning no disrespect to the little chap, but he does have an uncommonly fat rump. Absorb any number of blows I should think. The bruises are certainly vile, though I doubt if he was ever given more than the customary six of the best. What sent him rushing off was a caning in front of his entire house following sentencing by a kangaroo court."

"I thought that sort of nonsense was outlawed these days."

"I'm sure it is in any decent school. It was certainly forbidden at St. Gregory's but still occurred from time to time. I imagine the same holds true at Archdean. Houses are run by the sixth form, prefects, and societies. They know how to form a court without attracting the attention of the housemaster. This particular one was held at midnight, in cloisters, the lower forms' study room. Ramsay was dragged out of bed to attend it. It was a frightening and humiliating experience and we feel certain he told us the truth."

"There's truth enough in a black-and-blue backside."

"Indeed there is, sir. He ran away the next morning before breakfast. That was three days ago."

"How on earth did he manage to get here?"

"He'd read about us in one of the tabloids and had been to Abingdon before. He had enough pocket money for a railroad ticket. Got here in a few hours . . . then lost his nerve. He hid in that old shack at the bottom of the orchard for two days. Lived off apples and a few buns he'd bought in the High Street with the last of his money."

"Resourceful chap."

"Yes. And he's only twelve. A bit young for Archdean, but he was academically advanced at prep school. I'd say that's about everything. May I go and have my tea now?"

"Yes, Jameson. And thank you."

Charles could visualize the scene as he walked to his study. The rough midnight justice of boys. All in pajamas and robes. Silent . . . filing down the dark corridors from the dorms under the watchful eyes of the prefects, their canes of office tucked under their arms. The court assembled in some candlelit hall. Judge and jury at a long table . . . the house captains, monitors, prefects, fag masters and bloods—the hierarchy of the sixth form. The oldest, biggest boys. The best of the athletes and scholars seated in judgment on Ramsay, D., the fat, untidy bed wetter whose appearance and behavior were giving the house a bad name. The court, by its actions and punishment, making clear that they did not appreciate *Dirt-ee Ram-see* as a member of their ancient and honorable house, or even of their school.

The headmaster of Archdean was cool but correct over the telephone. Ramsay, D.? He was well aware that the boy had run away, but unlike the previous time had not returned to his home in Wimbledon. The police had been notified. What on earth was he doing at Burgate? Caned and bullied? Certainly *not* bullied. Such behavior was forbidden at Archdean. As for having been caned, that was hardly surprising. A proper thrashing could work wonders on lazy boys with no sense of self-discipline. He would inform Ramsay's grandfather instanter. He would be relieved that the boy had been found—and a good day to you, sir.

IF MR. RAMSAY was relieved by his grandson's reappearance he did not mention it to Charles over the telephone. That Derek had appeared at Burgate House School was a puzzlement. *"Extraordinary. Most extraordinary."* He could not have sounded more bemused had the lad turned up in a brothel. *"I will drive down. You can expect me around eight this evening."* He did not say thank you, but did offer to reimburse the school for any expense incurred.

"Ramsay's grandfather will pick him up at eight," Charles said as he entered the common room. Simpson was there, reading a newspaper over a glass of sherry, and Marian Halliday was placing the day's sketches in a leather portfolio. Simpson only grunted, swallowed half the contents of his glass, and reimmersed himself in the sporting section of the *Times.*

"He fell asleep immediately after tea," Marian said. "Complete, but contented exhaustion. I don't think he'll wet the bed *here.*"

"I would doubt it."

"Eight, did you say? I shan't go home then. I would like a word or two with the man."

Her Irish was up, Charles noticed. The green eyes had a hard glint to them and there were high spots of flame on her usually fair cheeks.

"I can manage quite well, Mrs. Halliday, thank you all the same."

Her eyes mirrored some doubt. "I would like to point out to him that the hitting of a small boy with a stick, *many times,* can hardly be expected to improve his body *or* his mind. I would also like to mention that I think the custom is barbaric . . . and sadistic."

"It is also, I'm sorry to say, a firmly ingrained custom in English schools."

She stood rigidly before him. Anger made her nostrils flare. "Do you intend to say nothing? Just hand the boy over?"

"I certainly intend to hand the boy over. What other choice do I have? But I shall talk to the man . . . give him my opinion of schools such as Archdean."

"Fat lot of good that will do!"

"It's the best that can be done, I'm afraid." He lightly touched her arm. "Your outrage is admirable, but serves no purpose whatsoever. My advice is to go home and let me handle the matter—whether it does a fat lot of good or not."

"Oh, very well." She plucked the portfolio of drawings from a table. "But I shall stop off at the local first and have a very stiff gin!"

Simpson peered over his newspaper as she stalked from the room. "Spirited young woman, isn't she?"

"She's right, you know."

"Yes. But I doubt if the elder Ramsay will see it quite that way. A pity there aren't more Scorcher O'Haras in the country. She was telling me about her brother . . . when he was sent to a public school at thirteen. Seems the first day he was there he got in wrong . . . gabbing in class or something. The master hit him a tremendous blow across the hand with a metal-tipped ruler. Young Scorcher didn't like that at all. He reared back and socked the fellow from Wealdstone to Watford. Made him think twice about hitting anyone in the future, I would imagine."

"Yes, I'm sure it did." Through the windows he could see Marian Halliday walking with long-legged fury past the rose garden toward the back of the building where her car was parked. "I have a feeling the sister would have done the same."

T. C. Ramsay, Esq., arrived at eight fifteen in the back of a chauffeur-driven Daimler. The elderly man fitted the appearance Charles had imagined from hearing his voice—large, heavyset, with a jowly face and a ruddy complexion. John Bull in a business suit.

"Charles Greville, headmaster here."

"T. C. Ramsay." His handshake was perfunctory. He glanced at the imposing hall. "A larger place than I expected."

"It is large, yes. A private house at one time." Charles closed the massive front door. "I'm sorry we didn't find your grandson sooner, Mr. Ramsay. It would have spared you a couple of days of worry."

"I had the police out looking, but I had no dire thoughts. I assumed he was simply dawdling somewhere . . . afraid to come home and face me. Oh, well, it all comes out in the wash, I suppose. Where is he?"

"Upstairs asleep. He was exhausted and we put him to bed after tea."

The man cleared his throat loudly. "Yes . . . well . . . I'll take the lad off your hands. It's a fair drive back to Wimbledon."

"I think we should have a talk first."

"Do you?" His surprise was evident.

"There are some things I think you should know."

T. C. Ramsay studied Charles for a moment, taking him in with a banker's stare. "Very well. I can spare a few minutes. I would like Derek to be awake and dressed, however."

"Of course." He looked up the broad, curved stairs. "One of you chaps down, please."

There was a scuffling sound on the first-floor landing and then Manderson, still smarting over accusations that he had used undue force in tackling the runaway in the orchard, came barreling down the stairs several strides in front of his competitors.

"Only one," Charles said sternly. "Manderson will do nicely, thank you." A mob of boys froze on the stairs. "Manderson, this is Mr. Ramsay, Derek's grandfather."

The boy smoothed his hair and tugged at this shirt almost in one gesture. "My pleasure, I'm sure . . .. sir."

T. C. Ramsay only grunted.

"Find Matron, will you," Charles said. "Help her get young Ramsay up and dressed."

"I'll do that, Mr. Greville, sir . . . right away." He was off and running, clattering up the stairs.

"Eager fellow."

"We stress service here." Charles motioned toward one of the corridors leading off the hall. "Please come into my study, Mr. Ramsay."

He had no intention of taking a seat. He stood stolid in the room, large hands clasped behind his back.

"So you're Charles Greville . . . the Viscount Amberley. I had the pleasure of knowing your father at Westminster when I was M. P. for Chaterham before the war. And this is what you do, is it? Run this place?"

"This . . . *school,* yes."

"Your concept of a school is not the same as my own."

"Possibly not. But a school it is."

"More like a haven for misfits, if you ask me. I've read a good deal about Burgate House and have not liked one thing I've read. It's not my intention to be insulting, sir, but I'm a blunt man who speaks his mind."

"Jolly good for you. I find that refreshing in this day and age. Would you care for a sherry? Some of my father's private stock from Jerez."

The elderly man wavered, then gave in. "Perhaps a small glass."

"You know," Charles said as he poured the wine, "your grandson also read about us. It induced him to come here."

"The schoolboy's paradise, or so I hear."

"Hardly that, but not being flogged is heaven enough for some boys."

"I daresay." He scowled at the sherry glass when Charles handed it to him. "There's a purpose to caning. It's not simply blind, willful punishment. You know that, Greville. Where did you go? Eton? Harrow?"

"Eton."

"They caned at Eton, I daresay, as strongly as they did at Archdean. God knows I had *my* backside striped more than once in lower house. It's part of the ritual one goes through. It makes for obedient boys. Diligent boys. It is the making of men." He took a sip of the sherry, savored it on the tongue, and took another. "My son Thomas had many a thrashing. He was thirteen when I sent him to Archdean, the spring of nineteen eight. Discipline was ferocious in those days and a lad had to measure up if he wanted to keep any skin on his bottom. Tom measured up. He became, in time, captain of his house and captain of the school fifteen. Colors in footer and cricket as well. A fine, all-round boy. The custom today is to either sneer at discipline or wring one's hands over it. But, by God, it helped produce a breed I doubt we shall ever see again in England. Men who believed in *duty* and had *obedience* bred into their very bones. How else can one account for it, sir? The gallantry and self-sacrifice of those young men, those public-school boys, during the war? My own Tom . . . winning the V.C. at Zeebrugge . . . leading his men along the mole toward the German guns. Dying on his feet, but running on without a murmur until he dropped. Archdean produced that type of man, as did Eton, Wellington, Rugby—all the fine old schools. I want my grandson to measure up to that tradition. I don't need you to tell me that he's been caned, or even that he's been bullied. I'm quite sure that he has been, and will continue to be until he jolly well learns what's expected of him."

Charles poured himself another glass, noting with satisfaction that his hand did not tremble. How amber the wine . . . how clean and nutty dry. There had been one bottle left in his kit and he had poured it into the tin mugs of his platoon officers before the Delville Wood show where most of them had died. Good school fellows all. Eton. Harrow. Sherborne and Malvern. A Catholic lad from Downside. A jocular little Scot a year out of Glenalmond who used to sing in the mess after a whisky or two . . .

O, safe with thy soldiers up-grown
is thy honour, high Queen of the Glen,

And the battle shall seal them thine
Glenalmond, right mother of men!

. . . and who had died on the wire like a gutted pig. He moistened his dry lips.

"I'm sorry about your son, Mr. Ramsay. I know what you're saying and I know how strongly you believe it. I was in the war . . . the Royal Windsors. I'm well acquainted with the type of man the public schools bred. They were indeed brave, but many were both brave *and* foolish. The young subalterns of the Surreys who kicked a football across no-man's-land at the Somme and died doing so felt they were setting an example of coolness and bravery for their men. They would have better served their regiment and their king by crawling across on their bellies and not being shot to pieces by machine guns."

Ramsay scowled, drained his glass, and held it out for refilling. "You are quite right in that respect, sir. I won't argue the point. My own Tom was in the marines and he told me of many foolish acts of bravery on the part of fellow officers that served no purpose other than death at an early age. As a banker I revere caution. The junior officers of Drayton's Bank crawl on their bellies when under fire or, by God, I know the reason why they don't! This is an excellent sherry, by the way."

"Yes. It was given time—and patience—to age."

"Well put. But boys are not sherries. They go green into the world and are *taught* to become mellow and palatable. Notwithstanding the kicking of footballs into machine guns, I believe the public schools teach their lessons well."

"They teach some boys well . . . those that fit. Your grandson appears to be intelligent, but . . . at this stage of his life anyway . . . seems to be a square peg, and no amount of hammering is going to squeeze him into a round hole."

"I'm not a believer in square pegs, Lord Amberley. Hammer hard enough and anything will fit. I don't mean to be ungracious. I'm glad that Derek fell into your hands and not some roving band of gypsies as it were, but dash it all, sir, I can't go along with this so-called *progressive* school nonsense. I believe it panders to a child's proclivity to anarchy and self-gratification. My grandson is spoiled enough as it is, for reasons I need not go into. He needs solid guidelines and discipline." He set his glass on the table and turned toward the door. "Be so kind as to give my regards to Lord Stanmore."

And that was that. Derek Ramsay, still half asleep, was led to the car and driven away. Five days later he was back.

4

HE DID NOT hide in the orchard this time but came panting and puffing up the drive, footsore and weary after the five-mile walk from Abingdon station. Valerie A'Dean-Spender, running an errand for the soviet, was the first to spot him.

"Hello, Fat Chap!" she called out cheerily. "What brings you back?" She fell into step beside him. She was nine and small for her age. Her bright yellow hair cut in an Eton crop made her look like a delicate boy. "Run away again?"

"None of your business," he muttered.

"They'll only drag you back. I'd run off to sea if I were you." She skipped ahead of him. "Do you like cream buns and jam tarts? That's what we're having for tea." She raced ahead toward the front door, shouting back over her shoulder, "I'll save you some, Fat Chap . . . really I will."

It was a different boy who faced Charles in his study. No cowering into a chair now. He stood stiff-backed, chubby and resolute, hands balled into pudgy little fists at his sides. His school uniform was reasonably neat and unstained.

"I shall never go back to Archdean," he said with stubborn intensity. *"Never."*

Charles tilted back in his chair and tapped the end of a pencil against the rim of the desk. "You may well get your wish. I'd be greatly surprised if you're not expelled. But you can't stay here, Ramsay."

"Why can't I? I like it here."

"That's hardly the point. You have no say in the matter."

"It's not fair."

"It may not be fair, but it is fact. Come by train again?"

"Yes, sir."

"I'm surprised you were allowed pocket money, given your propensity for flight."

"They never look in my shoe."

"Care to tell me what drove you into exodus this time?"

He had not been beaten—there had hardly been time for it. He had been kept home for four days, to pull himself together and to be lectured on his "moral responsibilities," and then taken back to the school that Monday morning. His grandfather had spent half an hour talking with the headmaster and then had been driven away in the back of his shiny black Daimler to attend a business conference in Bristol. The car had been barely out of sight when he had walked from the school grounds, caught a bus going into Chippenham, and had taken the train from there. He had simply made up his mind to leave the school once and for all.

"Do you really think I'll be expelled, sir?"

"I'd say there was little doubt of it, unless your grandfather owns the place. You seem to have spent more time in railway carriages than you ever did in classrooms." He leaned forward and reached for the telephone. "What's your number at home?"

"I won't be missed at school until assembly at supper. And grandfather is on business. He won't be home until Thursday."

"There must be someone there I can talk to. The number, please."

"Roehampton . . . nine . . . three . . . five." He put a hand to his mouth and chewed a fingernail.

"Don't do that," Charles snapped. "It's a disgusting habit."

"I can't help it." The hand returned to his side.

"Of course you can. Just put your mind to it." He noticed the door to the corridor open a crack. "Is that you, Valerie?"

The door inched wide enough to frame her tiny face. "Yes, sir, Mr. Greville."

"Don't skulk about."

"I was just waiting. Everyone's going to tea and I thought . . ."

"Very well, go and have your tea and take Ramsay along with you."

She smiled broadly and flung the door wide. "Come along, Fat Chap. Jolly good tuck today!"

"His name is *Ramsay,*" Charles said coldly. "Or *Derek.* You didn't like it when Mary Henshaw called you Pencil Legs last term."

"I got the sow for it!" she cried, swinging her thin arms about. "Got her good *an'* proper!"

"Stop using slang. Now run along—and after your tea find Gowers and Wilson and place Derek in their care."

A maid answered the phone at the Ramsay house, asked

him to wait and put on a Mrs. Daintree who did not sound in the least surprised at what Charles told her.

"I said right along this would happen." She had an ancient voice, cracked and quavering. "He has no one to blame but himself. As the twig is bent the tree will grow. Told him . . . but would he pay any mind to me? I wash my hands of it. He'll be staying at the George Hotel in Bristol. He always does. The *George,* mind . . . and he won't be pleased, I can tell you."

Charles had poured a glass of sherry and was standing by the window drinking when Marian Halliday came into the room.

"Our wayward wanderer is back again, I see."

"Yes, and there'll be the devil to pay now, I'm afraid. We'll probably be blamed for exerting undue influence on the lad, or something like that. I placed a call to his grandfather . . . in Bristol."

"Anything I can do?"

"A touch of moral support." He stared morosely out at the garden. "I wish he'd never heard of Burgate House. Why didn't he run away to Summerhill?"

Marian laughed and walked over to him. "You should feel flattered that he preferred us. Just think what a reporter could do with all this . . . bullied and whipped little tyke determined to seek kindness and safety in Surrey progressive school . . . that sort of thing. Center section of the Sunday *Post.* Complete with photographs."

He swallowed some sherry. "God forbid."

"I'm sure the publicity would result in a flood of donations."

"You sound like Simpson."

"Well, we do think alike in that respect."

"I don't believe in soliciting. This is not a home for orphans."

She gestured toward the sherry decanter. "Mind if I help myself? I hate to see anyone drink alone."

"I am sorry. I forgot my manners." He set his glass down and poured one for her. "This Ramsay business is upsetting. He belongs in a school like this, but I don't know what to do about it."

"What can you do? It's not your fault if the boy has an *idée fixe.* All you can do is turn him over again and hope for the best. And by the way, I wish to apologize for my attitude last week. I was overwrought. It's not like me."

"Cool and collected."

"I try to be. I used to have a vile temper when I was married to Gerald . . . but then he had a peculiar talent for bringing it out."

He knew so little about her. Not much more in fact than the bare particulars . . . age thirty-one . . . divorced . . . no children . . . educated at the London School of Art and Design . . . seven years with the Old Vic. Of her life away from the school he knew nothing. Simpson and some of the other teachers had been to her cottage a mile or so from Abingdon, but he had not. She owned a huge ginger cat named Tartuffe which she brought to the school occasionally where it would follow her about like a dog and permit itself to be petted by all the children. A popular and vivacious woman—and certainly an attractive one with her red hair, green eyes, and slim, lissome body. Any number of suitors, he was thinking . . . although they were probably called "boyfriends" these days.

The telephone rang—a harsh, persistent sound.

"Him?" she asked.

"I'm rather afraid it might be, yes." He downed his drink.

"I'll leave you alone with his outrage."

"No," he said, reaching for the instrument. "Moral support, remember?"

He had a horror of confrontations and steeled himself for thunderbolts after informing T. C. of what had taken place, but there was only a painful silence for a few moments and then the man's voice, heavy with a weary resignation . . .

"I appreciate your call, Greville . . . and for looking after the boy. Sticky business this. I can't get away until tomorrow afternoon. Would it be putting you to too much bother to keep him overnight?"

"Not at all."

"I feel we must have a talk and I would find it easier in my own home. I realize it's an imposition, but if you could possibly come up to Wimbledon . . . any time after six tomorrow . . ."

"Certainly."

"The Willows, Woodvale Road. Derek will show you the shortcuts."

And that was the end of the conversation.

"He sounded rather abashed," Charles said, hanging up the phone. "Wants to have a talk tomorrow . . . in Wimbledon. I'll take Ramsay up. Leave here about four thirty, I expect. Not sure how long it will take me to get there."

"Days. You'd never get past Dorking in your car and the way you drive. I'll take you in mine."

"I can't ask you to do that, Mrs. Halliday."

"You didn't. I volunteered."

Derek Ramsay was not happy at the thought of going home. He had enjoyed spending the night at the school and a day of attending classes. *"Surprisingly well read and extremely bright,"* had been Simpson's evaluation. *"He belongs here,"* had been Marian Halliday's terse assessment. Derek felt the same way.

"I don't want to leave," he said.

"I'm afraid you must." The boy was looking over his shoulder as he stood beside Charles on the drive. There were children at the windows. Valerie A'Dean-Spender waving. "Are you afraid of what your grandfather is going to say to you?"

Derek chewed his lip and glanced at Charles with a worried expression. "He'll be very angry."

"Don't you think he has a right to be?"

"Yes . . . I suppose."

"Not everyone who goes to public school is bullied, you know. Most muddle through, or learn to get by. We expect new pupils to do their best here. We permit a certain latitude at first, a reasonable time to adjust, but our codes are as rigid in some ways as Archdean's. We don't tolerate students who will not at least *try* to live up to our standards. Do you understand what I'm saying?"

"Yes," he replied with a fierce intensity. "I would try. I *would.*"

Charles scrutinized the boy's face and saw a passionate determination stamped upon it. The cherubic mouth trembled, but the eyes gleamed and did not waver.

"I believe you, Ramsay. It may not come to pass, but I will do my best to have you enrolled here . . . that much I promise."

It was a little over twenty miles from Burgate House to Wimbledon as the crow flies, but crows had not laid out the winding country roads. Charles had only been driving for a few years and was still not comfortable steering his little Austin around sharp curves and past the thick hedge walls that turned narrow lanes into virtual tunnels. He drove with a tense, nervous concentration soon transmitted to anyone unfortunate enough to be driving with him. Not so Marian Halliday. She steered her Rover with all the verve and nonchalance of a professional, downshifting, turning, accelerating with such easy skill that Charles, seated beside her, could not take his eyes from her.

"You do this awfully well," he said.

"My brother taught me. He builds race cars as a hobby. I drove one of them once at Brooklands . . . got it up to a hundred and twenty."

Derek bounced with excitement on the back seat. "Oh, do it now, Mrs. Halliday . . . *please!*"

She laughed. "Not on this road, Derek. We want you home in one solid piece."

"I don't want to go home at all," he muttered, slumping back. "I shall only run away again."

Charles turned and looked at him. "No, not if you ever expect to come to our school. Your running away will solve nothing. Is that clear?"

Derek looked miserably out of the window. "I wish I were dead."

"Well, you're not, so make the best of it."

It was a large Victorian house on the edge of Wimbledon Common, the wooded hills of Richmond Park seen beyond its multigabled roof. A gravel drive flanked by rhododendron bushes curved to the front of the house from the street. A sign on the gatepost proclaimed it to be THE WILLOWS. Charles could not see any. Perhaps T. C. Ramsay had chopped them down.

A young maid opened the front door and Derek ran past her into the house. The maid watched him go and shook her head in wonder. "Cor! He's really 'ad it this time."

"Is Mr. Ramsay at home?" Charles asked.

The girl nodded in an abstract way and stepped aside. "Yes, sir. Will you follow me, please?"

She led them through a dark, wood-paneled hallway into a large room that had probably been furnished in 1900 and not altered since.

"Quaint," Marian said, taking in the horsehair sofas, wingback chairs, and expanses of polished oak and gleaming beveled glass.

"It's exactly the sort of place I imagined."

"Yes. Solid and sensible. Bank of England traditional."

A grand piano stood in a window bay, its lid covered by a lace mantle on which stood a dozen or more photographs in ornate gold or silver frames. Charles ambled over to it and studied the pictures in the pale orange light that filtered through the lace window curtains. There was an amber-tinted picture of a young man he assumed to be T. C. standing in front of a country inn, a pretty woman wearing a bonnet and a long dress standing beside him. There was a caption penned in white ink—*Jane and myself, Highmoor Cross, July, 1898.* Had Jane been his wife?

There were several photographs of his young son: wearing a straw hat and seated on a pony—*Tom at Longfield Farm, Summer, 1901;* standing in a boat with a punting pole in his hands, a background of willows trailing branches into the river—*Tom, aged 12, Henley, 1907.* And there was Thomas Ramsay through the years, growing older and taller; at prep school with a long, striped scarf wrapped around his neck; at Archdean in cricket flannels and the school cap—*Archdean vs. Charterhouse, 1912.* And there was a photograph of Thomas Ramsay in the uniform of a Royal Marine subaltern, an inscription scrawled in ink that had turned a rusty brown: *To Father with love and respect,* 15 *October 1915.* Two and a half years of life left to him before the raid on Zeebrugge. Dangling from the side of the frame on a faded purple ribbon was the Victoria Cross, the dull bronze medal inscribed with the simple explanation of its reward—FOR VALOUR.

There were no photographs of Derek.

T. C. Ramsay came into the room. He looked drawn and troubled, a man with a good deal on his mind. "Sorry to keep you waiting." The sight of Marian Halliday was unexpected and seemed to brighten his outlook. He smiled at her and straightened his tie. "I don't believe I've had the pleasure."

"Mrs. Halliday," Marian said warmly. "I teach art at Burgate House. Gave your grandson a lesson today, as a matter of fact. He seems to have a natural talent for sketching."

T. C.'s smile was bitter tinged. "He has a talent for most things—except staying in school." He waved a tired hand toward the sofas. "Please sit down . . . both of you. Would you care for a drink? God knows I would."

"Perhaps a small pink gin."

"And you, Greville?"

"Whisky soda."

"I'll join you in that." He shambled across the room to a sideboard and splashed liquor into glasses from crystal decanters. "I knew in my heart he would run away again. Your telephone call came as no surprise."

"Nor to Mrs. Daintree, I gathered."

"No. She told me I was making a mistake when I took him back to Archdean. Mrs. Daintree was his nanny. More than that, actually. My daughter-in-law was ill for many years. She died when Derek was eight . . . of a lung disorder . . . brought on by the influenza epidemic in nineteen nineteen. Nearly died then, poor child . . . as did Derek." He hesitated over his own glass and then sloshed in an extra dollop of whisky. "A sensible, no-nonsense woman, Mrs. Daintree. Yorkshire born and bred. The West Riding. A hard country. She saw her five brothers sent out into the world when they reached fourteen to sink or swim in the mills or the mines. But prepared for it from birth, you see. She feels that I sheltered Derek from the realities of life far too long. She may well be right."

"As the twig is bent . . ." Charles said as T. C. handed him his drink.

"She told you that, did she? Yes, her favorite aphorism where Derek is concerned. Well, I bent the twig all right. Best of intentions . . . but, the road to hell and all that." He scowled at his whisky and then took a drink. "Derek has been expelled from Archdean. I was just on the telephone to Dr. Grace, the headmaster."

"Probably for the best," Marian said quietly.

T. C. nodded. "Yes, quite so. Dr. Grace will write the expulsion down in soft pencil as it were. It will not affect Derek's chances of attending another school in a year or so . . . Charterhouse . . . Winchester, perhaps. We shall see. He's really too young for that now. And although I wouldn't go so far as to say that my grandson is eccentric, he *is* different . . . too vulnerable to the odd bully." He began to pace the room slowly, holding his glass tightly in both hands. "Derek was a rather special child. He was born three weeks after my son was killed. Tom dead. No reminders of him except a few photographs and a medal from the king . . . and then a healthy, bouncing boy. Yes, he took on quite an importance indeed."

It had been an age for death, the war grinding on through 1918 and then the terrible winter and spring of 1919 with influenza sweeping an exhausted world. Derek and his young mother had come down with the disease and had not been expected to live. That had been the supreme moment of despair for T. C. Ramsay. He had felt balanced on the edge of a chasm for the damned.

"Pamela never fully recovered," he said in a toneless voice. "A semi-invalid the rest of her short life. Derek had become a pallid, sickly little thing who required constant care until he was five. I kept him away from other children as much as possible. You see, I was still terrified of death. Children died of diphtheria . . . there was a German measles epidemic . . . what disease I didn't know I invented. The result was that I insulated the boy until I was convinced he was strong enough to withstand anything. I kept him home, with a tutor, until he was nine. By then he was as healthy as a horse and just about as broad. He read books the way a shark eats, had gutted my own library and every public one from Wimbledon to Richmond. I decided, finally, to send him to school as a day boy. I chose Larchwood in Roehampton, just down the road. He did well there, academically, at least, but lacked any sense of conformity. I realized that he was turning into something of an outsider and that it would not stand him in good stead later in life. He needed . . . oh, discipline . . . abiding by the rules . . . playing the game, one could say. That was when I enrolled him in Archdean. But, as Mrs. Daintree had told me many times, the twig had been bent. I can see now how foolish it was of me to expect Archdean to accomplish in one term everything that I had failed to do in twelve years." He paused by the windows, his large, oval body silhouetted against the sunset. "I rather libeled your school in my anger, sir. Called it a haven for misfits. Derek has more sense than I. He knows precisely where he belongs." He drew the curtains and switched on a lamp. "I might . . . merely as an experiment, you understand . . . place Derek at Burgate for the remainder of the term. *Might,* I must stress. I would have to look the place over."

"Of course," Charles said with studied casualness. "Any time."

"And not one of those tours where one is shown only bright work and no tarnish. I would wish to stroll about a bit on my own and poke my nose into the odd corner or two. Any objection?"

"None at all."

"This Saturday would be convenient for me."

"That would be perfect. Should we say eleven? You could stay for lunch. Sample the school cooking."

"I've consumed a good deal of school cooking in my time, Greville. The *culinary* qualities of your institution are of no concern to me."

He walked them to the front door. There was a slight scuffling sound coming from the upper landing and then Derek, wearing pajamas and a robe, peered over the railing.

"May I say something to Mr. Greville, Grandfather?"

"You may."

The round, pale face was strained and anxious. "I really *would* try, sir . . . do my *very* best."

Charles smiled up at the boy. "I know you would, Derek."

T. C. Ramsay cleared his throat loudly as Derek ran off down the landing, slippers thumping against the floor. "Well, now," he said, opening the front door. "I know what *he* wants, but we shall see . . . we shall see."

Marian started the car and shifted into gear. "Engaging little fellow. Do you really think he has a chance?"

"I don't know. I certainly hope so, but we'll have to pass muster first."

"I'm sure we'll come through with flying colors." They reached the end of the drive and she turned the car into the road. "God, but that was a depressing house. The piano. Like a shrine."

"It is a shrine."

"Poor, chubby Derek. Pictures of his father as school hero . . . war hero . . . the V.C. for bravery. Too many things to live up to. I truly feel sorry for him. But he's a scrapper in his own way."

"Courage takes many forms."

"I quite agree." They were driving past the great park with its shadowed woods and glades, deserted now under a pale rising moon. "I don't know about you, but I could go for another gin and something to eat. I know of a place in Putney, a pub where Swinburne did his modest drinking. Are you game?"

"I could go for something." He was looking reflectively through the window. They were passing a golf course, the deep, sandy bunkers catching the moon. "Tom Ramsay's photograph reminded me strongly of my brother."

"The horse-racing chap? I only met him once, but he doesn't look at all like Derek's father."

"Not facially. Same sort of man, though. Tom Ramsay and Willie. A cut from the same cloth. Both school leaders . . . caps and colors in everything . . . cricket, footer, rugger. Strong sense of duty to school and country. Willie joined up the moment he became eighteen. He was in officers' training here, oddly enough . . . where the links are now. Within walking distance to Ramsay's house. Curious." He looked away, took a cigarette from a box in his pocket and held it between his fingers, unlit. "There could so easily have been a photograph of Willie at home . . . on the mantel, perhaps . . . a posthumous medal dangling from the frame."

There was an odd tone to his voice as she glanced at him curiously.

"So many like William," he went on. "They'd come up to the front line at night with the replacements. Fresh as paint, eager to get at Jerry and win the war. They were impossibly young and full of high spirits. It was all a lark to them, you see. They were drunk on the excitement of it all. Most of them were dead or wounded within a week. I was acting colonel and I would write names into the roll one day and scratch them off the next. So many destroyed for no bloody purpose whatever."

"The war is over. Don't dwell on it."

"It's all right. Being able to talk is healthy. My problem for years was keeping everything to myself. I still do to a certain extent. A withdrawn personality."

"I wouldn't say that. Solemn, yes."

"Solemn as an owl. I'm really quite happy, though. I enjoy what I do and I believe I'm good at it."

"You're marvelous. Kind . . . patient."

"There were so many years when I couldn't function at all. Common knowledge around the school. I assume that Simpson or Wallis has told you."

She nodded slowly. "In an offhand way. You had a breakdown. A malady of the times."

"Everyone has a certain . . . *limit.* I reached mine one day and snapped. I didn't go howling mad or anything like that. I simply withdrew into a safe world of my own after doing something that I felt I must do."

"And that was?"

"Protest the war . . . the utter, useless carnage of it. Four hundred thousand men lost on the Somme, and a new batch being trained to take their places—my brother among them. A boy such as Willie . . . he would have leaped over the top as though hurrying to join a football match. Been shot down within seconds."

"Thank heaven that didn't happen. Just a game leg."

"He got it here on the final day of his training."

"An accident?"

"Not exactly. I put a bullet in his knee."

It was said with such dispassion that she wasn't sure at first if she had heard him correctly. She gripped the wheel tightly and drove on toward the lights of Putney.

"To keep him out of the trenches." Her voice was husky.

"I could think of no other way. It was wrong, of course. One shouldn't play God by interfering with the strands of fate. Willie hated me for it. Not now, you understand. He's grateful that he escaped the butchery. I wanted a full court martial on the charge of, quite literally, shooting a brother officer. My request was refused. The War Office had no intention of providing a forum where I could protest the slaughter in France. I was given a medical hearing instead. Quite a farce. The brass had already judged me shell-shocked . . . innocent by reason of insanity. I was committed to an asylum in North Wales where I sank into a stupor for four years."

The road curved past Putney Heath and there was the pub, light streaming through its windows. "A gin," she said firmly. "A very large, double-portion gin."

HE HAD NOT felt solemn in her presence, in the smoky pub where Swinburne had taken his daily pint of beer. He had felt oddly light-headed and buoyant, as though a punishing load had been removed from his shoulders.

And time remembered is grief forgotten,
And frosts are slain and flowers begotten,
And in green underwood and cover
Blossom by blossom the spring begins.

He had quoted that stanza from "Atalanta in Calydon" because it had seemed fitting somehow, and perhaps the ghost of the little poet lingered in the place. They had drunk gin and lime and eaten Scotch eggs, bread and cheese; seated at a small table perilously close to the dart board. He had told her things about himself that he had been incapable of telling the vicar's niece, or any of the other women that his mother had tried to bring into his life: of his brief, disastrous wartime marriage and the horrors of Gallipoli and the Somme that had led to his breakdown. Calmly objective as though discussing the trials of a stranger.

And time remembered is grief forgotten.

And she had told him of her childhood in North London, of her father, a flamboyantly spendthrift Irish tenor who had toured for years with the D'Oyly Carte company, and of her marriage to Gerald Halliday and the divorce—of which he had not read so much as a word, much to her surprise.

Yes, he was thinking as he finished his morning shave, a most enjoyable evening. He looked forward to seeing her and was glad that this was one of the days she would be at the school. He rubbed his cheeks with bay rum and got dressed, eyeing his shapeless tweed suit with regret. Wearing it, the image reflected in the mirror was drab and gray. The colorless tie did not help matters. He looked every inch the aging schoolmaster. A solemn owl indeed. He touched his forehead. Nothing much he could do about a receding hairline, but a new wardrobe was as close as a London tailor.

He sought her out after her last class and asked her to come to his study. She looked, he thought, very lovely in a pale green dress that complimented the rich chestnut of her hair, but found it difficult to tell her so.

"I had a fine time last night," she said easily, sitting in the chair facing his desk.

"So did I. I like old pubs . . . places with character."

"We should do it again. I understand there's an inn near Dorking where Nelson used to stay with Lady Hamilton."

"Yes. It's famous for its beef and kidney pies . . . and a beer the monks brew at Pebble Coombe. I'll take you there, if you'd like."

"Lovely! When?"

"Well . . ." He felt flustered. "Soon, perhaps." He leaned back in his chair and frowned at the ceiling. "I need some advice . . . this Ramsay business. Putting our best foot forward is easier said than done. I took a hard look at the school today, trying to see the place from T. C.'s point of view. A view not much different from my father's, I would imagine, and Lord knows I've heard his comments over the years."

"What exactly did you find to be the matter?"

"The very things that make us unique . . . the freedom of individual expression and dress . . . the total air of nonconformity about the place. Wallis, as only one example, was teaching his geometry class this morning on the west lawn, using string tied to croquet stumps. The class lounging about, laughing and joking, dressed every which way. Some still in their pajamas."

"It's a bright class all the same. Untidy except in mind. I would think that angles made with twine would be easier to comprehend than lines drawn on a blackboard. You could point out to Mr. Ramsay that Andrew Wallis may look rather eccentric in his shabby blazer and cricket cap but that he once chaired the mathematics department at the University of Glasgow and did not leave under a cloud to come here."

Charles waved a dismissing hand. "It's the tableau I'm referring to . . . the effect such a scene would have on Ramsay. So totally alien from his concept of a *proper* school."

Marian studied her fingernails. "If the scene is wrong, change the scene. An old saying in the theater."

"I gathered as much."

"It would seem to me that the only possible way to create the *proper* impression is to turn to theater for help."

"I'm afraid I don't follow you."

"It's quite simple. We put on a kind of play."

"A *play?*"

"Tom Brown's Schooldays . . . the Jolly Chaps at Greyfriars . . . the Eton boating song fondly remembered. That sort of thing. Children are natural actors and I can't see how we could go wrong. I'll take charge of it because I'm the obvious choice with my background. Wardrobe will be a slight problem, but then he knows we don't wear uniforms here." She stood up abruptly. "Not much time if we want perfection when the curtain rises on Saturday. I'll discuss my idea with the soviet right away. I know they'll jump at it."

Charles was leaning forward now, staring at her. "I don't have the foggiest notion of what you're talking about."

"Never mind. Just wait for the matinee and be pleasantly surprised." She headed for the door, then paused and smiled at him over her shoulder. "Though we will need you. The lead role. The part calls for a tall, handsome, wise, and compassionate headmaster type. Yes, I believe you'll do nicely."

"I'll be damned," he said as she left the room. Simpson had called her a "spirited" young woman. That was certainly an understatement.

WHEN THE BLACK Daimler rolled sedately up the drive at eleven o'clock on Saturday morning, the front doors of Burgate House opened and a file of boys and girls emerged walking two by two. They fairly gleamed in the morning sun with shiny faces, washed hair, polished shoes, and neat clothing. They were led by Mr. Simpson, splendid in the flowing black gown he had not worn since his years as a university don. Master and pupils nodded respectfully to the occupant of the car and continued their silent, ordered way across the gravel drive toward the far side of the building.

"Rather neatly turned out, I must say," T. C. Ramsay remarked, more to himself than to his chauffeur.

The hall clock had just finished striking eleven when Charles had seen the car coming up the drive.

"He's here," he had said to Marian Halliday. She had then told Simpson to move his group out. The forty or so children, who had been chatting and laughing among themselves, had fallen silent and marched out of the hall as actors onto a stage, with all the solemnity and pomp expected of their roles.

"Right on time, Mr. Ramsay," Charles said as he greeted the man.

"Punctuality is my obsession, sir." He drew a gold watch from his waistcoat and looked at it. "This shouldn't take too long. I'm expected in Guildford at one thirty." He closed the watch cover with a snap. "Well, let's get on with it."

The tour of the school began with a visit to the soviet in their chambers, where beef bouillon and biscuits were served. Extra chairs and a table had been brought into the room to give it a more businesslike atmosphere and the members conducted themselves with the poise of barristers.

"Soviet," said T. C. Ramsay with a scowl. "Not the most pleasant-sounding word. At least to *me.*"

"Only a word," Charles said. "When John Mastwick

founded the school in nineteen nineteen he let the children pick the name for the governing body. They could just as easily have chosen *parliament,* or *congress,* but they wanted something more modern and daring."

"To shock the establishment, I presume."

"Precisely. But what's in a name? It's the purpose that counts."

T. C. Ramsay asked a few pointed questions regarding the functions and duties of the soviet, listening attentively as they were explained, and seemed pleased with the answers.

"Novel, what? A true democratic body at work. And a most pleasant room in which to conduct business."

No one mentioned that he was standing on Lenin's carpet.

The dormitories—no more than four beds to a room—were pristine with not so much as a stray sock left lying about. In the study halls and classrooms the students sat in quiet groups, reading or writing in their notebooks. And from the chapel came the sweet sound of the choir at practice.

Mr. Simpson, imposing in his gown, came in on cue and offered to show the new science laboratory. And then T. C., visibly impressed by the lab, wanted to walk around on his own and "poke the nose here and there." He found nothing to put it out of joint.

"Quite impressive, Greville," he said as Charles walked beside him toward his car. "Not always so neat and tidy, I would imagine."

"Few schools are. Even Archdean."

"Visiting-day behavior. I know what you mean." He paused, thumbs hooked into the pockets of his waistcoat. "I'm a cautious man. I approached the idea of Derek entering here the way I would approach an application for a loan. I made a few discreet inquiries. Your school may have its detractors, but also its share of friends. I was surprised to discover that a member of my club, the managing director of the Manchester and Midland Bank, had sent his grandson here."

"John Laird. He's at Oxford now."

"You may have Derek. Let us say for a year . . . possibly more if I see a marked improvement in him. I still have hopes that he will be capable of enjoying the public school experience one day, but it's the boy's happiness and well being that is my primary concern at the moment. I'll send him down by train on Monday. I will ring first and perhaps you could meet him at the station."

"Of course."

"Though God knows he could find his own way."

THERE WAS A picnic in Leith Wood that afternoon, a closing-the-show party, Marian Halliday called it. It was a joyous, boisterous event, marred only by Valerie A'Dean-Spender falling out of a tree, cutting her leg and spraining her arm. Not a child to suffer in silence, her howls and wails coming from the depths of the wood had sent everyone fanning out through the dense stands of oak and beech to find her. Charles carried her back to the school for iodine, sticking plaster, and a sling.

"I must be getting home now," Marian said after helping Matron with the first aid. "I have my cat to feed."

"I'm sorry you have to go," Charles said. He smiled warmly at her as they walked down the corridor from Matron's room. "Everything worked out marvelously—thanks in no small part to you."

"Oh, I think he'd made up his mind. We could have been running around in paint and feathers and he'd have placed Derek here."

Charles laughed. "Paint, perhaps . . . no feathers."

"Definitely *not* feathers," she agreed. "Look here, if you have nothing better to do tonight why not take pot luck with me? There must be something in the larder I could whip into a meal."

"I would like that," he said without hesitation. "Very much."

She had bought one of the older cottages in Abingdon, a small but solid structure with fieldstone walls and a slate roof set in the midst of a rambling garden choked with flowers and wind-tattered yew. Her huge ginger cat waddled down a garden path to greet them as they got out of the car.

"Hello, Tartuffe," she called out.

"Unusual name for an English cat," Charles remarked.

"I was designing a Molière play when I found him. He was just a kitten then . . . skin and bones and chewed about by the Covent Garden toms. He's filled out in the past five years."

"Filled out? He's a horse!"

The cat trailed them into the house and sat patiently beside his empty feeding bowl in the kitchen.

"You might fix some drinks," Marian said as she picked up the cat dish and placed it on the sideboard. "You'll find a cocktail cabinet in the parlor."

The cottage had been decorated with the elegant simplicity of a modern London flat. Bright paintings and watercolors lined the white walls.

"You have a charming house," he said, handing her a drink.

"Thank you. It was terribly 'olde gifte shoppe' when I first saw it. All chintz and brass hangings. The owners were dismayed when I told them I didn't want the furnishings." She raised her glass to him. "Here's how."

"And to you. For your successful pantomime this morning."

"My pleasure. In fact, it started the wheels turning. There's something wondrously picturesque about the school. The building, the orchard . . . the old courtyard and the lawns. Can't you just imagine *Hamlet* or *Macbeth* played against such a setting? A Shakespeare festival in the summer, out of doors—a professional troupe, mind you. Split the box office. How does that strike you as a fund raiser?"

He almost choked on his gin and tonic. "You're incorrigible. You'll have us selling home-made jams next."

She sat on a sofa and cradled her glass in both hands. "I have a practical mind. It's from growing up on the genteel edge of poverty. I still think it's a good idea. Something the Old Vic might go for . . . two weeks every August. Draw the holiday crowds. Become an established institution in a few years."

"You miss the theater, don't you?"

"Some aspects of it. Working with certain directors I respected . . . reading glowing comments on my costume designs in reviews. The cast parties in Soho. I don't miss the shallow little friendships and the constant bickering and character knifing that went with it. But sometimes I think of going back. I had an offer just last week . . . a revival of a Shaw play at the Lyric in September."

He took a calm swallow of his drink. "We would hate to lose you."

"I'd rather hate to go, to tell you the truth. I'm content. A few days teaching, then puttering about here with my painting.

And besides, Tartuffe would loathe returning to London. He's quite the country gentleman now."

She fixed a supper of cold chicken, potted ham, mustard pickles and a salad which he helped her pluck fresh from the garden. She did not employ a maid, she said, because maids had a distressing habit of dusting her paintings with oily polish rags. And as for a cook, she had never found one yet who could cook as well as she. She waved a chicken wing. "Not that this poor bird is any example. I studied for a year in Paris . . . at the Comédie . . . and shared digs with an American girl who was studying at the Cordon Bleu. I'll fix you a *poitrine de veau farcie Gascogne* one night that will reduce you to tears. And my *canard à la Normande* will send you straight to paradise." She nibbled at the wing. "Have another glass of plonk."

"Plonk" was a chianti which she bought from a shop in Soho in gallon jugs encased in wicker. Red wine with chicken seemed a heresy to Charles, but after two glasses of the stuff it began to take on a mellow affability. He felt mellow himself, totally at ease. He sipped his wine and watched her as she talked, the lovely, expressive face, her long, slim-fingered hands moving to emphasize each word—gestures more Gallic than North London Irish. She had changed before dinner into American-style slacks and a blue cotton jersey. He watched her as she cleared away the dishes and carried them into the kitchen—slim hips and long legs, breasts moving softly beneath the vivid blue cloth.

"Let me help," he said, following her into the kitchen. "I know how to wash up."

"Do you?" she laughed. "I'm sure you've never *washed up* in your life."

"I'm willing to learn."

"Not with my Limoges, thank you. You can have a brandy and watch."

He poured Armagnac into a snifter glass and leaned against a heavy wood kitchen table.

"I've been thinking of Derek Ramsay. 'Fat Chap,' Valerie calls him."

"Oh, dear," she sighed. "Everyone will be calling him that now, I suppose. Valerie A'Dean-Spender is like the BBC."

"It won't matter. No malice to it. The kids love their nicknames. They wear them as medals." He swirled the brandy around in the bell-shaped glass. "Coming to Burgate is going to make a profound change in Derek's life. Mine as well."

She raised a quizzical eyebrow. "In what way?"

"I really don't know, but I have an odd sort of feeling about it. It's like chemistry. A tiny substance is added to a compound and that compound is changed utterly. A catalyst. I feel that Derek is a catalyst in some mysterious way. My standing here in your kitchen—"

"Little Ramsay's doing?"

"I think so. In a manner beyond explanation."

She rinsed the last of the plates and placed it in a wood rack to drain. "It's true you never came here before. Although you were invited. More than once."

"Something held me back. I apologize."

"No need. I can understand how difficult it can be sometimes to face social engagements. I went through a stage during my divorce when I didn't want to be around anyone."

"My . . . 'stage' lasted for years."

"Past tense now?"

He looked steadily at her face. Her eyes, he noticed for the first time, held tiny flecks of gold. "Very much in the past tense."

He poured another brandy and one for her, and then they went into the parlor, the sun's last rays touching the west-facing windows, glowing deep rose through the glass. Tartuffe lay on a chair, doglike, huge head resting on his paws. Marian sank back on the sofa with a sigh.

"I love this time of day."

"So does your cat, it seems."

"A highly civilized creature when night comes. No prowling about in the dark undergrowth for him. An easy chair, preferably a coal fire in the grate. I expect him to smoke a pipe one day and wear slippers."

Charles smiled and sat beside her. "I envy the beast."

"For living a hedonistic life?"

"For living it with you."

The sun dipped beyond the wooded slopes of the hills and a purple afterglow filled the room. Marian leaned forward and placed her glass on a table. "That was a charming thing to say."

"It's what I feel. A sudden, irrational envy."

"He won't mind. I certainly don't."

Her face was in profile, as sharply etched as a silhouette cut from black paper. The paper had substance, a perfumed warmth, velvet against his lips as he bent impulsively and kissed her cheek. "I have enjoyed this day," he whispered.

"So have I," she said with a throaty softness.

And her lips were soft . . . and her body soft under his gentle hands as she slipped back against the cushions and enfolded him in her arms.

The night wind stirred the curtains and moaned under the eaves. Tartuffe opened his tiger eyes, stared unblinking into the darkness for a time, and then closed them in sleep.

5

ALBERT THAXTON, ON his third day of the summer holidays and still wearing his school uniform, picked up the morning mail and brought the bundle of letters and newspapers into the dining room.

"Cripes! A fair amount in the post this morning, sir."

He placed the pile on the table next to Martin, who was pouring his first coffee of the day. Albert's cheerfulness in the morning took getting used to.

"Thank you. Had your breakfast?"

"Oh, yes, sir. An hour ago. Mrs. Bromley is a super cook. Sausages . . . bacon . . . eggs and fried bread . . ."

Martin winced and took a swallow of black coffee. The thought of food made him feel queasy. He'd spent the evening with Jacob Golden drinking martinis and discussing the problems of the world. The only problem worth considering at the moment was how to get rid of his hangover. He rang for the housekeeper and asked for a glass of tomato juice and a bottle of Worcestershire sauce.

"And anything else for you, Master Thaxton?" the woman asked. "There's some sausages left . . . and a gammon rasher."

"Oh, yes, please, Mrs. Bromley. That would be super. And perhaps a bit of toast and marmalade."

"God!" Martin grunted. "Where do you put it?"

Albert grinned and sat down at the table. "Making up for what they feed us at school. Porridge and treacle."

"And dry crusts and water, I suppose."

"Not quite so horrid as that." He toyed idly with the sugar bowl. "Were you able to discuss the matter with Mr. Golden, sir?"

"I was. He'd like nothing better than to put you on as a copyboy for the summer, but he's afraid there might be a few problems if he did."

"Problems?"

"Resentment from the other boys. The ones who have to work for a living. So many people out these days. I'm sure everyone on the paper knows someone who's desperate for a job."

"I can understand that. They'd put mine down to rank favoritism. I wouldn't want that. And it is true about the slump. I listened to the wireless last night before going to bed. The Board of Trade released the latest unemployment figures. Rather frightening." He pulled a small notebook from the pocket of his blazer. "I jotted it all down in shorthand, in case you'd be interested."

"Taken to carrying a notebook?"

"Oh, yes, sir. A conscientious reporter carries one at all times. I thought it would be a good idea if I got into the habit of it."

"You're really serious about all this, aren't you?"

The boy nodded vigorously. "More so than ever. I really buckled down to languages this term . . . and mastering Pitman. I practiced my strokes an hour a day, on my own time."

"Good for you. Don't be too disappointed. We'll work something out. I'll have a talk with Joe Johnson at INA. A wire service is not much different from working on a newspaper. Something might turn up there, if only for a week or two. It would get your feet wet. In the meantime, we can just knock about and enjoy ourselves. Ned said I wasn't to spoil you, but what the heck."

"Ned believes in hard work and no nonsense. Idle hands and all that. If he sees me spending an hour reading the *Times* he thinks I'm frittering my life away. What I'm actually doing is dissecting the method of putting a paper together. Not something they teach at school."

"I understand. I used to read every paper from cover to cover when I was in college. When I got my first job with the Chicago *Herald* I had the style down pat. Keep it up."

When Albert's second breakfast arrived, Martin avoided looking at the loaded plate and began to sort through the mail. There were the usual number of household bills which he set aside for Mrs. Bromley to check over; four or five letters requesting money for various charities; a couple of invitations to cocktail parties honoring people he had never heard of; a letter—sent airmail via the *Graf Zeppelin*—from an old girlfriend in New York that was as light as the blue onion skin paper on which it was written. He sighed and wiped his reading glasses with his tie. Hard to imagine by her frothy tone that only two years before they had been in the midst of a love affair of operatic intensity.

There was a letter from Germany, from Scott Kingsford, postmarked Hanover. It was, in the manner of all his ex-boss's letters, terse and to the point. More in the manner of a cablegram.

> Arriving London third August. Staying Ritz. Keep day open. Important matters to discuss. Though much is taken much abides. CBC Radio off the canvas at the count of nine and counterpunching like a sonofabitch. Dramatic . . . thrilling . . . revolutionary advancements here in radio engineering and CBC acquiring U.S. patent rights. Will discuss. Don't let me down.
>
> Scott

Curious. He folded the letter and slipped it into his pocket. The final envelope was buff colored, the Stanmore crest embossed on the flap. It was an invitation . . .

> The Earl and Countess of Stanmore request your presence at the 35th ANNUAL CHARITY BAZAAR AND FETE, Abingdon Pryory, 26 July 1930

His aunt's copperplate handwriting softened the formality . . .

> My dearest Martin,
>
> Come down on the Friday. Alex and her children arrive from America on the 23rd. Also, Fenton and Winifred depart for India in September. A long weekend party of welcome, of farewell—and to honor the Glorious Fourth, our own dear Independence Day.

He would phone her and tell her he would be bringing Albert. She would be delighted. The more the merrier.

"We're invited down to Abingdon Pryory this weekend, Albert. A Fourth of July celebration."

"*Fourth* of July?" He made a rapid calculation. "Saturday will be the twenty-sixth, sir."

"Yes, but my aunt isn't a stickler for dates. You'll enjoy yourself—and I've always wanted you to see the place."

"The country house where Ivy was in service?"

"That's right. Down in Surrey."

"Exactly what sort of maid was she?"

"What they called an upstairs maid. Then she became a lady's maid . . . the personal servant of my cousin Alexandra. Alex was eighteen . . . Ivy a year younger." He smiled in fond memory. "Boy, let me tell you, seeing the two of them together was seeing the two prettiest girls in England . . . bar none. You'll meet Alexandra this weekend. She lives in California now."

Albert crunched a piece of toast between his teeth. "Blond woman?"

"Yes. How did you know?"

"Mum used to keep a snapshot on her dressing table. Ivy and a blond girl, both in uniform standing in front of a tent. Lady Alexandra Greville. Is that right?"

Martin nodded. "That was Alex. She and Ivy became the best of friends. They served together in France for over a year on the hospital trains . . . Rouen to the Somme."

"Odd, come to think of it." He chewed slowly and took a swig of tea. "Their being friends, I mean. Never could have happened if it hadn't been for the war. Rather a democratic institution in its own horrible way. May I see the invitation, sir?"

He studied it, running a finger across the heavily embossed lettering. "Crikey. The Earl and Countess of Stanmore. How would I address them, sir?"

"A simple 'ma'am' will do for my aunt, though I imagine by the end of our stay she'll have you calling her Hanna. As for the earl . . . just call him 'sir.' God knows you won't have any trouble saying *that.*"

THEY TOOK THE three fifteen from Waterloo on Friday afternoon. Charles was on the platform to meet them when the train pulled into Abingdon thirty-five minutes later. There was a pronounced change in the man, Martin was thinking as he introduced him to Albert. His clothes for one thing. The baggy, shapeless tweeds had given way to white summer flannels and a dark blue blazer of faultless cut. But it went beyond mere haberdashery. His cousin's eyes had a sparkle and vitality that he hadn't seen in many years. There was a radiant air of cheerfulness and well-being about him.

"I must say, Charlie, you're looking good."

"Feel tip-top, old boy."

"End-of-term euphoria?"

"Actually, no. I keep the school open year round. There are always fifteen or twenty children who stay on for one reason or another. The place is rather like a holiday camp just now. Quite pleasant."

They reached the street and Martin looked for the Rolls-Royce and the chauffeur. Neither could be seen.

"Shanks' mare or taxi?"

"My car," Charles said.

"Can the three of us squeeze into it?"

"Not the ancient Austin. I bought a new one. A spacious and powerful Humber."

Martin looked dubious. "How powerful? Willie told me a few chilling tales about your driving."

"All true. I used to be a danger to both man and beast. Been taking lessons from someone who's a whiz with motor-cars. She says I'm progressing nicely."

"She?"

Charles beamed a smile. "Very much *she*. You'll meet her at the house. She's lending a hand with the bazaar—supervising the decorations."

"You'll have to tell me all about her, Charlie."

"I will . . . yes . . . she is really quite special."

Well, Martin thought as they reached the shiny new car, how quickly things could change.

The house awed Albert into silence as he followed one of the footmen down a long, spacious corridor toward the room he had been given. His suitcase, he noticed with a pang of shame, looked terribly small and shabby in the brawny hand of the liveried servant. A maid passed, hurrying along the passage carrying a stack of fresh towels, her starched uniform rustling as she walked. He smiled at her but she avoided his glance.

"Do you require anything, sir?" the footman asked after placing the suitcase on a wood bench at the foot of the bed.

Albert shook his head numbly.

"Very good, sir. The bell-pull is beside the door."

And then the man was gone and he was alone in a large, sunny room with a splendid view of formal gardens. He sat on the edge of the bed, not sure of what to do next. Wait for

Martin, he supposed. He thought of the maid with her load of towels. A pleasant-looking young woman doing what his sister had done in this house. An upstairs maid . . . making beds and changing towels. Ivy's daily tasks. And here he was, a guest to be waited on—if he had the courage to pull the bell-rope.

There was a tentative tap on the door and he jumped to his feet just as it opened. A blond woman wearing American-style slacks and a green silk blouse stepped into the room, smiling at him . . . rather sadly, he thought.

"So you are Albert Edward."

"Y-yes," he stammered.

She walked over to him and touched him lightly on the cheek. "I would have known even if Martin hadn't told me you were up here. You resemble Ivy Thaxton so much it's uncanny . . . a very *manly* image of your sister, let me add . . . but the same eyes, shape of face."

"Lady Alexandra Greville?"

"Yes. Mrs. Ross now . . . Alexandra to you, please."

"Mum . . . my mother . . . kept a picture of you and Ivy on her dresser."

"Taken in front of our quarters in Rouen. September nineteen sixteen. You were two years old then. Ivy and I were always knitting things for you in our spare time—not that there was much of that, I'm afraid—sweaters and little woolly caps. And now here you are, practically a grown man." She took hold of his hand and gave it a squeeze. "Had your tea?"

"No. I haven't even unpacked yet."

"I'll have father's valet do that for you."

"Please don't bother," he said quickly. "I can manage it

later." He had to laugh. It was all too absurd. "I don't know what a valet would make of my things."

She put an arm about his waist and led him toward the door. "I know, rumpled pajamas and mismatched socks. Come along then. Consider yourself in my charge. We'll have tea and I'll introduce you to everyone." She shook her head in wonder. "Ivy's baby brother. I can't tell you how happy I am that you're here. Dear God, if only she were here as well."

THE BOOTHS FOR the charity bazaar and fete were being set up in a large meadow half a mile from the Pryory. Volunteers from Abingdon, including men from local chapters of the British Legion, and Royal Order of Foresters were wielding hammers and saws while a crowd of women and children, including eighteen from Burgate House School, festooned the structures with red, white, and blue bunting—to Hanna alone the colors of the Stars and Stripes, not the Union Jack. Beyond the booths where food, drink, and a variety of crafts would be sold, a small traveling carnival was erecting a gaudy merry-go-round, swings, coconut shies, and other attractions of chance and skill.

"There she is," Charles said. "The woman on the ladder."

Martin gave Marian Halliday a long, educated look and liked everything that he saw—a slender, comely woman in slacks and sweater not afraid to stand on a ladder and tack bunting to a board. A woman who, when she spotted Charles, flashed a smile of such joy that it could only have come from the heart.

Martin whistled softly between his teeth. "Charlie, as they say back home, you've done yourself proud."

DEREK RAMSAY STRUGGLED through the trampled grass with a load of bunting in his arms, the red-and-white cloth unwinding from the heavy rolls and trailing after him in the mud.

"Oh, do watch what you're doing," Valerie A'Dean-Spender called out as she came along behind him carrying a roll of blue. "You'll get it all dirty, Fat Chap."

"No I won't," he replied stubbornly.

He was short for twelve with a chunky body and sturdy legs, but in the nearly eight weeks that he had been at Burgate House he had lost so much flab as to make his nickname virtually meaningless. One month after entering the school his grandfather had been delighted—and mildly dismayed—by a letter from Matron informing him that all of Derek's clothing was too large for him now and should be replaced. She had also informed him in a postscript that there had not been "even one unfortunate accident during the night." Happy and contented boys do not wet their beds. A scug no longer.

"Mrs. Halliday is going to be angry if you do," Valerie warned. "You'll see."

She was not angry as she looked down from her perch on the ladder, but she did admonish him gently for bringing the cloth to the wrong place. "That batch is for the pony ride fence, Derek. Don't you remember?"

"I told you so!" Valerie wailed. "Oh, you *are* an ass, Fat Chap."

"That will do, Valerie," she said sternly. "Better leave one roll here for now, Derek. They're much too heavy."

"I'll take it," a boy said. "I want to help."

Derek eyed the boy narrowly. He had seen him at the

school the day before. Mr. Greville's nephew from America. A Colin something-or-other . . . tall, sandy haired, and freckled. He was helping now; the not very strenuous task of bracing the ladder for Mrs. Halliday. He wanted to tell him to buzz off, that he was perfectly capable of carrying them one hundred yards across the meadow to where men were finishing the fence, but he could see the headmaster approaching.

"If you want to," he muttered, letting one of the rolls fall to the ground.

Valerie gave up there and then, setting down her burden and sitting on it. "It's not fair. We would have been there by now."

Colin Mackendric Ross touched the girl on the shoulder. "I can carry that one too, but not with you on it. Okay?"

"Okay!" she cried, springing to her feet. *"Yankee Chappie!"*

"Does she always give people names?" Colin asked as they walked away.

Derek nodded. "Yes. And we call her Pest."

"How old is she?"

"I don't know. Nine, I think. How old are you?"

"Ten . . . going on eleven."

Derek stopped walking and looked at him. He was a head taller than himself and carried the two rolls of bunting as though they had no weight whatever. "*Ten?* Is that all?"

"Big for my age . . . that's what my mother says. My father was tall, she said. Six foot three, or something like that. I guess I take after him."

"You never knew him?"

"He died when I was a kid. In Canada. That's where I was born. Toronto. He was a doctor and had a heart attack . . . I think it was. Yeah, a heart attack."

"My father was killed in the war. He won the V.C. Do you know what that is?"

"Sure. The Victoria Cross. Was he a pilot?"

"I don't think so. Royal Marines."

"Pilots won the most V.C.s I bet. Shooting down zeps . . . dogfights over the lines . . . that sort of thing. Have you ever been up in a plane?"

"Lots of times," he lied. "All sorts."

"Same here. My father—that is, my new father—he builds them. He has a factory in San Diego."

"Is that in Spain?"

"Spain? Heck no, California."

He tried to remember his geography. California was where Drake had stopped in the *Golden Hind* while sailing around the world. San Francisco. Hollywood was in California someplace. He had never heard of San Diego. He felt foolish for asking if it were in Spain. Why would the man have a factory in Spain and live in America? He trudged on, his arms leaden. He was getting tired and would like to have stopped and rested for a minute, but the red-headed ten-year-old would have to stop first. He showed no sign of doing so, striding along, whistling, the bundles thrust under his long arms. Derek had to trot in order to keep up with him.

"Say, can you ride a horse?" Colin asked.

"A horse? I . . . I suppose so. Why?"

"I have a horse at home. We have a ranch in La Jolla. Not a big ranch . . . not like a pal of mine at school. His father has a ranch in Escondido that's thousands and thousands of acres. I have this horse, Gunboat I call him, a palomino, and I can make him jump and everything and he loves to gallop along the beach and splash in the surf. Gosh, I wish I could have brought old Gunboat over here, but my grandfather has lots of horses. Heck, let's drop this stuff off in a hurry and go up to the stables."

They ran the last thirty yards, gave the bunting to the men erecting the fence, and then headed off across the meadow toward the distant stables. Derek, struggling to catch his breath, pretended to turn his ankle and sat down in the deep grass. Colin squatted on his heels beside him.

"You hurt it bad?"

"I . . . don't . . . think so." He gasped, making a show of rubbing his ankle. "Be . . . all right . . . in a minute or two."

"I do it lots of times when I play baseball. I catch my spikes sliding into second. But, heck, everyone does that . . . Gehrig . . . Al Simmons . . . everyone. Just spit and keep on playing."

Derek continued to rub his ankle, looking at Colin Mackendric Ross out of the corner of his eye. He still felt uneasy around boys bigger than himself. None of the bigger boys at Burgate House were bullies, but almost all of the ones at Archdean had been. The "Bloods," the athletes, swaggering about with their badges and blazers and special caps and scarves, pushing anyone who annoyed them. It seemed incredible that this boy was only ten years old. He smiled at the thought of an Archdean Blood pushing this Yankee Chappie around.

"Are you staying at the earl's house?"

Colin plucked at the grass. "He's my grandfather. We come over every year and stay for a month, and he and Grandmama come to us every Christmas . . . though I don't think they'll come this year because he was sick." Reaching out, he touched Derek's foot. "Do you think it's better now?"

"I think so, yes."

"Feel up to a ride, then?"

"I . . . better not."

"Why?"

"Because I don't know how." He could feel his face burn. "I've never been on a horse. Never been up in a plane, either." He stiffened in expectation of a hoot of derision.

Colin tossed some grass into the air and watched it drift in the wind. "Heck, I could teach you. Riding a horse isn't hard. And flying isn't such big stuff. Noisy as heck, though. My brother, John . . . he's seven . . . he won't go near a plane. The sound hurts his ears. He had an operation a couple of years ago. Mastoid . . . or something like that. Wouldn't you like to know how to ride?"

"I suppose so."

"Come on, then. There's no horses here."

Gardway was inspecting a batch of ponies that had been culled from farms throughout the Vale of Abingdon. There were sturdy Welsh and Connemaras, nimble footed Dartmoors, and even a sprinkling of Shetlands, not much taller than large dogs.

"Hello, Master Colin," the head groom called out cheerfully. "What do you think of 'em?"

"More of them than last year, Mr. Gardway."

"Right you are, lad. It's the most popular attraction with the young'uns."

"Any large ones?"

"One. Mrs. Herbert's Flossie . . . from over Bigham way."

"Could you saddle her up?"

The man laughed, tipped his cap to the back of his head.

"You, Master Colin? You're a fair way beyond a pony now, even a ruddy big one like Flossie."

"For my friend here. He's never ridden before."

"You don't say so?" He eyed Derek with something close to pity. "Well, I never. Still, it will have to wait, I'm afraid. I can't let you take the old dear out alone, Master Colin. I'm responsible to Mrs. Herbert, I am. You can have the cob."

"Too high a gait for a beginner," Colin said. "I rode Flossie last summer, Mr. Gardway. Remember? She knows me and I'd look after her."

"Sorry, lad. Not now. I have all this bunch to water, feed, stable, and make ready for tomorrow."

Colin watched the man walk off, shouting orders to the stable boys.

"Sorry."

"That's all right," Derek said with a sense of relief.

"Do you live at my uncle's school?"

"I'm staying on through the summer, if that's what you mean."

Colin bent his head and whispered. "We could come back later. At midnight."

"Midnight?"

"Sure. You could sneak away from the school and meet me here." There was a tremulous excitement in his voice. "Be a full moon again tonight . . . bright as day. Be lots of fun."

"I . . . I don't know . . . sneaking away . . ." His mouth felt dry.

"I'll go out my window, shinny down the drainpipe. How will you get out of the school?"

Derek swallowed hard. "Same way . . . I guess."

"We'll take Flossie into the meadow. Boy oh boy, I bet I teach you to ride in ten minutes flat. Midnight. Right here. Okay?"

"Okay," he whispered.

"Shake hands and spit on it."

He could shake hands, but there was no spit in the brass roof of his mouth.

VICTORIA WOOD-LACY TOOK her time dressing for dinner, primping in front of the dressing-table mirror, pinching her lips to get a deeper red into them, not daring to use the lipstick she kept hidden in the bottom of a purse.

"Did you notice his eyes when he looked at me?"

"When was that?" Jennifer asked, stifling a yawn.

"When we were introduced, silly. He stared at me . . . with a fierce intensity. With . . . *bedroom eyes.*"

"You're such an ass. Bedroom eyes indeed! You got that from one of your trashy novels."

"I don't read trashy novels. Never!"

"Oh, yes you do. You hide them under your mattress . . . *Her Flaming Passion* and *The Playboy and the Gold Digger.*"

Victoria turned on the bench and tossed a tortoise-shell comb in the general direction of the window seat where her sister was seated, staring down into the garden below. "Sneak!"

"Those sort of books will rot your mind."

"They're quite educational in a way." She looked back in the mirror and ran her fingers across her eyebrows. "Women, that is ultrachic women, are always plucking their eyebrows in books."

"I wouldn't try it if I were you."

"Do you think I dare wear the silk stockings I bought at Woolworth's?"

"Mother and Daddy would notice right away. I do not think they would be overjoyed."

"Oh, dear," she sighed. "I'm secretly glad they're going off to India."

"You are a proper fool. Do you honestly believe that the headmistress of Tolmers Park is going to be more tolerant than they are? It's a boarding school, you know . . . and an *Anglican* boarding school at that, not a Parisian brothel for *jeunes filles.*"

"Don't you think he looks like Ivor Novello? So dark and handsome. What a horrid thing it was to name him Albert. If I were he I'd change it. Roderick would be nice . . . or how does *Byron* Thaxton strike you?"

"I shall strike *you* in a moment if you don't bloody well get dressed."

THE BRIGADIER POURED a whisky for Martin and one for himself. The late afternoon sun slanted through the glass of the library windows and made lozenge-shaped patterns on the carpet.

"Here's how," he said.

"And good luck to you, Fenton."

"Thanks. Going off to India in September is rather an appalling thought, but at least Winnie will be setting up house in the Kashmir with a view of the cool Himalayan snows."

"And you'll be where?"

"The staff college in Quetta. Dealing in theory mostly until they ship out the new light tanks from Vickers—that is, *if* they ship them out . . . or find room in the bloody budget to purchase them. Still, it doesn't matter. We can make do with lorries and armored cars. It's the tactical concepts of the force that're important in the long run. The nuts and bolts of radio communications, infantry, armored vehicles, and aircraft."

"All the things you did in Iraq eight years ago."

"Quite so, but on a larger scale and with official sanction this time. It was a stroke of luck getting this assignment . . . although I sense Jacob's fine hand somewhere along the line."

"Not taking the girls, I hope?"

"Lord, no . . . not now. I hope the turmoil will quiet down, but not before Gandhi is released I'm afraid. Well, we shall see. Hate like hell to leave them behind, but Winnie can always fly back and visit them. Thanks to Imperial Airways it's not the far side of the world any longer, is it? Only seven days to Karachi. You could even fly out yourself. Enough happening to satisfy your pen I should think."

"More than enough." He swirled the whisky in his glass as he would a fine brandy. "I hope they don't waste your talents in guarding salt works and breaking strikes."

Fenton grimaced. "I shall try to divorce myself as much as possible from the problems of the raj. The Punjab bureaucrats got themselves into this unholy mess after Amritsar and they can bloody well get themselves out of it without any help from me. My job is to work quietly in Quetta and help modernize the Indian army, not badger the followers of a little man in a loincloth."

"And if ordered to do so, Fenton?"

He stared at Martin with his unblinking hawk's eyes. "*Or-*

dered? Heaven forbid, old boy. But if I am, I shall run their bloody nappies off."

CHARLES TOOK THE latch key from a pocket of his dinner jacket and opened the front door. Tartuffe ambled in from the kitchen and sat in the parlor cleaning his paws.

"And where is your mistress?" he called out.

"I don't know about his," Marian shouted back, "but yours is in the bath."

She was chin deep in soapy froth, her raised knees jutting above the water like smooth white islands.

"You look comfortable," he said, leaning against the doorjamb. "Is that what you are, my mistress?"

"Neither yours nor the cat's. It was just too good a remark to pass up. Be a dear and toss me the luffa."

He took the fibrous sponge from its resting place across the water taps and plopped it in the water. "You're expected for dinner, you know."

"I shan't be late." She sat up and scrubbed her back with the sponge. "Every muscle in my body screams with anguish."

"Mother is more than pleased. She told one and all that you did a magnificent job today." He glanced at his watch. "We usually sit at eight—sharp."

"We'll be there by half past seven."

It was steamy in the bathroom and he removed his jacket, hanging it on the back of the door. How beautiful she looked in the huge iron tub. Dwarfed by it. The cottage had once been owned by a farmer who had weighed as much as a heifer. The tub had been specially cast for him by a firm in Coventry. Thick, blackened metal and the slender softness of her body, soap flecked, the firm breasts draped with a residue as delicate as lace.

He cleared his throat. "I was thinking of the packing. I'm sure Mother would be disappointed if you didn't stay over."

"We already discussed it. I'm packed and my neighbor will look in on Tartuffe and keep his bowl filled. Persuasive woman, your mother. Not that I needed much persuading to spend the weekend in such a lovely house. She said she was giving me the Amalfi suite—whatever that is."

"Bedroom, dressing room, and bath; Italianate furnishings and décor, lovely view of the sunken gardens—and a door, normally kept bolted, leading to my rooms."

"I see," she said quietly, lying back in the water. "I suppose she ran short of space and had to put me wherever she could."

"There are forty bedrooms . . . give or take."

"A perceptive woman, then. Or did you tell her about us?"

"Only in the most general way." He moved a wicker stool and sat beside the tub, resting his folded arms on the hard, damp sides. "I wanted her to know that it was pointless to keep inviting the vicar's niece for Sunday tea in expectation of my seeing a great light one afternoon. I told her that I have become fond of someone."

"Fond. Romeo could hardly have said it better."

He touched the warm, soapy smoothness of her skin. "I did not tell her that I wish to spend every remaining moment of my life with this person. That I want, terribly, to—"

She sat up, shaking her head. "No. Please don't go on. I can't bear the thought of being proposed to naked."

He bent and kissed the side of her neck. "Then hurry and dress, my love."

Lord Stanmore tapped a spoon against the wine glass for attention. "May the twins be permitted a small glass of Moselle, Winnie?"

"I don't think it would hurt them. Do you, Fenton?"

"Good heavens, no. I certainly drank a wee bit on occasion when I was thirteen."

"Nearly *fourteen,* Daddy," Victoria hissed.

Her father laughed. "Quite so. Nearly sixteen if it comes to that!"

Victoria, blushing, glanced over at Albert Thaxton. The boy was staring intently up the table at the earl. There would be dancing after dinner and she had made up her mind to tell him that she was fifteen. Quite impossible now unless he hadn't heard. Damn Papa and his parade-ground voice!

Jennifer, seated beside her, inclined her head and whispered sweetly, "That put a fly in the old ointment, didn't it?"

The wine was poured around the table and the earl stood up. "There was a moment a few months ago when I . . . but I shan't dwell on that. I am here tonight after all, by God's grace—"

"Hear, hear," Charles murmured.

"—facing, as that poet chap wrote, dear friends and gentle hearts."

"How nicely put, Tony," Hanna said.

"Yes, well, not to place too fine a point on it, I raise my glass to everyone at this table . . . dear hearts, dear old friends, and dear new ones . . . your health."

Hanna raised her glass. "And, we hope, to new family."

"New family?" the earl said, frowning. "What on earth do you mean, my dear?"

Charles glanced at Marian and then smiled at his mother. "I'll answer for you, if I may."

"I would be honored."

Charles, holding Marian tightly by the hand, stood up. "I asked Mrs. Halliday to be my wife. I'm happy to say she accepted."

ALBERT, WHO SEEMED to know more about wireless than anyone else in the house, managed to fine tune the big set and pick up Radio Paris broadcasting the music of Paul Whiteman's band from the Lido.

"How terribly clever you are," Victoria said. "Is it really coming from Paris?"

"Transmitting from the Eiffel Tower. Super clarity."

"Oh, yes, marvelous." She waited expectantly. "That's a Gershwin song . . . from *Lady Be Good.* Very easy to dance to."

"Is it?"

"Don't they teach you how to dance at school?"

"The waltz . . . with broomsticks."

"Broomsticks?"

"Yes, as our partners . . . one-two-three-glide."

"I can teach you the foxtrot." She held out her arms. It was unladylike to ask a boy to dance, but she felt reckless, sensing Jennifer's eyes on her from across the ballroom. "Care to give it a whirl?"

"All right," he said.

VICTORIA'S ECSTASY COULD not be contained. She almost swooned across her side of the bed, emitting a long, passionate sigh. "Have you ever known such a night, Jenny?"

Jennifer only grunted, turning her back on her sister, and pulled the blanket around her shoulders. "Go to sleep."

"Impossible! I will never sleep again." She switched off the bedside lamp and luxuriated in the moonlight flooding the room. "I think Marian Halliday is so beautiful . . . and Charles is such a handsome, distinguished man. He could have been our father, do you realize that?"

"Oh, *do* shut up."

"But he wasn't in love with Mama nor she with him. It was Grandmama who wished them to marry . . . join the two houses . . . the Suttons and the Grevilles . . . so medieval, don't you think? But true love triumphed over all."

Jennifer made a retching sound and drew the blanket over her head.

"You have no romance in your soul, Jenny. You'll be an old maid, withered and dried like Miss Stackpoole the post-mistress at Lulworth . . . the one with the sharp chin and no breasts at all. You'll see. And they taught him to dance with a broomstick! Can you imagine it? And he held me so stiffly with Daddy watching us, but I know he wanted to foxtrot out to the terrace and crush me in his—"

Jennifer rose from under the covers and in one swift, exasperated movement brought her pillow firmly down on her twin's head.

THERE WAS A light under Albert's door as Martin came down the corridor toward his own room. He opened the door and stepped inside. The boy was sitting in bed writing in his notebook.

"Putting the day down on paper?"

"Just for practice, actually."

"Don't stop on my account."

"Oh, no, sir. I'm finished."

"Enjoy yourself today?"

"Oh, indeed, sir . . . a super time. Lord Stanmore gave me a tour . . . rather like being in a museum. Did you know they have paintings by Constable, Reynolds, and Van Dyck? Crikey! And all those silver cups and things for riding. A very *nice* man, Lord Stanmore."

"Yes, he is."

"And I rather liked the brigadier. Quite different from what I imagined a military chap to be. Smashing daughters, by the way . . . but odd about twins. So identical in looks and so opposite in personality. Victoria is . . . oh, warm and friendly, while the other . . . well, I don't think she likes me at all."

"Girls often go through a stage of not liking boys."

"They're usually over that by fifteen, aren't they, sir?"

Martin drew slowly on his cigar. "Fifteen?"

"*Nearly* fifteen, Victoria said."

"Ah, how time flies."

THE DOOR LEADING to the Amalfi suite was unbolted. Charles tapped lightly and stepped inside. Both the sitting room and bedroom were in darkness, but he could see Marian in the moonlight seated on a chaise longue facing open windows. She was still wearing her dinner dress.

"Woolgathering?" he said as he bent to kiss her forehead.

"A bit." She took hold of his hand and drew him down

beside her. "I had a long talk with your mother. Just left her rooms as a matter of fact. An honest and candid woman."

"Yankee directness."

"I admire that. I grew up calling a spade a spade."

"And what did you discuss?"

"You . . . us. Your happiness as her main consideration. She feels I worked a miracle on you and is grateful for that. She also made it clear that the divorced wife of an actor would not have received her blessing, let alone your father's, before the war."

"No. But then a great many things were different before the war . . . if one can remember such a misty past."

"As she pointed out, I will no doubt be Countess of Stanmore one day, so she talked of practical matters . . . presentation at court being one. The approach, she said, would have to be handled with the utmost discretion."

"Yes. Our beloved monarchs view divorce with incomprehension."

"She believes she can manage it. Is she really a cousin of the queen?"

"Second or third cousin . . . through the German branch of the Rilkes . . . the von Rilkes of Mecklenburg-Schwerin. When Mother has the will she will always find a way. Does the thought disturb you?"

"A little. So does the thought of being mistress of this house. I hope your parents live to be a hundred."

He put his arms around her and hugged her close. "But you're not marrying this house. You're marrying a country schoolmaster. *That* thought would disturb most women these days."

"Not when you're the schoolmaster. I love you very much, Charles."

"And I love you. Rather a comforting coincidence."

She rested her head against his shoulder and watched the slender branch of a plane tree, the leaves silver under the moon, move gently against the window. From somewhere in the house came the melodic chiming of eleven. "I shall remember this day . . . *always.*"

COLIN MACKENDRIC ROSS heard the sound of bells through the depths of his dream. He was with Elmer and some other boy. The other boy was lagging far behind and he kept yelling at him to hurry up, that there were hobos down in a jungle beside the railroad tracks . . . hairy, ragged men boiling coffee in tin cans, waiting for the northbound freights. And he was riding Gunboat up the trail through the yuccas toward Soledad peak and on the heights he could see the ocean forever and the U.S.S. *Saratoga* steaming out past Point Loma and the boy he could not place was running up the trail behind him . . . shouting, waving his arms . . . and the bells of the old mission were ringing . . . ringing . . . ringing . . .

DEREK, UNCOMFORTABLE AND hot in his clothes under the blanket, heard the tall-case clock in the downstairs hall chime eleven. He got out of bed and fumbled with his shoes in the darkness. There was only one other boy in his dorm, a fellow named Winslow whose father had a job in Kenya and left him in the school year round. There were only eighteen boys and girls in the school now—and one master, Mr. Wallis . . . not counting the headmaster. Matron had gone on holiday and Mrs. Mahon had assumed that function, but she slept like a log. He could go down the stairs and out the front door—but what if it were locked? He sat on the bed and laced his shoes. Of course it would be locked, he reasoned. Bound to be . . . as well as all the other doors. He could wake Winslow and ask him to help, but he was sleeping soundly, snoring gently through open mouth, a shaft of moonlight falling across his face. He walked to the window and looked down. There was a flagstone courtyard below. An awful long way and a terribly hard surface at the bottom. But there were any number of windows on the ground floor. He slapped his forehead with the palm of his hand at his stupidity.

His shoes creaked as he tiptoed down the hall toward the main stairs. He was so intent on being silent that as he crossed the corridor leading to the girls' dormitory wing he tripped over a carpet runner and went sprawling on his face with a loud grunt of surprise and pain.

A door opened down the passage and the slender beam of a flashlight wavered over him.

"Fat Chap!" Valerie's voice. "Are you running away?"

"Don't be daft," he muttered, sitting up and rubbing his knee. "And turn off that ruddy light, can't you."

She padded down the corridor in bare feet and squatted beside him, legs tucked under her long, white cotton nightdress. "If you're not running away, what are you doing then?"

"Meeting the Yank, if you must know."

"Where?"

"None of your business."

"Oh, do tell me," she whispered excitedly. "Don't be a beast."

"No."

"I'll scream the place down if you don't. Really I will. I'll say I thought you were a burglar."

He knew she would. It was just like the Pest. "All right. I'm meeting him at the stables at midnight . . . the stables at the Pryory."

She clutched his arm feverishly. "Oh, let me come, Fat Chap . . . let me come."

"No. It . . . it's too dangerous for girls."

She stood up and turned toward her room. "I'll just get my gym shoes."

The moment she was gone he scrambled to his feet and bolted down the stairs, across the main hall, and along a corridor to the classroom where Mrs. Halliday taught art. The windows there were wide and opened onto a tree-shaded stretch of ground that led to the upper meadows of Leith Common. He was through the window in a flash and running hard for the meadows. As he climbed a low stone wall he could hear a soft patter of footsteps coming up behind him.

"Wait for me, Fat Chap! Wait for me!"

He tried to ignore her and to think of ways to explain her presence to the Yank. And to top everything off she looked silly in gym shoes and nightdress. He felt mortified.

"Are you going to look at the horses for the pony rides?" she asked as she trudged along beside him across the meadow. "Are you? I love horses. I had my own once . . . I named her Angelica. I loved her dearly. That was when I lived with my father in Devon. He doesn't live there any longer . . . he lives in London and goes to New York all the time. Mother lives in Paris . . . or Monte Carlo . . . places like that. Father called her a tramp."

Derek stopped walking long enough to glare at her. "Must you keep talking? You'll give the game away."

"What game?" She went wide eyed. "Are you going to cop a horse? Sneak it from the stables?"

"Maybe." He looked away from her. "It's the Yank's idea. I . . . I'm going to ride it."

"Do you know how?"

"There's nothing to it."

"Grab a saddle and bridle, too?"

"I . . . suppose so."

"It's jolly hard to ride without a saddle, but I've done it lots of times on Angelica—but she was gentle and she loved me so."

"Hush," he said.

They had reached a long line of fence, the white-painted rails curving off across the meadow, enclosing pasture land. There were small signs at intervals—DO NOT TRESPASS. It was bright as day with the full moon and a cloudless sky. Going on at a crouch, they followed the fence toward the long, low outline of the stables, half hidden by elms. From far across the common came the sound of midnight church bells.

There was no sign of the Yank. Derek leaned back against a tree while Valerie sat on the ground. A dog barked fretfully and then another. A horse nickered in one of the stalls. Half a dozen ponies stirred in an open pen.

"Which one are you going to take?" Valerie whispered.

"I don't know." They looked large to him in the dappled shadows, even menacing with the moonlight glinting from their eyes. There was an empty feeling in his stomach and his legs felt weak. He thought of his bed . . . of Winslow's placid snores. The distant church clock struck the half hour. The gravel path leading from the stables to the great, dark house lay deserted. "He's not coming."

"Will you do it by yourself? I could help you."

"No. I . . . I think we should go back. Don't you?"

"Whatever you say, Fat Chap." She yawned and got stiffly to her feet. "I'm cold."

He peeled off his sweater and gave it to her. The dogs began a frenzy of barking. A light snapped on in one of the stable buildings and a large man stumbled out into the yard cursing loudly. Slowly, very slowly, the two children moved away through the shadows of the trees and then ran along the line of fence into the meadow. Halfway to the school Derek's legs gave way and he flopped onto his back in the tall grass.

"Tired, Fat Chap?"

"No."

"I am." She slumped down beside him. "It was jolly good sport, though. Sorry you didn't get your ride, but it was clever to leave when you did. I don't think that man would have liked it."

Laughter bubbled in his throat as elation replaced fear. He stood up and looked off across the fields. The thin white line of the fence could barely be seen.

"I was there, wasn't I? Right on the stroke."

"You were and he wasn't. If I see him at the bazaar I'll jolly well tell him, too!"

"No, Val. It doesn't matter."

He had been there. That was all that mattered. In the darkness and the silence with the whole world in bed. He . . . Sir Derek of Ramsay who had ventured forth at midnight on a quest with his faithful squire. He helped the bedraggled girl to her feet and felt quite different than he had a mere hour before. Older . . . strong . . . immeasurably tall.

6

It began to rain as Martin crossed Green Park, the dark clouds rolling across what had been only minutes before a pristine August sky. He hurried along the path toward Piccadilly and the Ritz Hotel, one hand clamped on the top of his straw hat to keep it from skimming away in the wind. Lightning scorching the air and a clap of thunder sent people hurrying from their canvas deck chairs to the dubious shelter of the great trees. Martin began to run and reached the marble-and-gilt lobby of the Ritz a few steps ahead of a cloudburst.

He found Scott Kingsford in the bar, patiently trying to explain to the barman how to fix an American-style martini.

"A waste of my time and his," Scott said as the man walked off. "You'd think a country that invented gin, for chrissakes, would know how to use it properly." He held out a huge hand, callused as a sailor's. "Well, Marty, you're a sight for sore eyes."

It had been over a year and a half since Martin had last seen him, and their meeting at that time had been cool, if correct. He had gone to Scott's office on the twenty-second floor of the CBC building on the corner of 64th and Madison Avenue in New York City to hand in his resignation—which had been accepted. An awkward moment for both of them. But that had been then. A great many things had taken place since that bleak February day in 1929. A world had changed, profoundly and forever.

THE COLLAPSE OF Scott Kingsford's Consolidated Broadcasters Company in December 1929 had not come as any surprise. It had been a season for failure. Numbed investors who had once scrambled to purchase CBC stock for as much as 392½ had watched with morbid fascination as the value of their holdings sank within two months to less than 85¾ a share. Dying dreams linked to the pulsebeat of a ticker-tape machine.

Scott Kingsford went into the radio business because he was bored. By 1921, the year of his forty-seventh birthday, the wire service he had started twenty years earlier, International News Agency, had become second only to the Associated Press. He was many times a millionaire and INA ran like a well-oiled machine. He had hired the best journalists money could buy to head the various bureaus—John Hammet in the United States, Peter Overholt in Asia, Martin Rilke in Europe—and there was little if anything for him to do. He looked about for a new challenge and found it in a radio set.

The potential grasped . . . the vision seen. The artful manipulation of a cat's whisker across a lump of crystal brought sound out of the nothingness of air. A human voice speaking into a microphone in New York City emerging in an instant in the most remote cabin in North Dakota. It would take money and it would take time, but there would be millions to be made in the sales of radio sets and in the selling of air time to advertisers. Not everyone shared his vision of the future and few rushed to buy stock in his Consolidated Broadcasters Company at $3\frac{3}{8}$ a share when it went on the market in the autumn of 1921. He formed a small financial syndicate composed of himself, Paul Rilke, and three other financiers. Together they put five million dollars into building radio transmitting stations and a radio manufacturing-and-research company with the grand name of Meradion Neutrodyne. The sale of radio sets, of which Meradion Neutrodyne captured the lion's share, reached the astonishing figure of sixty million dollars in 1922. Two years later that sum had rocketed to three hundred fifty-eight million. Radio was becoming an industry and Scott Kingsford had it by the throat.

By January 1929, the annual sale of radio sets in the United States had touched the seven-hundred-million-dollar mark, and was rising. More radios meant more listeners, and more listeners meant higher advertising rates for air time. Anyone owning a radio station couldn't help getting rich, and anyone owning a great many radio stations would get a damn sight richer. Scott Kingsford owned a great many stations.

After its modest beginnings Consolidated Broadcasters Company had grown into the largest radio network in the country. More people tuned into CBC than into all the other networks combined. This popularity was reflected in the value of its stock. All stocks were rising on a flamboyantly optimistic bull market, but CBC's rise was spectacular, touching the three-hundred-dollar mark after several years of stable growth with its stock in the fifty- to sixty-dollar range. Stock-market analysts sagely predicted that CBC would go to the blue sky within a year and investors eager to get in on this gold mine flocked to their brokerage houses, cash in hand. CBC stock lunged ever upward.

Scott Kingsford took this as a sign that gave credence to his vision. It was not enough to be big, he had to be overpoweringly dominant. It was possible to control the radio market, coast to coast and border to border, to drive his competitors into insignificance. To do this required nothing more than buying every independent radio station he could get his hands on, and building newer, more powerful stations in key areas. The sums required would be enormous, but Wall Street would finance. They knew a good opportunity when they saw one and his CBC holdings were gilt edged and sound as the dollar.

Stock pledged for cash. Cash spent for stations. Pledge and buy and pledge some more. And day after day the value of CBC rising on the Big Board.

There were men in congress who worried over the ethics, if not the legality, of Scott Kingsford's grab for control of the radio-broadcasting industry. There should be regulations of some sort, or did it already fall under the provisions and restraints of the Sherman Antitrust Act? No one could say for sure. And outside of a few, no one really cared. At the level of Rotary and Junior Chamber of Commerce there was outright approval. If Ford could manage to beat Chalmers out of the marketplace . . . well, where was the harm in that? Business was business. It made the world go around. It was, in the words of Bruce Barton, a holy thing that, like any solid and respected religion, should not be tampered with by government interference.

There had been warnings and danger signs, and some people had heeded them. "What goes up must come down," was heard in more than one corporate board room. But they were the doom criers, or the bears. "Be a bull on America," was more widely expressed. A delicious fever began to sweep the country, an "itch to get rich"—as easily and as quickly as possible. "Why, everybody ought to be rich," said John J. Raskob, and proceeded to tell people how to achieve this enviable state in the *Ladies' Home Journal.* The secret was in buying good common stocks. But then everybody knew that—and just about everybody knew a broker.

It was this national craze to invest that had so worried Paul Rilke. He had studied Wall Street for half a century and knew a thing or two about stock prices and earning ratios. The market was shaky, it fell with alarming suddenness, only to rise again a few days or a few weeks later as bullish as ever. It had a life, yes, but it was like some overgrown monster kept from expiring by constant infusions of blood from millions of Frankensteins. When housewives began to pool their bridge earnings to buy four shares of Continental Can on margin, he knew it was time to start getting out of the market—and so advised his friends and relatives.

Martin had been chief of the CBC news department since 1924 and had gone on the air every Saturday at 6 P.M. Eastern Standard Time as a news "commentator." His opening remark . . . "Hello, America, this is Martin Rilke speaking to you from New York City . . ." became something of a catch phrase, as familiar to the radio listener as Graham McNamee's fervid cry of *"And he did it! Yes, sir, he did it!"* at every Babe Ruth home run or Notre Dame touchdown.

It had not been his Uncle Paul's warnings or any personal qualms over the great bull market that had induced Martin to sell his CBC shares. It had been a dispute with Scott over sponsor interference with his news broadcast. He had sold his stock at 305½ the day he resigned from the company.

Scott had thought him a damn fool. Not for quitting, because he had anticipated that, but for selling the shares at such a low price. "It's going to hit a thousand, Marty."

But not in this world.

THE BARMAN PLACED a glass containing a pale yellow fluid on the counter. "Here you are, Mr. Kingsford. The classic martini cocktail. Two parts gin to one part vermouth . . . stir gently, serve with a twist of lemon peel."

Scott's expression was bleak. "*One third* vermouth? That will not be a *dry* martini, George."

Martin ordered a whisky and soda. "Not exactly like Gilboy's."

The big, gray-haired man sighed and took a small sip of his drink as though it were medicine. "Ah, Gilboy's. A pitcher full of ice . . . pour in vermouth, pour out vermouth . . . fill with gin. Now *that's* classic in my book. They raided Gilboy's a week after you left New York. Sloshed all that good hooch down Third Avenue."

"That must have been a sad day."

"Not as sad a day for me as the day you went off the air. Old 'Hello America' heard for the last time."

"I don't imagine Goldfield shed any tears."

"Hell, you just waded into politics. Gordon Benn of United Tobacco was angling for an ambassadorship. Some of your comments irked Hoover. So, tough. You had a right to your opinion, it's still a free country. The trouble was, old friend, there's a disease in radio known as please-the-sponsor, and I caught it bad. I should have backed you to the hilt and told Goldfield to go puff on their smokes."

"That's water over the dam."

"Sure. But it still hurts. I may not have stabbed you, Marty, but I twisted the blade."

"Don't go gray over it."

Scott chuckled softly and tore absently at a box of matches with the hotel's crest embossed on the lid. "Just a clash between my hubris and your integrity. But virtue is always rewarded in the end. I'm glad you cashed in your chips when you did. How does it feel to be one of the rich Rilkes for a change?"

"Pretty damn good."

"I understand you've built a very comfortable ivory tower with your money. I haven't read any of your books, by the way. I don't share your faith in the innate goodness of the human soul." He tossed off his martini and made a wry face. "I better stick to Scotch. Even this booze jockey can't screw that up."

Martin rolled his glass between his palms. "Why did you want to see me, Scott?"

"I'm sure you can guess. It's a new CBC. Not *my* CBC, you understand. That's long gone. The banks, brokers, and a million lawyers saw to that. They carved it up like a boardinghouse chicken. But they let me run it . . . what there is left of it."

"You still have some good shows."

"Oh, sure . . . Mick and Mary and a new group of loonies called the Happytime Boys . . . Saturday night, coast-to-coast hookup. Folks appreciate a chuckle these days. Nothing funny in guys selling apples. Ad revenues are way down, but I got hope." He reduced the matches to sawdust between his powerful fingers. "I lost a bundle in the debacle, Marty, but I'm far from busted and damn far from through. Give me five or six years and I'll make the network the only one worth tuning in."

"I'm sure you will."

"Innovation. Capture the imagination of the listener. Take the news . . . on all networks . . . most of it out of date, stale . . . yesterday's headlines. One or two good commentators, and with you gone . . . well, you left a big void."

"I'm not coming back."

"Oh, hell, I know that. I'm not asking you to come back. I'd like you to stay here . . . be CBC's man on this side of the pond. No network has a regular overseas news broadcast. Too many technical problems involved. But we can solve those problems with new transmitting and receiving equipment . . . and a wire recording device that has a clarity you wouldn't believe. Your German relatives make the stuff. Rilkefunken in Hanover."

Martin swallowed some of his whisky and looked toward the tall windows at the far end of the room. The rain had stopped, the leaves of Green Park glistening like polished jade in the sun.

"Does Paul fit into this some place?"

Scott snorted and toyed with his little pile of crushed matches. "Of course. He's become a major stockholder in the new CBC. Your uncle's a carpetbagger at heart. But that's okay, he can be chairman of the board for all I care. I get along with the old bastard. And I'll say one thing for him, he's smart . . . he looks down the road. We both agree that in ten, fifteen years, radio will knock newspapers right out of the ring. No one will buy a goddamn paper except to read the Macy and Gimbel ads."

"Was it Paul's idea to hire me?"

"Hell, no." He swept the matchbox residue away. "I don't need him to tell me who's the best in the business. Martin Rilke . . . why, that's a twenty-four-carat name, on a by-line or a broadcast. Why, you're a drawing power, Marty. You make people tune in—and they'll sure as heck tune in this show, believe me. It has novelty . . . and excitement . . . like talking pictures. Good folk who have never been fifty miles from Tulsa or Pocatello in their entire lives can sit back every Sunday night and have Martin Rilke speak to them from London . . . Paris . . . Moscow . . . Berlin. The world in their front parlor. And with these new wire machines you can prerecord things days before the broadcast. Not just interviews with famous people, but the *sounds* of the city you're broadcasting from. The changing of the guard at Buckingham Palace, say, or Bastille Day in Paris with a million people along the Champs-Élysées singing the Marseillaise while fireworks pop all over the goddamn sky!"

Martin laughed. "Don't get carried away."

"Hell, I am carried away. I tell you, Marty, those Kraut engineers know what they're doing. I've been to the factory in Hanover and seen all the prototypes demonstrated. They're going to make what we have in the States look like crystal sets. The technocracy is here and we have it, bo. We should start getting delivery from Rilkefunken in six or seven months. But there's a hell of a lot to be done in the meantime. CBC News, Europe, is just something on paper at the moment. It has to be fleshed out with people. You'll need correspondents, legmen, reliable stringers. You can get some of your top people from INA—Wolf von Dix, Carlos Medina . . . guys like that. I know that Eddie Miles is an old pal of yours, but I hear he's back on the sauce and—"

"Now just hold it a minute, Scott. You're talking as though I've taken the job."

"That's right, bo." A huge grin split his craggy face. "You may not know it yet, but you've signed on. Oh, hell, yes . . . you've joined the crew!"

THE CONTRACT HAD been a handshake and a toast to success, the handshake more bonding to Scott Kingsford than a fifty-page document hammered out by a Philadelphia lawyer. Martin thought over the terms as he took a taxi home. They gave him carte blanche in all matters—staff, content of the broadcasts. Sponsor be damned. *His* show. But he would be as objective as possible, having been a journalist too long not to be able to look at all sides of a question. And he would avoid the trap, common to some radio commentators, of being blatantly opinionated. The whole idea increased its appeal the more he thought about it. The wire recorders, if they worked as well as Scott claimed, would open up limitless possibilities.

Rilkefunken, GmbH, was part of the sprawling industrial empire of the German Rilkes. The collapse of Germany and the devastating inflation after the war had nearly ruined them and they had been forced to sell patents and foreign manufacturing rights to many of their varied products to their cousin, Paul Rilke of Chicago, for solid American dollars. It had been Paul's greatest financial coup, leading one of his many critics to say that it was the biggest robbery every committed without the use of a pistol.

Martin lit a cigar and settled back in the seat as the taxi crawled along Piccadilly in the afternoon traffic. He would be working for his uncle in a manner of speaking. The major stockholder in CBC and not a man to refrain from dipping his paddle in the stream whenever he felt like it—not that Martin had any qualms about that. Paul's advice had always been sound. He had not become one of the ten richest men in the United States because of poor judgment.

One of the ten richest men. He drew idly on his cigar, thinking of Paul's success over the years. Luck, astuteness, and the ability to grasp opportunities when presented seemed to sum up the man's secret. They were, he thought, the very qualities his father had lacked. Not that he could recall his father with any great clarity. He had just turned eight when he had killed himself. There had been a faded tintype his father had kept in his Montmartre studio to remind him of Chicago. It had been taken some time in the early 1880s and had shown him with his brother and sister in front of their home on Prairie Avenue. Their lives were in their faces. Hanna doll pretty, a future fairy-tale countess even then. Paul tight lipped and heavy lidded, a young man who seemed to be weighing the contents of his purse, thinking of profit and loss, the Rilke breweries, and the rise and fall of the Chicago exchange. And there was his father, apart from the others, lounging against the porch steps with his indolent bohemian manners and mocking smile, looking as though he already knew he would be disowned one day, would fail as an artist and end in a pauper's grave—knowing it and not giving a hoot in hell.

THE GIANT BIPLANE, an Armstrong Whitworth Argosy of Imperial Airways, lumbered down the runway at Croydon, gathered speed, and then, all three engines howling, rose smoothly into the still morning air—to the incredulous relief of at least one of its passengers.

"Oh, I say, sir," Albert said in a choked voice. "We're off the ground."

Martin, relaxed in the wicker chair beside him, lowered his newspaper. "We'll be at five thousand feet in a few minutes."

"Five thousand? Crikey!" He pressed his face to the window's cool glass and looked down. The lower wing obscured some of his view, but he could see the Lilliputian roofs and roadways of southeast London and the emerging fields of Surrey. "How fast are we going, sir?"

"Fast enough. We'll be in Paris in two and a half hours."

"Good Lord." His breath left a patch of fog on the glass which he wiped away with the palm of his hand. An engine, suspended between the two wings, belched a brown stream of exhaust and occasional spurts of yellow flame. "Safe . . . I imagine."

Martin smiled at him and raised his paper again. "Safe as a London bus. Settle back, Albert. The steward will be serving tea in a few minutes."

Settle back! Easy enough for him to say. Probably been up

in an aeroplane dozens of times. Old hat. He stared down. A train was a toy so far below, trailing a painted plume of smoke. It was soon lost to view, sliding away behind them. A cathedral underneath now, the soaring spires puny and insignificant from this height. A cloud swept into the whirling blades of the propeller and obscured the window with gray vapor. He had always imagined clouds to be of greater substance.

Special assistant to Mr. Martin Rilke, CBC Radio (Europe)

When they arrived in Paris, Albert wrote that heading on the first page of a new notebook he purchased in a shop on the rue St. Lazare. He still could not quite believe it. *"Two pounds a week and found,"* Martin had said. *"And if that be nepotism, make the most of it."*

His duties were unclear. General errand boy and all around dogsbody. Every morning he picked up Martin's favorite cigars at the tobacconist across the street from the Opéra . . . sent messages through the *pneumatiques* . . . answered the telephone in their suite at the hotel . . . and traveled around Paris as Martin worked to hire a staff and find office space for the news bureau. Two hectic, exciting weeks and then, at the beginning of September, they went on to Berlin. Again by air, Le Bourget to Tempelhof in a Junkers trimotor. He was more blasé about it now and no longer awed by the misty fragility of clouds.

There were squads of police milling about outside the passenger terminal building at Tempelhof. From across the road flanking the airport greasy plumes of smoke rose above the flat roofs of dingy tenements. Albert was wide eyed.

"What do you think is happening, sir?"

"Street fighting, probably. Communists and Nazis." He placed a reassuring hand on the boy's shoulder as they walked toward the terminal. "But you won't find it happening everywhere in Berlin. The street gangs stick close to certain districts, I understand—Neukölln, Wedding, Lichtenberg—places to stay away from. Some things never seem to change in this town."

Wolf von Dix, a gray-haired, courtly man, was waiting for them when they cleared customs. A renowned correspondent for the *Frankfurter Zeitung* during the war, he had been for the past ten years Berlin bureau chief of Kingsford's INA.

"Welcome to the city of brotherly love," he said with a wry smile. "Herr Goebbels printed an item in *Der Angriff* yesterday saying that Trotsky was flying in today from Norway to help the reds steal the election. Only an idiot would believe it . . . and a few hundred did. The Brownshirts went berserk."

"Burning the buildings?" Martin asked.

"No . . . automobile tires. The clashes always look worse than they are." He smiled at Albert. "And you, of course, are young Thaxton. Martin wrote me and said you wish to become a journalist. Is that so?"

"Yes, sir."

"And that you speak German quite well—probably with a Chicago accent if he has been helping you. Kindly tell me about yourself . . . in German."

Albert talked as they walked to Dix's car. The story of his life—dull as it was. He hoped he wasn't boring the man with tales of Morborne and its long history, of his successes there as captain of the eleven and of winning the Montaigne prize the past term for excellence in French.

"Your German is excellent, too," Dix said as they drove from the airport. "It's obvious you have an ear for languages. I recall Morborne. Several of my students had gone there. I was a teacher of German at the University of London before the war . . . nineteen ten to nineteen fourteen. Ah, those were lovely years. I had a flat in Regent Square and I would sit in the garden on Sunday mornings and write my weekly articles for the *Frankfurter Zeitung* and the *Berliner Tageblatt.* I was a stringer for those papers. Do you know what a stringer is, young man?"

"A person who writes for a paper without actually being on salary?"

"That is correct. They paid enough for my articles to keep me in good English beer and roast beef with Yorkshire pudding!"

They drove toward the center of the city, through Neukölln and Kreuzberg, past endless rows of ugly brick tenement houses that had been designed, Dix explained to Albert, not by an architect but by Berlin's police chief in the middle of the nineteenth century. Dark, gloomy, fetid warrens. From windows overlooking the alleyways and sunless courtyards hung flags, red banners with hammer-and-sickle emblems or red flags with a white circle containing a black swastika.

"Enemies to the death," Dix said, "but companions in misery."

No misery was apparent on Wilhelmstrasse or Unter den Linden. The trees shimmered in the afternoon sun and the crowded cafés with their outdoor terraces were in dappled shadows. Dix pulled up his Benz touring car to the Adlon Hotel and a uniformed attendant hurried to open the doors.

"I'll just check in, Dix, and then we can go on to the office and have a talk. Would you like to come with us, Albert, or stay here? I won't be too long."

"The INA office, sir?"

"Yes." Martin smiled. "Your answer is in your face."

THE INA OFFICES occupied the entire second floor of a modern building in Neu Königstrasse. It was everything that Albert had imagined a newspaper office to be—not that INA was a newspaper, but it did supply news to papers all over the world. And not just from Germany. Outside of London, the Berlin bureau was the largest in Europe and drew its sources from Austria, Poland, Czechoslovakia, the Balkans, and Russia through its desk in Moscow. Banks of teletype machines chattered constantly, keeping two copyboys busy tearing off the sheets and rushing them to editors, reporters, and rewrite men. A dozen typewriters hammered away; men yelled over telephones or across the room at each other. Noise . . . a haze of tobacco smoke . . . shouts for a messenger to deliver copy to "Auntie Voss"—the *Vossische Zeitung*—the *Berliner Morgenpost,* or *Tageblatt* as the local deadline crept closer. Teletype operators tapped out the day's news onto the wires, sending it on to London, New York, Rio de Janeiro. It was a heady atmosphere to Albert. He stood out of the way as the chaos swirled around him. He wondered what momentous event had taken place in the world for there to be such frenzied activity. He could see Wolf von Dix through the glass walls of his office slouched in a chair, feet on desk, talking to Martin. No sense of excitement or urgency there. He took a deep breath for courage and tried out his German on a copyboy of about his own age who paused for a moment at a nearby water cooler.

"Did something important take place today?"

The lanky, red-haired boy shrugged. “Not that I know of. Just the usual stuff.”

“You mean it’s always like this? Everyone in such a rush?”

“Sure . . . most of the time.” He was eyeing Albert curiously. “You talk funny. Do you come from East Prussia or some place like that?”

“I’m English.” He could feel his cheeks starting to burn. “I . . . I’ve only been studying German for a year.”

“A year! You have the gift then. I’m trying to learn English. I go to the English flicks once a month. How about this . . . *Tip top, old sport! Time for tea! Oh, rawther!*”

A man in shirtsleeves glanced up from his desk. “Get your thumb out of your butt, Kessler!”

“I’m Rudy,” he whispered before hurrying back to work.

Martin lit one of Dix’s cigars, blew a stream of smoke, and scowled at the ceiling. “I was hoping you’d be my top man, Dix.”

“Sorry, Martin . . . old dogs and new tricks. Emil Zeitzler is the one for you. You remember him, don’t you?”

“Of course. Helped me cover the Beer Hall Putsch. A damn good reporter. Is he still with INA?”

“He joined the *Stuttgart Tageblatt* a couple of years ago. He also does a news-and-interview show over Radio Stuttgart once a week that’s become quite influential.”

“Influential in what way?”

“For moderation and political sanity. Emil hasn’t changed. A good Social Democrat. He’s the man you need to put a staff together. No doubt of it.”

“I’ll go and see him.”

“Yes, do that. I have his address.” He turned his head and

glanced at Albert standing beyond the glass partition. "Your brother-in-law is a fine boy. Is he serious about his choice of career?"

"Seems to be."

"Is he learning much with you?"

"At the moment, no. How to buy cigars and answer the phone."

"Well, that's something. When does he go back to school?"

"End of the month. Why?"

"Because I could use him. Copyboy, general flunky. A few weeks in this office might alter his view of journalism."

"No, Dix. Working for you would set it forever."

EMIL ZEITZLER HAD changed little since Martin had last seen him in 1923. He was a thin, intense man of thirty and he peered thoughtfully at him through his thick glasses. "A most interesting proposal, but I must decline."

"Oh? Why?"

"Dix may not have told you, but I am managing the reelection campaign of Otto Haushofer. Both the Communists and the Nazis would like his seat in the Reichstag so we are, as you Americans say, in a dogfight at the moment. I think he'll win, but it will be close. If it came out, only two weeks before the election, that I had taken a job with an American company . . . well, you know they would make hay out of it. Especially the Nazis. Goebbels would say that American money was pouring into the Haushofer campaign, that he was a tool of the Wall Street Jews."

Martin laughed and poured himself another small glass of schnapps from the bottle on the table. "That's crazy."

"Many things are crazy today, Martin. Ominous times."

There was nothing ominous about where they were; a bright, sunny apartment in Stuttgart overlooking the Schillerplatz with a fine view of the castle. Emil's pretty wife, heavy with pregnancy, sat knitting in the parlor, keeping one eye on their two-year-old son who was playing with a wooden train on the carpet.

Martin sipped at his drink. "I'm a bit out of touch, I'm afraid. How do you view the election?"

"With dread. Bruening was foolish to talk the president into dissolving the Reichstag. He opened the door to the Nazis and reds. The Nazis only had twelve seats. The reds fifty-four. They're both bound to gain at the expense of the center."

"How many do you think?"

"Oh, twenty or so from the Communists . . . perhaps as much as fifty from the Nazis. Goebbels and Hitler have pulled out all stops this time. Posters and pamphlets blanketing the country, mass meetings and speeches every night . . . in the cities, the small towns . . . everywhere. God knows where they get the money. And then all this Horst Wessel nonsense of Goebbels . . . the first Nazi saint!"

"Horst Wessel?"

"A young storm trooper thug in Berlin who was living with a prostitute. He got into an argument one night with the girl's ex-pimp who just happened to be a communist. They both drew guns and Wessel wasn't quick enough. He died a few weeks later and Goebbels sent him to heaven with a roll of drums, calling him a National Socialist Christ! That was in February. The fellow had written a poem about the glory of being a Brownshirt street fighter and Goebbels had it set to music. You hear it everywhere these days. They have all the trappings now; flag, armbands, song, *and* a martyr. A perverse sort of genius, Herr Goebbels. Did you know that he once worked for INA as a stringer? Dix told me—back in nineteen twenty-one—but he had to let him go for grossly embellishing his stories. The novelist *manqué.* He's never forgiven Dix for that . . . or INA for that matter."

The schnapps was mellow. Pigeons cooed on the window sill. "My problem, Emil. Can you help me at all?"

"Oh, yes. I can give you the names of half a dozen men, good reporters and broadcast people. After the elections . . . well, we shall see. I might be able to join your group." His eyes looked troubled. He stared out across the rooftops. "It all depends how the wind is blowing."

A column of young Nazis marched across the Schillerplatz, none of them much older than boy scouts and just as courteous. They toted bulging knapsacks and a few carried the flag of the Hitler Jugend on long poles. One boy played a guitar as they marched toward the Swabian hills. The boys began singing . . .

Comrades shot dead by Red Front and Reaction
march in spirit within our ranks!
Raise high the flag!

" 'The Horst Wessel Song,' " Emil said in a flat voice. "One hears it everywhere now."

THE ENGLISH TEAM that Karl Voegler, the sports editor, wanted interviewed at the Sportpalast before the start of the six-day bike races turned out to be two Scots; short, sandy-haired men from Aberdeen with burrs so thick Albert could barely make out half of what they said. It was his first lesson in creative journalism and he made the most of it, typing up the story from shorthand notes and his imagination.

HIGHLANDERS VOW SIX-DAY FLING AT RACES

"Catchy," Voegler murmured. His eyes flicked over the copy, his blue pencil slashing here and there. "Not bad. Give it to Kerner . . . and then go down to Peli's and bring me back an apple strudel and coffee. Quick now!"

From a reporter to an office boy with the flick of a hand. He complained bitterly to Rudy Kessler when they left the office that evening.

Rudy laughed and retrieved the cigarette he had been keeping behind his ear most of the day. "What did you expect? A Pulitzer prize or something?" He grinned and lapsed into his terrible English. "*Bad sport, old chap! Not cricket!* You'll never get a pat on the back from Voegler, or any of the old-timers. It's the sad lot of the flunky, let me tell you." He snapped a match with a fingernail and lit his smoke. "Tradition, my man, tradition. Treat the copyboys like dog droppings. We underlings also have our traditions . . . first one to get a writing assignment must buy the beer and sausages. How much money do you have?"

"Ten or twelve marks," Albert muttered.

"A fortune! I'm walking with a Rothschild! We'll go to the

Kurfürstendamm and watch the girls." He gave Albert a hearty poke in the ribs. "Maybe even latch on to a couple. Sixteen is too old to be a virgin."

The ten days that he had worked for INA—six days a week, twelve to fourteen hours a day—seemed more like ten weeks to Albert. He had become immersed totally in both job and city. A true journalist—Karl Voegler's attitude notwithstanding—and a real Berliner. He lived in a large boardinghouse for men, where Rudy stayed, a place popular with young men who worked in the newspaper and publishing business and the nearby stock exchange. A substantial dinner came with the price of a room, but neither he nor Rudy ate there often, preferring the small, smoky cafés frequented by actors, writers, painters, and all the polyglot intelligentsia of this teeming, restless city.

They squeezed their way into the Romanische Café on the Tauentzienstrasse. Two blond girls in tight dresses who might have been actresses, or young whores, or both, sat at a table with two empty chairs.

"Mind if we sit down?" Rudy asked with almost Prussian correctness.

One of the girls gave him a hard stare. "Piss off, sonny."

Rudy, not at all abashed, moved on through the crowd. "I didn't like their looks anyway. Too skinny. I like girls with lots of moving parts on them."

"A good country girl who milks the cows."

"Exactly! I should have stayed in Regensburg."

They managed to grab a small table, to the annoyance of a waiter who grudgingly took their order for two small beers and a plate of bratwurst.

"This is the life," Rudy said, looking around the café. "Rubbing shoulders with celebrities and then on to more exciting things. What shall we do tonight? Piscator's theater? Another stab at some girls?"

"How about a flick? *All Quiet on the Western Front* opens at the cinema on Nollendorfplatz."

"We'll never get a seat. Sold out completely, I hear."

"We could try. No harm in that."

HE WENT UP the stairs to his room on the top floor after making sure Rudy was all right. The side of his face throbbed and he wondered if his jaw was broken. The top-floor bathroom was unoccupied and he went in, turned on the light, and locked the door behind him. He studied his face in the glass above the sink. A purple bruise flowed like a wine stain from his right ear to the point of his chin. He moved his jaws from side to side and then opened and closed his mouth. There was no increase in the pain when he did so. He remembered the agony Tim Pakenham had felt when his jaw had been broken playing football . . . Morborne versus Winchester. No, he decided, not broken, thank God. He ran water into the sink up to the brim and then bent low, turning his head, and immersed the side of his face. He winced at the pain, especially from his ear, but after a few minutes of ducking in and out of the icy water his face felt better. He patted himself dry with a towel and went to his room.

He lay on his bed in pajamas, stared at the ceiling, and fought back tears, his throat aching with the effort to keep from sobbing. Then he sat up with a start. Damn! Mr. Rilke wouldn't lie on his bed and bawl. No *real* journalist would. He switched on the bedside lamp, found his notebook and pencil in the top drawer of the bedstand, and began to write in Pitman . . .

Berlin, Friday night, September 12, '30

The usual crowds along the Kurfürstendamm and in all the streets leading off from it. Rudy Kessler and I made our way to the Romanische where we had beer and wurst. A waiter gave us cold stares and tried to hurry us out because he could sense he wouldn't get so much as a pfennig tip from us. He was right, of course, but we would have sat there all night if there had been nothing better to do with our time. There isn't a waiter alive who can intimidate Rudy Kessler.

I read *All Quiet on the Western Front* at school. I think Mr. Remarque's book is better than Barbusse's *Le Feu,* despite the fact that Barbusse had fought in the trenches and Remarque had not. It's odd how some of the best books about war and man's courage in the face of death were written by men who had never heard a shot fired in anger. Stephen Crane . . . Count Tolstoy . . . although I believe Tolstoy served briefly with the Russian army when quite young, but on the frontier, protecting villages from Tartar bandits—hardly the type of provincial service to serve as inspiration for Borodino! Rudy lent me his copy of Remarque in German . . . *Im Westen Nichts Neues* . . . and I felt it was even more powerful than the English translation. Simon Kahr, INA's motion-picture and theater critic, had seen the American picture while in London. He told all of us in the office that it is the most stunning war flick ever made, better by far than *The Big Parade.*

There was such a large crowd in the Nollendorfplatz, jamming the pavement in front of the theater and spilling out into the street, that police had been called to keep the traffic moving. A good deal of shouting, pushing, and shoving was taking place under the marquee and it seemed obvious that Rudy had been right, that we wouldn't have the remotest chance of buying tickets. Rudy suggested we go around the corner to the UFA house which was showing *The White Hell of Pitz Palu* with Luis Trenker and Leni Riefenstahl, but I'm not fond of mountaineering flicks.

"Something is up," Rudy said. "Too many cops."

As we walked closer we could see a solid line of policemen in front of the theater; tall, imposing men in buckled greatcoats and leather-and-brass helmets. Lights from the marquee gleamed off their shiny boots, belts, and holsters. They stood as a wall between two groups of people—men and women going into the theater and a much larger group, men only, milling around in the street, waving their arms and shouting. All of the latter were wearing white shirts.

"Storm troopers," Rudy said. "Brownshirt bastards."

It has become the costume of the Nazi SA since the government forbade the wearing of uniforms in Berlin until after the elections. On the second button of every white shirt dangled a brown rubber band so everyone would know who they were.

A White Shirt stepped out of a doorway and stood weaving in front of us. He was a short, thick-set man with a grizzled face and breath like a brewery.

"Where are you two going?" he shouted.

"See a flick," Rudy said casually.

The man jerked a thumb at the marquee. "Not that one."

"What's wrong with it?" I asked.

The man spat at our feet. "A rotten pack of lies. A Jew in Hollywood made that shit—one of our own Jew boys, too—from Laupheim—my town—may the son-of-a-bitch roast in hell!"

We brushed past him and he made no move to stop us. He stood swaying in the shadows, cursing Carl Laemmle, spitting obscenities about the international Jewish bankers who had stabbed the German army in the back.

A policeman gave us a cold stare when we said we had tickets to the showing. Rudy told me that most of the Berlin police are sympathetic to the Nazis. They do their job because Germans obey orders, but they find it mortifying that their commissioner of police is a Jew and that the Nazis taunt them as "Isador's Army." We had no tickets, of course, but figured—rightly—that in all the confusion we could slip by the doorman. As it turned out, there was no one at the door and the box-office window was shuttered.

Groups of people in the lobby—some angry and defiant, others clustered in tight, nervous groups. The theater seats well over a thousand people, but we could see no more than a few hundred. Along one wall there was a long banner—NO MORE WAR INTERNATIONAL—BERLIN CHAPTER. Beneath it was a table piled high with Erich Maria Remarque's book in both English and German, and Mr. Rilke's book, *An End to Castles,* in English only. I bought a paperbound copy for Rudy for a mark fifty and told him I would have Mr. Rilke autograph it for him, that it might serve as an incentive to learn English.

A tall, white-haired man wearing a dinner jacket thanked everyone for coming and spoke angrily of the intimidation they had faced ". . . from a mob of ignorance and unreasoning hate." He then asked us all to take our seats and the motion picture would begin. Frightened ushers closed the front doors on a final howl of invective from the streets.

It was the book, alive on the screen. I knew them all—squat, ugly, powerful Katczinsky; thin, lugubrious Tjaden; and boyish Paul. I mouthed the dialogue in the darkness as though I, too, stood weary and hungry in front of the field kitchen demanding that the rations be served—the double rations—for we are the Second Company even if half the men the cook has prepared to feed lie in the dressing stations or dead in no man's land. And I could feel the terror as the shells howled down from the night sky as we strung barbed wire. And the agony of the wounded was my pain. My palms were damp as I clutched the armrests on the seat. I glanced at Rudy, and his face was pale in the flickering light from the projector and his eyes were fixed on the terrible images of war. And the young soldier Paul, who is no one and everyone, reached a gentle hand through the wire to cup the delicate butterfly . . . and the hand closed so softly in death.

The Nazi mob was gone when we left the theater, but a few knots of police could be seen standing about on the far side of the square or in the center of the traffic circle. Taxis lined the curb and our fellow moviegoers hurried to them. Rudy and I walked slowly toward the Kurfürstendamm subway station, our collars turned up against the wind. We did not speak, both of us lost in our own thoughts.

"Enjoy the show, Jew boys?"

We had not heard the footsteps behind us. We stopped and four men in shabby raincoats faced us in a semicircle. One was not much older than we, the other three had the hard, craggy look of ex-soldiers. We could see their dirty white shirts beneath their coats, the rubber bands looped on the buttons.

"I'm not a Jew," Rudy said.

"You think like a Jew," one of the men said with a quiet intensity.

We tried to move on but they crowded in on us, forcing our backs to the metal grille of a shuttered store window. One of them stuck his face close to mine.

"I read that damn book, sonny. Not a word of truth in it. We never broke . . . we never cried for our mothers. Give us guns and we'd go back tomorrow and finish the job. Do you think I wept when I stuck a goddamn Frenchie in the guts? Shit, boy, pure shit."

"Get away from us," Rudy said.

"You whine like a Hebe." The youngest of the group licked his lips and glanced nervously up and down the street. "You're nothing but a red-headed turd, that's what you are."

"Call me that when your friends aren't around! I'd kick your fat ass all the way to Potsdam!"

The three older men chuckled softly. "Go for a walk, Hans," one of them said. "Wait for us around the corner."

The man who had his face close to mine smiled. "Kids today. All talk and no balls. You look a good sort. Act like a real German and don't fall for that pacifist turn-the-other-cheek crap."

I didn't want to tell him I was English. Maybe he bore a grudge against the tommies. I could only stare into his eyes. It was like looking into dark water.

"Kids like you don't know what to believe. The Bolshie Jews tell you what to believe. No one to set you straight. If you were my son and went to see shit like that—" He moved his hand back a few inches and slapped me on the side of the face. It was like being struck with a hard leather strap. My head snapped back against the grille. Rudy shouted something and one of the other men drove a fist into his belly. I must have turned toward him—to help him—I can't remember—and the man slapped me again, putting his strength behind it this time. Lights exploded in my eyes and the next thing I can recall is being on my hands and knees on the pavement. The men had gone. Rudy was kneeling by the curb, bent forward, vomiting in the gutter.

He put the notebook aside and turned off the light. There was still pain in his jaw but he felt better having written about it. He sat on the edge of the bed and listened to the night sounds of the city, the rumble of traffic along Neue Friedrich Strasse and the bridges of the Spree. He thought of automobiles filled with contented people on their way home from theaters or restaurants, the men in dinner jackets and the women in furs, whizzing past the dark shadows of narrow streets where men in shoddy clothing prowled like wolves.

LIGHTS BURNED IN the early morning hours in the offices of all the wire services and newspapers throughout Berlin. By four in the morning of September 15 the election results, except for a few provincial districts, had been received. The figures were stunning.

"Nearly six and a half million votes so far for the Nazi party," Dix said in a toneless voice. "Quite a gain from eight hundred thousand they received two years ago."

Martin peered over his shoulder at the clattering teletype machine. "How many seats?"

"Over a hundred, I'd say."

"A hundred and seven for certain," one of the editors remarked. "That makes them the second largest party in the Reichstag."

The three men stared numbly at the machine, the names of cities, candidates, parties—the tally of votes—appearing in typed blocks on the white paper.

"Hofhauser lost in Stuttgart to the Nazi candidate by two thousand votes," Dix said. "Poor Emil."

Martin shook his head. "Poor everyone."

"And your kinsman won in Munich . . . Werner von Rilke . . . but no surprise there. The Nazi paymaster."

Martin turned away from the machine and poured a cup of coffee from an alcohol-heated urn. The coffee was bitter and scalded his tongue. To think of Werner was to think, in a symbolic way, of Germany itself. Werner had marched off to war in 1914 as a twenty-three-year-old infantry officer loyal to kaiser and fatherland. He had been horribly wounded in the abdomen by a grenade and had been brought back to a Germany plunging into revolution and anarchy. The defeat, the continuing allied blockade, the humiliation of Versailles, the French occupation of the Rhineland, the despoiling of his country—even by his own relative—had embittered him. Paul Rilke had bought for six million dollars family holdings worth twenty times that amount. But the dollar had been king as the mark tumbled into the rat hole of inflation. Werner had spent his share in seeking political solutions to the overwhelming problems of the Reich. Among the myriad splinter parties he had backed in 1922 had been Adolf Hitler's National Socialist German Workers. It had obviously turned out to be a sound investment.

Dix joined him at the coffee urn. "Will you be making a broadcast today?"

"I hope at midnight . . . six P.M. New York time. I asked for fifteen minutes on the shortwave, but I may only get five."

"And what will you tell America?"

Martin shrugged and slurped at his steaming coffee. "What can I say? Facts and figures, I suppose. It's too early to speculate on what this is going to mean to Germany."

"Not too early," said Dix quietly. "Too late."

ALBERT FINISHED PACKING his suitcase and Rudy insisted on carrying it downstairs for him. Frau Bernstorff, who managed the boardinghouse, met them in the main hall and kissed Albert on the cheek. She was a plump, jolly woman who fretted over her "young men" and pampered her favorites.

"Be sure to come back next year," she said in English. *"Mein jung Englander."* And kissed him again.

He liked Frau Bernstorff. She was a woman who had known

far better days. Her husband Klaus—who puttered about and did the bookkeeping—had been a hotel owner who went bankrupt during the inflation years.

"I'll try, Frau Bernstorff," he said, knowing in his heart that he would never want to come back to Berlin. He noticed that a photograph of Adolf Hitler had been hung next to the one of President Hindenburg on the wall behind the concierge's desk. The old field marshal and the corporal side by side. He mentioned the photograph to Rudy as they went out to the street to wait for the taxi.

"Oh, that," said Rudy airily. "Bertha Kiss-Kiss has great faith in him. The savior of Germany, she says. But she hates the Brownshirts. Scum, she calls them . . . feels certain they'll be eliminated once Hitler gains the support of the army."

"Do you believe that?"

Rudy shrugged. "Makes sense. Why hold on to those gangsters if he doesn't have to?" The taxi pulled up at the curb and he opened the rear door. "Friedrichstrasse Bahnhof," he told the driver, then turned to Albert and clasped him by the arms. "Goodbye, my friend, and good luck. I'll think of you slaving away at school while I'm drinking my beer at the Romanische! As we English fellows say . . . *cheerio and pip-pip, old cock!*"

BACK TO SCHOOL. The thought was depressing. There would be something of a fuss made about his returning two weeks late, but he could justify his absence by having "been abroad." Travel, he would claim, was most enlightening. He had also brought a leather-bound volume of Heine's poems for his housemaster.

The soft, pallid face staring out from the frame on the wall. The little mustache and lank hair. The sightless eyes. Field Marshal Paul von Hindenburg, president of the Republic, hanging beside him. The fleshy jowls and the white hair . . . the vacant, senile stare.

And Adolf Hitler telling the country in his bad German what they wished to hear. His speech in Leipzig, pledging his allegiance to the army and promising the German people that he would come to power through the ballot box, swearing that he would fight against the Treaty of Versailles even if he had to do that through illegal means. What had he meant? What sort of *illegal means?* And vowing in his harsh, near hysterical voice that *once* he came to power—no doubt there; the stating of an inevitable fact—he would form a National Socialist Court of Justice and heads would roll. Whose heads? All the shadowy enemies of the Reich, Albert supposed as he gazed through the window of the taxi. The enemies alluded to in all of the Nazi speeches; the Jews and the liberals; the "degenerate" artists, writers, and poets; the international bankers—the so-called scum and parasites who had stabbed Germany in the back during the war.

People crossing the Friedrichstrasse into Unter den Linden. People shopping . . . going to and from work . . . seated in the cafés . . . standing in front of the restaurants. A city like any other going about its mundane affairs in the pale October sunshine. Rough boards covering the broken display windows at Israel's department store. JUDE painted across a wall. Brownshirt pranks, Rudy had said. But the gangsters would go when Hitler achieved his aim of becoming president, or at least chancellor, through the process of ballot box, law and order.

And he had seen them take their seats in the Reichstag, standing high in the press gallery with Mr. Rilke and Wolf von Dix. One hundred and seven new delegates to the parliament of the land, respectable gentlemen all in their dark blue business suits. And then, unaccountably, they had all risen to their feet and walked out, leaving the remaining members talking among themselves in confused speculation. They returned a short time later, the blue suits gone, one hundred and seven men now dressed in the brown uniform of the Storm Troops, the swastika brassard on their arms, red and black—the colors of blood and iron. And the roll being called and one hundred and seven voices shouting in their turn . . . *Present! Heil Hitler!*

He thought suddenly of Abingdon Pryory, that summer evening after dinner . . . Lord Stanmore rising to give a toast. *Dear friends and gentle hearts.* The words ran through his head like a litany as the taxi crawled through the traffic toward the railway station. *Dear friends . . . gentle hearts* . . . words so meaningless in this time—in this place.

Teletypes

Torchlight and sweating faces. Hysterical eyes. Bonfires in the public squares. Berlin and Munich. Nuremberg and Weimar. Students clogging the Haupstrasse in Heidelberg, beer-filled and arm-laden—burning the books. Shadows writhing on the ancient buildings, the stones of Heine, Goethe, and Schiller.

Black cars in the silent streets. The locked doors and the closed shutters. The midnight raids. The disappearance of the man next door . . . the quiet woman down the hall. A beginning—a New Order—and a thousand endings in dim-lit cellars or the hastily nailed and wired compounds at Oranienburg and Dachau.

"Whatever happened to Wolf von Dix? . . . Emil Zeitzler? . . . The elderly couple who owned the restaurant next to the Schiffbauerdam? . . ."

Do not ask such things. There is nothing to be done, even if one knows, or cares.

Protests. Debates in Geneva. Committees formed and

abandoned. A wringing of hands. Mute rage. Shrugged gestures of impotence. Fear.

"It's going to be a lousy decade," Martin Rilke says in the Schwarzenberg Café in Vienna the day Chancellor Dollfuss orders tanks and artillery to crush the Social Democrats in the Karl Marx Hof. Democracy dead in Austria. Dollfuss dead with it five months later, the Nazi gunmen pumping their Lugers into the little man and letting him bleed to death on a couch. No room for two German-speaking dictators.

"Capone would understand," Martin says, mixing gin and vermouth for the CBC Radio team in the bar of the Hotel Crillon in Paris. *"Hitler would be right at home in Cicero, Illinois."*

Martin Rilke in Paris . . . London . . . Brussels . . . Copenhagen . . . Rome . . . Leningrad. Anywhere at all but in Germany. *Persona non grata* by order of Goebbels. No CBC Radio team in Berlin. No INA . . . the offices on Neu Königstrasse house a travel agency featuring cheap tours of the Bavarian Alps. No point in trying to file a worthwhile story in Germany anyway. The censors go over everything. Reliable sources dry up. Gestapo informers are everywhere. *"One must be so careful. My own sons . . . I'm sorry."*

News is where you find it. In the agony of China . . . bullet-whipped Shanghai and burning Chapei. The League of Nations imposes sanctions against the Japanese but they are meaningless. Rome has as much contempt for the league as Tokyo. Mussolini begins his own adventure in the wastelands beyond the borders of Italian Somaliland and Eritrea.

A hard country. The Gojam . . . Gondar. A boy on a camel takes the dispatches from the high desert to the Sudan. The world reads the reports of a twenty-two-year-old correspondent for London's *Daily Post* and looks up Abyssinia on the map. They read of barefoot armies with spears hurling themselves against machine guns and armored cars. They read of guerrilla war . . . the roving bands of Haile Selassie and Ras Desta Demtu . . . the Fuzzy Wuzzy sword wielders bounding through the bush out of a page of Kipling.

A. E. Thaxton in Abyssinia—by wire from Khartoum.

The older correspondents, the wiser ones, travel with the accommodating Italians from the coast. They file their stories in Addis Ababa and sleep in clean sheets. It takes a young man hungry for a by-line to trail along with Ethiopian camel riders through the stony wastes and the fever trees. The stories he writes are painful and dramatic. Courage and futility. The Italians do not fight face to face any longer. They send the planes instead—the Caproni and Marchetti bombers with their loads of fragmentation bombs and mustard gas. It is the summer of the Olympic games in Berlin. The summer of Jesse Owens. Abyssinia ceases to exist. There is no news from Italian East Africa fit to print.

The teletype machines clatter away. Impersonal. Printing of beauty queens crowned and kings deposed. A revolt against the Spanish Republic by the garrisons in Burgos, Seville, and Saragossa. A General Francisco Franco flies in from Morocco to join General Emilio Mola in leading the insurgent forces. Heavy fighting in Talavera and Toledo. The Alcazar besieged . . . *exclusive report of Madrid fighting by A. E. Thaxton.* American baseball . . . the New York Yankees of the American League defeated the New York Giants of the National League in World Series play four games to two.

"I think nineteen thirty-six is the worst year I can remember," says Martin

Rilke following a broadcast from Barcelona that has probably been jammed. His companion in the restaurant gazes out at the Ramblas, deserted in the rain except for a few militiamen and Carabineros. *"I think next year will be worse,"* she says.

The machines clatter endlessly. Boys tear off the copy and deliver it to the desks. Deadlines come and go. Leaves turn brown and fall in city parks. Trees bud again. Alfred Lunt and Lynn Fontanne warmly received by London theatergoers in *Amphitryon* 38 at the Lyric. Laurence Housman's *Victoria Regina* has at last reached the Berlin stage, but all references to Benjamin Disraeli have been excised from the play. Will Don Budge conquer Wimbledon? Nazi triumph in Austria. Cheering millions greet Hitler in Vienna following bloodless *Anschluss* with German Reich. Dramatic increase in number of suicides among Austrian Jews, but report cannot be confirmed at this time . . .

The machines write on.

Book Two

A FUTURE ARRIVED

1938–1940

7

SEPTEMBER 1938

Albert Thaxton woke at dawn, a shaft of pale light filtering through a gap in the curtains and falling across his face. Rolling onto one side he groped for the rumpled package on the nightstand and fished out the last of the French cigarettes he had bought in Port Vendres after crossing the border. It was an obligation to the men of the O'Hara Detachment of the International Brigade to whom cigarettes had been more important than cartridges for their Mausers. *"Smoke some decent fags for me and the lads,"* Corporal Knott had told him on the morning he had left with the pack mules and the stretcher cases for Tarragona. He smoothed the cigarette with his fingers, lit it with a match, took a few puffs, and then ground it out in a crystal ashtray. His final link with Spain snuffed out. Dead in the bowl of glass as surely as the corporal and his men were dead by now in the bomb-holed wastes along the Ebro.

A servant brought coffee in a silver pot, toast, and a newspaper on the stroke of seven. He was dressed and shaved by then, standing by the open windows and looking out on the magnificent grounds of Abingdon Pryory.

"Good morning, sir," the man said, placing the tray on a table. "Breakfast will be served on the east terrace at eight thirty."

"A perfect day for it."

"It is that, sir. A good omen when September dawns fair."

"Is it my imagination or do I hear shooting?"

"Partridge season opened today. That would be hunters out Bigham way. A fair number of birds on the heath."

That made him feel better as he drank his coffee and munched toast. The distant popping and thud of gunfire had carried over from his dreams and touched still uneasy nerves. Reading the paper was not cheering. A Jacob Golden editorial was splashed across the front page. HITLER MUST BE STOPPED—NOW! It was Jacob at his most fervid, calling on the prime minister to order the immediate mass production of four-engine bombing planes, heavy tanks, and Spitfire fighters.

> . . . Mr. Chamberlain must let Hitler and his henchmen know that Great Britain will back to the very hilt its commitment to the freedom and independence of Czechoslovakia. There can be no compromise with the forces of terror, no appeasement to those who would hurl mankind back a thousand years . . .

As persistent in his outcries as Marcus Porcius Cato crying *Delenda est Carthago* before the Roman senate. Though not as respected nor heeded. To many, just the Jew Golden slashing out at the Führer in a fit of pique. But the wire-service reports from Prague were not Jacob's inventions. A.P., U.P., INA, Reuters, all reporting the same ominous stories of Nazi demonstrations in the Sudetenland and of German troop movements along the Czech borders. Hitler screaming in a radio speech his willingness to go to war in order to "protect" the Sudeten Germans from their "intolerable suppression" by the Slavic race. British negotiators in Prague urging Dr. Beneš to give in to Hitler's demand for the Sudetenland and by so doing create a more "homogenous" Czechoslovakia—also a Czechoslovakia stripped of its mountainous borders and elaborate concrete forts and antitank barriers. A nation shorn of its defenses and left naked to its enemies. A photograph on page 3. The British ambassador in Berlin smiling toothily at Hermann Göring. The *Post* caption: WHY IS HENDERSON SMILING? Why indeed.

He wandered down to the terrace and strolled hands in pockets beside the carved stone balustrade. Maids were setting the table for breakfast while footmen carried chairs through the open French doors of the breakfast room. The sun was warm and a slight wind stirred the trees. At the end of the terrace, stone steps curved down to the sunken Italian garden with its cypress and yew, roses, hyacinth, and marble statuary. He could see Lady Stanmore, a wicker basket over one arm, clipping long-stemmed blooms, and he walked down to her. "Good morning," he said. "You're up early."

She gave him a warm smile from under her floppy straw hat. "Good morning, Albert. Yes, it is a bit early for me. Fact is, I woke at a heathen hour and couldn't get back to sleep. Mind racing like an engine. So many things to do before this evening. Large parties are a trial, but I do enjoy them so."

He nodded at the basket. "Doing the floral arrangements?"

She laughed. "A bunch for my own enjoyment." She eyed his tall, slender frame critically. "You look as though you've put on some weight."

"I'm certain I have. Feel tip-top."

"Not too tip-top I hope, or Jacob will send you back to Spain."

"I doubt that, Lady Stanmore. Nothing left to write there except an obituary. The storms shift."

"The whirlwinds." A troubled look crossed her face like a shadow. Then she brightened and turned back to a rose tree. "I've enjoyed having you here the past few days. I'm very glad Martin talked you into coming down. What shall I do when you leave? No one to speak German to! It's a beautiful language."

"Yes, it is."

"Schiller's *Don Carlos.* Heine. Rainer Maria Rilke . . . no relation, I'm sure, but one never knows. Such a sensitive, mystical poet." She held a rose to her forehead. "*Fühlst du die Rosen auf der Stirne sterben?* Do you know, I've been married to Anthony for nearly fifty years and he's never learned to speak a word of it." She dropped the flower in the basket and moved slowly along the path from bush to bush. "We went to Germany once. Nineteen twelve . . . and we stayed for four months. Everyone at my cousin Friedrich's spoke English. They took pride in that, so I suppose it wasn't necessary for Anthony to learn a few words, but I do think it would have been a nice gesture on his part."

"Where did your cousin live?"

"Outside Berlin . . . in the Grunewald. Oh, my, I thought

we lived on such a grand scale here at the Pryory, but Friedrich lived like a prince . . . and a prewar prince at that. I think that even the servants had servants! And every one of them in their own special livery according to their task. There was even a boy whose sole function was to polish boots, dressed to the nines in a tight green jacket with brass buttons and a little pillbox hat. So long ago now. I've never been back. I considered going after the war, but . . ." She sighed, clipped a rose and laid it gently in the basket. "How could I? So much hate and bitterness. A gulf between us that seemed unbridgeable. They were in ruin and we were the victors. Though God knows, where pain is concerned there was little to choose between us. Friedrich had two sons, about the same age as Charles. Nice boys . . . they stayed with us one summer. Otto was killed in the war and Werner was wounded. A Nazi now, Martin tells me."

"Yes. Minister of munitions, or something on that order."

She smiled bitterly and clipped a dead stalk. "Ironic. A minister of the very things that destroyed his world and his body. Is it so impossible to learn something from the past? If all of us who remember the war banded together in one body we could make war impossible . . . sweep it onto the dust heap of history with all the other forms of human sacrifice."

"I wish it were that simple."

"So do I. But one can always hope." She took his arm and they began to walk toward the steps and the terrace. "I'm sure you will be going back to work soon. The news must be reported or what would we do over our morning coffee? Try to remain objective, Albert. Jacob has become so strident lately . . . so bellicose . . . like Mr. Churchill. I trust my heart. I know there must be millions of people in Germany who are as dismayed by

Hitler's excesses as we are. The nation of Goethe, after all, as well as Nietzsche. Those people must be encouraged to add their voices to the cry for peace."

He said nothing, holding on to her arm as they climbed the steps. She was nearly seventy, still beautiful, a light in her eyes as she talked of sterling dreams. He thought of the young Luftwaffe pilots of the Condor Legion sweeping low over the vineyards at Tamarite de Litera in their new Messerschmitts, strafing the workers just to test their guns.

Lord Stanmore was sitting down for breakfast, helped into his seat by his grandson, eighteen-year-old Colin Mackendric Ross. Colin, six-feet-three-inches of lanky height, wore faded blue jeans, a cotton check shirt, and shiny boots. A red bandanna was tied loosely around his neck.

"You look almost excessively American this morning, Colin," Hanna said.

"Exactly what I told him," the earl grunted.

Colin grinned broadly. With his reddish hair and tanned, freckled face he looked like an illustration in a cowboy novel. "What's your opinion, Albert?"

"Picturesque. Gary Cooper in *The Plainsman.*"

He straddled a chair as though swinging into a saddle. "Thought I'd show off my new Texas boots." He extended a foot. "Genuine Gila lizard."

His grandfather grunted again and avoided looking at them. "Are you joining us this morning, Hanna?"

"I don't think so, dear. I had some cocoa and toast. I'll take the flowers now, Albert. You sit down and have your breakfast."

"She eats like a bird," the earl said as she walked away.

"Like Mama," Colin said. "Always watching her figure."

"And a figure worth watching," the earl said, smiling for the first time that morning. "A grand old girl."

Colin winked at Albert. "Not so much of the 'old,' Grandpa. She might hear you."

Footmen brought the food on heated silver trays: kidneys, Yorkshire ham, eggs, local sausage and bacon, white bread toasted to a pale gold. Perfectly prepared and elegantly served on Meissen breakfast plates. The warm wind carried the scent of the rose garden—perfume, fertilizer, and damp earth. Different scents in Catalonia, Albert was thinking. Boiled mule meat if the men were lucky, and the perfume of the dead. He ate his breakfast without dwelling on the difference or suffering any pangs of conscience. He had just turned twenty-five, a war correspondent and as much an old campaigner as the men he wrote about. And old soldiers took their pleasures as they came and were grateful for them.

"What were you and Hanna chatting about in the garden?" the earl asked.

"Oh, one thing and another. War and peace . . . Hitler's Germany."

Colin made a wry face. "Holy Mo! What a subject on a sunny morning." He turned his face to the sun. "Why can't England be like this every day in the year?"

"We're quite grateful for the odd week or two. This is not California."

"You're telling me, Gramps."

"Yes, Colin, that is precisely what I am telling you. When in Rome, and all that. I trust you will change before our guests arrive. And kindly stop referring to me as *gramps!* It sounds like a disorder of the bowels."

The earl picked at his food, drank a cup of tea, and then excused himself from the table.

"Talk about Grandmama eating like a bird."

"He doesn't look well this morning."

"He's okay. Just sulking. His new doctor wouldn't permit him to get up before dawn and go tramping out with guns. I don't understand the joy in blowing some poor old partridge to pieces anyway. But, to each his own." He rolled a fragment of toast into crumbs between restless fingers. "How much longer are you going to be on the sick list?"

"Off of it now. My boss is coming tonight and I'll be given an assignment I expect."

"Where?"

Albert shrugged and took a sip of coffee. "The Berlin desk would be my first choice, but Goebbels may revoke press credentials for the *Post.* That's the rumor. A Jewish, warmongering rag, he calls us. I'll probably go to Prague, unless the crisis blows over."

"Storm in a teacup, if you ask me." He rolled another piece of toast into pellets and flicked them from the table with his thumb. "You always wanted to be a newspaperman, didn't you?"

"Since I was sixteen."

"Martin told me once that you had a scholarship to Balliol and turned it down. Why?"

"I didn't feel I needed the Oxford experience. I went to London University, did odd jobs for INA . . . free-lanced for the *Post* . . . got a practical education and then went my merry way."

"I feel the same about Cambridge. I dread the start of term."

"It won't do you any harm."

"The only person I'll know there is my friend Derek Ramsay, and he'll be two years ahead of me. I'll be odd man out."

"You will in lizard-skin boots, that's certain. They'll probably call you Tom Mix." He could tell by the somber expression on the boy's face that this was not a laughing matter. "You really are concerned about it, aren't you?"

"Sure. I don't belong in Cambridge. I'm not smart enough."

"You were smart enough to pass the examination."

"Yeah, with a discreet pull from Uncle Charles. The bursar is a fellow classmate from Eton. My going to an English university was my mother's idea, and I got talked into it."

"Where did you want to go? Stanford?"

"Nothing that grand." He tilted back in his chair, long legs stretched out, hands clasped behind his head. "I'm like you, Albert. I've known what I want to be since I was a kid. Mama has always wanted me to go into medicine, but I'm not cut out for it. I'd like to be a *professional* flier . . . the air races . . . test pilot . . . jockey a Clipper to Manila. Why not do what I'm good at already? Heck, I soloed before I was fifteen. I could learn to fly anything built."

"I can't see your mother approving of that."

"Neither can I. She'd take a lot of persuading. But there's more to it than being a pilot. I could start my own airline one day. Not passengers, freight. That's where the money's going to be. Transport everything from oil pipe to orchids."

"A good idea. Put me down for a quid when you start selling stock. In the meantime, spend a year or so in college. It won't make you a better flier, but it will round you out as a human being."

"Yeah, I suppose so. That's what Dad says." He sat forward and toyed with the silverware. His nervous energy was like an electric charge. "Anyway, I'm committed now. Pembroke College . . . founded before Columbus sailed the blue. I'll get used to it, I guess. What are you doing this morning?"

"Nothing. Lie around and read."

"Want to ride over to Burgate with me? I promised Charles and Marian I'd lend a hand."

"I'm not much for horses."

"I'll have Gardway hitch something gentle to the trap."

A DIRT PATH, hard and dry, meandered across the fields in the general direction of Burgate House School. The horse knew where to go and Colin let the reins dangle as he slouched in the seat, eyes closed, face to the sun. Albert sat beside him, watching the broad chestnut rump of the horse as it plodded along, feeling uneasy, expecting it to burst into a gallop at any second. But all the horse did was to stop as a small boy darted suddenly into its path from the tall grass. He wore nothing but shorts and canvas shoes. In his hands was a crooked stick that he brandished like a gun.

"Stand and deliver!"

Colin opened a baleful eye. "Beat it, kid."

"Your money or your life!" the boy cried, waving the stick violently back and forth. An older boy suddenly appeared, running through the grass. He grasped the would-be highwayman from behind, plucked the stick from his grasp and tossed it away.

"Sorry," he called out. "It's only Bertie."

The boy named Bertie struggled and kicked in a paroxysm of fury. "You! . . . You! . . . blitherin' bloomin' blinkin' bleedin' bastard!"

The older boy only smiled, turned Bertie upside down, and shook him like a rag. When he plopped him on the ground, Bertie sat there, quiet and dazed.

"He gets that way sometimes," the older boy explained with a gap-toothed grin. "But he's better than he used to be, aren't you, Bertie?"

"Aggressive," Albert said.

"Yes, sir. He's my cousin and I look after him. Don't I, Bertie?"

Other children were coming over the slight rise and down to the path, an orderly group, some with canvas satchels slung over their shoulders, others with butterfly nets and glass jars. Kate Wood-Lacy shepherded them along. She was sixteen, a tall, full-breasted, wide-hipped girl with a round, pretty face still plump with baby fat. Soft brown hair hung in wavy masses to her shoulders, complimenting her faultless complexion.

"Hello, Colin," she said. "Mr. Thaxton."

Colin climbed down from the trap and jerked a thumb at the boy on the ground. "That little nut could have spooked the horse."

She blushed and pushed a strand of hair away from her forehead. "Sorry. He can be a handful at times."

"Not your fault."

"I am in charge."

"Hey, don't take being a counselor too seriously. You don't have to go down with the ship, you know."

"You . . . look nice today, Colin. Are those cowboy boots?"

"Sure. Genuine Gila-monster skin." He lifted one leg. "I'll take one off if you'd like and you can show it to your group."

"That's all right," she said, blushing deeper. "We're only doing butterflies today."

Charles Greville splashed gin into two glasses, added a few drops of bitters and handed a glass to Albert. "Colin give you a gentlemanly drive over?"

"Grandmotherly, as a matter of fact."

"You're fortunate. Sometimes he races that trap like a crazed Roman in a chariot race."

"Only one incident. A tyke tried to hold us up."

"Ah, Bertie. We always have one or two of those. Has parents who have no time for him. Too many other delightful things to do. A good many of the truly rich should be sterilized at birth."

"He got bounced on his head and then walked away hand in hand with the Wood-Lacy girl, gentle as a lamb."

"Kate keeps them all calm. A sweet child."

"Shy."

"Well, painfully self-conscious at the moment. Suddenly bloomed into a woman since last summer."

"Has a crush on Colin, I think."

"Does she?"

"Judging by the way she looked at him in silent adoration. I think he's oblivious to it."

"He would be." He took a swallow of gin. "It's been a couple of years since you've seen him. What's your honest impression?"

"Ingenuous . . . confused . . . a boy in a man's body."

"Restless. I suggested he go up to my brother's place in Derbyshire, muck about with the horses for a couple of weeks before the start of Michaelmas term. Did you ever meet William's wife, Dulcie?"

"No."

"A grand girl. Bright as a florin, outspoken, unconventional, involved in every conceivable liberal cause. The atmosphere up there quite different from the Pryory, if you get my drift. Mother and Father love the lad, but they are set in their ways . . . dressing for dinner, that sort of ingrained formality. Colin is like having a large Airedale romping about the place."

"He seems to be in his element now," Albert said, pointing his glass toward the tall windows of the common room.

Stagehands from the Royal Theatrical Company swarmed across the grounds, arranging lights in trees and shrubbery, unloading props and wicker baskets packed with costumes from large vans, and setting up folding chairs for the audience. Colin moved among them, tall in his slant-heeled boots, a hefty roll of electric cable slung over one shoulder.

"Yes, that's Colin," said Charles. "Raising a sweat and dirtying his hands. That's joy to him."

The annual Burgate House Drama Festival, now beginning its sixth season, had become an established summer event. Charles had opposed the idea at first, fearing that poor critical reception might hold the school up to ridicule. But Marian had persevered and he had finally relented. The first year's production, *A Midsummer Night's Dream* performed by the London Shakespeare Ensemble, had been greeted by every important theater critic with unqualified enthusiasm and delight. Not only did the festival raise money for the school and sundry charities, but the very name Burgate House had taken on a new connotation in the public mind. The old image of antiestablishment radicalism wafted away on the wings of Shakespeare, Sheridan, and Shaw.

"Will you be staying for lunch, Albert?" Marian asked as she came into the room, looking happy but disheveled. Six-year-old Christopher Michael Greville trailed after her cradling a ginger kitten in his sturdy little arms.

"Lunch? I just had breakfast . . . and now cocktails at ten in the morning!"

"I know," Marian sighed. "We're all topsy-turvy here. Tomorrow's opening night and everything is total confusion."

"As it should be," Charles said. "You told me that yourself."

"True, dear. The worse the rehearsals the better the show. This one should be a stunner." Her son tugged at her skirt and she had to lift him up, cat and all. "There's a dress rehearsal this afternoon, Albert, if you'd care to watch it."

"I'll wait for the opening. Will you be at the party tonight?"

"Lord, yes. Wouldn't miss it for the world. What a mixed bag! High-church pacifists and Mayfair lowlifes."

"All in a good cause," Charles said. "Spanish Relief is bound to attract a few odd lots. Will we be hearing from you, Albert?"

"If asked," Albert said with a shrug. "I imagine your mother expects me to give a short talk. War is hell, that sort of thing."

"As if one needed to be reminded. When are you riding back into the lists?"

"I'll probably know tonight. Jacob should be coming down with Martin."

"Feeling healthy enough to take on Mr. Goebbels?"

"For fifteen rounds—bare knuckle. He's outdoing himself with outlandish fabrications lately."

"Do you think Hitler's serious? That speech of his the other night in Berlin. Blatant propaganda, or is there a kernel of truth? Will there be war?"

Albert swallowed his gin. "I don't believe Hitler wants war with Czechoslovakia just now, Charles. They're too strong. Skoda makes as good a gun and tank as Krupp. A military setback, even a temporary one, would destroy the carefully contrived myth of Nazi invincibility. He's relying on Chamberlain and Daladier to back down and hand him the Sudetenland on a plate. The Czechs seem willing to fight, but not without positive support from their supposed protectors."

"Please!" Marian wailed. "There are enough problems with *As You Like It* without worrying about that horrid little man Hitler." She held out young Christopher to her husband. "Look after Kit and cat for a while, Charlie. I promised Joan I'd give her a hand with the costumes."

He held his son in his arms. The cat crawled from the boy's grasp and sat on Charles's shoulder like a parrot on a sailor. "Is there any way out of this impasse?"

"I believe so. It means sticking it out, come hell or high water."

"Bluff him to the brink of war, in other words."

"Exactly. Full mobilization here and in France. But that won't happen. Chamberlain doesn't have the stomach for it and too many people believe in giving Hitler whatever he wants as long as it's east of the Rhine."

Charles had a faraway look in his eyes as he gently stroked

his son's head. "A dishonorable price, perhaps . . . but peace."

"No, Charles. Just a dishonorable lull."

JENNIFER WOOD-LACY STRUGGLED to concentrate on the itinerary and travel schedule for the Reverend Donaldson and Captain Winters. It was complex, calling for them to appear at peace rallies in five cities within eight days. They were by far the most successful fund raisers and peace-pledge gatherers that No More War International and Calthorpe & Crofts had ever sent out. The Reverend Donaldson and the captain had been world-famous athletes in their youth, both winning silver medals at the 1912 Olympic Games in Stockholm. The Reverend Donaldson, rector of Worley-on-Tyne, was a burly, hearty man who stood well over six feet in height and had a voice to match. Captain Winters was just as hearty and bugle voiced and would have been equally as tall had he not lost both legs at the hip during the battle of Neuve Chapelle in 1915. They made a remarkable team, a blend of classic evangelism and music-hall turn. They had the ability to reduce an audience to relieved laughter ten seconds after that always awkward moment when the good rector wheeled the truncated captain on stage in his little rolling cart.

She stared at the railroad timetable. Birmingham to Sheffield. Her thoughts wandered. The sun streamed ferociously through the window in her tiny office, scorching the fragile flower on the window sill, the only splash of color in an otherwise drab room. She rose from her desk and went to the window for a breath of air. Tree-shaded Bloomsbury Square lay below, littered with the inert bodies of office workers seeking temporary relief from London's unexpected heat. Her cubbyhole was rapidly turning into a furnace. Leaving, she walked down the corridor to the toilet where she splashed water on her face and dried it with a towel which, along with the ancient sink, was none too clean. She made a mental note to speak to Tommy about it. He was a good enough office boy, but his janitorial duties left much to be desired.

So did her appearance. She stared at her reflection in the badly blotched mirror above the sink. She was twenty-one, tall with a willowy grace, slim hipped and small breasted. Her raven-black hair, dark eyes, and ivory complexion imparted a foreign air. She had often been mistaken for Portuguese when she had lived in India during her father's second tour of duty there. She dabbed at her hair with stiff fingers. It was rich, thick, and shiny, but there was far too much of it. She looked, she thought ruefully, permanently windblown.

She could hear Mrs. James having one of her interminable squabbles with the office boy and she poked her head into the reception room before continuing down the corridor to Arnold Calthorpe's office. The overgrown seventeen-year-old lounged in a chair, munching a chocolate bar.

"When you can find the time, Tommy," she said coldly, "you might do something about the W.C. It's a disgrace."

Mrs. James snorted and pulled a plug from the telephone switchboard. "He's busy biting the hand that feeds him, that's what *he's* doing!"

The boy grinned and munched. "Just expressin' an opinion, Mrs. James. It's still a free country. As for the loo, Miss Jennifer, I'll get to it, never you fear."

"The lad tore up his peace pledge, he did."

"Now, Mrs. James, I didn't say I did and I didn't say I didn't. All I said was that Golden's editorial was bang on. Might just give notice and try the bloomin' army. Three squares a day and a bit of the old adventure thrown in. Maybe your da would put in a good word for me, Miss Jennifer."

"Not ruddy likely. Join the navy."

She felt distinctly out of sorts as she went into Calthorpe's untidy office and flopped into a leather chair by the open window. The publisher glanced up from the manuscript he was reading and smiled at her.

"That was a deep sigh, Jenny. Having problems?"

"Only in getting them on the proper trains."

"It'll work out. And Reverend Donaldson is a resourceful man. I admire your sense of duty, but there was really no reason for you to come in this morning. Drive down to Abingdon now, why don't you? Spend the rest of the day in clean country air. What time would you say things would be getting started?"

"Eightish, I imagine. Knowing Lady Stanmore, there'll be a smashing buffet, so don't miss that."

"I'm certain Hogarth would be devastated if we did. You might take a few dozen copies of his poems with you. Set them up on a table or something and he can autograph them after the reading. Mrs. James and Tommy sound as though they're at it again. What's the flap this time?"

"Tommy tearing up his peace pledge under the influence of the *Daily Post.*"

"Ah, well, quite a few others doing the same I warrant. It's not easy to remain steadfast in this confusing age. Tides of belief in surprising shifts, so to speak. Jacob Golden went to prison in nineteen seventeen rather than fight in a war he referred to as 'an obscene mockery imposed by kings' . . ." He pointed to the shelves lining every square foot of wall space. ". . . And Martin Rilke's *An End to Castles* continues to be one of our best sellers. Yet neither man believes rearmament or war to be obscene when applied to stopping Herr Hitler. They have, you might say, torn up their pledges as young Tommy has torn up his."

"They may have a point."

Calthorpe rubbed a thumb across the deep hollow of a scar where a German sniper's bullet had once plowed his cheek. "God grant them wrong, Jenny."

She turned her head and looked down on the square. Girls in light cotton frocks. Men in their shirtsleeves. Children. Baby carriages and dogs. "Yes, God grant that."

SHE SHARED A large two-bedroom flat in Mayfair with her sister. It had not been her idea of a London apartment, being far too modern for her tastes, but Victoria had insisted on leasing it. Her objections to it had dissipated during the winter when the American-style central heating had proved such a blessing. When she came in she found Gerald Smith Blair sprawled on the drawing-room sofa reading a copy of *Picture Post,* a cup of tea balanced on his stomach, a cigarette dangling from his lips. He was a tanned, curly haired blond of twenty-four who seemed to spend more time racing his yacht than reading for the bar. He was Victoria's fiancé, or ex-fiancé. It was difficult for Jennifer to keep track of his current position in her sister's life.

"Hello," he drawled.

"And to you, Gerald. Where's Vicky?"

He scowled and flipped a page of the magazine. "Getting dressed—for the past hour."

Victoria was in her room, seated half naked on the bed painting her toenails. When they had been children in boarding school and had worn uniforms they had been virtually impossible to tell apart, but no one mistook them any more. Victoria was silk to her sister's tweed, a stylishly coifed, chicly couturiered Mayfair deb.

"Hi ho!" Victoria called out cheerfully. "You're home early. Get the sack?"

"No such luck."

"Why don't you chuck it in? What's the point anyway? Working for a living must be bad enough—working *unpaid* for Arnold Calthorpe is absolute madness. I think you're a masochist at heart." She scowled at her wet, splayed toes. "Do you think this color does *anything?*"

"Not to me."

"I'll ask Gerry."

"He thinks you're dressing. Why don't you oblige him?"

"In due course. And, oh, we're not heading down till after eight. We're going to a cocktail party first . . . Jacques Heim's new showing in Grosvenor Street. You should come along, might give you some idea of style. What are you wearing, by the way?"

"Haven't thought about it. I'll find something appropriate."

Victoria raised a dubious eyebrow. "Take something of mine. The pale green Schiaparelli with the leg-o'-mutton sleeves. You'll look a charmer."

"I have my own clothes, thank you."

Victoria bent forward and dabbed at a toenail. "So I've noticed."

She tossed a few things in a suitcase. Her closet was Mother Hubbard's cupboard compared to her sister's, but then Victoria's only passions at the moment revolved around keeping in style and stringing Gerald Smith Blair along.

The mood of depression that had dogged her all morning faded rapidly as she drove her little two-seater Sunbeam out of London. Leaving the main highway, she darted along narrow country roads to Abingdon, the canvas top folded down, the wind whipping her hair into a tangled black nest.

Quite a few guests had already arrived and she parked her car among ponderous Daimlers, Packards, and other chauffeur-driven behemoths, including the limousine of the bishop of Guildvale. One of the Stanmores' footmen carried her suitcase to the house, along with the carton of books which she asked him to place in the ballroom.

Getting her hair back to reasonable neatness was her first priority. The windows of her room looked down on the west terrace, and as she stood there combing her hair she could see a number of people that she knew, including the bishop and other pillars of No More War International sipping tea and chatting away with Hanna. She didn't feel up to conversing with anyone at the moment and made her way downstairs through the servants' stairs and the back passageways to the ballroom. Preparations for the buffet were being made, with servants setting up long, cloth-covered tables along one wall. There was a small table to one side of the bandstand and she began to unpack the slim books and stack them on it. While she was doing this, setting up some books so that the title showed, *Spanish Cross* by Hogarth Wells, and others to display the poet's famous portrait by Augustus John on the back cover, a man wandered in from the terrace and stood near her, scowling slightly at the book jacket. He was almost excessively good looking with pale violet eyes and the longest lashes she had ever seen on a man.

"Would you like to take a copy?" she asked.

"I don't think so," Albert said. "I know most of them."

"Surely not. The book hasn't been released yet."

"In Spain. Hogarth was in Barcelona last year . . . briefly. He used to recite his new poems in the bar of the Hotel Florida." He leaned forward to take a closer look at the portrait. "John painted that in nineteen thirty. Unbelievable how much a man can change in so short a time. Debauchery plain and simple. Too much whisky and too many girls."

She forced a smile. "Are you one of the Quakers from the Friends for Peace?"

"Good Lord, no. I've nothing against debauchery as long as it doesn't lead to dissipation. My name's Thaxton, by the way . . . A. E. Thaxton."

"Jennifer Wood-Lacy."

He gave her a thoughtful stare. "Yes. You're the general's older daughter . . . one of a perfectly matched set. We've met before."

"Have we? I'm sure you must be mistaken."

"Right here. About eight or nine years ago. I'm not sure which one you are. One smiled and danced. The other did neither."

"I'm probably the latter."

"You don't look at all like young Kate."

"She takes after Mother. Victoria and I are in Father's mold."

"Daughters of The Hawk."

"In looks only." She found his eyes to be hypnotizing and glanced away. "When did you meet Kate?"

"The other day . . . at Charles and Marian's. Marian told me that she knows as much about biology as their regular teacher."

"She's the brains of the family." She fussed with the books. "Are you a relative of Marian?"

"No. I'm Martin Rilke's brother-in-law."

"Of course." She gave him a quick glance of recognition. "I remember you now. You wore a school blazer with a large crest embroidered on the pocket. You danced with my sister and she had a crush on you."

"Did she? Outgrew it by now, I suppose."

"Knowing Vicky that would be hard to tell. Are you staying here?"

"Resting up. I'll be leaving soon." He picked up a book and leafed idly through it. "Nicely printed. Do you work for Calthorpe's?"

"Not really. I do odd jobs for NMWI. Arnold Calthorpe is chairman of the U.K. chapters . . . cochairman actually with the bishop of Guildvale."

"No More War International," he murmured, turning the book in his hands. "Hogarth is keen on it. Quite pointless, actually."

She stiffened. "I'd hardly call it that."

"I'm sure you wouldn't. My own personal observation. It

might make some sense if Hitler became a member. Otherwise . . ." he placed the book back on the table ". . . it's a movement of futility. As hollow and meaningless as Hogarth's poems."

She drew in her breath sharply. "What a rude and cynical remark."

"Rude, perhaps . . . but nothing I wouldn't say to Hogarth's face—and have. I told him in Barcelona that what he is writing is claptrap. Spain as metaphor . . . all those allusions to bleeding crosses and dying bulls."

"I found his poems to be very poignant."

"I suppose they are in a maudlin kind of way. They confirm one's belief in the tragedy of war. But the significance of what's happening in Spain goes much deeper than that. The bombing of Guernica shocked the world, and rightly so, but one squadron of Hurricanes could have prevented that particular tragedy. What's truly shocking is that England never sent modern fighter planes to the Loyalists, they sent Hogarth Wells instead."

"You really dislike the man, don't you?"

"Good heavens, no. I love and admire him. I was one of his students for three years at London University. But he was a different poet in those days. He wrote about what he knew and understood so well. The forgotten Englishman . . . the bloke on the dole. Compare *In Nottingham Town* to that Spanish fantasy and you'll see what I mean." He took her arm in a gentle grip. "Look here, I don't know about you, but a terrace swarming with bishops and other ecclesiastics fills me with terror. Would you like to go for a walk in the garden?"

She wasn't sure whether she would or not. The amethyst

eyes sparkled. His fingers were cool against the smooth skin of her arm. "All right."

They avoided the terrace by going through the conservatory with its black-and-white tiled floor and potted palms and then out through a glass door into the gardens.

"It's good to meet old friends after so many years," he said.

"Is that what we are?" she laughed. "We were barely introduced."

"A minor point. I saw you arrive in your little green runabout. I was having a cup of tea on the terrace with some monkish fellow in a serge suit and I thought to myself, I wish a girl like that was a good friend of mine . . . and lo and behold she is . . . or will be, I trust."

"A charming sentiment. And you just happened to find yourself in the ballroom to meet me."

"Not exactly. I wandered about looking for you."

"You seem to be a man who goes after what he wants."

"The mark of a good reporter—and I am a good reporter."

"I know. I've read your articles in the *Post*—including the one you did on my father in Egypt."

"Ah, yes . . . that was a long time back. When I was on my way home from Ethiopia. Were you in Cairo then?"

"No. He was only there for a short time . . . maneuvers of some sort. We were in India."

"How long were you there?"

"Two years."

"Like it?"

"Some aspects . . . not others." She plucked at a full-blown rose and tossed the heavy, waxen petals in her palm. "When one is so much a part of the raj one sees India from rather an unreal perspective. All pomp and palaces . . . the lancers riding ahead of Father's motorcar. That type of thing. I wandered around a bit with some Indian friends from the University of Delhi and glimpsed the other side."

"How long have you been a pacifist?"

"I'm not sure I am one . . . at least not with the dedication and commitment of most people in the movement. I'm not evangelical about it, Mr. Thaxton, but I do have my firm beliefs."

"Albert," he said. "Albert Edward. My close friends call me Thax."

"Albert, then. I believe in nonviolence and that war of any kind is an obscenity."

"That's true, it is—but then, so are concentration camps in Brighton and firing squads in Trafalgar Square."

"I've heard that retort many times. I don't believe it could happen."

"That's what the Czechs believe."

"There is a . . . *moral* force sweeping the world that's just as powerful as guns, perhaps more so."

"Well, moral shields are all right in their way, so long as one keeps a sword in the other hand."

"Now you're being cynical again. I had a glimpse of the power of moral force and it quite altered my life."

"On the road to Damascus?"

She flushed and let the petals fall from her hand. "On the road to Lahore as a matter of fact. Gandhi and his followers on a pilgrimage to Amritsar. Trouble was expected and there were troops and armored cars all along the route. Nothing happened, just an overwhelming radiance of love and peace."

"Your naïvetè is touching."

She stopped walking and turned to face him, her body stiff, color spots of anger on her cheeks. "You have a talent for irritating people."

"So I've been told. I'm sorry, I'm not scoffing at your beliefs. They're noble and civilized, in a world that is rapidly becoming neither. At least we British have learned to be somewhat tolerant. Our General Dyer massacred Hindus at Amritsar in nineteen and now we let the Mahatma march past our armored cars and place flowers on the machine guns. If he did the same in Germany he'd be shot out of hand, and his followers right along with him. So much for moral shields where the Nazis are concerned."

She began to turn away. "It's been nice meeting you—again. I enjoyed our little talk, but I must get back."

"I'll go with you. Perhaps I can give you a hand."

"I doubt it," she said, walking toward the house. "I have to get dressed."

"I'll see you at the party then. Perhaps you'll save me a dance or two."

"I doubt that also, Mr. Thaxton. I never did learn how."

He watched her go, kicking idly at the blossoms she had strewn across the path. They had not, he thought ruefully, hit it off too well.

JAPANESE LANTERNS HUNG the length of the terrace and swayed gently in the warm evening wind. The hundred or more guests drifted from the terrace where drinks were being served to the ballroom with its tables loaded with countless delicacies. A string quartet played softly in one corner while a swing orchestra from London waited in the wings.

There were speeches by the bishop of Guildvale and a former cabinet minister now devoting his life to international pacifism. Hogarth Wells, a rotund, sad-eyed little man in a crumpled corduroy suit, recited his poems in melodious Welsh tones. Albert Thaxton gave a firsthand description of the plight of orphans in Madrid and Barcelona, Seville and Bilbao. The head of the British Red Cross made his appeal for funds to help their Committee for Spanish Relief. It was all very apolitical and impeccably humanitarian and checks or pledges came from a broad spectrum of people with diverse views—"Spain" meaning all things to all men. When the talks were over and the amount of money raised had been announced by Lady Stanmore in a short speech of gratitude, the orchestra took its place on the stand and swung into a spirited medley of Benny Goodman tunes.

"Stompin' at the Savoy" made discussion and autographing next to impossible, and so Jennifer asked two footmen to carry the table of books into the conservatory. She stayed there with Hogarth Wells and Calthorpe until the last slim volume of verse had been signed and handed out to admirers, mostly elderly women who seemed to find the cherubic-faced man more interesting than his current poetry. At last the table was cleared and Wells, badly in need of at least a double whisky, fled to the terrace and the makeshift bar set up under the Japanese lanterns.

"You look charming tonight, Jenny," Calthorpe remarked, smiling at her as he smoothed a cigar between his fingers. "Hie thee to a ballroom and dazzle the swains."

"Well, I'll go to the ballroom at least."

She didn't feel dazzling. Her cocktail dress of pale mauve silk, made for her in New Delhi two years before, was decidedly out of date—a "colonial" dress, Vicky called it—and her hair had reverted willfully to its usual windblown state. Not that anyone would notice or care, she was thinking as she pushed her way through the crowded room. The orchestra was now playing the score from *Roberta,* with just about everyone hurrying in to dance to "Smoke Gets in Your Eyes." She spotted Victoria dancing with Gerald—just like them to arrive after all the speeches—and Colin, looking stiff and uncomfortable in a tuxedo, dancing with Kate. Kate looked beautiful and grown-up in a chic gown that revealed her blossoming figure to perfection.

"What do you think of your sister?" Marian asked, coming up to her by the buffet table.

"Which one?"

"Kate, of course. I made the dress for her."

"You should make one for me. Where's Charles?"

She made a wry face and helped herself to a chilled lobster claw. "Staying as far away from the dance floor as possible. Talking politics with Martin and Jacob Golden." She poked at the cracked lobster claw with a thin silver fork. "Good heavens. There must be a quarter pound of meat in this. Have you eaten? You look harassed."

"I haven't eaten, and yes, I am feeling harassed . . . from keeping Hogarth Wells away from the drink all evening. Thank God his little turn is over."

"Dreadful poetry."

"Did you think so?"

"Lord, yes. Impassioned but shallow. Not the Hogarth Wells of a few years back."

"Someone else was saying the same thing."

"He was right. A pity."

She had known that in her heart when Arnold Calthorpe had given her the galleys to read. She might have agreed with A. E. Thaxton if he hadn't been so curt and abrasive in his criticism. He had simply rubbed her the wrong way.

"Let me fix you a plate," Marian said.

Jennifer glanced at the table—oysters, lobster, and scampi, beef, ham, roast partridge, and plovers' eggs. She felt queasy. Too many people . . . too much noise. "I . . . I think I'll get a breath of air first—and something with gin in it."

He came up to her on the terrace as she stood against the balustrade, sipping at a gin and french and staring moodily at the moon-flooded lawns beyond.

"Mind if I join you?" Albert asked.

"No, of course not."

"Everything went quite well, I thought. I want you to know that I congratulated Hogarth for a fine reading. There's a good deal of the actor in him and he carried it off nicely."

"I'm sure he was grateful."

"He seemed to be." He leaned back against the carved stone. "Is it true that you don't know how to dance?"

"A girl can't be eighteen and living in a military cantonment in India and not know how to dance. The junior officers wouldn't permit it. One thing they do very well in the British army is foxtrot."

"I wish the same could be said of me. However, I would like to have one dance with you . . . while they're playing something reasonably slow."

She set her glass down on the stone rail. "All right."

The orchestra was playing "Lovely to Look At" and they slipped easily into the swirl of dancers, Albert holding her with unself-conscious familiarity.

"You dance very well," she said after a few moments.

"Thank you. A bit heavy footed."

"Not at all. You can have more than one dance if you'd like."

"I would, very much, but I have to get packed. I'm leaving in half an hour."

"Leaving? Now?" She felt an odd sense of disappointment.

"Yes. I'm driving back to London with Mr. Golden. He's sending me to Prague."

"When?"

"I fly out tomorrow morning . . . from Croydon. Martin's going as well, with his radio team. So this is our last dance, I'm sorry to say." The music ended, but he continued to hold her in his arms. "May I call you when I get back?"

"Certainly."

"I have no idea when that will be."

"It doesn't matter. I'm in the directory."

"Good." He kissed her on the cheek and then he was gone.

Victoria hurried over to her through the crowd. "Who was that utterly devastating man?"

"Thaxton," she said quietly.

"A sexton? In the *church?*"

"Albert *Thaxton.* Martin Rilke's brother-in-law."

"Oh, I say. You must introduce me."

"He's just leaving. Besides, you've already met. Years ago. You had a crush on him."

"Did I? I can easily believe it. We must have him up for dinner one night."

"We? When Gerry's out of town, I suppose."

"Now, darling. Dear Uncle Martin's relative. Practically one of the family."

DODDS, THE STANMORES' butler since Mr. Coatsworth had retired in 1925, brought up her coffee in the morning.

"I took the liberty, Miss Jennifer."

She sat up in bed and reached for her robe. "And very good of you to do so, Dodds. How do I rate such an honor?"

"By special request of Mr. Albert."

"He's still here?"

"Left last night with Mr. Rilke and some other gentlemen." He placed a wicker bedtray beside her. A single rose, still damp with dew, stood in a slender crystal vase beside the coffee pot. "He asked me to cut a rose for you this morning. A task, by the way, I have not done since the twenties. Young men were more, shall we say, *gallant* in those days."

"How lovely," she murmured.

"He left the choice of bloom to me. I selected a Royal Darlington . . . what won the silver cup at the Holmwood flower show last summer." He drew an envelope from his pocket and placed it against the stem glass. "And he asked me to give you this."

She opened the envelope after the butler had left the room. The note inside was simple, scrawled in haste. *"For the twin who dances, but still does not smile. Can I possibly change that?"*

She held the note for a time and then folded it and leaned back against the pillows, smiling.

8

DEREK RAMSAY TURNED his motorbike off the Abingdon road and into the driveway leading to Burgate House School, the dusty sidecar, containing a leather suitcase and a golf bag, rattling and swaying as he made the sharp turn.

He had first entered this long, gravel drive at the age of twelve, walking then, a chubby, round-faced boy in short pants and blazer running away from Archdean School for Boys in anger, humiliation, and pain. The sight of the Gothic building at the end of the drive had drained his courage and he had hurried into the orchard flanking one side of the driveway to hide and to wait amid the leafy gloom of the trees.

The orchard was still there, and the buildings rising above the trees, but any resemblance to that small, frightened boy was long past. He was twenty now, a man of average height with a large chest and broad shoulders. His nose, broken by a cricket ball when he was sixteen, imparted to his gently handsome face a pugnacity at variance with his character. A leather flying helmet covered his thick, wavy hair, the streaked goggles obscuring his merry brown eyes. He wore white flannels and a baggy cricket sweater with the crest of Pembroke College, Cambridge, embroidered on it. He smiled when he saw the buildings. His old school that had once been both sanctuary and home and, for the past two summers, where he had worked as a counselor.

The savage snarl of the machine coming up the drive brought some of the summer students running from the orchard to the front of the main building, to stand in awe as Derek brought the bike to a stop in a drifting haze of gravel dust and exhaust smoke. He pulled the helmet from his head and grinned broadly at the children.

"Hello! I remember some of you from last summer. Is that you, Bertie?"

Bertie nodded sullenly and scratched his thin, bare chest. "You didn't show up this year. We have a blinkin' *girl.* Blinkin' *Kate!*"

"Lucky you."

"May we carry your bags inside for you, Mr. Ramsay?" one of the older boys asked.

"I'm not staying, Clifton, but you might keep an eye on them for me."

Bertie picked at his nose. "You going to take me for a ride on the bike?"

"No, Bertie. And stop that disgusting habit. You should have outgrown it by now."

The boy glared in defiance. "Well, I haven't, so there!"

Derek slipped his helmet over the handlebars and combed his hair with his fingers. Kate Wood-Lacy was coming out of the orchard with the rest of her group and he strode toward her.

"Well, well," he said. "Kate the counselor!" He put his arms around her and gave her a quick hug. "My, my . . . not little Kate any longer. Like squeezing Mae West."

She flushed scarlet and pulled away from him. "Oh, put a cork in it."

"Such language."

"Two months at this job and I've learned to swear like a trooper."

"Bertie?"

"Very much Bertie. There are times when I could just kick the little beast."

"Go ahead and do it. I set my hand across his rump ten minutes after I met him."

"No corporal punishment at Burgate. Remember?"

"A smack on the backside is not punishment. It is a catharsis for the counselors." They walked slowly across the drive toward the front doors of the school. "Outside of Bertie, are you enjoying being the teacher and not the taught?"

She nodded. "Very much. Charles said I can come back next summer if I'd like. Do you think you'll work here again?"

"No, Kate. They keep me too busy at Pembroke. Study . . . and then the Cambridge air squadron most of August. No time for it." He paused for a moment and looked up at the main house and then off across the gardens at the new building, all modern glass and brick. Christ, he thought, how the old place keeps growing. "Had some happy times here, though."

Charles was in the hall talking to Colin when they strolled in. Colin, holding a suitcase in one hand and a canvas duffel bag in the other, was wearing his Levi Strauss pants, lizard boots, and a worn leather flying jacket with the emblem of the U.S. Navy over the breast pocket.

"Hello, Yank!" Derek said.

"Hi yourself." He grinned at his friend and held up the bags. "You have room for these in that rattle wagon?"

"We'll cram them in somehow."

"Are you sure you won't stay and have some lunch, Derek?" Charles asked.

"No, thank you, Mr. Greville. I had a whopping breakfast."

"Are you going to stop over at my brother's or go straight on?"

"Spend the night, sir, then head up to Scotland in the morning."

"Two weeks at Gleneagles playing golf," Colin said. "The lucky stiff."

"I'd have preferred a run through the south of France, but the old boy is looking forward to my joining him."

"Give your grandfather my best," Charles said. "He seems to be enjoying his retirement."

Derek laughed. "He is, sir. Playing more golf these days than Byron Nelson."

They shoved and pushed Colin's bags into the sidecar and tied them down with a leather strap. A semicircle of boys and girls stood watching, some of the boys hesitantly stroking the powerful machine. Kate plucked at Colin's sleeve. "I . . . I'm sorry you're going."

He turned to face her and touched her shoulder awkwardly. "That's how it goes."

"Do you think you could find the time to drop me a

line? When you start at Cambridge, I mean. How you're getting on . . . that sort of thing."

"Sure, Kate. Sure I will."

"Cheltenhurst Girls' School . . . Coombe, Dorset. You won't forget?"

He looked away from her anxious face. "I won't forget." He climbed onto the double seat behind Derek. "Maybe you could come to Cambridge next spring. During May Week. Jenny or Vicky could bring you if you can't come by yourself. Derek told me it's a lot of fun. Boat races on the river . . . dances . . . all sorts of things."

She brightened instantly. "That sounds super."

"May Week then. Is it a date?"

"Yes," she said fiercely. "A . . . date."

Derek brought a foot down hard on the starter. "We're off!"

The engine sputtered, backfired, then caught with a roar. They moved away at high speed, the children running after them down the long drive, shouting and waving. Kate stood watching until the thin haze of the exhaust could no longer be seen above the hedgerows and the trees.

THEY TOOK THE Great North Road, out of London, through Hatfield and Welwyn and on into Bedfordshire—mile after mile with Derek hunched over the handlebars and Colin clinging to his back, the engine hammering beneath them. Colin finally pressed his mouth close to Derek's ear and shouted that he was getting hungry and needed to piss. They turned off the road to Leicester and stopped at a pub set back from the road at the edge of a forest.

"Hard on the ears," Derek said as he switched off the engine.

Colin nodded, shaking his head like a swimmer coming out of the water. "Tougher on the kidneys."

They bought sandwiches and ginger beer and sat at a rickety table in a small garden.

"How are your grandparents, by the way?" Derek asked.

"Fine. They went up to Harrogate to take the waters, or something." He finished his sandwich in two bites and reached for another. "I'll tell you the truth, Derek, I'm not looking forward to this . . . Pembroke, I mean."

"We're a friendly bunch. You'll fit in."

"I hope so. When can I join the air squadron?"

"Not until your second year, I'm afraid."

"Rats. You solo yet?"

"Of course. I have ten hours."

"In what?"

"Tiger Moths."

"Kid stuff."

Derek bit into a pickled onion. "We can't all have stepfathers who build ruddy big patrol bombers for the ruddy United States Navy. How is the plane? They let you fly it yet?"

"The Colorado's a honey and, no, they won't let me do anything except sit in it."

"Sell many?"

"About thirty on order. Not enough to warrant expanding the plant just yet. Poor Jamie spends most of his time in Washington these days buttonholing congressmen." He played absently with a crust of bread. "I saw you talking with Kate. She say anything about me?"

"Such as?"

"Oh . . . nothing, I guess. You know girls."

"Ah, ha." He leaned back with a knowing smile. "Kiss and tell?"

Colin nodded and flipped the crust from the plate with his thumb. "I don't think she would."

"And she didn't, old man. Well, you have nice taste. Kate's a smasher. When did all this take place?"

"*All* this was about ten minutes of petting in Grandpa's old Rolls, for crissakes. It was dumb of me. She's just a kid."

"Is she? Doesn't look like a kid to me."

Colin peeled another crust from a sandwich and tossed it to a fluttering colony of sparrows. "There was a party last week at the Pryory. Kate came . . . in a dress that Marian had made for her. It was some dress. Sort of low in front and back. She looked swell in it. Older, if you know what I mean."

"I think I get the picture."

"Anyway, we danced a few times and had some laughs and I offered to drive her back so that she didn't have to leave early with Uncle Charles."

"Very decent of you."

"I had nothing in mind, and that's the honest truth. I've known her since she was a baby."

"All right, take the chip off your shoulder. What happened?"

"I took her for a drive and we talked about this and that. Went all the way to Ashdown and then started back. I parked on Leith Hill for the view and then . . . well . . . she looked so great in the moonlight in that dress, so I kissed her."

"You would have been less than human had you not. And she, of course, fought you off like a tigress."

"She kissed me back."

"How surprising."

"Shove it, Fat Chap!"

"Sorry. I don't mean to sound facetious. Do go on."

Colin glared at his plate. "One thing led to another damn fast. She started getting worked up and saying that she loved me. That's when it hit me. *Kate* of all people. I slammed on the brakes."

"And that's it?"

"It's enough. Now she has a hot for me. I don't want to hurt her feelings, but I don't feel the same way. I've got to let her down easy."

"That might be harder than you think. In the words of old Tommy Moore . . . And when once the heart of a maiden is stolen, the maiden herself will steal after it soon. Unquote."

"The heck with that."

"Absence, as they say, makes the heart grow even fonder. Frankly, old chap, inviting her up for May Week was not a sound idea. She'll be counting the months and days."

Colin tossed bits of bread to the flock of sparrows darting along the ground. "Maybe she'll meet another guy. One her own age."

"At Cheltenhurst Girls' School? Hardly. And as for her age, she'll be seventeen by May. A marriageable woman in most cultures."

"You can really make a guy feel swell all over."

Derek stood up and put on his flying helmet. "Come on, young Lochinvar. Back on the steed. There may be countless eager virgins waiting beyond the next hill."

Colin gave him a withering scowl. "You know something,

Fat Chap. You could become a number-one arsehole if you worked at it."

THE BISCUIT TIN Farm covered nearly seven hundred acres of rich pasture and woodland on the edge of the Peak District. Shallow, clear streams meandered across the meadows imparting a richness to the grass. It was an ideal place for raising thoroughbred horses, as the profusion of cups and ribbons in a small trophy building next to the stables bore out. The mighty Halbedier, four-time winner of the Queen Alexandra Stakes at Ascot, stood at stud there, as did several other celebrated stallions along with a harem of high-born brood mares. The Earl of Stanmore had inherited the land from an uncle in 1895 and had given it to his youngest son in 1921. The Hon. William Greville had done well with the property over the years, building miles of fences, paddocks, ultramodern stables and foaling barns, a half-mile training track and a fine stone-walled, slate-roofed house. As a trainer of international renown, William had spent as much time in France, Ireland, and the United States as he had in Derbyshire. Not so his wife. Dulcie loved the horse farm as she would have loved a child and rarely left the place for more than a week or two at a time.

Colin could understand why, as could Derek.

"Like a small piece of paradise," Derek murmured. He stood by his motorbike in the early morning, putting on his leather helmet and gloves and watching the yearlings race across a meadow after their mothers. Banks of white clouds drifted over the dales and the distant peaks of the mountains. "I wish I were staying on."

"Scotland should be fun," Colin said, placing his friend's bags in the sidecar. "Shoot a hole in one for me."

"I'll give it a try." He held out a gloved hand. "Well, old boy, see you in three weeks' time at jolly old Pembroke. Leave your cowboy suit in the trunk though. We don't want you to be too conspicuously Yankee."

Colin grinned. "Maybe I'll wear a Comanche war bonnet and paint my face yellow."

"It wouldn't surprise me in the least. Nothing you did would surprise me." They shook hands. "Keep the old pecker up, that's the good chap."

"As the showgirl said to the bishop."

He stood in front of the house watching Derek ride away, the backfire of the engine cracking like gunshots across the dale but not disturbing the horses in the slightest.

"Nice chap," William Greville said, coming out of the house and standing beside him. "If he'd stayed the day Dulcie would have tuned that motor for him."

Colin laughed. "Is there anything she can't do, Uncle Willie?"

William shrugged his massive shoulders. "Not too much. And what she can't do isn't worth doing." He stretched his arms and yawned. "We foaled a colt in the night. Care to see him?"

"Yes. I wish you'd woken me. I would have liked to see it happening."

"It was Ronay's Queen Bess. Her seventh, and the old girl gets terribly windy around strangers. Just Dulcie, me, and the vet allowed. Sorry."

They walked down a gravel path toward the foaling barns, William limping slightly, the knee stiff in the morning chill.

"God, it's beautiful," Colin said.

"Your mother loved this spot. We spent a couple of summers here when we were kids. It wasn't anything like it is now . . . just an old farmhouse, a few horses, and lots of sheep. A cousin of some sort lived here. An eccentric but harmless chap. He thought he was Napoleon or Wellington, not sure which. Alex and I adored him."

Dulcie was in the stall with mare and foal, the mare standing calmly, neck bent to the feeding bin, the colt, all wobbly legs and great staring eyes, standing shakily under Dulcie's arm as she rubbed his still glistening coat with a towel.

"Isn't he a love?" Dulcie said, smiling at Colin. "I'm going to name him California Collie, after you."

Dulcie Greville was thirty-six and had the figure of a young girl, leggy and slim in her jodhpurs and riding boots. Her red hair reached the small of her back in tight braids, like the tail of a chestnut mare in a show ring. Her age showed only in her face, in a network of fine lines caused by sun and wind and the hard Derbyshire winters. Colin had seen her only rarely during the many summers he had spent in England. He had known *of* her, of course, Uncle William's wife, the bishop's daughter who had become an activist in all kinds of radical causes. He had once spent a few days at the farm when he had been thirteen, and Dulcie had spent an occasional weekend at Abingdon Pryory—reluctantly, because she did not like the place. Uniformed footmen and other displays of great wealth offended her. She thought it feudal. And although Hanna loved her because she had made her youngest son happy, she dreaded having her as a guest. Dulcie was apt to say the most outrageous things with the candor of a precocious child.

Once, at a tea party, the vicar, while discussing with Charles the varied problems inherent in running a school, had foolishly remarked that young boys must be shielded against the "temptations of Onan." Dulcie had picked up the man's fatuous inaccuracy. "But onanism does not mean masturbation, Vicar," she had said in her high, clear voice. "It means ejaculation outside of the vagina . . . a rapid withdrawal of the penis before orgasm takes place. Quite an effective, if personally unsatisfying, method of birth control."

Neither the vicar nor Hanna had been amused.

"California Collie," Colin said, grinning across the breakfast table at Dulcie. "I hope he turns out to be a winner."

"He will."

William grunted and stirred sugar in his tea. "All one can do is hope. Breed the best to the best and pray like hell."

"I could feel his heart," Dulcie said. "Strong and steady. Not a drop of fear in the little thing. An Ascot winner for certain."

William slurped his tea and then glanced at his watch. "I'd better start getting packed."

"Just get yourself shaved and dressed," Dulcie said, "and leave the packing to me, if you don't mind." She shook her head in bemusement as she watched her husband leave the room. "With all the traveling that man's done he still can't pack properly. Tosses in shirts any which way."

"Why aren't you going with him, Aunt Dulcie? Paris should be lovely this time of year."

"Oh, Paris is all right in its way. It's the people he has to meet I can't stomach. A bloated old rajah with pockets full of diamonds and a head filled with straw, and a French count who wears a black ribbon in his buttonhole to mourn the passing of the Bourbons. Now, I ask you, can you see me hobnobbing with that sort?"

"No." He laughed. "Why does Uncle Willie?"

"Business. They want to buy one of the colts. Some utterly staggering sum so he really must go I suppose. An unraced, untried yearling worth thousands of pounds, and skilled men a few miles from here trying to raise their families on pennies. Odd sort of world, Colin."

They drove into Chesterfield, where William would take the train to London.

"How long will you be gone, Uncle Willie?"

"About a week in Paris. And then over to Ireland. There are some horses I'd like to take a look at in Killarney and Limerick."

"The Goliath filly among them?" Dulcie asked.

He nodded as he got out of the car, motioning to a porter to take his bags. "I hope I can persuade Merrivale to sell. We'll see."

Dulcie tilted her face to be kissed. "Good luck."

William kissed her, then winked at Colin in the back seat. "Look out for her, Colin, old man. Keep her out of mischief."

Colin helped Dulcie and the elderly maid in the kitchen, shelling peas and peeling potatoes for dinner. The maid had a married daughter living in California. "Long Beach," she said. "My Daphne is always after my comin' over and livin' there."

"You should go, Agnes," Dulcie said, sprinkling a leg of lamb with rosemary.

"A terrible way it is that."

"You'd like it," Colin said. "Sunny almost all year round."

"Sun is it? I'm not a flower. I can do without sun. I was born in these hills. I'll not have me bones laid to rest in *Long Beach.*"

After dinner they took the dogs for a run, walking slowly up the long grassy hill behind the house, the dogs coursing off, chasing rabbits in the fading light. He found Dulcie easy to talk to, receptive, and understanding. He expressed his doubts about entering Cambridge, and he told her about Kate Wood-Lacy, her infatuation for him and that evening in the car after the dance.

"Oh, dear," she said. "Growing up is a terrible process, filled with awesome peaks and valleys. But one must be firm and plow ahead. Of course you must go to college . . . and of course you mustn't let Kate become too enamored. You're both at the age, you see. Hormones boil through the blood and quite upset rational thinking. You did the proper thing in putting on the brakes, as it were. Getting carried away is not an idle phrase, I'm sorry to say. The number of girls impregnated in these hills on warm summer nights would astonish you as much as it dismays me. Many of them run off in their shame to Manchester or London—others marry their boys. Of the two groups it's hard to say which is the more tragic. Although I would choose the latter. At least there are well-funded societies in England for the care of unwed mothers. There's something so terribly sad in seeing young people burdened with four or five kids and trying to feed them and themselves on thirty bob a week from the dole."

"Is that one of your causes?"

"I belong to the Margaret Sanger Society, yes. It's certainly not a popular undertaking. Lecturing on birth control rarely is, but I feel it's necessary."

"I'll say one thing for you, you've got plenty of moxie."

"Moxie?"

"Guts . . . nerve."

"Oh." One of the Irish setters brought back a stick in place of a rabbit and dropped it at her feet. She picked it up and tossed it as far as she could. "It's not guts it takes, Colin, but patience. It's quite frustrating and boring most of the time. I'll be taking a day's swing through some of the towns on Thursday. Would you like to come with me? I give a lecture and pass out pamphlets and samples."

He cleared his throat and stared at his feet. "Well . . . I don't know . . ."

Her laughter rang like a bell. "Oh, dear Colin, I think you're blushing. A lecture on nutrition and personal hygiene! You'll help me give out vitamin charts and toothbrushes."

"Sure," he said. "*That* I can handle."

IT WAS A side of England that he had never seen and only vaguely knew existed. There was, Dulcie said as they drove through the dales, the England of the southern counties with its middle-class prosperity, and the England of the north. No prosperity here, only padlocked factory gates and pinch-faced men standing about on street corners. The England of the dole and the dreaded Means Test. The England where hope and promise had long fled and only apathy remained.

Bowsby-on-Tree was a typical small town in the district,

Dulcie explained as they drove slowly across an ancient stone bridge and into the High Street. It had been a sleepy village until the mid-nineteenth century when a Manchester textile king had built a cotton mill there, using the driving force of the swift little river to run the machinery. The sprawling, ugly mill buildings dominated the town, rising above it with all the grim arrogance of a medieval castle. Housing had been spawned by its existence—rows of ugly brick houses lining narrow, cobblestoned streets. There had been a time when the sound of the mill machinery could be heard from one end of the town to the other, twelve hours a day, six days a week, year in and year out. A haze of lint had drifted through the streets like finely powdered snow. But that was no more. It was silent now and the air was clean. The mill had been shut down since 1930.

"No one who worked there loved the place," Dulcie said. "God knows they didn't, but the mill meant a pay envelope every Saturday afternoon and a joint or roast chicken on the table for Sunday dinner. But a pay packet meant more than just food and clothing—they had a pride in their jobs. They were union people, paying their way, holding their heads up with the best of them."

Men, old and young, walked slowly through the silent streets in groups, or stood in patient lines outside the labor exchange. It was a daily ritual. There was no work. There were only women and children inside the union hall, listening in apathetic boredom to Dulcie's lecture on vitamins. An occasional flare of anger and resentment . . .

"I'd 'ate to see what my Tom'd do if I give 'im raw cabbage an' spuds t' eat."

"Not raw, dear. Boiled *gently* until just fork tender and then chopped together with a bit of marge. Boiling vegetables for hours destroys the vitamins."

"Boiled down proper is 'ow my Tom likes it."

"Yes, dear, perhaps he does, but I'm sure you can see how much more nutritious . . ."

It was all quite hopeless. Their mothers had boiled vegetables into watery shreds, and their mothers before them. And her demonstration—in a frying pan over a Primus stove—of how to sauté a sheep's liver so as to retain all the goodness of the meat fell on stone ears and, slice by succulent slice, into reluctant mouths. Liver they tossed into smoking fat and fried until it could have been nailed to the sole of a boot.

"It must be very discouraging," Colin said after the women had left.

"Oh, I'm used to being ignored. When I was in college I joined a Communist group for a while. That was in nineteen twenty and we were pressing for diplomatic recognition of Lenin's government. We spoke on street corners and in Hyde Park on Sunday afternoons, but no one paid the slightest attention to us."

As they were leaving, an elderly, portly man wearing a neat but threadbare suit and a plaid wool cap came into the meeting room. Dulcie introduced him to Colin as Harry King, a union steward. "Well, Dulcie," he said. "Still at it, eh?"

"Still trying, Harry."

"Oh, aye, aren't we all. You hear about the march yet?"

"What march?"

"News travels slow through the dales, I take it. It's come Saturday week. As many good lads as we can got a hold of. All the Board of bloody Trade rogues are meetin' in Manchester, includin' Lord Don't-give-a-damn. We're goin' to beard the boogers with the petition before takin' it down to Westminster. I spotted your car as I come oop High Street and figured you'd not be wantin' to be left out."

"And right you are, Harry. Thank you. I'll be there."

"It's not a long march, just enough to attract the press. The plan is to start off from here on Wednesday and be at Manchester Town Hall Saturday afternoon. The way I figure it, should be well over a thousand of us . . . skilled men from all the trades."

"That's fine, as broad a spectrum of journeymen as possible."

"Oh, aye, that should make them sit oop and take notice. Smudger Smith's bringing a couple hundred machinists from Sheffield and Rotherham. Should be a right smart showin' I figure."

"It should indeed. I'm looking forward to it."

Colin carried all the gear back to the car and checked the ice chest to make sure there was enough ice left to keep the liver from spoiling. "Where to now?"

Dulcie got into the car and sat for a moment behind the wheel looking thoughtful. "I think I'll forget about the other towns today, Colin. Presenting the petition to the Board of Trade in Manchester is a good idea, but I can't trust Harry King to alert the press about it. His idea of press coverage would be the *Barnsley Weekly Advocate.* We need the London papers. I'll get home and start making some phone calls."

"What petition are you talking about?"

"Twenty-five thousand people in three counties signed one

calling for the government to give contracts for rearmament work so that more factories can open. Take this mill. Among other things, they wove khaki cloth for the army since the Boer War."

"Gee, Dulcie, I always thought you were an ardent pacifist."

"I was," she said flatly, starting the car. "Hitler changed my mind."

THEY CAME FROM the mills and the factories, the great "works" of South Yorkshire, Lancashire, and Derby. Quiet men in neatly patched clothing with the unmistakable air about them of the undernourished and the unemployed. There were a scant thousand in all, mostly men, but a few mill girls among them, banded together in a group and looking forward to the march. Harry King was disappointed at the turnout, but there had been so many marches in the past few years, all of them coming to nothing, that many had stayed away out of apathy. This one began on Wednesday morning from the football field outside Bowsby-on-Tree. A breakfast of tea and cheese sandwiches was provided by private citizens and the town council, and then the cavalcade started out on the long, meandering route to Manchester. Dulcie and Colin trailed the marchers in a Ford estate wagon carrying first-aid supplies. When the marchers reached the town of Haddlesfield in the late afternoon, two medical students from the University of Manchester joined them and set up shop in the back of the wagon.

"Foot inspection," one of them explained to Colin. "Very important to nip any problems in the bud. We've been on marches before. Went all the way to London last year with three thousand from Leeds and not so much as an inflamed bunion among the lot of them."

The press was waiting in Haddlesfield as well, a small group of bored men who had covered protest marches many times. The only novelty in this one was that it was heading for Manchester and not London. Snaring the Board of Trade chiefs in the provinces was a new wrinkle. Lord Runcy and his colleagues might just be foolish enough to try to avoid confrontation by canceling their meeting with the Mayor of Manchester and going back to their inner sanctum in Whitehall. *That* would make a delicious headline . . . *Lord Runcy flees wrath of idle factory hands.* It was worth sticking around to see what developed.

The reporters found Dulcie quickly enough. "Well, well," one of them said. "Might have known you'd be here."

"Hello, Sam. Thought Beaverbrook sacked you years ago."

"He's kind to dumb animals."

Another reporter, a florid-faced, overweight man from *Foto-Mail* named Archer, eyed Dulcie as something of a curiosity. "You're Will Greville's wife?"

She smiled as sweetly as possible. "As if you didn't know. You did a piece on me three years ago."

"Not me. I just joined. Nasty bit, was it?"

"Not exactly kind."

"Sorry. Perhaps we can do better for you this time. I'm rather fond of your husband. Won a hundred quid on one of his nags at Goodwood."

"Some nag," she said dryly.

"A wee slip of a red filly. A fair description of you, Mrs.

Greville, come to think of it." He spotted Colin leaning against the car, watching. "Hello, what have we here? A Wild West show come to Haddlesfield?"

Colin ambled over, hands thrust in the back pockets of his jeans. "The name's Ross, Colin Mackendric Ross. I'm just tagging along with my aunt."

The reporter gave Dulcie a glance. "Your side of the family or the Grevilles'?"

"Does it matter?" she said.

"Not to me, but my readers might be interested." He eyed Colin's boots. "Fancy bit of leather that. What is it?"

"Lizard."

"Ruddy big one. Hate to meet him in the dark. You're American I take it. Where from?"

"La Jolla . . . near San Diego. California."

"I know San Diego . . . Coronado Hotel. I was there once when the Prince of Wales was on a world tour. Nice place to be from. Tell you what, Colin. I'd be interested in your views of all this . . . from the American perspective. Might be interesting, don't you think? Mind if my lad Garth takes a few pictures first?"

"No."

He motioned to a young man with a Speed Graphic. "Get the road in the background, Garth." He turned back to Dulcie as the photographer began shooting. "We just came up from London. They're starting to dig slit trenches in Hyde Park and set up antiaircraft guns. Chamberlain's flying off tomorrow to see Hitler in Berchtesgaden. We're on the brink, lass. You people should be praying, not marching."

Dulcie only smiled. "If the armament factories had been

opened two years ago, Hitler would be flying to London to see Chamberlain."

"Well, that's one way of looking at it. It's what makes horse racing . . . a nice, healthy difference of opinion."

Archer did his interview with Colin, low key and pleasant, and then walked down the street and into the White Hart Inn where he had taken a room for the night before driving up to Manchester. He had five hours to deadline and phoned his editor in London to tell him that the motorcycle messenger was on his way with Garth's plates. "Not much of a march" he said, "but the timing is interesting with the P.M. going off to meet Hitler. We can get some play out of it . . . the country crying for peace while the trade unions march for rearmament and war, that kind of slant. And have the morgue call me. I want whatever they have on Lord Stanmore's daughter . . . Alexandra Greville. Married James Ross of Ross-Patterson Aircraft over in the States. A bell rings on that union from a long time back . . . when I was with the *Express.* Might give me a wrinkle. God knows I could use a bit of spice."

THE WEATHER STAYED glorious through Thursday and Friday and the demonstration took on all the aspects of a holiday stroll through the countryside. It gathered in numbers as they went along, unemployed men from Liverpool and the ring of factory towns around Manchester coming down to join them. At least a dozen men had brought accordions and there were scores of mouth organs. There were tunes as they marched, and singing—"Tipperary" and all the old soldier songs that half of the men had once sung along the dusty roads of Flanders. Dulcie slept at night on an air mattress in the back of the Ford, but Colin and the two medical students joined other young men and some of the mill girls and slept in haystacks or barns after sitting up half the night around a campfire, shooting the breeze and sharing bottles of beer.

"You seem to be having fun," Dulcie said as Colin cheerfully prepared breakfast on the Primus stove.

"Best time I've had since coming to England. One egg or two?"

Up and down the City Road,
in and out the Eagle,
that's the way the money goes . . .
POP goes the weasel!

A thousand or more voices sent the song rollicking through the streets of Manchester on the morning of the last day. The long column, marching no more than three abreast by order of the police, serpentined its way to the town hall in a light rain to await the arrival of Lord Runcy, due at noon for the ceremonial luncheon with the Lord Mayor. All of the London papers were at the newsstands and copies were soon being circulated among the crowd. As each newspaper reflected the political thinking of its owner, the headlines ran a gamut of views. The prime minister's dramatic departure for Germany dominated the front pages of all the papers, but the march to Manchester received its modest share of coverage—little of it sympathetic except from Jacob Golden's *Daily Post* and one or two other liberal dailies.

"They could have said more about us," Colin muttered.

"Not with Chamberlain in the lion's den," Dulcie said.

Foto-Mail was widely passed about. A lurid tabloid, its circulation was second only to the *Daily Post.* Its headline reflected its point of view of the crisis.

TELL MR HITLER WE WANT PEACE

> Neither moral nor historical grounds bind England to Czecho-Slovakia. The Sudeten Germans have the right to self-determination and their wishes should not be . . .

Colin skipped the pages.

TRADE UNIONS MARCH FOR GUNS NOT BUTTER

There was a photo of the marchers streaming into Huddlesfield on the afternoon of that first day. The editor had artfully chosen a shot of the minuscule Communist Party group holding up a hammer-and-sickle flag. That set the tone for the article which Colin merely glanced at. What held his attention was his picture on the opposite page. It was a good one, worth sending to his mother. He was pictured standing by the Ford, smiling at the camera, one foot resting on the bumper so as to show off his lizard-skin boots. There were men walking along a road in the background, but there was something odd about it. They were different men on a road other than the one in Haddlesfield. These men weren't jaunty. They were shabby, cold-pinched, bitter-faced wraiths. Men starving on a strike, perhaps, in some bleak coal town in Wales. The heading gave him a twinge in the gut.

EARL'S YANKEE GRANDSON NOBLESSE OBLIGING

He read Dalbert T. Archer's caption in growing fury.

> . . . Americans may well smile, their homeland being three thousand miles away from any possibility of being bombed by Herr Hitler's awesome Luftwaffe. Young Master Colin Ross of San Diego, California, is the grandson of the Earl of Stanmore and finds the current crisis amusing—or so it would appear. Colin, 18, and entering swank Pembroke College, Cambridge, in October, reveals his love for the common man by following the marchers to Manchester in a spiffy Ford estate wagon with gleamingly varnished wood body. Perhaps his love for the "lower classes" is inherited. His mother, Lady Alexandra, showed her noblesse oblige by marrying her father's chauffeur in 1922 and dashing off to live in our late, but hardly lamented colonies.

"You son-of-a-bitch." He crumpled the paper in an angry fist.

Dulcie, reading it beside him, touched him gently. "Don't pay the slightest bit of attention, Colin. It's only a rag and not worth getting upset about."

"That bastard pulled a fast one on me, Dulcie. He *lied.*"

"No, dear. He jumbled the facts and wrote things that are unfair and uncalled for. That, my boy, is one facet of British journalism that takes getting used to. I've been tarred with the brush once or twice and I simply gritted my teeth and ignored it."

"I'd like to shove this paper up his . . . nose!"

"Revealing that you're upset would be more grist for their mill. And they go just so far, you see. They know the libel laws to the last dot and comma."

Nothing libelous, he was thinking as he walked away to try and cool his anger. Jamie *had* been a chauffeur and his mother *had* married him. The fact that his stepfather had been a chauffeur before the war and a noted aeronautical engineer when he had married his mother had not been mentioned, but didn't have to be. They had printed no lie, just a snide smearing of the truth.

Flashbulbs popped along the edges of the crowd. Colin could see several press photographers standing on the town hall steps, taking pictures of the demonstrators and an approaching cavalcade of gleaming black Daimlers. He recognized one of the photographers as the man who had taken his picture in Haddlesfield. And then he spotted Dalbert T. Archer among a group of reporters waiting behind the police line at the curb for the arrival of the motorcade bearing Lord Runcy and the Board of Trade ministers. Still clutching the tightly folded and twisted newspaper, he shoved his way through the throng.

The reporter seemed amused by his lanky, angry presence.

"All in the spirit of fun, lad. That's what *Foto-Mail* is all about. We mustn't take ourselves too seriously."

Colin shoved the newspaper at him. "Do you know what you can do with this bilge?"

The reporter flinched. "I know what you can ruddy well do

with it, Yank. You can ruddy well stop poking me in the chest with it. Now hop it, I've got work to do."

"*Work?* Is that what you call it? More like shoveling *shit* if you ask me!"

One of the policemen turned and gave him a stony look. "Now, now, lad. Mind your tongue."

"Not easy to do, is it?" Archer sneered. "All you ruddy Americans have big mouths."

He neither hit the man nor pushed him. What he did was toss the newspaper at him, and Dalbert T. Archer, startled by the move, jerked his body backward, slipped on the wet pavement, and went down hard on his bottom. The policeman saw only a member of the press on the ground and the tall young man—obviously one of the marchers—standing over him in what he would later describe to a magistrate as ". . . a threatening manner." The policeman was a large, experienced man and he put an armlock on the perpetrator and hustled him quickly from the scene.

IT TOOK DULCIE three hours to find out what had happened to him, and another hour to locate a solicitor that she knew. It was late in the afternoon when Colin was brought before a magistrate and informed that D. T. Archer, journalist, of Foto House, Fleet Street, London, had pressed charges against him for assault. He was released without bail to the custody of his family.

The solicitor was wryly amused. "I saw your Mr. Archer. There wasn't a mark on him."

"Because I didn't hit him," Colin said bitterly. "Never laid a hand on him."

Dulcie slipped her arm around his waist as they walked from the building. "I believe you, darling. You mustn't get upset by this. I'm sure he'll drop the charges after they get a bit of fun out of it. We'll give Jacob Golden a ring. He'll know what to do. Who owns *Foto-Mail,* Dan?"

"Part of Lord Rotherlow's chain now, I believe," the solicitor replied.

"Jacob must know the man. All publishers belong to the same clubs. He'll set things right in no time."

"Sure," Colin muttered.

He felt angry and humiliated. It was raining harder now and lights were going on in Deansgate and John Dalton Street, watery blobs in the gathering dusk. A gray city, cold and bleak. He thought fiercely of La Jolla . . . the bougainvillaea spreading crimson across the whitewashed walls of the house. The palm fronds rustling in the wind and the surf booming against the cliffs of that beautiful coast. Homesickness crushed him like a blow to the heart.

"I'd like to go home, Dulcie," he said softly as they got into the car.

"Yes, dear. It's not too long a drive. Agnes will have the fire lit and we'll have a good hot cup of tea."

He looked away from her, smiling thinly at the rain-streaked window. His people and his heritage, but he would never understand the British if he lived for a thousand years.

9

The twin-engine de Havilland came in low over the outskirts of London and landed at Heston Aerodrome five minutes ahead of the plane bearing the prime minister. It was five thirty in the afternoon, September 30. The de Havilland, painted a pale green with the words DAILY POST stenciled discreetly on the sides of the fuselage, taxied slowly across the tarmac toward the hangars, keeping well away from the huge crowds waiting in growing excitement for Neville Chamberlain, their paladin of peace.

"Bloody well makes me ill," Thompson grunted, loading the Contax he had bought in Munich. "Look at the silly bastards. Cheering their ruddy heads off. If there was half a mind among the lot of 'em they'd be getting ready to hurl eggs at the old gaffer."

Albert Thaxton was the only other passenger. Dr. Goebbels, in a grudging concession to the cause of Anglo-German good will, had permitted "that Jew rag" to send one reporter and one photographer to the Munich meeting.

"They don't understand," Albert said.

"Don't they just!" the photographer sneered. "What my dear old mum would have called lily livered. Ye yeomen of Little Britain . . . the thin yellow line!"

Half the press corps in the British Isles was at Heston, and Albert could see no point in his staying. What could he add to the coverage anyway except his own dark and bitter view? The cheering of the crowd sounded like a great wind threshing a forest. The Lockheed Super Electra had just rolled to a stop in front of the terminal building and Chamberlain was emerging. He had rarely flown, one of his aides had told Albert, and had found the flight to Germany in the luxurious Lockheed plane most exciting. "As thrilled as a boy," the aide had said. He wondered how thrilled he was now. Ecstatic, he supposed, with that piece of paper in his pocket. Hitler's signature, as solid as Keats's—which had been writ in water.

ALBERT TOLD THE *Daily Post* driver to let him out at Hyde Park Corner and to leave his bags at the paper. Crowds were streaming down Constitution Hill toward the Mall. He joined them. He had been in at the beginning of this mission to save England's green and pleasant land from Hitler's wrath and he supposed it was only fitting that he witness its ignoble conclusion. He managed to get through the crowds packed into Horse Guards Parade by showing his press credentials to a police sergeant and enlisting his aid. The burly man cleared a path for him all the way to Number 10 Downing Street.

"Well, well, if it isn't A. E.," said a correspondent from *Picture Post.* "Enjoy your German holiday?"

"Not overly."

"I wouldn't be too depressed by it all, Thax. There's a bright side, you know. Euphoria can fade quickly . . . and perhaps we've bought a little time. I had lunch with Winston. Those are his words."

"They won't give much comfort in Prague tonight."

There was a long delay before the prime minister arrived. He had been met at Heston by the Lord Chamberlain who carried a message from the king, an invitation to Buckingham Palace. But the more ecstatic crowds thrust their way into Downing Street, and when his car finally appeared the singing began, warm and heartfelt . . .

For he's a jolly good fellow!
For he's a jolly good fellow . . .

"Good old Neville!" went the cry.

The prime minister hurried through the door of his residence and then a short time later his storklike form appeared in an upper window. He waved a sheet of paper at the crowd and called out in his reedy voice: "My good friends, this is the second time in our history that there has come back to Downing Street peace with honor. I believe it is peace for our time."

The man from the *Picture Post* frowned. "When was the first occasion, Thax?"

"In the eighteen seventies. Disraeli had a meeting with Bismarck . . . I'm not sure what it was about. Leave it to Neville to choose the obscure."

He tried to clear his mind of it as he walked back to Hyde Park Corner. There were groups of delirious celebrants going into the park, streaming along the moonlit paths, past the slit trenches and the sandbagged guns. A banner had been tied to the iron railings at Albert Gate . . .

GOD BLESS YOU, NEVILLE!

OUR THANKS

NO MORE WAR INTERNATIONAL

He paused for a moment to look at it, thinking of Jennifer Wood-Lacy. When he reached Knightsbridge he went into a pub and looked up her name in the telephone directory . . . J. Wood-Lacy, Mayfair 5672 . . . no address listed. He called, shielding the instrument with his hand to try to deaden the noise of the place. Some young soldiers, looking embarrassed and half drunk, were being plied with drinks by a group of boisterous businessmen wearing red, white, and blue rosettes in their buttonholes.

"Hello?" she said.

"Jennifer Wood-Lacy? Albert Thaxton. I hope I'm not disturbing you."

"Not at all." There was a pause. "Are you at a party?"

"No. I'm in a pub across from Knightsbridge Barracks. There's some sort of victory celebration going on. I'm not part of it, but I may have a large whisky just the same."

"When did you get back?"

"This afternoon . . . one jump ahead of the prime minister."

"I see." Another long pause. "You can have your drink here if you'd like. I might join you."

"I would like that very much."

"Fifty South Audley Street. Shall we say half an hour?"

"Half an hour it is."

A large woman at an upright piano began to sing "I Didn't Raise My Boy to Be a Soldier."

"Have fun while you're waiting," Jennifer said before hanging up.

He took a taxi to South Audley Street. She lived in a concrete building of modern design on the edge of Grosvenor Square. A porter took him up in a small elevator and he walked along a thickly carpeted hallway to her apartment. When she opened the door he was slightly taken aback by the sight of her. She looked even lovelier than he had remembered. Her hair was shorter to begin with, and she was wearing a silk hostess gown that could have been made only in Paris.

"How lovely you look," he murmured.

"Thank you."

He was suddenly conscious of the fact that he hadn't changed his shirt in two days and that there was a coffee stain on his tie. "I . . . just got in," he said lamely.

"So you told me." She gestured him into the apartment. "Please. I rarely entertain in the corridor."

He glanced about the drawing room as she mixed the drinks, a gin and tonic for her, a whisky for him. "Posh digs you have here."

"Vicky's taste. Very Syrie Maugham. I prefer Sheraton and good, serviceable, country-house English."

He accepted a large, potent-looking glass of whisky. "You look rather more Parisian salon than country house in that dress."

She touched the flowing chiffon. "This? Oh, just something to lounge about in." She sat on the sofa, he in a chair. "I want to thank you for the rose."

"Ah, the rose. That seems an age ago. I hope Dodds picked a nice one."

"It was beautiful. He has good taste in flowers."

"The best to the best." He raised the glass, squinting at it. "Strong-looking stuff."

"My grandfather's stock. He buys it in Scotland by the barrel. It's what the crofters drink on hard winter nights."

He took a sip. It coursed through his body like flame. "It must give them the feeling they're in the tropics."

"Pure malt, Grandpapa told me. I don't know very much about Scotch whisky, but Vicky's boyfriends seem to like it."

"She must have some two-fisted friends." He took another small swallow. After the initial shock, this one had a mellow charm. "This would appear to be a good day for the peace movement. I'm surprised you're not out celebrating the triumph."

"Is that what it is?" she asked, frowning at her glass.

"To some people. They were romping through Hyde Park with banners. I'm glad you're not among them."

"I resigned today. Tore up my pledge."

"And may I ask why?"

She eyed him for a moment, her expression somber. "It's hard to explain . . . even to myself. But I feel a sense of shame at what we've just done. They trusted our honor and commitment and we sold them out."

He downed his drink. "Peace at any price. No one said it would come cheap."

"What have we bought?"

He shrugged, toying with his empty glass. "A little time, perhaps. That is, if we look at it that way and do something about it."

"We're not dealing with a sane man, are we?"

"Hitler? Biting carpets and all that? That's too simple a judgment of the man. It raises false hopes of his going round the bend at any moment and being carted away in a strait-jacket. The true horror of the man is his icy sanity. There are no demons howling in his head. No delusions. He *knows* he's the savior of Europe . . . the founder of a super race. He'll go about creating his *new order* with all the zeal and righteousness of a Torquemada." He held out his glass. "May I have another one of these? Those Scottish crofters must have some grand times."

"Help yourself."

He stood up and walked, a trifle unsteadily, to the side-board. He had not, he suddenly realized, slept a wink in the past thirty-six hours. He poured two fingers worth. "I'll be going in a minute—I'm really out on my feet. Would you have dinner with me tomorrow?"

"I'd love to."

"Marvelous. I talked with Martin before leaving Munich. He's planning a broadcast to America at the BBC. Air time mid-night. He'll be interviewing Churchill, Jacob Golden . . . one or two others, including myself. I think it should be interesting. We can have dinner at, say, nine and then go on to Broadcasting House. Be a late night for you. Sure you won't mind?"

"Not at all. It sounds exciting."

"Jacob will probably toss an after-broadcast get-together, so don't expect to get to bed before dawn."

"That suits me fine. I've become an insomniac the past few days."

"Haven't we all." He downed the whisky, wishing instantly that he had not. It was time to leave before he staggered out. He set down the glass and walked toward her, with fierce concentration, and held out his hand. "I'm so glad . . . that . . . we've met again."

"So am I." She took his hand with a smile. "There's a taxi stand in Mount Street in front of Scott's."

"I know," he said thickly. "I . . . like Scott's. Best . . . oysters in the West End."

"You're a wonderful journalist . . . *Thax* . . . but as a crofter I doubt if you'd survive a winter."

She curled up on the sofa after he'd gone, nursing her tepid gin and holding a book. An hour later Victoria let herself in and flopped beside her, dropping her black beaded handbag on the floor.

"Lord, what an evening! Gerry was utterly boring . . . more so than usual. We had dinner with Noel and one or two others at Mario's. Noel talked about his new play and Gerry kept steering the conversation around to centerboards and spinnakers! I could have kicked him. *Non sequitur,* but why are you wearing my dress?"

"I had someone up for a drink."

"*You* did? I don't believe it. Who?"

"Oh, just a friend of the family."

"Your usual attire for friends of the family is either skirt and sweater or bathrobe and slippers. What caused you to filch a gown that just cost me a small fortune?"

She gave her a hard, straight look. "Because I wanted to look *extremely* pretty."

"For whom? Aunt Minerva's second cousin Bessie or someone like that?"

"Albert Thaxton, if you must know."

Victoria drew in her breath sharply. "He of the long lashes and bedroom eyes?"

"He's . . . very interesting and . . . extremely intelligent."

Victoria gave her a pitying look. "Do you really care about his mind? Oh, dear, it's not fair. He's going to be totally wasted on you."

"You have Gerald Smith Blair, Esquire."

"Yes," she sighed. "Worse luck. Oh, well, I won't be greedy. You do look ravishing in the dress. You can keep it if you like. Balmain designed it . . . just in case anyone should ask."

"It's very lovely. Thank you."

"And you'll be needing some other frilly things if you're starting an affair."

"Vicky! What a ridiculous remark."

"Sorry. I keep forgetting your vows of chastity." She yawned and stood up. "Well, I'm for bed. Staying up much longer?"

"Another chapter."

"I find Proust hard to take . . . especially when read upside down." She took the book from her sister's hands and turned it right way up. Then she bent forward and kissed her on the cheek. "That's all right, darling. Men. Sitting and thinking about them is half the fun."

MARTIN HAD BEGUN preparing for the broadcast while still in Munich. His recording engineer had set up a Rilkefunken wire recorder in the lobby of the Regina Palace Hotel and had described the arrival of Neville Chamberlain and his party. Chamberlain himself would not consent to an interview, but one of his aides had answered a few questions before hurrying off. The recording machine had then been taken to the Königsplatz across from the towering Führerbau where the conference with Hitler was to take place. The sounds of the city, the cheering crowds, the military bands, would add color to the broadcast. Martin, script in hand, sat at a table with Jacob, Churchill, Albert, and a Czech diplomat. The red second hand on the clock above the glass control booth flicked toward midnight. An engineer in the booth pointed his finger at Martin as a red light went on.

"Hello, America. This is Martin Rilke speaking to you from London . . ."

Jennifer listened to the broadcast in a visitor's lounge down the corridor from the studio. There were several other people in the room, men whose faces seemed familiar to her. Churchill's entourage, she suspected, by the way they smiled and nodded when he spoke. She found herself smiling when Albert answered some questions put to him by Martin. She had always thought Martin Rilke to be a quiet, humdrum man, like a well-meaning but ultimately boring uncle. Over the radio he was all snap and fire, leading his guests through the show with the verve of a symphony conductor—asking the right questions and easing into their replies if they started to ramble. The show covered a great deal of ground and seemed far longer than the scant fifteen minutes of allotted time. Martin had the final summation . . .

"And so Czechoslovakia has ceased to exist as a democratic nation. Tonight, German armies march unopposed across its once strongly defended borders. In the ceded territories, Sudeten Nazis raise the swastika flag and roam the streets marking the doors of Jewish and Czech homes and shops. Yesterday, Austria. Today, Czechoslovakia. And tomorrow?" Under his voice, faintly at first, then growing to a chilly crescendo, came the sounds recorded in the Königsplatz—the rhythmic tramp of hobnailed boots, trumpets, drums, the crowd roaring *Heil Hitler.* A moment of utter silence, followed by Martin's crisp sign-off . . . "Goodnight from London."

"Rather powerful," said one of the men. "A pity no one in this country heard it. I thought Winston was bang on form."

"Perhaps it might shake up the Yanks a bit."

The Churchill group left the room en masse and Jennifer waited alone, seated deep in a leather chair.

"Sorry you had to wait in here," Albert said as he hurried into the room. "I'd hoped you could have sat in the control booth, but they wouldn't allow it."

"It doesn't matter."

"Could you hear all right?"

"Perfectly. Your voice sounds different over the radio."

"Not too shrill, I hope."

"Far from it. Deep and resonant, like an actor's."

He laughed and helped her from the soft clutches of the chair. "I certainly didn't feel like an actor. I can't speak into a microphone without breaking into a cold sweat. I don't know how Martin can do it week after week."

He led her into the studio where Martin was waiting for the feedback from New York. It came . . . Scott Kingsford's voice booming at them . . . "Reception better than okay. Damn good show. Tell Winston I'm sending him a box of cigars."

"I should think so," Churchill growled as he stood up to go. "I can think of better places to be at midnight than the BBC."

"Care for a drink with us?" Martin asked.

Churchill shook his head. "I would like nothing better, but I must have a talk with Duff-Cooper. Some other time, mister radio man . . . some other time."

They went to Jacob Golden's townhouse in Berkeley Square. It was one of a row of fine old mansions, most of which had been converted into flats or office buildings. Jacob's house was a combination of the two. He maintained a spacious residence on the upper floors and had turned the lower into what he liked to call his command post. Teletype machines and shortwave radios kept him in touch with all branches of his far-flung press empire by day or night.

He led Jennifer on a tour of the new communications room where the night staff tended the chattering teletype machines.

"I don't see enough of you these days, Jenny . . . or of your mother. How is she?"

"Very well. Busy."

"She must be pleased that Chamberlain . . . pulled it off, as they say."

"I don't know, I haven't talked to her about it. But knowing her sense of fair play I think she may have mixed emotions."

"Yes," he mused. "She may at that. Winnie was always more of an idealist than a pacifist anyway . . . but don't tell her I said so." He gave her hand a quick squeeze. "I must say, I was surprised to see you arrive with my man Thax. How long has this been going on?"

She felt her cheeks burn. "Nothing's . . . 'going on,' Uncle Jacob."

"No? Pity."

They went upstairs where drinks were being served and a cold supper had been laid out. There were a dozen or so guests, most of them members of Martin's CBC radio team. Martin took Jennifer in hand and introduced her to them. They were young men, easygoing and casual, referring to Martin as either "Chief" or "Pop." They had spent most of their time on the Continent and were unfamiliar with London. Clustering around her, they wanted to know where the best "hot spots" were to be found. She answered as best she could, but they would have been better served by her twin. Vicky knew every dive in London. Albert, bearing a glass of champagne in each hand, extricated her.

"The most popular girl at the party."

"The *only* girl. That might account for it."

"So you are. I hadn't noticed." He handed her a glass. "Something very Edwardian about serving champagne and oysters at one in the morning."

"I could do without both."

"There's a duck pâté that looks good."

She took a small sip of her wine and set the glass on a table. "I don't really want anything. Fresh air, perhaps."

"Not feeling well?"

"Claustrophobic all of a sudden. I don't know why."

"Would you like to go home?"

"I think so. I'll just slip out."

"Don't be daft. I'll go with you."

"It's not necessary. It's only a short way."

"I know, but the streets are crawling with white slavers at this hour. Seriously, I wouldn't think of allowing you to go home by yourself. Chivalry may be dormant in jolly old England, but not totally dead."

It was beautiful in the square, clear and brisk. Taxis rattled past on their way to the May Fair Hotel in Berkeley Street.

Jennifer looked up at the stars and took a deep breath. "That's better. I love London at this time of the morning. The air feels so fresh."

"A million buses off the streets."

"I'm sure that has something to do with it." She started to walk in the direction of her flat and then hesitated. "I don't feel like going home. Are you up to a walk?"

"Fine. Where would you like to go?"

"Oh, I don't much care. Just around."

"I believe all walks should have a destination."

"You choose, then."

"Soho. I'll show you my digs and brew some coffee."

"You don't seem the Soho type."

"I'm not," he said as they started across the square. "I'm too gainfully employed for the neighborhood. But Martin leased me his old flat years ago. It's a big place above a Russian restaurant in James Street. It belonged to Jacob Golden at one time, before the war."

"I don't imagine you spend much time in it."

"Not since I left university. But I'll be using it now . . . at least for the next six months or so. Jacob's decided to keep me in England."

"Oh? You don't sound happy at the thought."

"I would have preferred a foreign assignment, but he believes I can be of more use here. The *Post* will be starting an all-out campaign to get Churchill back into the government and to thrust the rearmament program into full gear. I'm not sure how we're going to do it, but he's given me a week's holiday to think it over."

"I'm sure you could use a holiday. Fatten yourself up. Where are you going?"

"I have no idea. I might take a run up to Cambridge for a day or two and see how young Colin is settling in."

"But haven't you heard? Colin's left . . . he sailed for New York three days ago."

He stopped walking and stared at her. "Gone? But why?"

She told him of the trouble in Manchester as they walked on toward Regent Street, of how the reporter had dropped all charges, but not before writing a mocking story in *Foto-Mail* about the "Cambridge Cowboy." The whole experience had embittered him so much he had decided to go back to California.

"Archer," Albert said. "That horse's arse. If I ever run into him he'll have a *real* assault case to write about. It must be upsetting to Lord and Lady Stanmore."

"Mother talked to them. They're philosophic about the whole thing—it's Kate who was devastated. I never realized how fond she was of him . . . a major crush, it seems. She went back to school in utter misery."

The Soho streets were crowded, all the restaurants and private clubs ablaze with lights. At the Café Moskva, singing and music spilled into the narrow street in a melodic flood. Albert unlocked a door beside the café's entrance and led Jennifer up a steep flight of dimly lit stairs. He switched on a lamp, revealing a spacious, comfortably furnished room with crammed bookshelves rising from floor to ceiling.

"Interesting," Jennifer said, glancing about. "The place has a good deal of character."

"That it does. A perfect flat for anyone who appreciates balalaikas. I only pay Martin a token and I'm rarely here, so it would be foolish to find anything more modern and less noisy at this stage of my life."

"A place to hang your hat."

"Exactly—if I owned one to hang."

He made coffee in a brass contraption that looked like a miniature ship's boiler. "Something Jacob brought back from Bulgaria in the twenties, I understand. Looks fearsome, but produces a unique brew."

She took a tentative sip. It was thick as syrup and bitter as gall. "*Unique* is the proper word."

"You don't like it?"

"Perhaps if I were Bulgarian . . ."

"I usually lace it with Drambuie or Grand Marnier."

She held out her cup. "By all means use both."

Jennifer carried the potent mixture around the room, looking at the books. Albert trailed along beside her.

"Cheap editions mostly. When I was at university I used to haunt the used-book shops in Charing Cross Road. The better-looking volumes belonged to a long-time tenant of Martin's, a writer and a recluse. He was trying to write the definitive history of mankind, a twenty-volume work, but gave up in despair halfway through the first. Killed himself, poor chap."

"By drinking the coffee?"

"Quite possibly," he laughed. "Off London Bridge, actually. Anyway, I was glad he didn't do himself in here. I didn't relish his anguished ghost knocking about."

She stood still, head cocked, listening. "I can hear groaning."

"Downstairs. The Russians. They get drunk and maudlin about now and start singing dark songs of the Volga."

Jennifer finished her drink and handed him the cup. "One more of these and I'd be joining them."

"Feeling light-headed?"

"A bit."

"They affect me the same way. Must be the Drambuie. Would you care for a glass of water?"

"No thanks." He took the cups into the kitchen and dumped what was left of the coffee. It flowed down the sink like oil. When he came back she was seated on the couch, her head back and eyes half closed. The shaded lamp threw a soft wash of pink across her throat.

"You must be exhausted," he said, looking down at her. "I'll go scare up a taxi."

"Not just yet. I was listening to the music. There's something so sad and . . . lost . . . about Russian melodies."

"That tune certainly is. It's always the last one of the night. I asked old Vassilievich about it once. He owns the place . . . an ex-colonel in the Imperial Russian Guards . . . although they always say they were something grand. He was probably a cook. Anyway, he explained it was a folk song about a dying Cossack dreaming of the homeland he will never see again."

"One can't get much sadder than that."

He leaned toward her and pressed his lips against her throat. She opened her eyes and stared at him, almost in curiosity. "I hope you didn't mind," he said.

"No. Should I?"

"Taking advantage. Balalaikas and brandy. An unfair mixture, like moonlight and roses."

"I suppose it is . . . yet pleasant."

"Certainly that." He sat on the couch and drew her to him. Her lips and body were rigid as he kissed her. Then she was soft against him, pliant as wax. His tongue felt the moistness of her mouth. She pulled back from him with a throaty gasp.

"I . . . should go now."

"If you wish."

"It's best . . . I think."

"Yes. It's terribly late."

"If you would call a cab . . ."

He smiled at her and touched her cheek. "One doesn't call cabs at this hour. We walk around the corner to the White Mouse Club where the taxis wait."

"What's the White Mouse Club?"

"A private social spot for well-heeled businessmen. A nunnery in the Shakespearean sense of the word."

She stared at him, brushing a strand of hair from her forehead. "I see. An interesting neighborhood."

"A bachelor's paradise—or so they say."

"Not to you?"

"I'm not here often enough to find out."

He took hold of her hand as they went down the stairs under the appalling gloom of the low-wattage bulb. The hand seemed quite lifeless to him, rigid as a mannequin's. In the street, he could see her expression in the brighter glow of the lights. Her face, he thought, was a mask of either boredom or indifference. He did not attempt to hold her hand, or to touch her in any way, as they walked around the corner into Bridle Lane where taxis were lined up in front of a darkly shuttered building. Albert stepped into the road and whistled for one of them.

Jennifer broke the silence between them as the taxi plunged into the now deserted streets of Mayfair.

"I had a most enjoyable evening."

"I'm glad. I know I did."

"I'm sorry your holiday plans were spoiled."

"That doesn't matter. I'm just sorry for poor Colin. I'll find things to do. Day trips to Clacton-on-Sea, and other such thrilling excursions."

There was an eternity of silence and then she said: "I'm rather at loose ends. Perhaps we could do something together."

"I would enjoy your company."

"And I yours." The taxi pulled up in front of her building and she got out. "Why don't you phone me on Monday and we'll work something out."

"I'll do that."

"Good." She shook his hand with a crisp formality—but the hand lingered, the fingers touched.

HE TELEPHONED HER on Monday morning and she suggested a drive in the country, to Lulworth Manor in Dorset. Would that be all right with him?

"Whatever you'd like to do," he said.

"Good. I knew you'd agree. I ordered a hamper for us from Fortnum and Mason."

"A what?"

"A picnic hamper . . . sandwiches, cold chicken. Much nicer than those horrid little roadside inns. I'll pick you up at eleven."

She was there on the dot, pulling up in front of his door in her little green Sunbeam, the top folded back, a wicker basket strapped to the luggage rack. She was wearing slacks and a sweater, a green bandanna tied around her head to keep her hair from blowing. He got in beside her.

"You can drive if you'd like," she told him.

"No, no. You look too enchanting behind the wheel."

She pressed the gas pedal and shot away, threading into the London traffic.

It was impossible to talk over the snarl of the engine and the howling wind, so Albert sat back, face tilted to the sun, and enjoyed the drive. She turned off the main highway at last and drove along narrow lanes through a lush, verdant countryside and past hamlets of thatched-roof houses. An iron gate barred the end of one particularly deserted lane and she stopped the car, leaving the engine running, unlocked the gate and swung it open.

"Where are we?" he asked as she got back into the car.

"Lulworth Manor."

"Which is?"

"My grandfather's estate. No one lives here now except a caretaker and his wife. It's a lovely old house, though, and the grounds are beautiful in a wild, overgrown sort of way."

She was right on all counts. The house came into view, a Georgian mansion of gray stone perched on a hill with a magnificent view of the Channel and Lulworth Cove. Unpruned evergreens and the tangled thickets of what had once been a garden surrounded it. The house seemed to be rising from a jungle of native European flora.

"Good Lord," he said. "What on earth are the caretakers for?"

"Not much. They're quite ancient. Keep the inside of the house from being swallowed in dust, I suppose. None of the family have lived here in years and no one seems willing to buy the place."

"Make a smashing resort hotel."

"That's Grandfather's fervent wish. It's a horrible white elephant, but I do love the place."

She stopped at the caretakers' cottage to pay her respects to them—a pleasant couple who seemed as weathered as the stones of the house, and as strong—and then drove on for half a mile and parked on the edge of a meadow that sloped toward low cliffs and the sea.

"Chicken in herbs," she said, unpacking the basket and placing the items on a blanket. "Potted shrimp . . . deviled eggs . . . sliced ham . . . French rolls . . . cheeses . . . a bottle of Chablis, a bottle of claret . . ."

"Stop! Did you invite six other people?"

"You should put on some weight. I think you're far too thin."

"I've seen an infantry company exist on less food than this." He filched a pickled onion from a jar. "Looks jolly nice, though. Must have cost you a ruddy fortune."

"A pretty penny, as the saying goes." She snapped her fingers. "But who counts the cost for an occasion such as this?"

"What sort of occasion is it?"

"Being with good company on a sunny, windy day. God in

his heaven and all that." She bit into a chicken wing and gazed across the wind-tossed grasses. The Channel was gray-green and flecked with whitecaps. "I used to swim in that cold sea when I was a child, even at this time of the year. I would hate to do so now."

"God forbid." He rummaged in the basket. "They even provided a corkscrew and two glasses. White or red?"

"Red. It warms the blood better."

"Chilly?"

"Not yet, but it's time to get fortified. Those clouds blowing in will cover the sun in about an hour."

The clouds did more than that and in less time. They brought a misty rain swirling in on the wind. Albert struggled to put up the canvas top while Jennifer hurriedly repacked the basket and carried it to the car. There were no side curtains and they huddled in the seats with the picnic blanket drawn around them like a tent.

"It'll blow over in a few minutes," Albert said.

She shook her head. "I know this coast. It'll get a good deal worse before it gets better. We could go to the caretakers' cottage. They'll have a fire going."

"Do you want to?"

"Not unless you do. I'm quite cozy here. Is there any claret left?"

"Nearly half a bottle. I stuck it behind the seat."

He half turned to reach back for it, brushing against her as he did so. She placed her hands against his chest, moving her palms lightly across the softness of his sweater. She arched her back and strained against him as he put his arms around her and kissed her, her hands sliding to the small of his back, pressing him closer.

"You're very lovely," he whispered against her mouth. "Beautiful."

She pulled her head back, eyes closed, lips parted. "I've never felt quite this way."

He smiled and kissed the hollow of her throat. "Deviled eggs and red wine."

She rested her head on the back of the seat and studied him with a grave, thoughtful expression. "I couldn't get you off my mind yesterday. Found it hard to go to sleep last night. I kept thinking of you . . . that flat . . . the Russians and their sad songs. I'm really not myself today."

"Aren't you? I rather like you this way. How are you usually?"

"More . . . in control of myself."

"You seem calm enough to me."

"Not inside. I . . . I think I'm falling in love with you, Thax."

He drew away from her and watched the rain pelt against the windshield, driven almost horizontal by the wind. "I *know* I love you, Jenny. Knew it the moment I saw you that day at Abingdon Pryory. A reporter's instinct."

"Have you ever been in love before?"

"Every second Tuesday when I was in college."

"What were they like?"

"I can't remember one face. Just girls to go to the pictures with or the pubs, argue philosophy and the state of the world. Undergraduate romance. Intense but shallow."

"Yes. I felt the same way about a man in India once. A Lieutenant someone-or-other. He had a small mustache."

"Well, there you are. Can't take a chap with a small mustache seriously, can you?"

"I can take you seriously," she said, the words barely audible over the rain.

He tapped his fingers against the dash. "Not the wisest idea, perhaps. Journalists and sailors."

"What my sister would refer to as 'no-strings.' None at all."

He looked at her and she was staring at him. He could feel her intensity, her need. He reached for her hands and squeezed them between his own. "Shall we go back to London, Jenny?"

"Yes," she said firmly, leaning toward the starter button. "As quickly as possible."

HE LAY NAKED on the bed under a sheet and watched her come into the room in his bathrobe. The light had faded and the glow cast by the restaurant sign bathed the room in soft green and gold. She walked slowly to the bed and sat beside him, one hand holding the edges of the robe together. He smiled at her and said, in mellifluous tones: "And now Miss J. Wood-Lacy looking a vision in this season's fabric rage . . . tattered terry by Prince Albertino of Milan."

She did not laugh as she curled her body beside him and rested her head on his chest. Her hair was still damp from the bath. "I feel . . . so odd all of a sudden, Thax."

"Do you?" He stroked her shoulder, the familiar cloth, threadbare and in need of a wash. "Nothing odd about feeling odd."

"I've never . . . made love before."

"Really? What a shocking surprise. And you ten times married and only twice divorced." He sat up on one elbow and brushed his lips across her cheek. "No wonder you're nervous. Nothing like rituals to take the starch out of anyone. Do you trust me?"

"Yes," she whispered.

"Then get dressed. We're going downstairs for dinner. Borscht with sour cream . . . shaslik or stroganoff . . . solianka, and pony glasses of ice-cold vodka. How does that sound to you?"

She raised her head, smiling at him. "Lovely."

"And then, my darling, you can drive to your cozy flat in your cozy little car, or you can come back up here." He teased her lips with his. "Either way . . . I love you."

HE STOOD IN front of the window at dawn and glanced out across Lower James Street. It was silent below except for the gentle gurgle of rain down the drainpipes. Beyond the shadowed buildings he could hear the steady, never ceasing hum of the city, constant as blood coursing through living veins. Walking back to the bed he looked down at Jennifer sleeping peacefully under the blankets. Her face was in profile on the pillow, mouth parted, a wisp of dark hair across her forehead. She held the pillow in her arms and this movement had pulled down the blankets below her bare shoulders to reveal one small, uptilted breast.

He put on the terry-cloth robe—that now and forever held the scent of her body—and went into the kitchen. He put water on the gas ring and then walked into the drawing room and turned on the lamp over the large table he used as a desk. All the papers that had been sent over by messenger on Sunday were stacked beside his typewriter along with a note from Jacob. He glanced at the note again while waiting for the kettle to begin singing . . .

Thax: Just a few things for you to read while on holiday. These are the very latest figures on aircraft, ship, tank, weapons, etc., production in U.K. and the counterpart production figures from Germany. Cannot totally rely on the German figures as being completely accurate or up to date, but they do give a relationship between what they have and we have which is frightening in its implications. A sense of defeatism is endemic here, as you know, and is constantly being fed by statements from Col. Lindbergh and the American ambassador, both of whom see Germany . . .

The kettle whistled for him and he made a small pot of tea which he took to his desk.

. . . Thax, the widely accepted "fact" that six hundred thousand English men, women and children would die in the first Luftwaffe raid is utter nonsense. Such a figure would only be possible if we had not one fighter plane to oppose them and if the great mass of our population stood dumbly in the streets and allowed themselves to be massacred. Your articles must stress need for continued air-raid precaution drills and stress and stress again the deterrent factors of (1) Spitfire-equipped fighter squadrons and (2) the four-engine bombers still in desultory planning stage, planes capable of hitting any

part of Germany with fourteen-thousand-pound bomb loads—six times the capacity of their Dorniers. You must also point out . . .

He sipped his tea. A clock ticked on the mantel. He could hear the *clop-clop* of the milkman's horse entering the street from Golden Square. Seven-ton bomb loads and Spitfire fighters! Death's gray instruments.

He set his cup of tea on the table, switched off the lamp, and went back into the bedroom. Jennifer was still deeply asleep, lying on her back now, arms flung behind her head. He took off the robe and slipped under the covers, pressing his body against the warm loveliness of her, fingers touching the smooth, rounded flesh where blood pulsed and life flowed.

10

SHE WAS DISCREET but knew it would be only a matter of time before it dawned on someone in her family that she was having an affair. She had lunch with her mother at the Savoy one afternoon in early November.

"I had a long talk with Vicky yesterday," Winifred said, toying with the orange in her Manhattan. "She told me she doesn't see much of you lately."

"I know, but I've been terribly busy."

"Doing what?"

"Oh, a million things. Research mostly . . . organizing notes and material . . . typing and using a Dictaphone machine. Honing the skills I learned at Calthorpe's."

She eyed her daughter closely. "I must say, the work seems to agree with you. I've never seen you look so . . . radiant."

"Thank you, Mama. I feel radiant, as a matter of fact."

"And who are you doing all this work for?"

"A journalist on . . . one of the dailies." She picked up the menu and studied it. "How does the *coquilles St. Jacques* sound to you?"

"Does he pay you much?"

"Not too much, but money's not important, is it? I mean to say, if one is happy at a job . . ."

"Do you work in Fleet Street?"

"Fleet Street? Not exactly."

"Where then?"

"Really, Mama, why this sudden curiosity?"

"I hardly relish being an inquisitor, Jenny, and I know that it's none of my business. You are free to do what you wish, but it's not like you to be anything but forthright. You've pretty much moved in with him, haven't you?"

"Yes. I spend a lot of time with him."

"Vicky put two and two together and came up with Albert Thaxton. Is that right?" She could see the answer in her daughter's eyes. "He was a charming boy and I imagine he turned into a charming man. Why are you ashamed of him?"

"Ashamed? He's the most wonderful person in the world."

"Then why be so circumspect? Sharing a quiet love affair is hardly a hanging offense."

Jennifer stirred her martini with the speared olive. "I was going to tell everyone about him sooner or later. When I felt certain this would last."

"Last? Affairs either end or turn into something far more complex."

"I feel certain this one will turn into something grand. It's not just sexual attraction."

"I hope so, although passion can be a powerful reason to stay together. But passion, to the degree you obviously feel it now, can't last forever. What turns a love affair into something richer is love itself . . . the love of sharing . . . common goals and purposes . . . the unselfishness of blending two lives into one."

"I understand, Mama. I enjoy being with him, helping him with his job, being around him. I believe with all my heart that we can make a go of it."

"Well," Winifred said, raising her glass, "you certainly have my blessing."

"Thank you. I hope Daddy is as understanding."

"Dear Jenny," she laughed, "if he could cope with Vicky all these years he can certainly adjust to you."

They led a quiet life, rarely going out or having more than four friends in for dinner, but as the new year approached Jennifer decided they should throw a party.

"How do the hors d'oeuvres sound to you?" she asked one night, coming into the drawing room with a notebook in her hand. "Caviar, smoked Scotch salmon with capers on toast squares, assorted canapés and pâtés."

Albert, hunched in front of his typewriter, glanced up in bemusement. "I beg your pardon?"

"You didn't hear one word I said."

"Sorry. I was thinking of something."

"What?"

"The Churchill-Baldwin debates of 1935."

She put the notepad on the table and sat on his lap. "That's what I love about you, Thax. I need help with the menu and you're drifting in the past with Stanley Baldwin."

He slid a hand inside her silk pajamas. "I've always found something highly erotic about Baldwin and his thick wool suits."

She pushed his hand away. “Stop, please. You’re always trying to turn me into a wanton.”

“I don’t have to try very hard.”

“No. I’m easily aroused and you ruddy well know it.”

“Menu,” he said. “Fish and chips will do nicely.”

“Be serious.”

“I’ve already discussed the matter with Vassily. A dinner fit for a czar, he said. He just needs to know how many to cook for.”

“About thirty, I expect.”

He whistled softly. “Can we cram that many in?”

“With a little rearranging of furniture. A man with your vast circle of friends will need a larger place one day.”

“With room for a nursery?”

She got slowly from his lap and leaned back against the edge of the table facing him. “I promised no strings, Thax. Remember?”

“Yes.”

“Is this a proposal?”

“Let’s say it’s a proposal for a proposal. I wouldn’t want to spring anything on you. Girls should be prepared for all sorts of surprises . . . clean undies in case of an accident. That sort of thing. We love one another. There has to be more to a marriage than that, but at least we’ve passed the first test with colors flying.”

“Three months. Still honeymoon fever.”

“In a manner of speaking.” He reached out and drew her to him gently. “And a delightful fever it is, too.”

“Yes,” she said, touching his face. “More satisfying than I ever thought possible.”

SHE SANK INTO sleep, his body curved against her back, an arm around her in comforting possession. But in her dreams there was only an immense hollowness . . . shadows of emptiness. She was standing in a room, windows flung wide to face an empty sea. The room seemed endless, vast walls and floors stretching away forever. All empty. And there was such sadness, a longing for something irretrievably lost. She sat up with a strangled sob, hands pressed to her mouth. Perhaps the cry had only been in the dream. He had not stirred. His breathing as gentle as the snow drifting against the windowpanes.

"Is that the last article?" she asked at breakfast.

He glanced from the typewritten sheets propped against the sugar bowl. "Of this series. I have to go to the office this morning for a conference with John, Farnsworth, and Jacob. Map out what's needed for the next group."

"Any ideas?"

"A few. Along the lines Jacob discussed. Resurgent, vital Britain. Rising employment and humming factories; a commitment to defend our shores and our skies; an assurance to foreign investors and customers that we will never be added to Hitler's list of enslaved people."

She clapped her hands. "Bravo! When are you standing for Parliament?"

"Very amusing. Anyway, you get the idea. It will mean a few trips to Coventry, Birmingham, Sheffield, and etcetera. You're more than welcome to come along."

"All the garden spots of the realm."

"Sorry. I'll try to do my next research on the Riviera."

She poured them both coffee. "How long will this take?"

"I'm not sure. A month or two."

"And then?"

He shrugged, reaching for the cream. "Journalists and sailors, remember? Always prepared to sail where the wind blows."

"Not all journalists. Take John Baker . . . or Farnsworth."

"Editors, my pet. A different breed of cat."

"I think you'd make a marvelous editor."

"Thank you. Perhaps in twenty years . . . when my old backside yearns for a padded swivel chair." He caught sight of the wall clock. "Cripes, getting late."

She watched from the drawing-room window as he hurried toward a taxi, fending off the sleet with his umbrella. A man going to work—as thousands of others were doing on this cold London morning.

THE GREAT BELLS rang the hour—the final midnight of the year. From St. Paul's and St. Clement Danes and on across the city, peal by jubilant peal. In Soho, people took to the streets with rattles and paper horns. From the Café Moskva came the strains of "Auld Lang Syne" played on balalaika and violin. The sound drifted to the upstairs flat.

A correspondent from Reuters, who had been with Albert in Spain, raised his glass and expressed the sentiments of just about everyone in the room. "Farewell nineteen thirty-eight. Jolly glad to see you go!"

"I will always cherish nineteen thirty-eight," Jennifer whispered as she gave Albert a kiss.

He smiled and kissed her back. "I shall cherish the year as well."

SHE DID THE driving on the wintry roads while Albert huddled beside her, working on his notes or coaxing the heater to give a little more warmth. Coventry and Birmingham, Sheffield and Manchester—a similarity of bleakness. Factories, foundries . . . aircraft assembly plants, rolling mills. Nights in provincial hotels, correlating the day's notes, typing the rough drafts. A hard but exciting trip for Jennifer, seeing a Britain she had never seen before. Oldham and Merseyside, Newcastle and Jarrow. Albert collected the background material he needed in three weeks and they returned to London.

Her sense of unease began to grow the closer he came to finishing the articles. The clatter of his typewriter in the small hours of the morning seemed almost ominous to her as she lay sleepless in bed. When she did fall asleep, she would often have the dream . . . the empty rooms and deserted landscapes . . . the aching feeling of loneliness.

He took her down to the paper as the edition carrying the first article in the series started through the giant presses. He handed her a copy, still smelling of ink. There was gaudy artwork . . . the British lion baring its fangs . . .

THE LION HAS TEETH

A. E. Thaxton

"You can keep it as a souvenir," he shouted in her ear.

She yelled back: "I will. A lot of my own sweat went into it."

He put an arm around her and led her out of the cavernous room, the presses thundering like the machinery of some gargantuan ship.

"You need a suitable reward," he said as they took a lift up to the ground floor. "Let's say . . . champagne and dinner at the Ritz."

"Let's settle for pink gins and a mixed grill at that chop house in Magpie Alley."

"Jolly good for you. Spoken like a true Fleet Streeter."

The interior was dark oak, smoky, and pungent with the smell of beer, whisky, and meat spluttering on red-hot grills. It had been the haunt of Fleet Street journalists and lawyers from the nearby Temple for over a century. They squeezed into a corner booth near the long, crowded bar.

"To you," she said, lifting her glass.

"To us."

John Baker, a hefty, red-faced man of forty who looked like a rugby player and dressed like a Piccadilly dandy, leaned toward them from the bar, a whisky soda clenched in one beefy paw. " 'Allo, Jennifer . . . Thax. Bloody good opener, what? The lion has teeth, indeed! Eye catcher."

"I hope so," Albert said quietly.

"And congrats to you, Thax. Your name's on the list. Jacob the golden one passed *me* up, but that was to be expected, what?"

Albert downed his drink and signaled a waiter for another. "Too useful where you are, Johnnie. No one could run the city desk like you. It purrs like a watch."

"Or ticks like a cat, old lad. Yes, I know what you mean. There is oft a penalty for being too bloody good at what one does. I shall no doubt get a hefty raise if I know Jacob. Compensation for the slight, which I will squander on pointless frivolities."

"God broke the mold when he made him," Albert said after the editor had moved off down the bar.

"What was he talking about? Congratulations for being on what list?"

"Oh, nothing much to speak of. A guessing game going on at the paper."

"About what?"

"It's hardly worth mentioning. Let's order. I'm starved."

"I really would like to know," she persisted.

The waiter brought his drink and he ordered two mixed grills. Sipping the gin, he looked at her and noticed the tautness of her expression, the anxiety in her eyes. "Very well. Jacob's forming a new venture . . . *Weekly Post.* A news magazine, fairly condensed stories of the week's happenings. On the order of the American weeklies. There will be an editor-in-chief and four sub-editors. At least ten people that I know of are in line for the jobs."

She let out her breath slowly. "And you're one of them?" Her hand impulsively found his. "But . . . how wonderful. How completely and absolutely marvelous!" She sat back against the seat with a deep sigh, as though relieved of some terrible burden. "I'm certain Jacob will choose you. Foreign-affairs editor . . . that would be perfect for someone with your qualifications."

"There are many men with my qualifications."

"I'm sure there must be, but you could do the job as well as any of them. Didn't Jacob say anything about it when you saw him yesterday?"

"He dropped a hint or two . . . and I let him know my feelings. But let's get off the subject. I was thinking that we could do with a week's holiday. What would you say to this . . . fly to Paris in a few days and take a suite at the Crillon—the honeymoon suite, Jenny."

"Well," she said softly, "not the most romantic atmosphere for a proposal. No moon or starlight, not even a violin."

"Lamp chops and sausages spluttering on a grill."

"Original. But then you're different from most men in all ways. Yes, Thax. I rather like that idea."

"I realize that Vicky and Gerald will be having a stylish wedding at St. George's, Hanover Square . . . bridesmaids and rice. Sorry to make you settle for a registry office."

"I like registry offices, not that I've ever been in one, but they sound so solidly official. The awesome power of the British civil service behind our *I dos.*"

The food came—chops, sausage, grilled kidney and tomato, crusty potatoes. Jennifer ate with gusto and exhilaration.

"I was thinking," she said. "We should redecorate the flat. To be practical, we shouldn't rush a nursery for a year or two. Soho may not be as chic as Chelsea, but one couldn't find a flat there of that size for love or money. And besides, Colonel-Cook Vassilievich would be desolated if we left. We could turn the spare bedroom into a proper office for you. Bookshelves on three walls, some good oak files. Replace *all* the furniture. We could take a run down to Lulworth Manor and loot what we wanted. There are so many lovely pieces enshrouded in dust cloths . . . Sheraton and Hepplewhite . . ."

Albert picked at his food. "I think that's a good idea. It will keep you occupied."

"*Us,* dear. The week may belong to Uncle Jacob, but your weekends belong to me—and I shall tell him so. No seven-day labors for you."

He pushed his plate aside, the meal barely touched. "I told Jacob yesterday that I wouldn't join the magazine staff. I told him why and he agreed with my reasons. My name was on that list, Jenny, but it's scratched off now."

She could only stare at him numbly for a moment. "I don't understand."

"I'm not suited to be an editor of other men's work. I'm a reporter, foreign correspondent—call it what you will. I find the story and write it. It's what I do and I do it well. It's what I want to do now."

"*You* want to do," she said hollowly.

He felt shaken, looking at her beautiful, stricken face. "I know you'd prefer me to work in London, but that's not possible."

"Yes it is." Her voice had an edge of anger to it.

"Hitler's on the verge of taking over Bohemia and Slovakia, Jenny, not Kent and Surrey. The story is in Prague, and if all the guesses are right, Warsaw in a few months' time."

"Any number of reporters could go."

He attempted a smile but found it difficult. "I know how disappointed you must feel. It's been wonderful being together the past few months, but I won't be going away forever."

"How long were you in Spain?"

"Thirteen, fourteen months, but . . ."

She shook her head. "I won't let you go without me."

"That's just not possible. The situation there is too perilous, even if I could get you a travel permit. Look, Jenny, there are going to be many trips we can take together, but not to countries that are on the brink of war. I won't be gone too long and when I get back—"

"Stop it!" she said fiercely. "You sound like my father. My mother had to listen to that all her life. I won't be an . . . *army wife!*"

She slid out of the booth and stood up. He reached out and held her arm. "Where are you going?"

"I must get some air. Please don't follow me. I want to think this out alone."

He reluctantly let go of her sleeve. "Will you be coming home later?"

"Home?" A bitter little smile hardened her mouth. "We don't have a home, Thax."

THE MARQUESS OF Dexford lay dying in his London house. He was eighty-two and had lived a good life. He was experiencing a slow but painless decline and there was nothing to be done that would reverse the inevitable. He lay sleeping in his bed, nurses in constant attendance watching over him.

The doctor slipped the stethoscope from his ears and straightened up. "No change," he said to Winifred. "I see no point in giving him any more digitalis."

"No," she said, reaching down and touching her father's cheek. "He looks so peaceful."

"He is—and thank God for it."

They left the room and walked down the winding stairs to the front hall.

"I'll call back this evening."

"It's almost over now, isn't it?"

"Yes, Winifred. Just a matter of time. Could be days . . . or even hours. Do your brothers know?"

"They're flying up from Capetown. Should be here tomorrow."

"Not that he'd know. Still, it's nice to have one's family

about you." He caught sight of Jennifer standing in the open door of the library. "Hello, Jennifer . . . or is it Victoria?"

"Jennifer, Dr. Powell."

"Brought the two of you into this world and still can't tell you apart. You're the oldest . . . by about five minutes."

"I wondered why I felt so ancient."

She poured two cups of tea while her mother was seeing the doctor out. "I took the liberty," she said, handing a cup to her as she came into the library.

"Thanks," Winifred sighed. "I need it."

"How's Grandfather?"

"The same. Dying."

"I'm sorry. It must be an awful strain on you."

"He had a long, good life, Jenny, and he's just drifting away in sleep. I'm grateful for that."

They sat side by side on a sofa, Jennifer stiffly, holding the cup between her hands. "You haven't said a word about my going back to stay with Vicky."

"I assumed something happened between you and Albert and that if you wanted to tell me about it you would."

"He left for Prague yesterday. He wanted to marry me before he left. I said no."

"I see." She took a sip of her tea. "Actually, I don't see at all. I was under the impression you loved him."

"I do."

"Then why?"

"Love isn't enough. I want more out of a marriage."

"It would suffice for most people."

"Was it always enough for you, Mama? Weren't there times . . . when it was not nearly enough?"

"We . . . had some difficult periods, yes."

"The plight of the army wife."

"My early years with your father were more difficult than most. We were separated often, and for such long stretches of time. That was before Kate was born. He was always a stormy petrel and the War Office wanted to be rid of him. So they gave him the worst possible tours of duty in an attempt to force him out. God knows I was on their side and tried my best to make him resign. Nothing would have made me happier than to have seen him with a job in a civvy street. Father had lined up a position for him with an insurance company." She laughed. "Can you imagine your father going off to work every morning in a dark suit and a bowler?"

"You didn't laugh at the idea then, did you?"

"No. Not then." She looked away to the tall windows. An oblong of pale, March sky. The trees of Cadogan Square. "I shall be candid, Jenny. There were moments when I hated him for the type of life he forced me to live. He hung on to his commission through stubbornness and pride and we both suffered for it. There was even a time when I thought I could leave him."

"Jacob Golden," Jennifer said in a flat tone.

Winifred stiffened. "Why do you say that?"

"A child's perceptions. A way you would glance at one another. It's true, isn't it?"

"Yes. We had an affair. Brief. Intense. I wished with all my heart that I didn't love your father as much as I did. I felt that I could be happy with Jacob. He sensed my turmoil and confusion and used his political power to force the army into recalling Fenton from Iraq and appointing him to the staff college. It was Jacob's ultimate gift of love."

Jennifer set down her teacup and put her arms around her mother, resting her head against her shoulder. "I'm glad you told me. What do you think would have happened if Papa had left the army when you wanted him to?"

"It would have destroyed the very qualities I loved. I had married a soldier—for better for worse."

"Oh, Mama, I don't know what to do. I feel so torn. I always swore that my children would never live my sort of life—no proper home, always moving or being separated. Those officers' wives in India used to haunt me. Frittering away their days at the club while their husbands were off on the frontier for months at a time. Playing too much bridge. Drinking too much sherry. Having their sordid little affairs like Major Bill's Dora. I would think, God, don't let that happen to me. I used to envy Cynthia Morrison with a passion because her father was in civil service and came home every night."

Winifred smiled, turned her head, and kissed her on the cheek. "Dear Jenny. You're just angry because Albert didn't fit your perfect dream. He had the temerity to want to live his own kind of life. But you knew what he did. He doesn't work in an office. A foreign correspondent, and according to Martin and Jacob one of the best. I can't tell you what to do now. I can only tell you what *I* would do."

"And that is?"

"Follow my heart."

TELETYPES

IT IS MARCH 15, 1939—the ides of March—and the assassins strut through the streets of Prague. German motorcycle troops and panzers roar across the Charles Bridge above the icy blue Moldau. Adolf Hitler gazes down on the city from the ancient castle of the Bohemian kings. It is snowing and cold but he is as elated as a child with a new toy. He has swept another country into the Reich without firing a shot. He has liberated the Czech people from the clutches of Jews, Bolsheviks, and democracy.

BRITISH NEWSMAN JACKBOOTED OUT

Prague (UP) March 18, 1939. A. E. Thaxton, veteran war correspondent for London's *Daily Post,* was ordered to leave Prague today by order of the German Gestapo. No reason was given for . . .

There is apathy in France. A shrug of the shoulder. A gesture with the hands. Hitler will take what he wants. There is no point in treaties. The Maginot line stands sullen and powerful from the Ardennes to the Swiss border. There is no danger to the west. Hitler would never bloody his legions against French cannon.

Neville Chamberlain is stunned and humiliated. The press, even his own cabinet, has rebelled against his infuriatingly conciliatory attitudes toward Hitler's move. His umbrella of peace has become as much a caricature as Colonel Blimp in his bath towel. *Babes in the Wood* plays at London's Unity Theatre. The witty satire on the bumbling politics of appeasement has theatergoers rolling in the aisles. It's all in fun, but no one at Number 10 Downing Street feels any inclination to laugh. It is finally too much for the prime minister. He is an honorable gentleman with a deep, passionate hatred of war. But he has been played the confidence trick, cheated and lied to. In a speech in Birmingham he turns no cheek.

> What has become of Herr Hitler's assurance, "We don't want Czechs in the Reich"? Is this the last attack upon a small state, or is it to be followed by others? Is this, in fact, a step in the direction of an attempt to dominate the world by force?

Winston Churchill could not say it any better.

HITLER DEMANDS POLES RETURN DANZIG
AND PERMIT HIGHWAY TO EAST PRUSSIA

Warsaw—March 30, 1939 A. E. Thaxton, in an exclusive interview with Polish ambassador to Germany Jozef Lipski, reports . . .

Neville Chamberlain, the man who more than any other handed Czechoslovakia to the German Reich, thus ensuring Poland's indefensibility against German attack, stuns the House of Commons and the world by proclaiming that Great Britain will come to Poland's aid in case of such an attack. He even persuades a reluctant France to join him in a bilateral agreement.

"I've 'eard that one before," says the man on the street. More words on paper. More exchanging of ceremonial pens.

"All very well," says Major General Fenton Wood-Lacy, *"but I'd like to know what we're supposed to go to war with."*

He is saying this to Martin Rilke as they watch an exercise of the general's armored division on Salisbury Plain. The light tanks with their two-man crews and single machine gun look eminently stoppable. Bren gun carriers dash back and forth with the zeal of terriers. *"Oh, they look dashing enough—and they'll do the job if we can persuade Jerry not to shoot at the little darlings."*

The Mark II tanks, the Matildas, look more impressive, but there are so few of them—and so many teething problems. The treads break down after a hundred miles, and the radio, in those that have one, is erratic.

"I'm not overly impressed," says Martin. *"Thank God you have a navy."*

Home defense is of more importance to the prime minister—the need for the right little, tight little island. Antiaircraft guns ring the cities. Sluggish barrage balloons, which provide so many jokes for the music-hall comics, float serenely over London. The projected number of RAF fighter squadrons has been greatly increased—to the annoyance of the air marshals who firmly believe that only bombers win wars. Women work extra shifts stitching fabric to the frames of Hawker Hurricanes. The all-metal-skinned Spitfires crawl with agonizing slowness along the production lines. Young men to fly these planes are being trained through the university air squadrons, the Auxiliary, and the Volunteer Reserve.

The euphoria of Munich is not even a remembered dream. In the offices of Calthorpe & Crofts, Arnold Calthorpe sees the orders for pacifist books dwindle to nothing. His vision of universal peace shattered, his business on the brink of ruin, he publishes a novel sent to him by a middle-aged spinster in Yorkshire. It's an absurd tale of wanton women and lusty men in eighteenth-century England. The pure escapism of it strikes a chord in a nervous, if committed race, and the book shatters all records for sales in the history of the British publishing industry.

The French troops sit in the Maginot line and gaze toward the Rhine. The Paris press dub it the "Shield of France." The men in the line call it *le trou*—the hole. They wait deep underground in air-conditioned comfort. Well fed, lying naked under sun lamps once a day. They are bored, indifferent. *Je m'en fous* is the current saying—to hell with it. None of them want war. The cold shadow of Verdun touches them all.

"There is something disturbing about the Maginot line," says Martin in a broadcast from London to the United States in August:

> *It is not so much a line of fortifications as it is a state of mind. A philosophy for survival. A talisman against disaster. Walt Disney's little pigs in their straw house. It covers the least likely route of invasion should France be attacked. A route ignored utterly by the German general staff in nineteen fourteen. It is vast, awe inspiring, deadly, impregnable to assault. Observing it, I could not help but think of a huge battleship—*

embedded in concrete, incapable of shifting its firepower where it might be needed most.

DAILY POST EXCLUSIVE

A. E. THAXTON WITH POLISH AIR FORCE

The young Polish fliers are dashing and superb pilots, but their planes are slow and obsolete. The Polish army is dashing as well, especially the cavalry, the huge squadrons of horse soldiers wheeling and thundering across the plains, pennons fluttering from the lance tips.

HITLER-STALIN PACT—WARSAW IN SHOCK

WAR FEARED IMMINENT

A. E. Thaxton, reporting by telephone Wednesday morning from Poland's capital, described the reaction . . .

All roads reach an end somewhere. This road begins in the palace of Versailles in 1919 where frock-coated diplomats squabbled over the war spoils like so many shysters over an accident case. It ends in the harbor of the Free City of Danzig in the early morning hours of September 1, 1939. The old German battleship *Schleswig-Holstein,* which had last fired in anger during the battle of Jutland in 1916, trains its eleven-inch guns on a Polish army barracks and the firing switches are pulled. The thunder rolls across the dark water, past the sleeping city, and on and on over the fir forests and the Polish earth. The frontier with Germany throbs and shimmers with the flashes of a thousand guns and a new road begins, hammered out by the iron tread of the tanks.

IT IS QUIET in London. Sunday, the third of September. A balmy, sunny day. The cabinet has been meeting most of the night, and at nine o'clock in the morning instructs the British ambassador in Berlin to give the Germans two further hours in which to decide whether they will withdraw their troops from Poland or face war with Great Britain and France. The ultimatum is scorned. At eleven fifteen the prime minister broadcasts to the nation. There is no cheering in the streets as there was in 1914. Neither is there panic and despair—despite the inadvertent sounding of the air-raid sirens. A quiet, almost relieved acceptance of reality.

In the evening, the king speaks to his subjects over the radio in his painful way, struggling not to stammer. No one yet knows what iron grit and courage fills every pore of this shy, spare man. ". . . *We can only do the right as we see the right and reverently commit the rest to God.*"

And so be it.

A Day in October 1939

The Norwegian freighter *Hjelmeland,* battered and salt rimed after a stormy crossing of the North Sea, docked in London with a cargo of dried herring, lumber, and canned sardines. Among the twenty-three passengers were nine Polish and Czech fighter pilots who had managed to make their way to Norway, and Albert Thaxton.

Albert pointed up the Thames. "The Tower of London."

The Poles nodded solemnly. "Where they cut off the heads?" one of them asked.

"Once. A long time ago."

A whip-thin Czech tried out his English. "The RAF is please . . . ?"

"Anywhere," he said in German. "Just tell the immigration officers who you are and what you are."

He couldn't leave it at that. They looked lost, bewildered. He showed his papers to an elderly man in uniform.

"Thaxton, eh?" the man said. "Welcome back. I read your stuff in the *Post.* Bloody good it was too."

"Thanks." He pointed off. "That group there. Poles and a couple of Czechs. Pilots. Shot down a dozen Jerry planes between them. They hate the Nazis more than you'll ever know. Look after them will you? They want to join up."

"Don't worry about that, son. Two Polish *destroyers* came upriver last month. It's like the ruddy Foreign Legion in old London now."

He had lost all of his luggage when the Stukas had found the train twenty miles from Posen, howling down out of the dawn sky and dropping their bombs with such uncanny accuracy on the tracks ahead that the Polish officers had been shocked. A second wave of dive bombers had come for the train as soon as it stopped, plummeting steeply with their sirens shrieking. Gaunt birds of hell. He had spent the rest of his time in Poland in the clothes he had been wearing and with the money he had in his wallet—and a hundred-pound-note rolled tightly and sewn into a seam of his coat. The hundred pounds had paid for passage on a fishing boat from Gdynia to Sweden for him and six air force pilots. The British embassy in Stockholm had looked after him from there on and he now looked, riding in a taxi to Fleet Street, like a prosperous businessman.

"Take off a few days," Jacob said. "Write your adventures. Stirring, *Boy's Weekly* prose. Then get down to the War Office and see a Colonel Maitland. I'm having you accredited to the BEF. Maitland will brief you on all the dos and don'ts of the job. And by the way, I increased your salary while you were away."

"I'm sure I'll find a lot of ways to spend it in the trenches."

Wartime London. Not much changed, he was thinking as he left the *Post* building and taxied on to Soho. A few buildings along the Strand with their fronts sandbagged. Windows criss-crossed with tape. The ubiquitous barrage balloons floating limply in the dull gray sky. A great many men and women in uniform. Otherwise no different from busy afternoons past. He thought of Warsaw burning under the bombs.

He sensed her presence the moment he reached the top of the stairs. Her perfumed bath powder. Her silk robe tossed across the foot of the bed. A teacup and saucer, a plate and glass in the draining rack in the kitchen sink. Food in the fridge. Her clothing in the closet.

"Well," he murmured. "Curious are the ways."

He got out of the heavy wool suit and into his work clothes of slacks and rumpled pullover. He had started typing the article Jacob wanted when he heard her close the front door and come up the stairs. He tilted back in his chair and waited for her. She came into the room, looking very lovely in a sweater and skirt, a Burberry over one shoulder like a cloak. There was a heavy briefcase in her hand which she tossed onto the couch with her coat.

"You're wearing your hair longer," he said.

"It gave me something to do—watching it grow."

"Are you surprised to see me back?"

She shook her head, gazing at him. "Jacob's been keeping me informed. He called me at work and I left early."

"He didn't say a word to me—about you."

"I made him promise."

"Are you back with Calthorpe?"

"No. I managed to snag a job with the Ministry of Information. The we-would-never-lie-to-you gang, we call it." She walked up to him and cradled his face between her hands. "God, I'm glad you're back."

"My feelings about you, Jenny."

Bending, she kissed him lightly on the lips. "Sun's over the yardarm and we're well stocked with gin."

"*We* are?"

"Yes. *Our* home, Thax."

It was getting dark in the room and she started toward the windows to draw the blackout curtains. He stood up before she could do so and took her into his arms. "I'll be going away again. Covering the BEF in France."

"I knew you would be."

"I have no idea how long I'll be gone."

"Millions of men are saying that, darling. We'll have to make the most of the time we have and not waste a second of it."

"It seems so wrong to ask you to marry me now, Jenny."

She draped her arms around his neck and pressed her body tightly against him. "Oh, Thax, it would be so terribly wrong if you didn't."

And the darkness fell over London, over the dim streets and the blacked-out houses. And far above the city a balloon rose trailing its snapped cable—higher and higher, its silver skin catching the last rays of the sun, glowing a dull orange until it faded from sight in the winter sky.

11

1940

The seven Colorado flying boats floated serenely at their moorings on the placid waters of San Diego Bay. They were painted a light blue-gray and bore the roundels of the Royal Air Force on fuselage and wings. The sight of airplanes with foreign markings had once caused people to stop and gawk, but the novelty was long past. England and France had been at war with Germany for nearly six months and San Diego had become one of the arsenals of the allies.

Colin Mackendric Ross drove his mother's canary-yellow Packard convertible through the main gate of the Ross-Patterson Aircraft Company. The long corrugated-iron buildings of the old plant were silent and deserted—there was no Sunday shift—but a score of construction workers swarmed over the new buildings where the Colorado 2Bs, an amphibious version of the long-range patrol bomber, would soon be built.

"Wow," he exclaimed to his mother, "they're sure putting that baby up in a hurry."

Alexandra said nothing in reply. Her eyes were on the line of planes in the Channel. It was a morning in early February, clear and dry with little wind. A few clouds drifting in from the sea. Perfect flying weather. Within an hour those planes would be thundering across the bay toward North Island, white spray feathering up behind them. Then they would rise like gulls, make a long, slow turn, and head southeast toward Pensacola. Then on to Londonderry in Northern Ireland via Bermuda and the Azores. Planes destined for the war. And her eldest son going with them.

"Did you pack the parcels?" she asked.

"That's about the tenth time you've asked."

"All right," she snapped. "I'm asking again."

"Yes, Mama," he said quietly. "I packed them." He drove slowly on to the administration building and parked the car alongside half a dozen others. Turning on the seat, he put an arm across his mother's shoulders. "Please try to understand."

She nodded grimly, not looking at him. "I do understand. That's the awful part of it, Colin. I understand you perfectly."

"It's not blind patriotism . . . England, home and duty. None of that stuff. I just want to be part of this. I have a skill that they can use. If Derek can join up, I can."

"It's all a great adventure to you," she said bitterly.

"That may be part of it. I won't argue. Anyway, the way the war's going at the moment they might call it off out of sheer boredom."

"You don't believe that and neither do I."

"Okay, I don't believe it. A Fred Allen joke. Look, Mama,

I'm not a good pilot, I'm a *goddamn* good pilot. I'm going to be just fine." He got out of the car and removed two large canvas duffel bags from the back seat. "Are you going to stick around and watch us take off?"

Alexandra slid over behind the wheel. "Maybe . . . maybe not."

"Sure," he grinned. He bent his great height and kissed her on the forehead. "If you drove off, I'd spot you on the road and buzz the car all the way to La Jolla."

Her hand touched his cheek, lingered there. "I'll go over to the tower and watch. Look after yourself. Please?"

"Like I was made of glass."

The preflight briefing was held in the conference room next to James Ross's office. It was conducted by a short, sandy-haired Englishman of forty-five named Fergus, a civilian sent to San Diego by the Air Ministry to test fly the planes and shepherd them home. Before the war, he had been the chief test pilot for an English manufacturer of large commercial flying boats. The other men in the room were American pilots hired for the ferry job. Colin was going along as a copilot and radio operator.

"Let's keep together," the Englishman said. "No straggling and no chummy chatter over the radios. The weather forecast for the next forty-eight hours looks quite good. Should be some heavy rains over Northern Ireland, but no storm fronts expected. All the ships are ticking away like hundred-guinea watches so I don't anticipate any problems."

"Where do we hit the Gulf?" someone asked.

"Corpus Christi. That should be marked on your maps."

"Right. It is. Sorry."

"Cheery-bye, then. See you in Pensacola for supper."

As the men filed out of the room, he walked up to Colin. "Your father tells me you're coming across to join up."

"If they'll take me."

"They'll do that all right." He looked up at him, grinning. "You'll be Pilot Officer Ross in no time, though God knows where you'll find a uniform to fit."

James walked slowly beside his stepson toward the dock where the motor launch was moored. He was nearing fifty, but was still as lean and wiry as he had been in his twenties, when he had been the Earl of Stanmore's driver. His spectacular success in America had not changed him either. He still wore coveralls when at the plant, and he usually had grease on his hands.

"I'm sorry to see you going," he said. "I'll not pretend otherwise."

"I know Mama's upset."

"She'd not be much of a mother if she weren't. You know, lad, there's more than one way to serve. They wouldn't take me into the army in the last war. Said I was of more value to England building aero engines than mucking about in the trenches. I felt a proper slacker at first, but it was machines that whipped the Kaiser. It'll be machines that cook Hitler's goose in the end."

"I'm sure you're right, Jamie."

"Some admirals I know feel it's only a question of time before Japan jumps in. If that happens there'll be a raft of planes being built on the West Coast and we'll be needing good men to test them."

"It's not what I'm looking for."

"I know. You have hot blood. I'm not trying to stop you, Colin, just make you aware that there are honorable and exciting alternatives to firing a gun."

"I'll keep that in mind." He turned to Jamie before boarding the launch that would take the crews out to the planes. "You're one heck of a father and a damn good man. Just in case I never told you before."

He didn't dare look back. He stood in the bow and stared fixedly ahead at the graceful twin-engine planes that in a matter of days from now would be carrying machine guns and depth bombs and flying operational patrols with RAF crews. The Ross-Patterson Colorados winging over the English Channel and the cold North Sea—a long way from sunny California.

RAIN SLASHED INTO the dark, sullen waters of Lough Foyle and slapped like buckshot on the curved metal roof of the Quonset hut. Through a small, steam-blurred window Colin could see a swampy wasteland dotted with similar huts and wood buildings. The bay could be seen in the distance, the seven Colorados and three deep-hulled RAF Sunderlands tied to buoys in the stream. It was the morning of his second day in Ireland and the rain had not let up for so much as a second. He was alone in what was facetiously called the "visiting dignitaries' hotel." The other pilots had left for Belfast where they would sail for New York on an American freighter.

He was scowling at the sodden landscape and wondering what the hell he was doing there when the door at the far end of the hut flew open, letting in a blast of cold, wet air. An RAF officer hurried inside, slamming the door behind him. The man plucked off his hat and shook the rain from it before clapping it back on his head at a raffish angle.

"You Ross?"

"That's right."

"Allison here." He removed a rain-blackened coat to reveal the two bands of a flight lieutenant on the sleeves of his uniform. He gave the coat a shake and hung it on a peg beside the door. "Lord! It's a bloody wonder kids in Ulster aren't born with gills. Do you have anything worth drinking or must we swim over to the club?"

Colin waved a hand toward a row of cots. "The guys left half a bottle, but I don't drink whisky."

"Really? A week here would fix that, I can tell you."

He was not much older than himself, Colin was thinking as he watched the man home in on the bottle and take a pull, but there was a weary, ageless quality about him. He looked like a man who had done a great deal of flying and little of it pleasant.

"Allison, you said?"

"Right. Kenneth Allison, Coastal Command. I'll be flying one of those beauties of yours to England."

"When?"

He took another long drink, then recorded the bottle and tossed it on a cot. "An hour or two. The weather chaps say we're in for a break. Not much of one, but enough to tell the difference between sea and sky. Get out while the going's good." He straddled a chair and rested his chin on the top rung. "Fergus tells me your father made those boats."

"That's right. Stepfather, to be correct."

"And that you've popped over to fly one for jolly old England."

There was something mocking in the icy blue eyes. Colin tensed. "Fly Spits . . . if possible."

"Of course. Spits. Everyone wants to fly those. Well, Ross, I don't know what you'll fly, or even if you *will* fly for the jolly old firm, but Uncle Fergus has persuaded me to give you a lift across."

"He told me he'd try."

"Tried and succeeded, chum. Quite against RAF regulations, you see, but as senior officer of the ferry detachment, I'm not above bending the old rules in a worthy cause. I'll jot you down in the log as a civilian engineer employed by the manufacturer . . . making unexpected adjustments. Where are you heading for in Blighty?"

"London. Stay with my grandparents."

"Oh? Bit of English blood in the Yank veins?"

"All of it."

"Do tell? Welcome home, then." He stood up abruptly, glancing at his wristwatch. "I'd better get my chaps briefed. You can fly with me if you'd like . . . number-two ship."

"Fine. Ever fly a Colorado before?"

"No, chum . . . none of us have, but old Fergie explained the little oddities to us. If one can fly a Sunderland, one can fly anything."

"Is that what you do?"

"Normally, yes . . . out of Loch Broom in Scotland. Long-range patrols. Western Approaches." A shadow of bitterness crossed his face. "They may talk of the 'Bore War' over in France and the 'phony' war in the London press, but it's bloody real on the North Atlantic."

FLIGHT LIEUTENANT ALLISON let him take over the controls as they crossed the English coast at Liverpool. A brace of Hurricanes burst through the overcast to have a look at them, waggled their wings, and then roared on ahead, barrel rolling before plunging back into the murk below.

"Ah," Allison said, "the fighter chums at their boyish sport. Envious, Ross?"

"Well, this is sort of like driving a bus."

"It is indeed." He leaned back in his seat and tipped his cap over his eyes. "Wake me when you spot the Thames estuary and I'll land her on the Medway."

There was no need to navigate. He simply held his position in the formation and kept his eye on Fergus in the lead plane. The weather became clear as they swung down across the midlands at eight thousand feet. A clean, snow-dusted landscape lay below, sparkling like a Christmas card in the wintry sun. The broad, ice-green mouth of the Thames estuary came into view and the middle-aged test pilot who had made a thousand landings on the Thames dipped to three thousand feet and gave instructions over the radio. Colin glanced at Allison and decided not to wake him. It was routine—monkey see, monkey do. The little squadron fell into a staggered line astern behind the leader, dropped to a thousand feet over Southend, and curved down toward the ancient fleet anchorage of the Medway past Sheerness. He touched the ship to the broad reach of the bay as gently as a feather floating into a bathtub. As he began to taxi after the others toward the seaplane base, Allison pushed his cap back and sat up.

"Neatly done, old chum. I'll drive her in from here. You fly well, but you're a bit too free and easy with the controls. This is not California of the balmy skies and tranquil seas. Winds can kick up as you're making your final approach and slap you arse over tea kettle into the drink. Happened to a chum of mine when we were in final training on the Solent last year. Quite altered his old-age retirement plans."

COLIN HAD ALWAYS liked his grandparents' London house at Regent's Park. It was one of two limestone houses designed by John Nash in 1812 for mistresses of the royal dukes. It was far smaller than Abingdon Pryory and had a warm, comfortable ambiance that was in sharp contrast to the formalities of the country house. He sat in the drawing room with its glowing Renoirs on the walls and watched his grandmother open the parcel he had lugged from home.

"But what on earth? . . ." Hanna said in bewilderment as she removed cans, boxes, and jars.

Colin laughed. "I tried to talk her out of it, but she's read about the U-boat sinkings and was convinced you'd be starving."

She held up a jar, looking puzzled. "What is this?"

"Instant coffee. A kind of syrup. You put one teaspoon in a cup and add hot water."

"Sounds perfectly ghastly."

"I have identical packages for Aunt Marian and Dulcie."

"I'm sure they'll be as delighted as I am. Your mother's intentions have always been good, so I can't be angry with her." She picked through the assortment. "Cook will welcome the sugar I'm sure. Spaghetti with meat balls? In a *tin!* I've never even *heard* of tinned spaghetti with meat balls. Have you, Tony?"

The earl glanced up from his magazine. "Don't be ridiculous."

She put the assortment back into the box. "I'll take these in to cook and let her figure it out. You men have time for one drink before dinner. You serve, Colin. Your grandfather has a heavy hand."

"One finger?" Colin asked as he picked up the whisky decanter.

"Have a heart. I'd give a boy more than that."

He poured a stiff whisky and opened a bottle of Guinness for himself. "Cheers."

"By all means. Cheers and good luck—the latter most heartfelt. It's good seeing you, but I wish in my old heart that you'd stayed in California."

"Don't you start, please. It's what I want to do."

The earl glared at the fire burning softly in the grate. "Bloody damn war. Rotten waste of a young man's time. Still, may not come to anything after all. The troops staring at one another from their Maginot lines and Siegfried lines. Queer sort of war if you ask me. How do you go about joining it?"

"There's a pilot recruiting office in Aldwych. I guess I just walk in and sign up, but Derek can give me all the dope when he gets here in the morning."

"They'll take you, I suppose," he said gloomily.

"They'd better. Let's drink to it."

"Sorry, Colin. I want to enjoy my whisky, not have it lodge in my throat."

PILOT OFFICER DEREK Ramsay and two other members of 624 Squadron got off the train at Charing Cross station and then went into the cavernous, Victorian splendor of the Charing Cross Hotel.

"Sure you won't join us, Ramsay?" one of the young fliers asked. "Forty-eight hours of pure hell raising."

His equally young companion smiled. "I didn't know one could raise hell at the Albert Hall and the British Museum."

"One can try, Barratt. It's a matter of putting one's mind to it. It seems a pity to waste two days' leave on intellectual pursuits."

"Try to combine it," Derek said, looking around the lobby. "But no, I can't join the party, old lads. I've my friend to meet. He should be here."

"What's he look like?"

"Civilian . . . tall as a tree."

"There's a chap over there . . . leaning against that pillar. Rather like Samson in the temple."

"That's him. Come on, I'll give you an intro."

The two officers had a shyness around strangers that bespoke their age. Schoolboys in uniform. Derek introduced them and they soon left.

"They look sixteen," Colin said.

"Eighteen. I feel downright middle-aged around those two."

"Any good in the air?"

"They try hard. They've only had twenty hours in Hurricanes." He placed a hand on Colin's arm. "But let me look at you. The terror of Fleet Street. Bash any reporters lately?"

"No," Colin grinned. "But I might bash someone from the RAF in a second."

"Hit a fellow officer? Not done, old boy."

"I'm not an officer yet. Hell, they may not be needing any more fliers the way it's going—or not going, I should say."

"Oh, it's going. The bomber boys are taking a licking every day, but there's nothing much about it in the papers. Jerry shot down eleven out of twelve Blenheims during a day raid over Heligoland last week."

"Thanks for telling me. Well, let's get on with it. What do I do first?"

"Let me check my kit someplace and we'll walk down to Aldwych."

"Leave the bag in the car. I have my granddad's trusty Rolls—complete with aged driver."

"Well, la-di-da. Nothing like enlisting in style."

The RAF recruiting officer was an elderly wing commander with ribbons from the first war on his uniformed chest. He smoked a heavy pipe that was black with age and talked out of one side of his mouth. "Your flying log is most impressive, Ross. We shall find steady employment for you, never fear. A spot of training and you'll soon be posted to a squadron."

Colin smiled politely. "I think I'll need more than a spot of training to fly Spitfires, sir."

"Spits? Oh, no, lad. You're a bit too tall for a fighter pilot, in my opinion. Awfully cramped little things. And besides, we don't get many new boys with multiengine experience . . . even fewer who know how to set a plane down on water. Just what we're looking for. I shall be frank. We have more fighter pilots in training at present than we have planes to put them in. I'm posting you to Coastal Command, and damn important duty it is, too. An island race, you know. Sea's our life's blood. Can't allow Fritz to cut the artery with his damn U-boats, now can we?"

He felt keenly disappointed as he left the building and walked to where the chauffeur had parked the car.

Derek was in the back seat, reading the *Daily Post.* "That didn't take long," he said, putting the paper aside.

Colin grunted, getting into the car. "I go for my physical tomorrow at half past three. But I'm scratched off as a fighter pilot. He thought I was too large to fit the goddamn cockpit! It's Coastal Command for me."

"Good. I'm happy to hear it."

"The rocking-chair air force," he said bitterly.

"Better than flying a bomber and being chopped about by Messerschmitts. U-boats don't pounce on you—you pounce on them."

"I'd been hoping to fly with you."

"Yes, I was rather looking forward to having you in the squadron. Quite a few horses around Kentish Hill. You could have taught me to ride one of them."

THERE WERE ONLY a few guests invited to welcome Colin back to England, and the dinner was set for a much earlier hour than was usual for one of Hanna's dinner parties.

"This damn blackout," she said in a burst of annoyance as Colin escorted her down the stairs. "So many of our friends simply won't venture out in it. Too dangerous, especially on foggy nights."

"It's not too bad, Grandmama—if you're careful."

"That's easy for you to say. When one gets old it's a different matter."

He gave her arm an affectionate squeeze. "Hey, who's old?"

"*Hay* is for horses. I'm old enough. Seventy-one. Too old to grope about in the dark without breaking my neck."

A small party then, for which Colin was grateful, recalling the forty or more for dinners at Abingdon Pryory. The stiff formality. The, to him, boring conversations at the table. They reached the hall just as Dodds opened the front door and the few guests entered en masse.

"It's a real pea souper out there," Gerald Smith Blair said excitedly as the butler helped him off with his heavy navy overcoat. "We jammed into one car and I *crawled* up Albany Street with Vicky leaning out the window to watch the curb!"

"At least you made it," Hanna said. "The navy always comes through. Where's Winifred?"

"She'll be here later," Vicky said. "She's expecting a phone call from Papa . . . from Rheims."

Hanna frowned. "I'll try to phone her first and tell her not to bother. It's far too dangerous."

"She has an army driver," Jennifer said. "The man can see like a cat." She smiled at Colin. "Welcome back, darling. I wish it was for a more peaceful pursuit."

He gave her a kiss on the cheek. "Thanks. And congratulations. Albert's a lucky guy. Where is he, by the way?"

She made a wry face. "Somewhere in France. He gets to London occasionally for a few days so it's not been too bad."

He noticed Kate for the first time, standing off to one side. She had changed. The baby fat was gone, although she was still full figured. The change was mostly in her face. Not a plump-cheeked, calf-eyed schoolgirl any longer. The eyes that met his own reflected a cool self-assurance. She had lost her prettiness and had become gravely beautiful.

"Hi," he said.

"And hello to you."

He stepped over to her, wondered if he should kiss her, and then thought better of it. He took her hand. "It's great to see you. Still in that boarding school?"

"No. I'm staying with Jenny . . . and seeing a tutor twice a week. I go up to Oxford in April. Trinity term."

"Really? Wonderful. Derek will be pleased to hear that. He's here, by the way."

Her face lit up with pleasure. "He is? Where?"

"In the drawing room having a drink with Grandpa."

She hurried off and he trailed after her, feeling an irrational flash of jealousy at her eagerness.

Everyone left before eight thirty. Lieutenant Gerald Smith Blair, R.N.V.R., steering them out into the darkness and the dense fog. Lord and Lady Stanmore yawned, said their goodnights, and went early to bed. Dodds locked up the house and went down to his room to listen to the nine o'clock news service over the BBC. Colin went into the pantry and brought four bottles of beer back to the drawing room.

"Guinness or Bass?"

"Bass," Derek said. He took off his uniform jacket and loosened his tie. "Damn nice little party. Best ruddy food I've had in six months."

"How does the RAF feed you?"

"About as well as the Chinese feed their air force I expect." He sprawled into a chair and took the beer Colin handed him.

"Lord, I'm bushed. They've been flying us from morning to night, fair weather and foul."

"Will they be sending your bunch to France?"

"No. We're an Auxiliary squadron . . . strictly home defense. Only the regulars are across the pond."

"What are the guys like?"

"*Men,* old boy . . . in their thirties most of them. Clannish lot. Been flying together for years. Every weekend and two weeks every summer until the balloon went up. They resented the Air Ministry weeding out the men over thirty-eight and replacing them with us—the two chaps you met and three others. I think they were afraid we might ruin the social tone of the mess."

Colin straddled a chair and nursed his beer. "Kate fell all over you like you were her long-lost lover or something."

"Lover?" he raised an eyebrow. "Uncle might be closer. I caught the shadow of a frown in your eye from time to time while she was talking to me. Thought you were cold on the girl. Little Kate—*of all people.*"

Colin shifted on the chair and studied the label on the bottle. "She was just a kid then . . . mooning over me."

"Hell, it was her first crush, what did you expect her to do?"

"She sure must be over it now. She didn't say four words to me all evening."

"Talked a torrent with me," he said through a yawn. "Her exam scores, the degree she would like to try for. A bit about you."

"Me? What did she say about me?"

"Oh, that she thought you'd changed. On the chilly side.

Not as happy-go-lucky. Wondered if you were embarrassed meeting her again."

"She said *that?*"

"No. I put in the latter. My own observation. I think you are. Just how far did you go with her that braw brecht moonlecht necht so long ago?"

"Far enough for her—I guess." He could feel his face burn and took a long swig of beer.

"Tell Uncle Derek, that's the good lad."

"You're a real crud, Fat Chap."

"Come on, don't be shy."

He glared at him. "I felt her tits. Okay?"

"Okay with me—and obviously okay with her. I doubt if she looks back on that night with pain and horror." He finished his beer and stood up, a trifle unsteadily. "I'm really going for a burton, old lad. If I'm not awake by noon just roll me over and let me sleep on."

Colin sat up for a while, drinking beer and staring into the fire. His thoughts were formless weavings. The Colorado touching down on the Medway, the icy spray splashing the windshield. Flip the wiper switch. Never lose vision. Keep a steadier hand on the controls in case the wind kicks the ship hard on the beam and a wing float gets buried deep in the water. Could cartwheel that way. Finis. Cold in England in early February. Guys body surfing this time of year at Pacific Beach. Lovely and warm that night on Leith Hill with the moonlight washing the tops of the shadowed trees. A hand inside her dress, a large, supple breast nestled against his palm.

He felt a pang of regret for that night. After he had cooled down in a hurry, realizing that he wasn't parked out on Point

Loma with some beach cutie, she had pressed herself tightly against him and had said that she loved him. What a bastard. He could have said that he loved her too . . . and respected her . . . but that he was going away soon and it would be better if it ended here, on a romantic note. The moon. A nightbird trilling in the woods. But no. He had to say something slick and laugh it off before driving her back to the school. And then he had done his best to avoid her.

"You're the crud, boy," he muttered to the dying coals.

COLIN PASSED THE physical. Signed a few papers, received instructions regarding uniforms, travel warrants, pay while training, when to report and where—and that was it. Royal Air Force, Coastal Command. He walked out of the building into the foggy darkness of early evening and groped his way along the Strand to the Savoy Hotel.

He found Derek in the bar.

"Kiss me, Mother," he said. "I'm queen of the may. I leave for the Isle of Wight the day after tomorrow. And, listen, you're not taking me to dinner, I'm taking you. All of us Yanks are rich, correct?"

"You're not, strictly speaking, a Yank."

"You're so damn technical. You're going to make one hell of a lawyer when this war is over. We should make a night of it. Why are you taking the nine o'clock train?"

"I already told you. I want to get back early and have a good night's sleep. We'll be flying more radio-directed interception exercises tomorrow."

"Sleep! That's become your preoccupation in life."

"It's going to become yours in the very near future."

It was getting noisy in the bar, as a group of army officers began an argument over football, so they took their beers into the lounge and sat in deep leather chairs.

"Do you mind taking a little advice, Colin?"

"From you? Heck, no."

"You have a lot of virtues, old son, but patience isn't one of them. Neither is restraint. A short fuse, in other words. I'm sure you're a good flier and you won't have any trouble completing the training course. But just remember that for the next three weeks or so you're strictly a probationer. RAF flying instructors are a crusty lot, full of bull and brass and addicted to King's Regulations and the flight manual. Do it the way they tell you to do it—from buttoning up your coveralls to following cockpit procedures to the letter. If you have to bite your tongue a few times, bite it. I don't want to find out that you've been booted out. Your stepfather may be an American citizen, but you have a British passport and just might find yourself digging holes for the army."

"Advice received and accepted. Now then, where would you like to have dinner?"

"Simpson's. I made reservations. Kate will meet us there at seven."

"Kate?"

"I thought it would be chummy."

" 'Chummy,' " he repeated in a flat voice. "Sure."

Her face was flushed and she looked out of breath when she arrived late at the restaurant. She had been in a taxi accident in Charing Cross Road and had continued on foot. "With *very* long strides. Sorry I'm late."

"Obviously you weren't hurt," Derek said.

"No, but I can't say the same for the taxi's radiator." She combed her hair with her fingers. "I must look an absolute mess."

"You look lovely," Colin said, meaning it.

After dinner, they had to hurry down the street to Charing Cross and Derek, waving at them over his shoulder, ran along the platform and caught his train just as it was pulling out.

"Sorry to see him go," Colin said.

"Yes," she said. "A sad place, railway stations."

They walked slowly through the cavernous structure. In front, arriving passengers were lined up waiting for the few available taxis.

"It might be easier to get one at the Savoy," Colin said.

"Plenty of them in Soho this time of night. Shall we walk? It's not too far, and I know a nice little coffee bar in Gerrard Street."

"Okay." He held her hand as they crossed into Charing Cross Road, the traffic signals subdued spots of light, the headlamps on the cars shielded into mere slits. "Life in the blackout. If the war goes on too long people will develop the sensory structure of bats."

"I wouldn't be at all surprised," she said with a laugh. "Londoners are half batty as it is!"

Colin continued to hold her hand all the way to Gerrard Street and she made no move to draw it away; did, in fact, give his fingers a little squeeze from time to time as though to emphasize something she was saying. She talked of how much she enjoyed living with her sister, and of how Jennifer was being assigned to the Crown Film Unit to do research for propaganda films. And she talked with a restrained excitement about entering Oxford.

"Be a horrid amount of work, but I don't mind. It's in a field I've always loved. Did you go to college when you went back to America?"

"For a little while, but got bored with it and dropped out. I got a job as a copilot with an air-freight line—a small outfit. We flew flowers mostly, to the eastern markets."

"That must have been interesting."

"Yeah, if you weren't allergic to roses."

Kate hesitated in front of a door. "This is it, I think. Yes . . . it's upstairs."

It was a smoky, crowded place that served Turkish coffee in small brass pots and Greek pastry. It was very popular with actors, she said. Vicky had introduced her to the place.

"Didn't she want to be an actress once?"

She nodded. "Just for a lark. She had a walk-on in a Noel Coward play and was perfectly dreadful."

Colin watched her take tiny sips from her cup and pretended to drink from his own. He didn't like Turkish coffee. It tasted like hot syrup. "Derek said you thought I'd changed."

"You seemed . . . oh, reserved. Not that I blame you. The fact is, Colin, I'm the one who's changed. A year and a half makes a big difference. I'll be eighteen next week. Not a girl any longer." She looked down at the table and turned the cup between her fingers. "I acted foolishly that summer . . . especially the night in the car."

He cleared his throat and broke off a piece of baklava. "I certainly didn't act very well, Kate."

"You did absolutely the right thing under the circumstances. You put the damper on and did your best to get my feet back on the ground. I was just carried away in a mad crush, a biologic urge, and confused that with love. I must have embarrassed you terribly."

"Not at all . . . really."

"We've known each other all our lives and it would be a pity if there were any uncomfortable feelings between us." She leaned back in her chair. "Good. That's off my chest."

He gave her his best Groucho Marx leer. "Some chest."

"That's my Colin," she said. "It was your wicked little grin that I missed most."

He walked her to Lower James Street and looked up at the building as she searched her handbag for the key.

"So this is where Jenny lives."

"Not much from the outside, is it? But it's a truly lovely flat. Full of antiques and things. I'd ask you up, but I'm sure she's asleep by now."

"When I get back from training."

"Lots of luck on that."

"Piece of cake." She had trouble with the lock and he opened the door for her. "They give you a couple of days' leave when you finish. Maybe we could get together . . . have dinner and take in a show."

"I'd love to."

"Swell." He pressed her hand. "And happy birthday. I'm sorry I'll miss it."

"You can give me a birthday kiss if you'd like."

"I would, Kate. I really would." He kissed her briefly on the lips. "Take care of yourself."

"You do the same," she said softly, then stepped inside and closed the door.

It was a long walk to Regent's Park, but he never gave a thought to hailing a cab. He walked with light steps and a joyous heart—thinking of her.

THE VENERABLE SARO London flying boat winged majestically over Swanage Bay at five thousand feet, Colin keeping her steadily on course despite a vicious cross wind whipping in across the English Channel. Rain behind the wind, black sheets of it blotting out the distant line of the French coast. He fought back the urge to open the throttles on the twin Pegasus engines and scoot merrily for home, but his instructions had been exact—ninety miles per hour on a two-hundred-mile triangular course. He checked the airspeed indicator—ninety on the button—and glanced at his watch: two fifty-seven. Right on time and right on course. The gimlet-eyed flying instructor in the second seat was doing the same—and also glancing out the side window at the approaching squall. "If you goose the old girl up a bit, Ross, we might miss this muck."

Colin's smile was inner. Not a muscle of his face so much as twitched. Silly bastard, he was thinking. "Chief Flying Instructor Bishop's orders, sir. Keep the ship at nine-oh airspeed."

"Mr. Bishop did not anticipate a ruddy monsoon, Ross."

"One can never anticipate anything on a mapped-out patrol, sir. Unless the aircraft is in obvious danger I shall stick to the flight plan . . . sir."

The instructor cracked a smile. It was like watching granite split. "Good for you, lad. You'd be surprised how many get a tick on that one."

Not me, he mouthed soundlessly as he began a slow descent toward the Solent, the Isle of Wight off to his right, already wreathed with mist.

Rain on the March wind pelted the seaplane base. The moored flying boats rocked in the bay; water sheeted off the Nissen huts and the old brick buildings. Colin, a raincoat wrapped around his white coveralls, sprinted across sloppy ground and into the Operations building. He hung the streaming raincoat on a rack and walked down a corridor to Wing Commander Jessop's office.

The portly little commander of the base rose from his desk, all smiles. "Sit down, Ross . . . sit down. Care for a sherry to dry out the bones?"

"That would be nice, sir. Thank you."

"Called you in, Ross, because orders have come through for you while you were in flight. And may I say that the report on your exercise this afternoon was first rate."

"That's good to know, sir."

"Not that you could possibly have doubted it, I'm sure. You've done splendidly here the past few weeks. Your pilot officer rings are secure on your sleeves." He perched on the edge of his desk, feet dangling a long way from the floor. "A new squadron has been formed. Number Thirty-four, based at Thurne Mere in Norfolk. Seven Ross-Patterson Colorados. The boats you helped bring over, no doubt. They should prove useful with all this sudden activity in Norwegian waters. You're to report to it as soon as you're qualified—which is now. Congratulations."

"Thank you, sir."

"Did I say as soon as you are qualified? Let me clarify that. You are entitled to three days' leave starting, officially, tomorrow. Report to RAF Thurne Mere first thing Monday morning. However, I won't keep you here unnecessarily. If you can pack up your gear in a hurry you should be able to catch the ferry to Gosport and be in London by nightfall." He stuck out a small, pudgy hand. "Goodbye and Godspeed."

GOSPORT TO SOUTHAMPTON. Train to London. Taxi from Waterloo in swirling rain through blacked-out streets, the driver cursing softly over the *tick tick tick* of the windshield blades.

"My goodness, Mister Colin," Dodds said in surprise. "You were not expected." He closed the front door and helped him out of his raincoat. "Lord and Lady Stanmore are in Derbyshire staying with Mr. William. We don't expect them back until Wednesday."

"Sorry I missed them. I only have a three-day leave . . . have to be in Norfolk on Monday."

"That is a shame. May I say, sir, you look splendid in uniform."

"Thank you, Dodds."

A maid had brought a ham sandwich and a glass of Guinness to his room while he had been taking a bath, the first really hot soak he had had in weeks. Sitting on the edge of the bed, he wolfed the sandwich and wondered if he should phone Kate now or just roll over on the luxurious bed. Derek had been oh, so right. Sleep was not an abundant commodity in the RAF. The bath and the beer, the softness of sheets and the warmth of blankets made up his mind for him.

"Tomorrow," he muttered—getting into bed and turning out the light—and was instantly asleep.

The storm had blown over by morning, and the weather report called for a windy but clear weekend. He spent it with Kate, playing the tourist: Kew Gardens, the Tower, Madame Tussauds—the wax image of Hitler being the biggest attraction. There were dinners and the theater.

"The nicest weekend I've ever had," she said.

Colin, standing by the window and looking down on Lower James Street, smiled and turned away. "Certainly the best I've had. I wish it wasn't Sunday, and Sunday evening at that."

Jennifer came out of her bedroom in a cocktail dress, the back of it undone. "What time do you have to be at that awful place, Colin?"

"I take the six-fifteen train to Norwich and someone from the base meets me there. God knows where Thurne Mere is. I couldn't find it on the map. A lot of water in Norfolk. It's probably the name of a swamp."

"Do me up, will you, Kate?" She sat on the couch next to her. "You two are certainly welcome to come along. Jacob would love to see you."

"Cocktail parties bore me," Kate said, pulling up the zipper. "Besides, I thought I'd show off my cooking skills. Lamb chops, mashed potatoes, and peas."

Jennifer smiled to herself as she stood up. "Have a pleasant time. I won't be in before ten thirty."

Colin straddled a chair in the kitchen and watched Kate

as she fixed the meal, smiling at her obvious anxiety as she checked the potatoes and peered for the fourth time at the chops sizzling under the gas broiler.

"Need any help?" he asked. "I know how to boil spuds."

"They're about done—I think. You can mash them if you'd like. That is, if it's not beneath the dignity of a Royal Air Force officer."

"Nothing is beneath my dignity where food is concerned."

Kate had set the table with care, using china, Georgian silver, and crystal wine glasses that Jennifer had brought from Lulworth Manor. The effect was not lost on Colin.

"Elegant."

"It's the food that counts. I hope everything is all right."

Colin cut into a chop. "Soft as butter." He looked at her across the table, the candlelight imparting an ivory warmth to her face. "Lovely dinner and a beautiful hostess. My cup runneth over."

"So does mine," she murmured.

Colin closed his eyes to fix the moment forever in his mind. The utter tranquillity and rightness of it all, with the fire glowing in the grate and Kate snuggled against him on the couch. She had suggested a game of cards after dinner, but he had preferred just to sit beside her, content with her closeness.

He stroked her hair, and she murmured something against his chest, a tiny sound of happiness and contentment.

"I'd better be off soon," he said. "Have to get up with the hens."

She raised her head and kissed him on the throat. "I'll get up, too, and meet you at the station."

"No. Please. That's an image I could do without. You alone on a platform, waving goodbye. This is all I care to remember."

A FLAT AND watery country. Canals and lazy rivers and broad inlets of the sea. A cold and windswept landscape with the North Sea beyond. The little Austin, painted RAF blue, turned off a narrow road and along a wheel-rutted track leading to RAF Thurne Mere—a new base, still under construction, an untidy scattering of huts, tents, and workshops. A long wooden jetty ran out into the wide, brackish reach of a lake, kept from the sea by a distant line of dunes. It was the most depressing place Colin had ever seen, or hoped to see again.

A tall radio aerial jutting up from the curved roof of a Nissen hut marked the squadron operations center, and the car pulled up in front of it. The commanding officer's office was a desk at the far end of the cluttered hut. The commander stood up as he approached and Colin realized that he had seen the slim, sandy-haired man with the icy blue eyes before.

"Flight Lieutenant Allison?"

"Squadron leader now. Promotions come rather quickly these days. Nice to have you with us, Ross."

"Quite a coincidence, sir."

"Is it? I spotted your name on the men-in-training list and put in a request for you. I've seen you fly, remember?"

"You'll find me a bit less free with the controls now."

"I hope so. Duty isn't easy here, Ross. Long, tedious patrols. Jerry's shipping iron ore from Sweden down the coast of Norway, keeping within neutral waters. Our job is to shadow their ore convoys. If any ships stray past the three-mile limit we alert our destroyer patrols. So far, the Jerry ships have not strayed an inch. We are also prepared to depth bomb any U-boats we come across, but we haven't seen one yet. Our biggest enemy is boredom and fatigue. So, you can see, I hardly did you a favor by picking you out of the crowd."

"I think you did. When do I begin flying?"

"Tomorrow morning. The only consolation here, by the way, is that the food in the mess is top hole. Our sergeant-cook once worked at the Savoy Grill."

He had been right about the food and right about everything else. It was the only consolation. He lay on a hard cot under rough blankets and his greatcoat feeling the deathly cold seep through the plywood walls of the barracks. He shut his eyes tightly, recalling the warmth of that room . . . the exquisite warmth of her against his chest. He could smile. He could sleep.

12

ALBERT THAXTON HEARD the rumor on the morning of April 9. He had been spending a few days in the small town of Quesnoy near the Belgian frontier as guest of the second Battalion, Durham Light Infantry. The battalion HQ was located in the basement of the town hall and when he entered it the duty officer, a thin, pink-cheeked lieutenant, said: "Old Adolf just invaded Denmark and Norway."

"Are you sure?" Albert asked.

"It just came over the blower from division. Think the real balloon's going up now, Mr. Thaxton?"

"Maybe. If that's true."

There had been many exaggerated reports of German actions during the past weeks. A six-man patrol probing French defenses in Moselle would cause wild tales of "massive" assaults and "heavy" cannonading. If a reporter took all of his news from what came over the field telephones he would find himself writing a story one day and retracting it the next.

The elderly lieutenant colonel commanding the battalion said the same at breakfast. "Everyone has the wind up. Bound to be some sort of move in the works. The Boche like the spring. Make sense if they went into Denmark and Norway, come to think of it. They'll need coastline bases. Still, I'd not take it as gospel on the basis of one call from some rabbity chap at HQ."

By noon it was official. The Nazis had marched into Denmark with hardly a shot being fired at them, and they had landed troops in half a dozen Norwegian cities and ports, from Oslo to Narvik in the far north. The news was stupefying.

"My guess as to how they pulled it off is as good as yours," the colonel remarked. "Rather clever, these chaps. I wonder if Mr. Chamberlain is wondering who missed the bus now? Hitler or him?"

Albert wondered the same thing as he walked beside the colonel on an inspection of his lines in the fields and woods west of the town. The men, loosely strung out beside the rusting tracks of a narrow-gauge railway, were in high spirits.

"This news is a tonic to the lads, Thaxton. The possibility of action for a change. Been a ruddy long winter with not a bloody thing to do. Kept them in shape by digging holes. Dig them in the morning and then fill them up in the afternoon. Dig and fill since November. Bloody boring for them, but it kept them fit. Not like the French army. Half drunk most of the time."

Albert left the battalion after lunch, seated in the back of a staff car compiling his notes . . .

With the BEF on Belgian frontier . . . Spirit of troops "superb," says A. E. Thaxton.

There was British transport on the road moving north from Lille, infantry on the march or crowded into the back of trucks. Bren gun carriers and a few light tanks clattered along the *pave.* The men cheered and gave the thumbs-up sign as the staff car passed them. On the move at last. It had been a long winter for everybody.

Major General Wood-Lacy's HQ was in a roadside inn five miles from Armentières.

"A lovers' inn, Albert," he said as he ushered him into the small bar that served as his office. "Designs of hearts and cupids on the bedroom walls. Would have been a nice place to bring Jenny for a holiday. Not a time for lovers now, is it?"

"I'm afraid not. Are you moving your division to the frontier?"

"Not at present. It's a wait-and-see situation for us. They're shifting half the corps up, though. If Fritz moves west we're to scurry into Belgium . . . take positions along the Dyle from Louvain to Wavre. Don't try to print that. All very hush-hush. Only about half the Paris taxi drivers know of it yet. Bloody silly strategy if you ask me. The high command have their heads in the sand."

He had always liked and admired the general even before he became his father-in-law. Outspoken, caustic, and cynical, The Hawk made good copy—not that much of it could pass the censors.

Fenton waved a hand at a bin filled with dusty bottles. "We have wine galore, but are flat out of whisky."

"Wine will do nicely."

"Not bad stuff, actually. Clos Vougeot." He uncorked a bottle and poured some into two glasses. "You know, it's so terribly odd. *Déjà vu* . . . is that what they call it? I wake up some mornings and think it's nineteen fifteen. I was camped just a few miles from here before the battle of Aubers Ridge. I hate to think of how many men I knew who are buried within walking distance of this spot."

Albert took a reflective sip of his wine. "My sister Ivy's grave isn't far away."

"At Poperinghe, I believe Martin told me once. No, not far." He drank his wine and poured another. " 'A richer dust concealed,' as the poet said."

Through an open window they could see a tank crew working on one of the Matildas parked under a tree, a soldier in black coveralls whistling as he pulled a cleaning rod through the barrel of the gun.

"Happy soul," Albert said.

"That lad's only nineteen and eager to put all his training to the test. He may enjoy combat. Oddly enough, a few men do, but I wonder if he'll be whistling a month from now."

"You believe we're in for something, don't you, Hawk?"

"Oh, we're in for something all right. Beyond anyone's imagining. Only a fool would think otherwise. The German method of warfare is hardly a secret—it's essentially my own. The only difference is that they have everything it takes to make it work in the field and not just on paper. If Hitler attacks he won't hurl his army against the Maginot line. The man fought on the Somme and at Ypres and doesn't want any more gains measured in yards and costing a hundred lives per foot. He'll slash into Belgium and Luxembourg long before we get official permission from those countries to step in and defend them. When we do move it will be too late. Jerry will cut through the

Ardennes, by-pass Maginot, and nip us off from any possibility of escape to the coast. A sorry kettle of fish, I must say."

"You paint a bleak picture. A shame you're out of whisky."

"One of the true horrors of war, Thax old lad. Supply failing demand."

"Any bright spot I can tell my eager readers?"

"There's a bright spot you could ruddy well tell me. I'd like a grandchild or two."

"I'll get to work on it—when I have the time. Anything at all?"

Fenton tipped his oil-stained beret to the back of his head and stared through the window with tired eyes. His pathetically undermanned, undertanked armored division lay scattered in the woods beyond. The young gunner was still whistling "The Lambeth Walk" in the pallid shadows of the gray afternoon. "You can tell them that all of us in command positions, great or small . . . Lord Gort . . . Thorne . . . Alexander . . . Holmes . . . Montgomery . . . me . . . have the highest faith in the poor bastards we lead. That they will *all*, when their day comes, do Britain proud—win or lose."

Albert was silent for a moment, oddly moved by Fenton's quiet, bone-weary sincerity. "I'll write that. Although 'poor bastards' will have to go and 'lose' will get snipped by the censors."

Fenton sighed and drew a flat tin box of cigarettes from a pocket in his coveralls. "I don't care about 'lose,' but 'poor bastards' is a pity. It's what they are, you know. Ours and theirs. Poor bastards all."

GREEN SECTION OF 624 Squadron was at readiness, three Hurricanes warmed up on the tarmac in front of the dispersal hut. There was no tension among the three pilots playing cards inside. They had never been scrambled yet except in practice and didn't expect to be now. The long afternoon at readiness on this cold, overcast day had been fatiguing and they played their cards listlessly.

"I wonder if the sergeant-fitter made any tea," Barratt said.

"Probably," Derek yawned. "It always tastes of machine oil."

"Does, now that you mention it." He discarded a trey.

"Ah ha!" The section leader picked it up. He was a heavyset flight lieutenant who had been with the squadron for nearly ten years. His name was Rodgers and his nickname "Jolly."

"You can go out, I suppose," Barratt said, glassy-eyed with boredom.

"Yes, old son. Chalk up another for me."

The loudspeaker on the wall suddenly hummed and the voice of the operations officer blared into the room. "Squadron six-two-four Green Section . . . scramble!"

Barratt whooped and knocked over his chair getting to his feet while Derek scattered his cards across the floor to the obvious annoyance of Jolly Rodgers. Within minutes they were airborne, the three fighter planes thundering down the runway and zooming up into the low clouds.

Derek concentrated to keep in formation. Jolly was a stickler for tight vics. He stayed close to the leader, flying wingtip to wingtip with Barratt. The radio hummed in his ear and he could hear Jolly calling Sector Control and reporting that they were off the ground.

"Righto, Green Leader. Vector nine-zero. Intruder off Sheerness. Are you receiving me?"

Rodgers replied that he was and asked for intruder identity, if possible. A Heinkel, he was told. Zero feet in the mouth of the Thames. Mine laying, Derek was thinking as he set his reflector sight to the bomber's wingspan of seventy-four feet. They burst through the cloud layer at twelve thousand feet into brilliant sunshine and set a course for the estuary.

"Don't lag, Green Three." Jolly's voice over the R.T.

Derek glanced to the side. Barratt was easing back, a thin plume of white vapor streaming from his engine.

"Green Three to Green Leader . . . I'm losing glycol, skipper."

"Return to base, Green Three. Hop it."

Barratt rolled out of the formation and was gone. Derek prayed he'd make it before his engine stalled from loss of coolant.

"Bloody hell," Jolly swore.

Derek shifted his position, boosting the engine to come up on Jolly's right side and slightly back.

"Let's go down, Green Two . . . take a look-see."

"Righto, skipper."

They dived as one back into the clouds. Derek watched his instruments, seeing nothing through the windshield except gray vapor that turned darker the deeper they flew into it. Eight thousand feet . . . seven . . . five . . . the airspeed indicator needle quivering close to four hundred.

"Level off at three zero, Green Two."

He pulled out of the dive at three thousand feet in thick sheets of scudding cloud. The sea and obscured patches of coastline below. Not a sign of Jolly Rodgers, only his voice in his ear over the R.T.

"Where the hell are you, Green Two?"

"Over the drink, Skipper. Herne Bay below me . . . I think."

"Then you're off course. Blast it to hell."

A weary acceptance in Jolly's voice. There was always something going wrong in the squadron's vintage Hurricanes. All the new models had been shipped over to France. The Auxiliaries were stuck with the ones that had been issued in the summer of 1939. A leak in Barratt's glycol lines . . . and now a compass out of whack. It would have been all right if he hadn't lost the leader in the clouds. On his own unless he could spot him. He eased the stick forward and dropped to twenty-five hundred feet. Visibility less than two miles. Not a hope. He eased the plane down to a few hundred feet over the sea. Clearer there . . . five miles at least, but no sight of Jolly. He kept the coast of Sheppey Island to his left and streaked toward the mouth of the Thames.

The Heinkel III was a surprise. All he saw of it was a shimmer of sunlight off its bulbous glass greenhouse of a nose. The rest of the big twin-engine bomber seemed to blend into the haze. They came at each other on a collision course at a combined speed of over six hundred miles an hour. He yanked back hard on the stick and shot up and over it, feeling the blood drain from his head and his jaw drag down, cutting into the chinstrap of his helmet.

"Green Two to Green Leader," he said thickly. "Bandit . . . am chasing."

"Shoot the bugger."

He rolled up and over and leveled out close to the water. The Heinkel was a long way ahead of him . . . a speck heading toward Margate. He slammed the throttle through the seals and the big engine howled at full revs, pushing him hard against the back of the seat as the plane surged ahead. He turned the firing button from safety and switched on the gunsight. "In pursuit now, Skipper . . . five miles off Margate . . . heading almost due east . . . compass going crazy."

"Good hunting," said Jolly Rodgers sadly, far away off Sheerness.

He was gaining rapidly on the bomber now. Two miles . . . a mile. The German's flight seemed leisurely. Was it possible the pilot had not even noticed the near collision? It had all taken place so quickly . . . a flash out of the mist. Or if he had been aware, perhaps he thought the fighter was miles behind him. He nursed stick and rudder, dropping so close to the sea that the prop was kicking spray behind him. But he was slightly below the Heinkel and to its left. Be difficult for the ventral gunner to spot him and he had the sun behind him, a pallid disk in the west.

Nine hundred yards. Too far. He wanted the fuselage and the engines fully within the lines reflected on the windshield. Four hundred yards minimum. Coming up too fast now with the engine on full boost. Ease off the throttle. Jig right . . . whip in on the beam. Now! He pressed the firing button and felt all eight guns shudder, the recoil slowing the plane, a stench of cordite drifting up from the wing roots. The tracer hosed under the belly of the bomber, well forward. Clean miss. He pulled back on the controls and zoomed over, catching a fleeting glimpse of a pale face staring at him from the teardrop bubble of the top gunner's position. He rolled and came around for a frontal approach. They were firing now, the streams of orange smoke slashing around him. The Hurricane shuddered and he could hear the snap of metal and wood, the shriek of wind across ripped fabric. The right engine and the bomber's nose filled the sights and he jammed his finger on the button and saw his fire thudding home. Chunks of plastic from the nose whipped away, boiling off in the windstream. Control column hard into his stomach—up and over in a gut-wrenching climbing turn to the right. When he leveled off, the Heinkel was below and ahead of him, staggering now, weaving back and forth with black muck vomiting from the right engine. He closed and gave it another long burst, holding his thumb down until he could hear the hiss of compressed air and the clank of empty guns. The bomber dipped its shattered nose to the sea and slammed into it, raising a geyser that slapped salt water against the windshield as the Hurricane swept through it, turning toward the coast and home.

SQUADRON LEADER POWELL, a well-known barrister in civilian life, smiled broadly as he hung up the phone. "Impeccable confirmation, Ramsay. The Margate lifeboat crew went out to the spot but there were no survivors. Congratulations. You bagged the squadron's first kill. I'll see that you get another ring on your sleeve for it. And Sergeant Cooper tells me your crate's a writeoff. It's a wonder your left wing didn't fall off on the way back. Someone on that Hun crew was a bloody good shot."

The thought began to nag at him as he raced toward London on his motorbike, his kit dumped in the sidecar. Seventy-two hours' leave. No plane for him to fly yet anyway.

Someone on that crew . . . In the excitement of it all he hadn't given a thought to it, but the adrenaline was out of his blood now. He was heading for London—drinks, a decent meal in a good restaurant—and out in the North Sea, entombed in a crumpled bomber, were the bodies of the men he had killed. Men of his own age, probably. Men who, except for that brief moment of bad luck, would have been heading off somewhere themselves tonight—into Wilhelmshaven or Emden, to drink beer, meet some girls.

"Poor bastards," he whispered against the cold wind.

THERE SEEMED TO be a feverish air of excitement about the town, an expectancy left unsaid. Hitler on the move at last. The end of the "phony war." There seemed to be more people than usual in the city and he failed to get a room at the Strand Palace. Not wanting to spend time checking the other hotels, he went to the Portland in St. James's Square, one of the three clubs where his grandfather had membership, and checked in there.

The Unicorn in Albemarle Street, Jolly Rodgers had told him. The RAF had taken it for its own. He dropped in there after a particularly satisfying meal in an outrageously expensive restaurant. It was one of the older London pubs, all warm woods and etched glass, and was jammed with people, the atmosphere opaque with tobacco smoke. There were some men standing at the bar that he knew from his days with the Cambridge University Air Squadron. They were, they told him, flying Spitfires out of Hornchurch, but hadn't done anything yet except training ops. Something prevented him from mentioning his afternoon kill. That pale face staring up at him from the gun blister . . . the shambled mess of the nose where the rest of the crew would have been. Four to five men on that plane. Dead on the bottom of the sea. He ordered a pint of bitter and shot the breeze.

"I say, Ramsay," one of the pilots drawled. "There's an absolutely smashing blond WAAF over there who can't seem to keep her eyes off you."

"Don't be daft."

"I mean it. I keep seeing her out of the corner of my eye. She hasn't stopped staring since you walked in."

He ventured a glance. Two WAAF sergeants seated at a table. A tall, dark-haired woman and a slender, petite blonde with a small, oval face and large blue eyes. Those eyes met his own in a cool, contemplating stare. He looked away.

"Probably thinks I'm someone else."

"Maybe she's an air marshal's bit of fluff looking for a good time."

Derek took a swig of beer. "She doesn't strike me as a bit of fluff."

"Only one way to find out, old boy. Direct and vigorous pressing of attack—that's the fighter pilot's creed. Come on, I'll toss you for the blonde, but, quite frankly, I don't care if I lose. I've always had a passion for tall, dark, beautiful sergeants."

They walked over, carrying their drinks. The pilot from Hornchurch bowed with stiff formality. "Good evening, ladies. May I take the liberty of introducing us. I am Pilot Officer Terrible Tommy Blythe, the scourge of the Luftwaffe, and this gentlemen is Pilot Officer Derek Destruction Ramsay, the only man who can fly upside down and backward. May we have the honor of buying you a drink?"

The dark-haired girl laughed. "You may. I'm Judy . . . Judy Davis. Are you really a *terrible* Tommy?"

"I like to think so."

"How marvelous! Do pull up a chair and sit down."

The blonde stared gravely at Derek. Then she smiled. Warm and faintly sad. "I thought it was you, Fat Chap. Do you remember me? Valerie A'Dean-Spender."

A group of pilots back from France on leave burst noisily into the pub waving bottles of champagne and it became impossible to talk without yelling. Derek impulsively took Valerie by the arm and led her out. Terrible Tommy was deep in mouth-to-ear conversation with the lovely brunette.

They brushed through the blackout curtain to the dark street.

"That's better. My God, what a racket." He turned to her in the gloom. "Valerie! I can hardly believe it."

"I recognized you instantly . . . or at least I felt reasonably certain it was you. You haven't changed that much, Fat Chap—except for the broken nose."

"Cricket ball . . . after I left Burgate. But, look, there's so much to talk about. Brown's is across the street. How about a brandy or something?"

"I'd love it."

"What about your friend?"

"Judy seems to be in good hands. We're not really together, I just gave her a lift into town."

He took her arm and they crossed the street to Brown's Hotel and into the small, quiet bar where he ordered two cognacs. She hadn't changed that much either, he was thinking. A nineteen- or twenty-year-old woman, but the same elfin delicacy and luminous eyes. Pest, he had called her in those days. Not a name he would use now.

"What drew you to the RAF?" he asked. "And what are you doing . . . and where?"

Her laughter was bright, musical. "One thing at a time. I joined up because I was bored doing nothing. I'm stationed, very comfortably I might add, in Bushey Heath. I work for Air Intelligence. Decoding . . . translating German radio intercepts . . . that sort of thing."

"How interesting. To be frank, Val, you never struck me as being much of a scholar."

"No, I was too busy being . . . a *pest.* Remember?"

"I didn't want to bring that up."

"I left Burgate just after you did. That would have been, let me see, nineteen thirty-three. My mother had remarried and won my custody in court. We went to live in the South of France—at Villefranche near Nice—and I was packed off to Switzerland to go to school."

"Like it?"

She wrinkled her nose in distaste. "Hated it—at first. I mean, after the marvelous freedom of Burgate I felt I was in an all-girls' prison. But I grew to enjoy it and I learned a great deal . . . German, Italian—French, of course—and music."

"Do you play?"

"Piano. Not concert quality, just well enough to brighten parties."

He grinned foolishly at her. God, but she was pretty. "I bet you're invited to a lot of them."

"More than enough."

"Have a boyfriend?"

She frowned at her drink. "I'm married."

"Oh." He looked at her left hand. It was ringless.

She noticed the direction of his glance. "I don't wear a ring. We separated a year ago."

"And what does he do?"

"He's in the army at the moment. A captain of Tirailleurs."

"French?"

"Yes . . . from Tours. His family is in the wine business."

"What's he like?"

She shrugged and drank some of her cognac. "Handsome. Very Gallic—also weak and family dominated. Qualities I ignored when he was rushing me off my feet in Cannes one winter. I was just eighteen and rather dotty with love and failed to notice the little flaws in his character. He must be quite useless in the army. His father was a great admirer of Franco and Hitler. Raymond dotes on his father's every word, so I imagine he shares some of his views, although he never expressed them to me."

"What made you leave him?"

"Something quite simple, actually. We lived in Paris. I was out shopping one day and stopped by his office. He'd neglected to lock the door and I found him naked with a woman. He became very angry with me. Said it was not a wife's business and that I had no right to drop by like that. I left him that evening and came to England . . . three months after my wedding."

"And took the king's shilling."

"Not at first. I stayed with my father and studied piano at the Royal Conservatory, but after I turned twenty it was becoming obvious to me that I would never be anything more than competent. When the war started I chucked it in—and here, dear Fat Chap, I am."

And for that he felt a gratitude he could neither explain nor express.

THE TWO COLORADOS returned at sunset after an eight-hour patrol over the North Sea. Unlike previous patrols, this one had contained a few moments of excitement. They had shadowed a strongly escorted German convoy crossing the Skagerrak in the direction of Stavanger and had been fired on by one of the warships—the shells exploding uncomfortably close to Allison's plane. Then, later in the day, as they were turning for home off Sunnhordland, they had witnessed the sinking of two German cargo ships and a patrol boat by a British destroyer.

"Jolly good for our side!" Allison had cried over the R.T., as though cheering a goal in football. Colin had stared down at one of the burning ships so far below. Men, tiny as ants, leaping into the freezing water in the mouth of the fjord. Most of them would be dead before they ever reached the barren shore.

They touched down in the broad, shallow waters of Thurne Mere, tied up at the buoys, and waited for the motor launch to take them ashore. Colin watched the squadron leader climb onto the wing of his plane and walk slowly along it as though looking for something he had dropped.

"Find anything out there?" he asked as the boat chugged toward the dock.

Allison nodded. "Thought I'd heard a twang or two. Some bits of shrapnel went through the skin. Learn through experience, old chum. Stay well away from Jerry cruisers in future."

After debriefing and a mug of tea, Colin went to his quarters, took a tepid bath, and opened a letter from Kate. She wrote to him frequently—bright, cheerful letters. This one made him sit bolt upright in the tub and he read it through twice. When Allison and two other officers came into the hut later to ask if he cared to join them for a booze-up in Ormesby, he said: "She's taken a flat in Norwich. She decided to put off going to Oxford until Michaelmas term and enrolled in some courses at a special school in Norwich."

"Who is *she,*" Allison asked.

"Her name's Kate. I thought I'd mentioned her."

"Not to me."

"Oh, I've heard of her," one of the officers said.

"The privileged few. How old is she?"

"Eighteen," Colin said.

"Pretty?"

"I think she is."

"Is she in Norwich now?"

"Apparently. Number Seven, Finch Grove. Flat D. She didn't give a phone number. Guess she doesn't have one."

Allison set his cap at an even more rakish angle than usual. "Ormesby is closer but Norwich is better. What say, chums? Shall we pass judgment on Mr. Ross's taste in women?"

"Oh, no," Colin said. "I'm not having half the squadron dropping in on her."

"Trot along by yourself, chum. But do try to bring her around for a drink. We'll be at the Sword of Nelson—as usual."

It was fifteen miles along a good, flat road. Colin had borrowed the duty officer's battered Austin and he drove as fast as he dared, considering the condition of the car and the pitch darkness of the road. It took him half an hour of groping through the blacked-out maze of Norwich streets to find Finch Grove—a narrow, dead-end street flanking the river. Number Seven was a three-story Victorian structure. Flat D was one flight up and in the rear of the building. She answered to his ring and opened the door, standing there looking beautiful in a simple skirt and blouse, her nose smudged and her hair messed.

"I was cleaning up," she said, sounding apologetic. "I don't think the previous tenant had ever heard of a dust rag or broom."

He leaned against the doorjamb and slowly shook his head. "What do you think you're up to, Kate?"

"Up to? Nothing. Are you coming in or not? This place is chilly enough as it is without leaving the door open."

He stepped in and closed it. "What's all this nonsense about not going to Oxford?"

She was on the defensive and it showed in her face. "My tutor thought it would be for the best. A few months' preparation here before plunging into university."

"This is the only school in England, I suppose."

"He thought it was the best . . . for what I need."

"He did, did he?" He stood in the middle of the small room and looked around. It was sparsely furnished. He could see part of a bedroom beyond a curtained alcove. "Not exactly the Ritz."

"I'll make it cozy. You'll see."

"What do your mother and Jenny think about this?"

She gave him a straight, unwavering look. "They consider me mature enough to do what I think best."

"Yeah, I guess you are at that."

"You're not happy to see me, are you?"

He was, terribly, and yet there was a gnawing doubt. "Sure I am, Kate." He put his arms around her in a brotherly fashion, but she clung to him fiercely, passionately, her lips warm, parted against his own.

"Oh, Colin," she whispered. "I just had to be near you . . . to see you once in a while. I won't interfere. I'm taking two very hard courses and I'll be studying most of the time. But I'll be here, just a few miles from you . . . and we can be together sometimes. Is it so wrong?"

"No," he said, smiling down at her strained, anxious face. He stroked her hair. "Heck, you're my girl."

She was happy to go out and meet his friends and spent half an hour putting on a little makeup, brushing her long brown hair, and selecting the right dress. He sat waiting patiently and thought, when she at last stepped from the curtained alcove, that the wait had been worth it.

"You look . . . a vision."

"Do I?" she asked anxiously. "The dress is all right?"

"Perfect. I think I'm an idiot to take you within a mile of that bunch."

SQUADRON LEADER ALLISON completed the briefing by seven thirty and the crews collected their chutes and walked in the morning chill toward the dock and the waiting launches. Five aircraft were going out today, each assigned a sector ranging from the southern tip of Norway to the Frisian Islands.

Allison, biting on an unlit pipe, fell into step with Colin. "Your Kate's a smasher, old chum."

"A nice girl."

"I have no doubt of it. What my ancient parent would call a pippin. I envy you, Ross." He turned his back to the wind and lit the pipe with a match. "Engaged, are you?"

"No," he said quickly. "Nothing like that. We enjoy each other's company."

"I see. Better that way, actually."

Colin's plane had the southernmost sector and flew low, no more than ten feet above the waves, so as to avoid detection by the German Freya radar on Wangerooge Island. Shortly before noon they spotted a strong German convoy heading out of Cuxhaven bound for Norway. They radioed back that information and then turned onto a course that would take them out over the North Sea, following the route taken by the bomber boys when they returned from their nightly leaflet raids over Germany. They stayed at seven thousand feet on this leg of the patrol to increase their range of observation.

"I think I've spotted something, Skipper," one of the gunner-observers in the waist called over the intercom. "Bearing six-o . . . five miles . . . small dot. Could be a U-boat's conning tower."

Porpoise more than likely, Colin was thinking as he altered course and flicked the safety catch from the bomb-release handle. Sergeant Pilot O'Conner in the second seat had his powerful binoculars out and was scanning the sea ahead.

"I see it, Skipper. Dead ahead . . . in a slight trough now . . . rising up . . . not a sub. Debris of some kind. No, by God . . . a rubber dinghy!"

Colin's heart gave a leap. "See anyone in it?"

"Hard to tell. Bring her lower and a bit to the left."

Colin dropped the nose sharply. He could see the speck of yellow on the sea now, rising and falling slowly in the swell. He leveled off at two hundred feet and circled it, banking steeply so that the men in the waist and Sergeant O'Conner could get a good look at it.

"Bomber's round raft . . . five men in it!"

The crew of a Wellington or Whitley. All had gotten out, so the bomber had probably not been attacked by fighters or hit by flak. A good many of the bombers sent as far as Berlin to drop their loads of propaganda leaflets simply ran out of gas bucking the westerlies on the long flight home to Norfolk or Lincolnshire. Going down in the small hours of the morning with a bone-weary crew. Down to a pancake landing on the cold, dark sea.

"Anyone waving?"

"Might be too done in for that."

"How does the sea look, Billy?"

"Swells, running north to south . . . two-footers, I'd say. Piece of cake."

He touched down, landing on the sea from west to east in the slight hollow of a trough, and then gunned his engines and taxied over the waves toward the raft, the hull bouncing and pitching and spray kicking up onto the windshield. He eased off on the throttles as they came close, the men in the waist sliding back the plastic blister and unstrapping the ten-foot boathook. The raft and its human cargo bobbed in the shadow of the left wing.

"Hold her steady, Billy. I'm going back and take a look."

He headed aft, noticing that the radioman and the navigator had left their cubicles and were now standing in the waist with the two gunners. The gunners had the rubber raft secured with the hook.

"Get 'em inside," he snapped.

The navigator gave him a dull stare and shook his head. "No point to it, Skip."

Colin pushed past him and leaned out of the side opening. The raft twisted on the end of the hook in the propwash. Five men in flying clothes sat huddled tightly together, arms about each other. They were all dead, salt-leathered faces turned to the sky, mummified lips pulled tautly over stark white teeth. Gulls had pecked out their eyes, leaving black sockets in the skulls. Through a rent in the heavily padded Irvin suit of one man he could see blue cloth . . . the weather-faded embroidery of RAF wings.

"Get 'em in," he said, his voice sounding alien. A terrible strangeness. "We're flying them home." The men stared at him, their faces the color of wax. He grabbed the boathook from the gunners and pulled the raft against the side of the plane. "In, I said! Goddamn it! *In!*"

SQUADRON LEADER ALLISON lit his pipe and tilted back in his chair. A hint of sun still tinted the windows of the Nissen hut.

"Twenty-four hours' leave, chum. For you and your crew."

"We don't need it," Colin said.

"I am in command here, Pilot Officer Ross. Kindly bear that in mind."

"Yeah," he muttered. "Sure."

"Bomber Command was grateful for what you did. The

chums were from a Whitley squadron at Swinderby. A paper drop in February. Don't be haunted by their eyes, Ross. Saw it once or twice on Western Approaches. The gulls never come until after they're dead."

"Thanks for telling me. I mean that, Allison."

"Now go on. You can borrow my car if you'd like. It's more reliable and comfortable than Taunton's old bus. Have a good booze-up. Get it out of your mind."

KATE WAS SURPRISED to see Colin when she opened the door. She was wearing a robe, her hair pulled back and tied with a ribbon. There was a way to reach her by telephone, but it meant calling the caretaker's flat. He had not wanted to do that.

"Sorry I disturbed you," he said.

"That's all right. I don't mind. You didn't tell me you got off every night."

She held the door open for him and he walked into the room and sat stiffly on the edge of a chair, twirling his cap in restless hands. "We can leave the base after patrols. Usually we just dash into Ormesby for a pint or two at the local. Special occasions bring us here. Like last night."

"What occasion was that?"

"Meeting you. Everyone thought you were swell."

"I liked them." She sat on the sofa opposite him and hugged her heavy robe about her. "Did you eat? I can make an omelet on the hot plate."

"I'm not very hungry. I have a twenty-four-hour leave. I wondered if you'd like to go into London."

"I have to register for my courses in the morning. I'm sorry, Colin."

"That's okay. I didn't want to go anyway. How about dinner at the Sword of Nelson . . . shepherd's pie and a shandy?"

"I'd like that."

"Okay. Get dressed."

She continued to sit, watching. She detected a change in him. A distant look in the eyes. A peculiar hardening of the mouth. "Is anything the matter, Colin?"

He shook his head and forced a grin. "Not a darn thing—now."

They walked to the pub, crossing a bridge into Westwick Street, moonlight shimmering on the little river. A full moon and a dappled sky. The bombers would be out tonight, he was thinking, holding her hand tightly, heading out across the North Sea and over Germany bearing their bundles of leaflets. There was a paper shortage in Germany. They were probably grateful for the shower of printed material fluttering down from the night sky. Grateful or not, it didn't stop them from aiming their flak guns or sending up the night fighters. Good training for the crews. There was a joke going the rounds:

RAF interrogation officer to bomber pilot: "You scattered your leaflets over Berlin very quickly."

"Oh, we didn't scatter them, sir, just tossed the bundles out."

"Good God, man! You might have hurt someone."

Not all the crews were flying. There were quite a few men in the pub from the Bomber Command field at Newton Heath, playing darts and making a large dent in the beer supply. There had been some bitter grumbling from some of the locals who resented the RAF taking over their favorite drinking spots. One of the small prices to be paid in the war.

If most of the men kept glancing at Kate, Colin kept glancing at them. His age, most of them . . . a few veterans with weathered faces and thick mustaches. He had lifted the first body out of the raft himself, expecting dead weight, shocked by the lightness—just bones and mummified flesh in the bulky flying clothes. Dead from the cold, the icy winds of February howling down from the Arctic. He wondered if they had watched the keening gulls before they died. Circling . . . knowing.

"You were very quiet," Kate said as they walked slowly back across the bridge to Finch Grove.

"Was I? Just thinking, I guess."

"Penny for your thoughts."

He pressed her hand tightly. "I was thinking of you. That's worth a thousand bucks."

"I wouldn't sell my thoughts about you for any price."

She asked him in and made coffee on the hot plate while he slouched on the sofa and leafed through one of her biology books. Glancing at him, she could tell that he was staring through it, not seeing anything printed there.

"You have an expressive face, Colin."

"Do I?"

"Yes. Eloquent. You'd make a terrible liar. I know something's wrong. I can see it."

"And what do you see . . . or think you see?"

"Oh, pain, anger . . . a gamut of emotions. When we were in the pub I watched your face while those chaps were playing darts. You had a haunted look in your eyes."

"Pretty smart, aren't you?" He closed the book and dropped it on the floor.

"Care to tell me? I'm a good listener."

"Okay." He sat forward, hands clasped between his knees. "We picked up some dead men this afternoon . . . a bomber crew that had ditched two months ago. All we should have done when we saw they were beyond saving was to take their identity disks if possible and get the hell back in the air. I had them loaded aboard. Took time . . . hauling them out of the raft . . . stowing them in the stern. God protects fools, I guess. If a Jerry floatplane had been on the prowl we would all have been dead men. Allison should have chewed my butt off, but he didn't say a word—not yet, anyway."

"I think you did the right thing. You couldn't just leave them."

"Could—and should. The dead have no priority. We were a sitting duck for damn near twenty minutes."

She sat beside him and rested a hand on his arm. "How do you feel about it, Collie?"

He closed his eyes for a moment, seeing the eyeless masks in the raft . . . the pink, smiling faces in the pub. A crew at rest . . . a crew at play. "I had to bring them home, Kate. I just wasn't tough enough to take off and leave them there."

Her hand touched his face and he turned to her and held her fiercely, face pressed against her breasts.

"Stay with me," she whispered. "Let me hold you."

"Sleep on the couch," he said. "So . . . damn tired."

She smiled and stroked the back of his head. "Have to take your legs off to make you fit. We can share the bed. And one day we'll share each other . . . for ever and ever."

13

IN THE EARLY morning hours of May 10, the sports editor of a Dutch paper awoke to the sound of planes. He was spending a few days on his parents' farm near Nijverdal, and the sound of the planes made the walls of the farmhouse tremble. He ran out into the dawn to see wave after wave of aircraft flying low from the direction of Germany. There was no telephone at the farm and so he jumped into his car and drove to the village where he phoned his paper in Amsterdam from the police station. He need not have bothered. Even as he was speaking Junkers and Heinkels were over the city, bombing the airport and strafing the roads.

WHAT CAME OVER the wires in the Paris office of INA during the course of the day was ominous and confusing. Trying to separate fact from panicky fiction was a guessing game that Martin, preparing his midnight broadcast to the U.S., was loath to do. He made endless telephone calls to his various sources of information and received nothing but wild speculation, darkest rumor, or euphoric wishful thinking for his pains. By six in the evening he had very little written. Then Albert called and asked him to meet him at the Café Alma in the rue Tronchet as soon as possible.

Albert was pacing the sidewalk in front of the café when Martin pulled up in a taxi. "About time," Albert said, opening the door for him. "I have a very nervous witness."

"A witness to what?"

"You'll find out. Just don't press him too hard or the bird will fly."

It was an appropriate allusion. The young man waiting nervously at a corner table on the terrace was a lieutenant in the French air force. He would not give his name, he said. His superiors had warned him to say nothing of what he had seen on patrol that day—not that they had believed him, he added bitterly. The war is a farce. We are going to be sold out by the Fascists!

Martin persuaded him to have a double cognac and quietly calmed him down. The pilot glanced around the nearly deserted terrace, swallowed his brandy neat, and began to talk. He had taken off that morning from his base near Châlons-sur-Marne for a reconnaissance flight over the German lines from Saarburg to the Rhine. He flew at fifteen thousand feet, but in the early light of morning he saw fleets of German fighter planes, an umbrella of them, about ten thousand feet above him. He dove quickly for the deck as his observer spotted Messerschmitts beginning to peel off. He flew on at treetop level, his twin-engine Breguet going flat out, nearly three hundred miles an hour. It was then that they saw the troop movements. Mile after mile of narrow roads clogged with German tanks and trucks, all heading into Luxembourg.

"And did you radio back what you had seen?"

But instantly! He had kept up a running comment for nearly three hours as they flew back and forth, inches above the trees, flying under high-tension wires and zooming up and over small hills. The columns of tanks, trucks, infantry, and horse-drawn transport stretched back farther than the Rhine . . . a hundred miles at least! Sluggish columns, jamming the few roads. On the way back to France they flew over the southern tip of Belgium and the Germans were there, heading for the Ardennes.

"Are you certain of that?" Martin asked.

The pilot nodded and asked for another cognac. Of course he was certain, and if his observer were here he would be just as certain. The tank columns were entering the forest. They flew low over them and were fired on for their pains.

"And when you landed in France?"

But nothing! He was in the reconnaissance section of Groupe d'Assaut I/52 and none of the bombers were even sent up until that afternoon, and then only to shift them to Montdidier for operations against *northern* Belgium some time tomorrow. A farce! A scandal! All those fat targets . . . all those juicy Boche columns jammed nose to arse on narrow roads. It was all too much for him. He was quite distraught.

"Well?" Albert asked after the pilot had gone. "What do you make of it?"

Martin swirled a dollop of cognac in his glass. "A clear light. It was what I expected they would do. The strategy according to Fenton Wood-Lacy. They'll push through the Ardennes and by-pass the Maginot line between Longwy and Sedan."

Albert reflectively chewed his bottom lip. "They'd have to cross the Meuse to do that."

"Hitler won't lose sleep over it." He swallowed his drink and shoved the glass across the table. "They know what they're doing. A high-risk plan, Albert . . . dependent on the Allies doing nothing for a few days—or doing it badly. They lobbed three pitches straight down the middle today and we just sat back and looked at them. One out . . . top of the first."

Albert shook his head. "You and your baseball analogies. I really must see a game one of these days to know what the bloody hell you're talking about."

Scott Kingsford was pleased, talking over the feedback from New York. "Good broadcast, Marty. No interference to speak of. It looks like Winston took over at just the right time. Poor sap. One day in office and now this!"

The French military censor, a gaunt staff colonel, had let the broadcast proceed without interference. It was, he told Martin and Albert, the orders of General Georges that had kept the French bombers on the ground . . . to avoid hitting civilian targets in Luxembourg. General Gamelin would soon rectify that error in judgment.

"Christ," Albert said as he left the radio station with Martin. "There's more animosity between the French generals than there is toward the enemy."

"A lot of old feuds and clashes in philosophy. What they need is another Foch to pull them all together, but there's no such man on the horizon."

They walked toward the Hotel Crillon where Martin was

staying. Paris that early May morning had never looked lovelier. A great many people wandered the streets or strolled through the gardens of the Tuileries as though seeking to impress this tranquil beauty on their memories forever.

The RAF liaison officer to the French High Command was walking his fox terrier in front of the Hotel Meurice. The gray-haired wing commander fell into step beside them. "Monitored your broadcast, Rilke. Quite accurate, as far as it went. Can't tell you this on the record, or you either, Thaxton . . . not that you could get it by the censors if I did. The RAF put up bombers yesterday afternoon. Sent over thirty Battles to hit the roads and bridges. Only nineteen came back, and those so shot up I doubt if any of them will fly again. Simply appalling losses and not a bloody thing to show for it. A complete washout."

"How do you see it, Peterson?" Martin asked.

The wing commander paused and looked down at his dog which was straining against the leash, eager to cross the road and romp in the gardens. "That we are in the wrong place with all the wrong things. I hate to play Cassandra, but I have the most awful feelings of doom."

They walked on in silence after the officer and his dog had left them. Moonlight flooded the Place de la Concorde.

"Care for a nightcap, Albert?"

"No, thanks. I want to get packed. See if I can catch some transport to the Ardennes."

"I don't think that's going to be a very healthy place to be."

"I think you're right. But an old war correspondent once told me that to write about war one must go where the war is."

Martin smiled ruefully. "I was afraid those words might

come back to haunt me. Take care of yourself . . . and never be too proud to duck."

DEREK RAMSAY MOVED his canvas deck chair out of the shadow of the dispersal hut and into the sun. He was in his shirtsleeves, his jacket with the new rings on the sleeves hung on the chair behind him. *Flying* Officer Ramsay—and a section leader now that Jolly Rodgers had been declared too old to fly fighters. The three Hurricanes of Green Section were dispersed across the flat, dry grass, engines warmed and ready to go. He eyed them with a sense of frustration. It was the 18th of May and all hell was taking place across the Channel. The squadron that had shared Kentish Hill with them had been sent to France the previous week and grim reports had drifted back. Eighteen aircraft had flown over and now only five were left—and nine pilots dead or prisoners of war. Half of Fighter Command was across the pond and here sat 624 Squadron on its duff with sixteen new Hurricanes. Not even an intruder scramble in the last few days. Jerry keeping his planes tight to the vest at the moment, like a winning poker hand.

They stood down at dusk, the ground crew pushing the planes into the antiblast revetments. Jolly Rodgers, raised in rank and made station commander as compensation for being grounded, came up to him in the mess.

"Met someone this afternoon who knows you, Ramsay."

"Who?"

"Stand me a whisky and I might say."

"All right, you blackmailing bastard."

"Now, now, lad . . . be respectful of age and rank. Had

visitors from the back-room boys. Chaps from Intelligence—perish the word. Bit of nonsense about installing some sort of recording device in the control center to capture the Huns' conversation over their R.T.s. Pawky lot, I must say. Pale-faced sods. One of them female, a corking WAAF, all blond hair and limpid blue eyes. Asked about you."

"Damn! I missed her."

"Still here, old boy. Over in ops."

He was out of the mess and running toward the group operations building, a squat concrete structure surrounded by a wall of sandbags. Valerie was there, standing with three officers he had never seen before. Squadron Leader Powell was talking to them, directing most of his remarks to her in his most charming London-barrister style.

"Oh, hello, Ramsay," he said. "I understand you know the lovely sergeant."

"Yes, sir. Old school chums." He grinned like a fool at her and she smiled back.

"Ramsay is the first man in our bunch to get a confirmed kill. Had a bit of luck off Margate last month. Splashed a Heinkel."

"Oh, I say," one of the Intelligence officers remarked in a high, girlish voice. "Jolly good for you."

The Intelligence officers had to return to Bushey Heath and Derek walked with Valerie to the car.

"You didn't tell me you'd shot down a plane."

"I have better things to talk about on the phone. When are we going to get together again?"

"I have Sunday off."

"Which Sunday?"

"Tomorrow's Sunday."

He stopped walking and impulsively took her hand. "But that's wonderful. So do I. Thank God my section had today's duty. What would you like to do?"

"Something simple and restful. A day in the country."

The officers were at the car, one of them looking back. "Whenever you're ready, Sergeant."

"I'll think of some place," he said as she hurried away.

VALERIE WAS ONE of six WAAFs billeted in a lovely old house near the edge of the common. It was owned by an elderly widow who took a motherly view of "her girls" and worried more about the possibility of their being seduced by swinish soldiers than she did about the war with Hitler. She was standing by the drawing-room windows and gave Derek a long, hard look as he came up the drive on his motorbike. He had spoken to her many times over the telephone when calling Valerie—she always answered—and he gave her a cheery wave. She did not wave back. Not so three girls leaning out of an upper window, wearing bathrobes, one of them with her hair in curlers.

"Show our Val a good time!"

He grinned up at them. "Do my best, girls."

Valerie came out of the house wearing a plaid skirt and a pale green sweater, her lovely hair covered with a silk bandanna. She carried a small wicker basket.

"What's that?" he asked.

"Sandwiches, cheese, apples from the orchard, ginger beer, and a bottle of Guinness. Gift from Mrs. Lamb."

He waved again to the elderly woman and this time she waved back—a barely perceptible raising of the hand.

"Odd sort of woman."

"Rigid and old fashioned . . . with a warm heart." She got gingerly into the sidecar. "I trust you'll keep to a modest speed. I'm not used to this."

"Hey," he said, kicking at the starter. "That doesn't sound like the Valerie I remember. You would have done handstands in that bucket at seventy miles an hour!"

"If you take a close look, Derek, you'll see that I've grown up a bit. I no longer fall out of trees."

"That's good. I thought we might climb one."

"Where are we going, by the way?"

He kicked the engine into stuttering life. "Back to school."

A large moving van pulled out of the drive of Burgate House as they approached. Another one, nearly filled, was parked in front of the school, the ramp down and two burly men carrying in desks and chairs. Marian and three boys, ranging in age from ten to fifteen, stood beside her watching the proceedings. They all hurried up to the motorbike as it came to a stop.

"Valerie!" Marian cried, holding out her arms. "Little Valerie! I couldn't believe it when Derek phoned and said he was bringing you down." She hugged her tightly as Valerie climbed out of the sidecar. "But not *little* Val any longer!"

"I've grown a bit, Marian. But you . . . you remain the same. Lovely as I remember you."

"Oh, dear, you are kind. I look a mess."

"But what's going on? Not closing the school, I hope."

"Moving it, dear. This is the final load. The War Office is taking it over for the duration for some secret reason of its own. We're moving into a sprawling old house now in Dorset. Lulworth Manor. A view of the sea. Quite pleasant."

The smallest of the boys stood awkwardly on one foot and stared shyly at Derek.

"Hello, Bertie," Derek said. "Cat got your tongue?"

"No, sir," Bertie said. "May I touch your wings?"

"How polite you are! You used to just reach out and grab."

"Oh, he's changed," his cousin said. "Haven't you, Bertie?"

"One of our major success stories," Marian laughed. "And you're another, Derek."

Marian got into her car with the boys after the second van had rumbled off down the drive. "Enjoy yourselves. The place is yours for the day. Just leave the front door keys under the mat for the army. And do *please* drop me a line from time to time, Val. Lulworth Manor . . . Lulworth, Dorset."

"I will."

They stood together and watched the car drive away, then Derek removed the wicker basket and a canvas bag from the bike.

"Let me get out of uniform and into some old clothes. Where shall we picnic. The orchard or Leith Wood?"

"Wood . . . a good, long walk."

She enjoyed her job, she said as they walked across the fields toward the high meadows and the woods. The only thing that she did not like about it was where she did it—deep underground in a warren of concrete rooms. "I burrow like a mole and you soar like an eagle."

"There are times when I'd gladly exchange places."

"What's it really like, Derek?"

"Oh, as the saying goes . . . days of pure boredom interspersed with moments of sheer terror."

"When did you shoot down that bomber?"

"The day I met you in the pub."

"Why didn't you say anything?"

"I'm not sure. Not very proud of it, I expect. Killing five or six chaps. Nazis, out to kill me . . . I know all that. Still . . ."

"You don't have to explain." She held on to his hand the rest of the way.

"Remember this glade?" he asked as they sat on the grass and opened the basket.

She looked around, nodding. "Marian's party for the school . . . the spot where I fell out of the tree."

"Care to try again?"

"No, thank you very much." She lay back in the grass and stared at the trees soaring toward the blue sky. "So peaceful here. Impossible to think there's a war going on."

"Hear anything of your husband?"

"Nothing. Half the French army is in blind retreat I understand. Total collapse. What one would expect from an army that could give Raymond a captaincy. Poor France."

They walked back to the school in the slanting rays of the afternoon sun—sunburnt, bramble scratched, and content. The house was cool and dim. Quite a few things had been left behind and they found a kettle, cups, a slightly cracked teapot, and a packet of tea in the kitchen. The gas and electricity were still on and Valerie made tea.

"We must explore," Valerie said. "I do hope they didn't take Lenin's carpet."

"Of course they must have taken it. What would the soviet do without it?"

"The soviet!" She hugged her teacup. "God, does that send

me back. Their trusted, ever-faithful messenger. I'd love to see that room again before we go."

"Come on, then. Finish your tea."

It was at the top of the house. Unchanged. The nursery wallpaper still on the walls. Lenin's carpet was gone, but a chair and an old horsehair couch with no back remained.

"So many memories," she said wistfully, touching the wallpaper. "I wonder where they are now? Jameson and Agnes Heath-Jones. And remember Gowers?"

"He's a solicitor. I ran into him one day in London and we had a drink." The fading sun streaming through the windows touched her hair, golden yellow, luminous as a corona. "You're a beautiful woman, Valerie."

She looked at him with her sad little smile. "Odd hearing you call me that. Odder still to think of being a woman at all in this place. Just the Pest and Fat Chap waiting for the soviet to come up the stairs from tea."

He touched the softness of her cheek, fingers lingering, trailing the delicate jaw. "I can't think of you that way."

"Nor I you . . . now."

Her body against him, hands clenching his back. Her lips were parted, pressing against his own with an eager intensity. He felt drunk, light-headed and reeling as he moved with her to the couch.

Blue and pink. The nursery at the top of the stairs. Rabbits and squirrels in stately dance across the papered walls. Children at their games. How exquisite she was with the sun touching her body. Ivory and spun gold. The firm, coral-tipped breasts. The sun set in burnt orange across the windows and she moved languidly on top of him, resting her head in the hollow of his shoulder. He stroked the orange velvet of her back and looked at the sunglowed sky that was so beautiful and so deadly and he thought—God—God . . . please hold this moment forever . . . never let it pass.

THE FIVE POILUS and the tall Senegalese corporal had been crouching in the culvert all afternoon, and only the Senegalese was willing to join Albert in leaving it at dusk.

"The planes will be back," one of the French infantrymen said.

"It's getting dark," Albert told him.

"The Boche are like cats."

There was no point in arguing with them. Their nerves had been shattered by the Stukas and he couldn't blame them. They were safe from the bombing inside the concrete tunnel and they were ready to surrender anyway. All of them, except the Senegalese, had thrown away their weapons. The ebony-black corporal slung his rifle over his shoulder and followed Albert out of the culvert and up the steep embankment to the road. It stretched away in the dark orange glow of the sunset like a road leading to hell. Shattered and burning trucks were littered around the craters along with the bodies of men and bomb-slaughtered horses. The eastern horizon glowed dull red from the flames of a burning village.

The corporal squatted on the road and turned his map to the flickering light of a blazing truck. His steel helmet was too small for his head and sat on top of it like a pot.

"Rheims. What is left of my regiment should be there. Yes.

Rheims, I think." He spoke good French with a musical lilt.

"Give me the directions for Arras," Albert said, adjusting the pack a major of Chasseurs had given him to hold his gear and portable typewriter.

"That way," he said, pointing a long finger to the west. "But I would not try for it, man. Damn Boche get you quick."

"I don't think so. They won't move their tanks at night."

"What is good at Arras?"

"The English should be there."

The corporal stood up, drew a revolver from the pocket of his greatcoat, and offered it to Albert butt first. "Kill Boche."

He shook his head. "Thank you, but no. I mustn't carry a gun."

The man looked mystified and returned the weapon to his pocket. "May your God go with you then, English man."

He missed the Senegalese as he struck out on his own, missed the company of any man who had a gun and seemed eager to use it. He pitied the German who ran into the huge corporal in the dark. He took the right fork of the road, walking carefully around the interlocking bomb craters that the Stukas had created early that afternoon when they had first plummeted on the retreating French column. The craters stank of high explosives and death. There had been two trucks filled with men on this spot when the bombs had slapped into it like bullets into a bull's-eye.

The narrow country road met the highway running south from Valenciennes and he could hear the movement along it long before he reached the junction. It was a sound that he had heard often during the past few days and hoped never to hear again. The sound of thousands of people fleeing from a battle that was quite impossible to flee from. They came in limousines and rattling Citroëns, in lumbering horse-drawn farm carts . . . on foot pushing wheelbarrows or baby carriages piled high with their belongings. He had even seen one man staggering along with a grandfather clock strapped to his bent back. This stream was no different from the others, except poorer. No limousines. No cars of any sort. Just weary people pushing carts through the darkness. He threaded his way through them and continued west on a silent, empty road. Shortly after midnight he reached a village that had been hastily abandoned and thoroughly looted, the cobbled street littered with bits of clothing, bed sheets, and broken crockery. He drank some water from the village pump, the handle making an unearthly squeal in the darkness. As he hurried on, a shape emerged from the shadows of a house at the end of the street.

"Haltez-vous! Haltez!"

He stopped, smiling to himself. The dreadful French pronunciation could mean only one thing . . . "It's all right! I'm English!"

A shielded torch flicked a thin shaft of light across him.

"Keep your 'ands up, mate."

There were two of them, short, stocky men in British battle dress, their hobnailed boots ringing on the worn stones as they came toward him. One of them held a rifle.

"Now then," the man with the torch said, flicking it on Albert's face. "What's a civvy doin' out 'ere?"

"The name's Thaxton . . . A. E. Thaxton . . . correspondent for the London *Daily Post.* My credentials are in my jacket pocket."

"Oh, they are, are they? Got a bloody grenade in there, too? What you think, Pincher?"

"I dunno, Bert. Chap I know says he saw ten Belgium nuns last week all wearin' German bloody army boots."

"That's just a story," Albert said.

"How would you bloody well know, mate?"

"Look, we're wasting time. Check my passes."

The papers were checked and the soldiers were satisfied. "Sorry, mate. You can get a bit windy out here on your lonesome. Where are you goin'?"

"Arras."

"Hop in with us, then. We were just pullin' out when we 'eard you down at the pump."

They were troopers of the Royal Lancers on a patrol in their Bren gun carrier. Albert got into the back of the squat little armored vehicle and they roared off, the caterpillar tracks chewing into the hard-packed gravel road.

Most of what was left of the British armor was in Arras, parked under dusty trees or scattered about draped with camouflage netting. The Luftwaffe had come over that day and dive bombed the town heavily. Some houses still burned at three in the morning and the streets were filled with the debris of shattered brick and plaster.

Major General Wood-Lacy's HQ was in a garage off the main boulevard, a noisy place crowded with overtired tank officers clustered in front of a wall map—a Michelin road map of northern France that was pathetically inadequate for military use. Soldiers cursed the squawking, static-ridden radio sets and the nearly useless telephones. It was an atmosphere of chaos but no sign of despair. Fenton, looking drawn and haggard, sat drinking a warm bottle of orange soda behind an oil-stained desk cluttered with Renault parts.

"I'm bloody glad to see you, Albert."

"Rather good to see you, too."

"Where have you come from?"

"The Ardennes and Sedan . . . carried along in the retreat."

"*Rout* would be a better word," Fenton said in weary resignation. He took a swig of soda pop and handed the bottle to Albert, who took it gratefully. "With the help of some French tanks we stopped a panzer column cold today . . . about three miles out of town. Only an advance group so we probably won't have the same sort of luck in a day or two."

"Is the BEF digging in here?"

"Christ no. We're just odds and sods. A holding action. Gort's pulling the army back to the coast—if there's still a coast left to fall back to. Jerry is between us and Paris and reached the sea today at St. Valéry and Noyelles. Nothing to stop them from rolling up to Boulogne and Calais. Bloody *nothing.*"

"And you're to hold on here?"

Fenton lit a cigarette and then immediately stabbed it out. "A counterattack is in the works . . . hit the panzers' right flank if possible . . . slow the bastards up a bit. Though how much we can slow them with sixteen medium tanks, some bloody useless lights, and a few odds and ends of infantry is not worth thinking about. 'Hawkforce' is the code name in case you want to write an obituary."

Morning came, hazy with smoke. A Bofors gun in a little park across from the garage began to fire, followed by the nervous chatter of machine guns, the sound of the firing drowned by the howl of Stukas and the heavy detonations of their bombs. Albert, who had managed to find a spot to sleep in the bottom of the lubrication pit, was advised to stay there by a knowing sergeant. "You won't find a better dugout, lad," the man said. "As good a bomb shelter as they come."

Albert ignored the advice and started for the narrow concrete steps leading from the pit. "I want to move out with Hawkforce."

"Too late for that, son. They left before dawn."

He spent the day being bombed, going hungry—except for some hardtack and weak tea—and attempting to get the story of the French army's debacle in the Ardennes down on paper. The sergeant, who had fought near this spot during the last war, knew the value of a hole in the ground. A bomb, landing in the park, had sent splinters into the garage killing two radiomen. The radios were now down in the grease pit along with half a dozen signalers, and Albert barely had room to balance his typewriter on his knees.

The long day finally ended, and so did the Stuka attacks. At dusk, what was left of Hawkforce began to trickle back into what was left of the once thriving town.

"We scuppered a few," Fenton said, climbing painfully out of the Bren gun carrier he used as a command car. "But it was a bloody balls-up just the same."

"Are you all right?" Albert asked in concern.

The general removed his steel helmet and wiped his smoke-stained face with a handkerchief. "Just stiff as a bloody post and fucking dead on my feet. We knocked out a dozen of their tanks and gave their infantry holy fits, but we had to cut and run."

"Attack again tomorrow?"

"No. We're to pull everything out during the night and get across the La Bassée canal."

"And then what?"

"Head for the coast . . . form a defense perimeter around Dunkirk."

"Dunkirk?"

"Yes. I was there once. Dreary little town. Not much of a port either, so I don't know what the hell the army will do there. Play in the sand I imagine until Jerry rounds us up."

THE SQUADRON THAT had been sent to France returned to Kentish Hill on the 25th of May—four pilots and a dozen ground crew on one of the last ships out of burning Calais. Every one of their Hurricanes had been destroyed, three of them by a German tank which had come bursting across their makeshift landing field all guns blazing. The survivors of the ill-fated squadron reported to Jolly Rodgers and were hastily packed off on leave.

"They were all in rum shape," Jolly said, convening a meeting of 624 Squadron in the mess that afternoon. "The first thing one of them said to me—and I shall not tell you this man's name—was that we might just as well pack it in. He told me that the BEF is bloody doomed now that Boulogne has fallen and Calais about to fall any minute. I will not tolerate that sort of talk as long as I am station commander. A squadron of Spits will arrive in the morning from North Weald and you will fly in concert with them. That's all I have to say, chaps. Powelly can take it from here."

Squadron Leader Powell then explained the current military situation in Artois and Flanders, enumerating the terrible facts as though summing up a case in front of a jury. "All plans for evacuating the army have been thrown out of kilter now with the loss of two major ports. They're backed up against Dunkirk and Jerry has been bombing the port facilities there. The hope is that a few thousand men can be drawn off at night by destroyers, but even that may not be possible unless the Luftwaffe can be slowed down a bit. We have not one plane left in France that can do the job. It's going to be up to us, and squadrons like us, here in England. The men coming in tomorrow from North Weald are all regulars and may not think too highly of the Auxiliary. I expect every man to show them that we're second to none. All right, eat, drink, and be merry . . . for tomorrow we *fly.* If I can be excused my little pun."

Pilot Officer Barratt looked puzzled as he walked from the mess with Derek. "What little pun was that, Ramsay?"

"Damned if I know," he said, not caring to explain.

"Going to the Red Bull?"

"No . . . not tonight. Meeting someone in Watford."

Or at least he hoped he would be. He hadn't seen Valerie since their Sunday together at Burgate, although he had managed to get through to her on the telephone one evening. It had been impossible to make plans. The squadron had been on continuous stand-by since the debacle in France, never knowing from one day to the next if they would be sent across to back up the decimated regulars. Had not seen her, but had never stopped thinking about her, living over in his mind the all too brief time in that little room. The horsehair couch . . . the exquisite feel of her body in his arms. "You seem to be smiling to yourself a good deal lately," had been the squadron leader's comment one night at dinner. He was smiling now, hunched over the handlebars as he raced the motorbike toward her at seventy miles an hour.

The Jolly Huntsman was the RAF pub in Watford, filled with staff and "back-room boys" from the vast and secret Fighter Command headquarters and communications complex at Bushey Heath and Bentley Priory. It was crowded in the early evening. The saloon bar was exclusively for the upper ranks, mostly middle-aged wing commanders and group captains. The more lowly officers and NCOs of both sexes jammed the less stuffy public bar. He spotted Valerie standing at the three-deep bar drinking a sherry and talking with the officers he had seen at the ops building the week before. She saw him elbowing his way through the crowd and hurried to meet him. She looked impossibly beautiful to him and he had to restrain himself from sweeping her up and sending her sherry glass flying.

"Hello," he said.

"And hello to you. This is a surprise."

"It's impossible to call first."

"I know. Impossible to call you. I just got off."

"Same here. First day we've been allowed off the base."

She nodded. "I know. My friend Judy Davis works in sector control. She keeps tabs on your squadron for me. I was praying you wouldn't be sent across."

They stood in the middle of the noisy room looking at each other and being jostled.

"Anywhere we could go and be alone for a few minutes?"

Her eyes were steady on his face. "Is that all the time you have?"

"No . . . hours. Well, until midnight anyway."

She set her drink down on a table and took his hand. "Come on then."

He did as she asked and cut the engine before entering the drive, letting the bike coast to a stop in the shadows of the house.

"Mrs. Lamb goes up to bed at eight. My room's on the top floor. The governess's room in the days when Mrs. Lamb had need of one."

"Is it all right for me to come in?"

"Of course it isn't. Do be quiet on the stairs. Don't, for heaven's sake, trip over a carpet rod."

He took his shoes off in the entry hall and they reached her spacious room without incident. She bolted the door behind them. "Safe and secure. Sorry I can't offer you a drink. I have some oranges, though. One of the group captains brought a bag back from Gibraltar."

He placed his hands on her shoulders and stroked the sensible uniform cloth which covered the vibrant flesh beneath. "I don't need a drink . . . nor an orange."

"No," she whispered. "Neither do I."

The bedside lamp threw a feeble light, tinged rose by the silk shade. She straddled him, thighs pressed tightly against his hips, back arched in ecstasy. He gazed up at her and ran his hands across the downy softness of her belly. "I love you, Valerie."

She bent down to him and touched his face. "Please don't. I don't think I could bear it if I fell in love with you."

His hands cupped her breasts, the taut nipples. "I think you are now . . . a little bit."

"A bit, yes . . . some. Making love. I'm not made of stone."

"Christ, no."

"You touch my heart, Fat Chap. I wish you didn't." She raised her hips and lay beside him, her face cool against his chest. "The terrible thing about the place where I work is that I will always know where you are . . . what you're doing . . . what happens to you. I made a vow with myself that I would never take a fighter pilot for a lover."

"God's little jest. I wanted to join my father's regiment, the Royal Marines, but the RAF grabbed me out of the Cambridge air squadron. If I had been a marine I never would have met you again. That, my darling Val, is fate for you."

"Yes," she whispered, stroking his body lightly with her fingertips. "I know all about fate."

THE SQUADRON FLEW at twenty-two thousand feet, three thousand feet below and a good way behind the faster Spitfire squadron that had joined them early that morning from North Weald. The smoke from Dunkirk was a thick, greasy black plume twenty miles to the south of them. Sector Control was vectoring them to cross the Belgian coast over Nieuwpoort to intercept the German bombers before they could reach the bridgehead and the nearly defenseless troops jamming the beaches.

The radio crackled in Derek's ears. Squadron Leader Powell's voice. "This is Fox leader. Angels two zero. Bandits. Don't break till I do. Echelon starboard. That's the good lads."

Derek glanced down and ahead. The German bombers were two thousand feet below and five miles ahead—a great black swarm of them in tight formations. Fifty at least. High above them were the Messerschmitts, whirling like bees as the fifteen Spitfires made their first slashing pass through them. That was the strategy. Spits to hit the fighters . . . Hurricanes to break up the bomber formations. They had flown a long way from Kentish Hill and had a long flight back. Derek checked the fuel gauge. Ten, fifteen minutes. That was the time they could safely stay over Belgium.

"Tally Ho!" Powell yelled over the R.T. "Buster!"

Wing over and down in a sickening plummet toward the packed masses of the bombers below. Dorniers. Pencil-thin bodies and short stubby wings. Derek flicked on the gunsight and turned the firing button from safety. Tracer whirling up from the German top gunners. Twitchy, he was thinking. Wasting ammunition. The green-and-black bombers grew larger with frightening rapidity. He picked one out, staring at the gunsight glow reflected on the windshield . . . the huge body . . . the black crosses filling the sharply etched lines. He pressed the firing button and the Hurricane shuddered with the recoil of the eight guns. Tracers thudding home, bits of the German's portside engine whipped away. Don't tarry . . . don't tarry . . . on and through . . . pick another. He was being hit . . . tracer coursing past the cowling. The sound of snapping metal behind him. A Dornier turning to his right. He fired ahead of it, holding down the button. Perfect deflection shot . . . the bomber flying straight into the bullet stream . . . the plastic greenhouse of the nose exploding into a million fragments. A clean kill. "Got one, Skipper!" he screamed over the radio. And then he was past them all in a wind-shrieking dive toward the green land below. Back on the stick, fighting the pressure on the wings. Out of it . . . the blood draining from his head . . . chin pulled down to his chest. He blacked out for a second and when his head cleared he was climbing back up. Ten thousand feet . . . fifteen . . . twenty. No sign of the bombers or his squadron. Voices over the R.T. "Got the bastard!" "Look out, Johnnie!" "I'm behind you, Skipper." "Break left . . . break left!"

And then he saw them. Ten miles ahead. The once tight bomber formation spread out now over miles of sky. A bomber dropping in a ball of fire. Another with one wing gone, twirling down like a leaf from a tree. The vicious little Messerschmitts and the Spitfires churning in and out among the bombers. A Spitfire went into a dive and never pulled out of it. One of the Hurricanes rolled lazily past, flames roaring out of the cockpit, through the black form of the pilot now mercifully dead. Squadron Leader Powell's plane. Then Barratt's voice through the cacophony of the radio.

"I've been hit! I've been hit!"

He looked wildly around but could not see him. Many of the bombers were jettisoning their loads now and breaking out of the fight. Time to go for all of them.

"This is Fox Green leader . . . Skipper bought it . . . break for home. Buster!"

He power dived for the coast and pulled out low over the sand dunes. A glance in the rearview mirror. Other Hurricanes behind him. He dropped lower, keeping twenty feet above the flat sea, and set a course for the Kentish coast.

JOLLY RODGERS SAT unmoving in his neat little station commander's office. The window was open and he stared unseeing at the bright grass of the airfield, the distant woods.

"We were always such a tight little group," he said in a dull, faraway voice. "Pals, Ramsay. All good pals together. Powelly and me . . . ten years. In the squadron every weekend . . . in the City during the week. I'm a solicitor, you know. Weeks, Parsons, Rodgers, and Bolton . . . Gough Square. I can't tell you how many cases old Powelly pleaded in court for me. Bloody fine lawyer. Finer man. Three kids. Not fair, Ramsay. Powell gone . . . and Shepherd. Young Barratt. Wilson saw him go. Plane looked okay. Must have been killed in his seat." He wiped a hand slowly across his forehead. He looked suddenly very old and tired. "They'll be sending a new skipper tomorrow and replacements. You're a level-headed chap. Natural flier. Two planes to your credit now. Damn good show." He sighed deeply and continued to stare through the window as though hoping to see Squadron Leader Jeremy Thomas Powell come skimming in over the trees in time for lunch. "If ops scrambles the squadron this afternoon, which they probably will, you'd best take command of it."

"Thanks. And I'm sorry, Jolly."

"Of course, old man . . . of course."

Derek walked toward the mess, still wearing his cumbersome Irvin suit and flying boots. The squadron leader of the Spitfire squadron came up to him on a bicycle and stopped. He was a tall, rangy-looking man with thick eyebrows. A regular. "Ramsay. Is that correct?"

"Yes, sir."

"Sorry we had such a brief meet-to this morning. Shame

about your skipper. You chaps did bloody okay this morning. Lost three, did you?"

"Yes, sir."

"We lost two of ours. But bloody pranged them proper, eh?"

"Not bad."

"Break the bastards up. That's the ticket, Ramsay. Give 'em a squirt and look for another. Rattle the bastards. Well, see you in the mess. Buy you a beer."

Derek watched him cycle furiously off. He paused for a moment and looked out across the field. The ground crew were working on the planes, fuel trucks—so damn few of them—moving from one to another. Fitters, mechanics, and armorers swarming over their particular plane. Getting them ready. Probably fly out in an hour or so. Back across. Today . . . and tomorrow. And all the tomorrows to come.

14

THE FEW MATILDAS that were left were run into the ditches so that only the turret and the two-pounder gun could be seen above the ground. The light tanks were parked in strategic spots among the rubble at the edge of the town to serve as machine-gun support for the infantry. Their engines were drained of oil and allowed to run until they smoked and died. There was no fuel left in the dumps to move them very far anyway.

"It's dig in and pray," Fenton said, pulling the cork on a bottle of wine. He walked around the shell-holed post office that served as his command post and splashed wine into the tin mugs of his junior officers. It was an hour past sundown, but the room was bright from the burning buildings across the street. No one was fighting the flames. There was no water and less time. "I want the buggers to pay for every foot of ground. Make that clearly understood, Tomlinson. No indiscriminate firing. Make every bloody shot count."

"Yes, sir," the captain said. He was a young man, his eyes sunken in a drawn face. He looked ancient.

"Forlorn hope," the general muttered, pacing the room with its counter and clerks' cage, the postal regulations set in a framed box on one wall, the glass long shattered. "I was a boy during the Boer War. One heard a good deal of that expression then . . . 'forlorn hope' . . . the gallant charge of doomed men. Boer words actually . . . *verloren hoop* . . . lost troop. That's us, lads, in case no one is aware of it."

There was some strained laughter and the men drank their wine and left.

"Not the most encouraging little speech I've ever heard," Albert said. He was seated on the countertop, legs dangling, nursing his cup of wine.

"I'd be a proper shit if I told them any different. They're good lads and appreciate the truth—even if it is a trifle nasty."

" 'Trifle'? You sounded like a Spartan general at Thermopylae."

Fenton snorted and downed his wine in a gulp. "The old Spartans prettied themselves up before battle. Did you know that? Plucked their body hair and painted their lips and eyes. Can you see my lot doing that? Take an order from the king to make them clean their fingernails. My boys won't die gloriously, they'll just die—scruffy and tough to the bloody end. You'll see." He frowned and opened another bottle with the corkscrew in his pocketknife. "To be frank, I hope you don't see. I'm ordering you off. Go back to Blighty and do your writing there."

"You can't order me to do anything. All you can do is kick me out of your area."

"Which is the blasted trouble with civilians. Never do what they're told."

There was a stir outside and a sergeant stuck his head through the jagged gap where a door had once been. "General White arriving, sir."

The elderly corps commander came into the room, stepping carefully over the rubble.

"Hello, Chalky," Fenton said. "Care for some plonk? A Cotes du Rhone. Modest, but pleasant."

"I don't think so, Hawk. Thanks just the same." He sat wearily on a bench, removed his cap, and slapped the dust from it. His kindly face was ingrained with soot and his mustache gray with ash. "Orders came in for you, Hawk. Direct from Downing Street. The French will take over your positions tonight. You're to pull your people down to the beach."

"Bugger that."

"An order is an order. If it were up to me I'd gladly sell you to Jerry for thirty pieces of silver—less, even. You can be such a pain in the arse."

"Now look here, Chalky—"

"No arguments please. I've been a firm supporter of your theories for over ten years. The tank is the key to victory. Everyone knows that now. Winston doesn't want his few experts dead or lolling away in prison camps. Don't be a fool, Hawk. Get your mob to the beach as quickly as possible. There'll be three destroyers coming in before midnight and you'd damn well better get on one of them."

Fenton poured wine into his cup and handed it to the general. "I would appreciate your judgment, Chalky."

The man took a sip. "Good body. Soft on the palate. You

might leave some bottles behind. The French will appreciate it."

They moved through the shattered, burning town and down to the beach. Night brought little relief from the bombing. Parachute flares drifted eerily above the harbor, bringing into sharp relief the wooden girders of the long pier. Stukas dived through the sulfurous mist of the flares, aiming for the pier and the long lines of shuffling men, but their bombs fell wide.

"A bloody charmed life that pier," one of the naval embarkation officers said.

Fenton eyed the rickety structure dubiously. "And we're to go out on that?"

"Afraid so. No other spot for the destroyers to dock. *Javelin, Verity,* and *Venomous* are due within the hour . . . or as soon as the hospital ship finishes loading on. You can stay here if you wish. I have your group down for *Venomous.* Four hundred and twelve. Is that correct?"

"More like three ninety—and one civilian."

"A civilian? Oh, I say. I wasn't told. Not Belgian royalty or anything like that I suppose?"

"Hardly. A newspaper reporter. Albert Thaxton of the *Post.*"

"Oh, dear. Probably be charged for the passage I expect. Be all right with him, do you think?"

Fenton merely stared at him until he hurried away into the flickering darkness.

"War," he said to Albert, "is truly the province of madness."

DAWN WAS BREAKING across a cloudless sky when the army staff car pulled up in front of the Café Moskva.

"Care to come up?" Albert asked.

Fenton shook his head. "Just give her my love. We'll have dinner together if at all possible."

Dinner together! It seemed unreal to Albert. He stood on the pavement in the cool quiet of the London street, the howls and shrieks of Dunkirk still buzzing in his ears. Unlocking the front door, he carried his gear up the stairs and left it in the hall. The bedroom door was open and he could see Jennifer's blanketed form. He sat on the edge of the bed and placed a hand softly on her shoulder.

She awoke with a jump and a startled cry.

"It's only me," he said.

"Oh, my God!" she sobbed, throwing herself into his arms. "*Only* you! Oh, Thax . . . Thax . . . Thax!"

"I'm as filthy as a tramp."

She buried her face in his shoulder and clenched his back. "I don't care. I don't care . . ."

"I do. I'm a fastidious man. Would you draw me a bath? I'm too tired to move another step."

She bounded off the bed, putting on lights, turning on the taps in the bath, boiling water for tea. He continued to sit on the bed, talking to her to keep awake and watching her darting back and forth in her nightgown. She helped him undress, clucking her tongue over the appalling condition of his clothes. "I think we'll have to burn this lot." She helped him into the tub and knelt by the side of it to scrub his back vigorously with a sponge.

"I think I must have died and gone to paradise," he said, sinking down under the foam.

"And then bed for you . . . sleep for a week."

"A few hours is more like it. I have to see Jacob."

"Jacob can come and see you."

"Either way. I must go back, Jenny."

"Why?" Her hand shook slightly as she began to shampoo his hair. "You've been through enough."

"It's the story of the century and I have to follow it up. I saw only one tiny piece of the picture falling back with your father. I want Jacob to fill me in, put it all into perspective. Then I'll go over again. That is, unless the Germans get there first."

He slept as though drugged. No dreams. An immense blackness. When he woke up it was to see Jacob seated in a chair by the window reading through the copy he had typed in France.

"Meet with your approval?"

Jacob removed his glasses and placed the sheets on a table. "Very much so. Jenny told me you're considering going back."

"If the army hasn't surrendered."

"Where did they drop you off?"

"Dover was full up so they took us to Ramsgate."

"Notice anything in the harbor while you were there?"

"An unusual number of yachts and motorboats."

"Part of the new plan, Thax. I just left the Admiralty. It's quite impossible to get enough men off the pier . . . taking too much time and we're losing too many destroyers doing it. They're going to start taking the men right off the beaches. Thousands of little boats are gathering. In Ramsgate . . . Dover . . . Folkestone. Everywhere. Yachts, trawlers, drifters, tugs . . . even large rowboats. All going across the Channel starting this afternoon. Civilians all, Thax. An armada of workaday seamen and weekend sailors . . . fishermen, tugboat captains, dentists, and clerks."

Albert sat up in bed. "Christ. Maybe something can be salvaged from the disaster yet."

"One man's disaster is another man's victory. I wish you could have known my father. He was the last of the press lords. Took an obscure little sheet called the *London and Provinces Daily Post and Times Register* and turned it into the largest paper in the world. He had a genius for putting the right slant to a story. The British army is no stranger to debacles. There was one in the last war . . . right at the beginning when the Germans forced the BEF to retreat from Mons. My father didn't want a headline that read 'retreat' from Mons, so he inserted the word *glorious* . . . the 'glorious' retreat from Mons. Made quite a difference, don't you think? We have the same situation now."

"Nothing particularly glorious about Dunkirk, Jacob."

"There will be if we can save the army."

"Wars, as they say, are not won by retreats or evacuations."

"Perhaps not, but the *will* to fight . . . the courage and pride to go on, can be won by them. We English have always taken a perverse pride in our military adversities—every schoolboy knows that. If those little ships sailing and chugging and rowing out of Ramsgate and Dover this afternoon can pull it off—well, there's a miracle for you. And there's nothing quite like a miracle for giving people faith."

SQUADRON LEADER ALLISON broke the news before the morning patrol. There had been some idle speculation among the crews for the delay in takeoff and now they knew.

"Ops are canceled for the day, chums. We're to have no part in this Dunkirk show. They're moving us to Beauty Firth."

"Where the hell's that?" Colin asked.

"Scotland, old chum. Hard by Inverness. It places us nearly three hundred miles closer to Narvik. The air chief marshal of Coastal Command has not seen fit to confide in me as yet, but I would say that our pathetic little force sitting in Norway is on the verge of being withdrawn."

"When do we leave?"

"After the briefing get your personal gear packed and stowed. We should fly out of here within the hour."

"What's Inverness like, Skipper?"

"Chilly and wet. And no one, as far as I know, has been laid there since Bonnie Prince Charlie. A spell of celibacy should do you randy chums a world of good."

Colin fell into step beside him as they walked toward the mess hall for the flight briefing. "Any chance of my ringing Kate? I was supposed to meet her tonight at the Nelson."

"Sorry. No telephone calls permitted. Leading Aircraftman Jones will be going into Norwich later to pick up the railroad warrants for the ground crew. Dash off a note to her. I'm sure Jones will gladly deliver it."

Colin strode along in silence for a moment, scowling at the ground; then he stopped and plucked Allison's sleeve. "Look here, Skip, I know that some of the guys screw around with the local tarts, but me and Kate . . ." He stopped, face red with embarrassment.

The faintest of smiles stretched Allison's thin lips. "That thought never crossed my mind."

"She's . . . well, something special."

"Of course. And I can quite see why."

"A real . . . friend."

Allison's smile broadened. "Ah, indeed yes. A particularly lovely and infinitely desirable . . . *chum!*"

RAF Beauly Firth was near Charlestown, across the broad firth from Inverness. It had been a small seaplane base before the war and, although construction was proceeding day and night, was hardly equipped to handle the number of flying boats sent there. A squadron of giant four-engine Sunderlands was moored on the slate-gray waters when Allison's group set down. Their officers, most of whom Allison knew, were crowded morosely in the ramshackle officers' mess.

"It's a real cock-up, Allison," their squadron leader said bitterly. "It'll be days before our ground crew gets here."

"The same with ours."

"Not to mention parts and spares. I think someone at the Air Ministry is running around without a head. Oh, Lord, here comes The Comedian."

The station commander entered the mess in a burst of ebullient good fellowship. He was a middle-aged, portly man who might have been a hotel manager or golf-club secretary in civilian life.

"That's the spirit, lads. Make yourselves at home. May I welcome you boys from Thurne Mere. Sorry we're a bit cramped here at present, but that will change shortly. I must also apologize for the dirth of maintenance facilities. The fact is, we were not scheduled to expect aircraft here for another two weeks, but we shall muddle through, what? I have just made arrangements to billet most of you in the local hotels and rooming houses. A lot of them about, don't you know. Popular spot before the war for the summer tourist trade, what with Loch Ness and its monster just down the road. If the squadron leaders will pop along to my office we can go over the details."

"Care to 'pop,' Allison?" the squadron leader whispered.

"Why not, old chum? He looks the type of man who would serve an exceptional sherry."

Colin was billeted in a rambling old hotel with splendid views across hill and firth. He put in a call early in the evening to Norwich and it took three hours before the operator in Inverness could put it through. He reached the caretaker who went up to Kate's flat and brought her down. She sounded breathless over the line.

"Oh, Collie, I'm just crushed that you're gone. Are you in Inverness?"

"Near there . . . Charlestown."

"But how long will you be away?"

"I can't say. No one knows anything. Quite a while I would think. I'm sorry, Kate. Not much chance of any leave at the moment."

"I'll come up there."

He gripped the receiver very tightly. "You can't do that, Kate. Impossible."

"No it isn't. I could come up just for the summer. My grandfather owned a hunting lodge in Glen Garry . . . Mama owns it now. I could stay there . . . bring all my books, study . . . see you from time to time. It's only forty-five miles or so from Inverness."

"Getting there would be difficult. Trains . . . all this Dunkirk business."

"Don't you want to see me, Collie?"

"Of course I do, you know that. It would be wonderful. I just don't want you to turn into some kind of . . . camp follower."

There was a long pause and then she lowered her voice and said: "It's not being a camp follower to want to be near someone you love. There. I said it. And it's not a schoolgirl crush this time. I love you, Colin."

He looked toward the windows, a mauve light lingering over the still waters of the firth. "I guess I love you, too, Kate."

ORDERS CAME IN constantly to be almost immediately canceled. A fog of confusion permeated the squadrons. Rumors swept the base and were squelched with difficulty.

"I'll trust the *Daily Post,*" one of the pilots said after breakfast on the last day of May. "This A. E. Thaxton chap has gone back and forth with the little ships. They're bloody well saving the BEF."

"The ruddy civvies are doing more than we are," someone remarked bitterly.

Morale in both squadrons had sunk to worrying lows in just a few days. Allison gave a talk to all the crews in the mess later that morning.

"Now look here, chums. There's no point in everyone slouching about with their chins down to their knees. We don't fly the type of aircraft that would be of much bloody use at the moment. We're here because someone at the War Office got terribly windy about our troops in Norway . . . envisioned an arctic Dunkirk with the poor old brown jobs being hurled into the freezing sea. The fact is, and I have this straight from an uncle in Whitehall and quite close to the situation, that our lads in Narvik are squatting in the town and the Jerry ski troops are hunkered down in the hills with nary a shot nor a cross word being exchanged between them. It is self-evident that our chums in Narvik will be withdrawn as soon as transport and naval escort can be released from the Dunkirk show. The powers that be are resigned to an embarrassing fiasco. What they did not want was another disaster. Our job will be to provide reconnaissance and assistance for the operation. In my own humble opinion, that task will not begin for another week or so. In the meantime, this nasty joke of a station may come to some sort of order and we may as well make the best of it until it does. The weather's good . . . the beer plentiful . . . the links at Munlochy available and the girls in Inverness far more acquiescent than I would have thought possible. Go, my chums. Enjoy your off hours with our blessings . . . but stay in touch."

Cheers rattled the windows and The Comedian scurried out of his office in the wild delusion that the war was over.

"Ross!" Allison called out. "Don't be in such a hurry to leave. Where are you off to anyway?"

"I don't know, Skip. Golf sounded pretty good to me."

"I would imagine that Miss Kate Wood-Lacy would sound better."

He stared at him blankly. "Kate?"

"A phone message of sorts on my desk this morning. None of the station sods know where anyone is. It was sent to my attention. Just her name and an address . . . Kinloch Lodge, Glen Garry."

"Jesus, she did it."

"You sound surprised."

"Yeah. I mean, I never thought she would actually come up here."

"Rather nice of her, I must say. Good to have a . . . chum nearby."

HE BORROWED A Baby Austin from one of the navigators in the Sunderland squadron, managed to squeeze his legs into it, and rattled off along the road to Loch Ness. A postman on a bicycle in the village of Invergarry gave him explicit directions and he found the lodge with no trouble. It was far larger than he had imagined: a two-story stone house with a slate roof and many chimneys. It stood alone on a rise of heather-cloaked ground overlooking the deep, still waters of Loch Garry.

She came out of the house at the sound of the car and stood stiffly in front of the open door. "I know you think I was wrong," she said as he walked up to her from the car.

"That's not for me to say, Kate. It's good to see you. I know that. Must have been tough getting here."

"A trial!" She smiled, her trepidation melting away. "They say that over two hundred thousand men have been evacuated so far from Dunkirk and most of them were going north by rail. Our little train was constantly being shunted into sidings. It seemed an age before we reached Glasgow. I took a bus from there to Fort Williams and the gillie met me with his van."

"Gillie?"

"Grandpapa's old gamekeeper. He has a cottage down the

hill and caretakes the place. His name's Archy Selenius. An unusual name for a Highland Scot, but that's what it is."

"Okay by me," he said, returning her smile. "Beats Macbeth any day."

Clouds, like an endless procession of woolly sheep, drifted in from the west. Their shadows moved across the loch and up and down the surrounding hills.

"We have fishing rights for two miles along the north shore," Kate told him. "Would you like to get out the tackle?"

"I'm not much for fishing. I like trout and salmon, but on a plate." He bent down, picked up a flat stone, and sent it skipping across the water. "Are you really going to stay here all summer?"

"If you'd like me to."

"I'd feel happier if you were back in Norwich. Going to school, making friends . . . filling your days." He gazed out across the slate-smooth loch, the empty hills. "This is a lonely spot, Kate. I hate to think of you being out here by yourself."

She pressed against his side and held his hand. "But you'd be here whenever you could. I wouldn't be lonely."

"It would be different if we were married, Kate. I don't feel right about it."

"I understand, Collie. Really I do. And that's quite a wonderful thought. I'd make a marvelous wife."

"Yeah, you can make an omelet . . . and toast."

"That's a beginning, isn't it? I can also brew tea, don't forget that. And speaking of tea, I could go for a cup. The wind is always cold here."

"Another reason to be in Norwich." He gave her Junoesque figure a pat and a squeeze. "Your delicate health."

They strolled up the hill toward the house, arms about each other's waist. "Have you heard anything from Derek?" she asked.

"Just a short note a couple of weeks ago. He didn't say much. I know his squadron's in the Dunkirk battle. A guy at the base has a kid brother flying Spits out of Kentish Hill. They're teamed with Derek's bunch. I worry about him."

"Yes, so do I. I worry about everybody."

"Not about me, honey. I'm a bus driver."

She made tea while Colin wandered about the one large ground-floor room. The stone walls were covered with antlers and the stuffed heads of Highland stags.

"Somebody liked to kill things," he said as she brought the tea in on a tray.

"Grandpapa. He was in the army when he was very young—Prince Albert's Own, the lancers. Fought in the Zulu War . . . or liked to say he fought. Daddy told me that was all humbug. He came down with fever in Durban and never even saw a Zulu. I suppose he took out his martial frustrations on the deer."

She sat on the edge of a sofa and poured the tea. She had made sandwiches of potted shrimp and ham and had sliced a Dundee cake.

"Quite a feast."

"I hope you're hungry," she said.

"I'm always hungry."

She leaned against the cushions and watched him eat, one hand toying idly with the locket at her throat. "Collie, would it be such a daft idea if we did get married?"

"Crazy."

"Is it because you're not sure if you love me? Please be honest. I won't be hurt."

He munched slowly and swallowed some tea. "It's got nothing to do with love. It's . . . oh, I don't know, responsibilities. When people marry it's to build a life together. A home . . . kids . . . sharing everything. I have no control over my life right now, Kate. A leaf in the goddamn wind. There's even a rumor that now that we've occupied Iceland we might be sent there, to patrol the convoy lanes from Canada. It could be just talk, but what if it isn't? What sort of marriage would that be? You couldn't hop a train to Iceland." He placed his cup on the table and turned to face her, his hands on her arms. "I do love you. I want you to know that and believe it. I knew I loved you when I woke up that night in your flat. Three, maybe four in the morning. Me in my shirt and pants . . . you in your robe. Your back was to me and you were sleeping like a baby. I stroked your hair for a minute and then rolled over and went back to sleep. You know what some dope asked me in the mess that next day? He wanted to know if I'd found a nice bit of fluff in Norwich to sleep with! Some . . . nice bit of fluff you are."

Her eyes never left his face. "Please kiss me, Collie."

How soft her lips were. And her body soft beneath the cashmere sweater, her breasts pressed tightly against his chest. To love her, he thought. To have her naked beneath him. To be inside of her. Buried deep in the warmth of her. He sat back and took a deep breath, exhaling slowly. Kate rested her head against his shoulder, her eyes closed.

"Allison expects me back by four," he lied.

"So soon?"

"I'm afraid so. A . . . training flight."

"When will I see you again?"

"I can't say. I don't know when I'll be able to get down to Norfolk. Go back, Kate. Don't miss any more classes. If you love me you'll do what I ask."

He stopped on the way back, by the banks of Loch Ness, and got out of the car. The water looked immeasurably deep and cold. He wondered idly if there really was a monster down among the sunless reeds and idly tossed pebbles into the depths.

THE NEW SQUADRON leader of 624 had lasted exactly four and one half minutes into his first fracas. A cannon-firing Messerschmitt had blown his tail to bits and he had bailed out, floating down into Belgium and captivity with an abashed wave of the hand. Flying Officer Derek Ramsay was made permanent/temporary leader.

"It's that type of gobbledegook that just makes me boil," Jolly Rodgers said after hanging up the telephone that evening. "What in God's name is a permanent/temporary when he's at home? Now answer me that. The wing commander should have given you the squadron and raised you a notch. It isn't fair."

"It doesn't matter," Derek said. "There are only ten of us now. Hardly a squadron if you come to think of it."

Jolly tilted back his desk chair and looked at the hollow-eyed young man standing before him. The 624 had gone over twice today and had shot down two bombers and a Messerschmitt 109 and damaged a couple more with only the loss of the squadron leader to mar the trips. Incredible, considering the losses in the past few days. "I'm restricting all men to base tonight, Ramsay."

"Because of what happened at the Red Bull last night? We didn't start anything, Jolly. Just a loud-mouthed, half-drunk infantry lieutenant. No one hit him, you know. Just a push or two."

"That's hardly the point. If any of your chaps want to know why I'm doing it they can gather in the mess in half an hour. First round on me."

It was a sullen bunch that greeted Jolly when he strolled in. He signed a blank tab for the first round of drinks and then leaned back against the bar and looked at the silent pilots. Twenty-two of them from both squadrons—and not many of them older than that.

"No point in your looking at me as you would at some wicked uncle. What happened last night has been happening all over southern England. And I think you know why. The brown jobs don't like us. The 'Brylcreem Boys' they call us. That's the army for you. They can't grasp what they can't see. They didn't *see* us over the beaches at Dunkirk. Ergo, we couldn't have been up there helping them out. Those that have come back can't wait to vent their spleen on anyone in RAF blue. That's a pity, but true. At the moment, only you know how bloody hard you've been fighting . . . and against what incredible odds. In time, when the true story comes out, the army will probably feel like shits. Until things cool down, avoid them before someone gets his head knocked in and *really* bad blood builds between us. And that's all I have to say. Drink up."

They were scrambled at seven in the morning, taking off two at a time and thundering up into the pale, clear sky of this first day of June. Sector Control vectored them to ten thousand feet and joined them with a Polish squadron that rose to meet them over the South Foreland. They were a wing now, three squadrons, thirty-five fighters in three waves heading across the Channel for the Belgian coast. Dunkirk, as always, lay to the south of them, the never ceasing black pall above it drawn across the sky like a smudge of soot across soft blue paper.

Radios began to hum and crackle as they leveled off at thirty thousand feet, the Kentish Hill Spitfires five miles ahead, squirting thin vapor trails from the edges of their graceful wings. Words snapped through the ether . . . *Cobra leader calling Fox . . . calling Zebra. Bandits below.* Thousands of feet down, dots of shadow across the checkerboard of fields. Junker 87s . . . Stukas . . . wave after wave of them. *Tally Ho!* And down they went.

THE 624 SQUADRON returned later in the morning, gunning their engines and sideslipping slightly over the trees. Jolly stood outside the ops building and counted seven. Three, he was thinking, were late. There had been nothing coherent coming over the radio for the past half hour. Some sort of minor malfunction in the receiver. Technicians were working on it. He shielded his eyes against the sun and counted more dots circling to the east. Spits forming their landing pattern. They were two shy. He turned his eyes back to the Hurricanes. All had fired their guns . . . the patches blown off, smoke trails along the wings. One was in difficulty, its hydraulics shot away. It landed belly down on the grass, spewing chewed turf and dust in a plume behind it before finally grinding to rest, one of the prop blades whirling on ahead like some monstrous boomerang.

The Spitfires came in, touched down, taxied to their end of the field. Jolly stared at the sky for ten minutes. Nothing marred its purity.

"Hello, Jolly." Higby coming toward him, a lumbering, tow-headed farmer's son from Lincolnshire. "Ramsay bought it. Went down flaming near La Panne."

"Ramsay," he said thickly. He was getting used to it. He tried not to put a face to the name. "Bad luck."

"And Sergeant Logan. I didn't see him, but Chester said he went into an awful spin. And Ginger ditched two miles from Dover on the way back. He climbed out on the wing and inflated his vest. The Dover lifeboat was on its way when I stopped circling, so he's all right."

"That's good. Go get a rest-up. Something to eat."

Jolly stood there and watched the sky. Larks darting and zooming. A hawk, motionless, very high, holding in the wind. It was certainly a glorious day.

He was dead because he was stupid. That was all Derek could think when the shock of the cannon shells jolted the stick from his hand. Flame licked from under the engine cowling and then the cowling tore away in a geyser of black smoke and great globs of steaming oil which splattered against the windshield to obscure his view. *Stupid! Stupid! Stupid!* He had been so intent on giving one final burst to an already smoking Stuka that he had failed to take a glance behind him. A 109 must have followed him down and been right on his tail.

"I'm *dead!*" he screamed. *"Shit!"*

The stick was useless, it wobbled in his right hand. Hand

and arm useless too—a numb block of meat from fingertips to shoulder. No feeling at all. Smoke drifted into the cockpit through the firewall, choking him. He managed to slide the hood back with his left hand and gulped air as he peered over the side, clots of oil slapping against the side of his helmet, scorching through the leather. He pulled back in a hurry, in pain and terror. He was horribly low. Roofs beneath him . . . streets of a village flashing by . . . people looking up at him. Five hundred feet. No more than that. Too bloody low to bail out. Stick flopping back and forth. Rudder pedals mush under his frantic feet. Engine dead and burning. The plane was a glider now at the wind's whim and fancy. He steeled himself for the final *coup de grâce* from his destroyer. The spurt of cannon shells did not come. The rearview mirror was empty of all images except placid sky. Good pilot, he thought crazily, burst them till they bleed then break away and look for another. His idiotic mistake for not doing the same. The plane glided on, losing speed, dipping and soaring. The flames had died out, only thick black smoke streaming past and white feathers of glycol from the cooling tank. A dead aircraft. A coffin on wings.

"I believe in God the Father Almighty, Maker of Heaven and earth . . ." he muttered, remembering a long forgotten childhood prayer. The Hurricane quivered on the point of stall, then rose, sailed over the spire of a church . . . dipped again. A paper plane tossed across a schoolyard. Swooping . . . banking . . . heading in for a landing on the mud-churned football ground.

The plane hit with a terrible crash and groan of smashed wood and snapping metal. Derek flew up in the seat, held cruelly by the safety harness, the straps cutting into him like steel bands. The plane bounced . . . wobbled . . . hit again and turned over. He blacked out as something slammed the back of his head. When he came to he had no idea where he was. An awful stillness . . . something gurgling close by. He closed his eyes to calm himself, then opened them and looked about. He was upside down, head a few inches from water. The gurgling sound was fuel pouring from the ruptured tank behind the engine, the stench of it filling his lungs. Please, God, don't let it explode . . . *please.* He fumbled with the release catch on his harness, tearing away the oxygen tube and the radio wires from his helmet and mask as he did so. The harness slipped off and he fell headfirst into the brackish water below.

The water was less than four feet deep. He went down to a bottom of sand, crawled through the tangle of broken wing, and then stood up in sunshine. He was in a pond ringed by sand dunes and could hear the ocean and the cry of seabirds. The plane lay belly up with its nose under water, the cracked fuselage hanging down like the broken spine of some prehistoric bird.

"Over here, mate!"

The words were indistinct on the wind. A soldier with a rifle crouched on the dunes, waving at him. He took off his flying helmet and rubbed his eyes. Hard to tell at this distance what he was. German? A tommy? Another soldier appeared over the rim of the dune, cupped his hands to his mouth, and shouted . . . "Get a bloody move on, carn't yer!"

Derek, sobbing with relief, sloshed on through the chest-deep water to the shore.

One of the soldiers helped him out of the water and out of

his bulky, waterlogged flying suit while the other lay warily on top of the dune with his rifle leveled.

"You're bloody lucky, mate. Me an' Flapper saw you come down. Them bastards over other side of the dunes must've seen you too."

"Germans?" Derek said through clenched teeth. His right shoulder was probably broken. The numbness replaced by pain.

"Jerry? Not bloody likely. Fuckin' deserters. Frenchies . . . some of our lot . . . a couple of bleedin' bints from a whorehouse. Wild as fuckin' crazy cats they are. Cut your throat for your bleedin' boots an' what's in your pockets." He glanced up the slope of sand and windblown grass. "Spot 'em, Flapper?"

His answer was four rounds of rapid fire.

The soldier grinned, revealing missing teeth. "Ol' Flapper don't talk much. I'm Lance Corporal Darby. Call me Sid. We're pullin' back with the rear guard. All mixed in together. We're with the Dorsets . . . Second bloody Battalion. You all right now, mate? Best get on other side of the dune. Easy walkin' along the beach."

"I think my shoulder's broken."

"Is it now? Lucky for you then you don't walk on it, ain't it? Come on . . . let's step lively like."

Dunkirk lay six or seven miles ahead along the beach, wreathed in smoke and haze. Columns of black smoke from bombed oil tanks rolled inland on the wind. French troops were digging in among the dunes, laying field guns and stringing barbed wire. They didn't bother to look up as they walked past them. Farther along the beach they met small, straggling groups of tommies, some with their rifles, most without. All of them had the dazed expressions of sleepwalkers. Lance Corporal Darby shouted at them, trying to form them into a cohesive unit, but all ignored him, stumbling on through the sand.

"Dunkirk bloody fever, I calls it. The poor sods don't know where they are."

The clean, tide-swept beach began to change after a couple of miles. Abandoned trucks and guns and a thousand odd lots of equipment came into view. Offshore, just beyond the gentle breakers, lay the burnt-out hull of a British destroyer, a wisp of smoke still rising from amidships. More wrecked boats farther along, the stern of a yacht bobbing on the water close to shore. SKYLARK painted in bright green across the white-painted wood. Someone's pride and joy.

"And little *Skylark* went to war," Derek muttered in his fog of pain.

"What's that, mate?"

"Nothing."

Lance Corporal Darby placed a strong, callused hand on Derek's good shoulder. "Keep your pecker up. Won't be long now."

Long files of filthy, shabby men snaked from the beach to the water, to small boats which ferried them out to larger boats. A major with walrus mustaches and a face the color of port wine was directing the operation with the awesome power of his lungs. " 'Ware plane!" he shouted.

The long lines of men did not need to be told. They hunched down in the sand as the Stuka howled out of the vivid blue sky. The bomb fell up the beach, exploding deep in the sand, jarring the earth but injuring no one.

"Where's your bloody friends?" the major bellowed.

Derek stared at him blankly, the man's vivid face inches from his own. "Sorry. What?"

"You bloody well heard me! On holiday, are you? Damn RA bloody F!"

"The young gentleman shot down a fuckin' Stuka . . . *sir,*" said Lance Corporal Darby with icy politeness. "We saw him do it."

The major, saying nothing, turned about and strode away—shouting at the men.

It was lovely on the sea in the summertime. *By the sea, by the sea, by the beautiful sea* . . . down the lazy Thames to Margate . . . Cliftonville and Broadstairs. Ices and licorice strings. Grandpapa smoking his cigar by the rail. The sun so warm. He smiled blissfully, rested his head against Lance Corporal Darby's shoulder, and fell deeply asleep.

15

Radio-Paris and the more powerful Paris PTT were off the air. Nevertheless, Martin finished typing his broadcast in the offices of INA on the rue Boissy-d'Anglas. Through the window beside his desk he watched a German staff car race down the empty street toward the Place de la Concorde, preceded by two soldiers on motorcycles, machine pistols strapped to their backs. The sight added to his gloom and marred the exquisite beauty of the June day.

"Maybe you can phone it to New York tonight," Charlotte Dale said from her desk across the room.

Martin eyed the attractive, leggy brunette morosely. "Not a chance. The German signal corps have taken over the exchange. No telling when things will get back to normal—not that they ever can."

"Not the way they were, anyway," Charlotte said, a distant look in her eyes. She had been chief of the Paris bureau for three years. "Do you think I should stay on here, Marty, or get the hell out and go back to New York?"

"Working with the German censors is going to be tough . . . being with INA even tougher. Goebbels hates this agency, you know that. The chances are good you won't be given a choice. If I were you I'd be packed and ready in case the Nazis give you ten minutes to get out of France."

"Sound idea. I'd been thinking the same thing."

Martin slipped the dust cover over the typewriter, folded his sheets of copy and slipped them inside his breast pocket. "I'll buy you a drink if any place is open."

"Sure, why not? Nothing coming over the wires anyway."

Paris lay paralyzed, numb with shock. The unthinkable had taken place after all. *Les Boches* were in their glorious city. A million or more Parisians had fled the capital, jamming the roads to the south. Terrible rumors had swept the city for days before the German columns had entered the suburbs. The city would be burned . . . the women raped in the streets . . . the men machine-gunned against the walls. Nothing of that sort had taken place. The soldiers of the *Wehrmacht* had arrived with a provincial shyness, painfully polite and self-conscious in this, the City of Light. They paid for their purchases of souvenirs in the few shops that had not closed their shutters and they posed in stiff little groups to have their pictures taken on the steps of Sacré Coeur, in front of the Madeleine, or against the soaring backdrop of the Eiffel Tower. They had conquered an ancient enemy, these boys from Bavaria, Westphalia, Saxony, and Prussia, and they felt a sense of pride at doing it, but no feelings of hatred or vindictive triumph.

"We are not Huns," a young panzer commander had told Mar-

tin that morning when he had interviewed him and his crew, their dust-streaked tank parked under the chestnut trees on the rue de Rivoli. The Gestapo and the SS had not yet arrived.

"I think Ricard's is open," Charlotte said as they walked up the empty street and into the equally deserted boulevard Malesherbes. Eerie to see the city streets empty of taxis, trucks, and cars, all bleating their horns in mad cacophony. There were German staff cars, trucks, and a line of commandeered buses parked by the Madeleine—more soldier tourists in *feldgrau* and soft forage caps, many with cameras. Ricard's was open, a few German officers drinking beer and wine at the little sidewalk tables. Not a Frenchman in sight except the waiter, and he turned out to be Spanish. They took a table at a distance from the Germans and ordered martinis.

Before the drinks arrived one of the officers walked over to their table and made a stiff little bow. He was a colonel of engineers and wore the Iron Cross First Class from the last war on his tunic. "Good afternoon," he said in guidebook French. "It is good . . . to see civilians . . . return to their . . . pursuits of pleasure."

"We are Americans," Martin replied in his pristine German. "Journalists. Would you care to see our identity papers?"

The colonel smiled and pulled up a chair. "Not at all. Your German is excellent."

"My father was German-American. My mother came from Alsace and spoke both German and French. I learned the language early in life."

"And your name?"

"Martin Rilke . . . and the lady is Charlotte Dale. She also speaks German."

The colonel made another sharp bow to Charlotte and then sat down, looking at Martin intently. "I read one or two of your books many years ago. I recall most vividly the one on the Somme battles . . . *A Killing Ground.* A good book. I fought there, at Montauban and Delville Wood." He shook his head in wonder. "After the horrors of that war I cannot understand why England so perfidiously would start another."

Martin said nothing and calmly picked up his glass when the waiter set the drinks on the table.

"Well," the colonel said, getting to his feet, "this one is now over. The English lost everything in Flanders. Those who got away left only with their underclothes. They will sue for terms in a few days. Kindly allow me to place your tab with mine. We will drink a toast to the memory of the last war. To no more killing grounds. To peace."

Charlotte toyed with her glass as the colonel returned to his table.

"Will Britain ask Hitler for peace, Marty?"

"Never."

"What in God's name will they fight *with?*"

"The English Channel and the navy. If the Nazis manage to get troops across, they'll fight with rocks and clubs if they have to."

She sighed and took a drink. "I hope I am bounced out of here. I have a sudden longing to go home."

"And where's home? New York?"

"Sacramento."

"Not exactly Paris."

"No," she said. "It's free."

When Martin entered the lobby of the Crillon later that afternoon it was to find all of his luggage hastily packed, dumped by the desk, and being watched over by an angry member of the CBC radio team.

"They kicked us all out, Chief. The German high command took over the entire hotel."

"That's okay. It's time we moved, period. Get over to London."

"Now you're talking, Pop! They haven't reached the south yet. We could get a neutral ship in Bordeaux or Toulon. Shall I run over to the embassy and see what I can come up with?"

"I talked with them this morning. An American liner leaves Cherbourg tomorrow afternoon. Makes a stop in Cork and then goes on to the States. The embassy is sending half their people home on it. There's nothing left for us to do here, Jim."

"Boy, you can say that again. But I'm sure going to miss the place."

He would not miss it, Martin was thinking as the motorcade swept through the streets toward St. Germain and the highway to Normandy. It was early morning, the soft yellow sun a glowing magic in the Bois and on the Seine at Neuilly. The Paris that he had loved for so many years, the city of his birth, was too painful to look at now. An elegant and beautiful woman stripped of her pride and forced into beggary. The Parisians were drifting back now by the tens of thousands, an endless stream of haggard, thirsty, worn-out people. On foot, in overloaded, radiator-steaming cars, jamming into and onto wheezing trucks and buses. A people returning because there was no other place to go. Life would come back to the city, but it was not a life that he cared to witness. The limousines, national flags of the occupants fluttering above them, crossed the looping bends of the river escorted by German motorcyclists. Americans and Brazilians, Cubans and Colombians—embassy staffs and newsmen going home or, via Ireland, to London.

"I hope we never have to do this any more," someone in Martin's car muttered.

"We won't," he said, his voice a growl of Churchillian intensity. "We'll never be run out of anywhere again."

THE MONTH OF June drew to a close with the usual routines, flying the daily patrols out of Beauly Firth on varied assignments. Flanking the southbound convoys from Newcastle-on-Tyne one day, roving far out across the gray wastes of the North Sea the next. There were moments of high excitement when a U-boat was sighted on the surface, or a raider detected attempting to break out into the Atlantic between Iceland and the Faeroes. But mostly it was endless hours of numbing boredom.

Eccentricity began to creep through the squadron and, because it seemed to have a positive effect on morale, Squadron Leader Allison went along with it. The eccentricity began with Colin, who appeared in the briefing room one morning wearing his lizard-skin cowboy boots.

"And what, may I ask, are those?" Allison had said.

"Riding boots, sir . . . from Texas."

"I see. Are you, by any chance, contemplating forming a troop of irregular cavalry?"

"No, sir. I've always found them comfortable when flying."

Allison had merely raised an eye toward heaven and let it

go at that. It had been both a mistake and a blessing to do so. The idiosyncrasies of pilots and crews knew no bounds. Men began wearing tam-o-shanters or glengarries over their flying helmets. Men bought, or had their girlfriends knit, long wool scarves in a bewildering variety of tartan plaids. His own navigator boasted a ten-foot scarf—the longest in the squadron until a waist gunner proudly turned up with one two feet longer. One flying officer, a hitherto dour and sober young Scot from Aberdeen, befriended a mallard and took it with him on all his patrols, the duck resting comfortably above the instrument panel. All of the men were reasonably cheerful for a change, but Allison lived in dread of some group captain or air commodore dropping by without warning. The Colorado Squadron began to be referred to by the ground personnel as the "Nuthouse Gang."

Colin came back from a patrol that had taken them west of the Shetlands to search for the crew of a torpedoed freighter. The gunner-observer had spotted a lifebuoy bobbing in the choppy sea and they had flown low over it, scanning it through binoculars. S.S. CARMARTHEN CASTLE—SWANSEA had been clearly seen in black lettering on the white ring. And that had been all. Not a sign of life, only flotsam on the water and wide drifts of oil. And gulls pecking at God knew what terrible garbage beneath the surface of the waves.

He felt tired and depressed as he returned to the hotel that evening with half a dozen other officers who were billeted there. A few of the permanent residents sat in the lobby reading or having before-dinner drinks. Someone rose from one of the deep leather chairs . . .

"Hi, cowboy."

"Fat Chap! Jesus H. Christ!" Colin stared at him. "I don't believe it. God*damn*, what the hell are you doing in Scotland?"

"I'm stationed here," Derek said. He pointed to the boots. "Join the Texas air force?"

"I have an understanding skipper." He gripped Derek's hand and noticed the two broad rings on the sleeve of his uniform. "A flight lieutenant. You son-of-a-bitch. When did that happen?"

"While I was in hospital."

"I'm sorry I couldn't get down to London to see you, Derek."

"That's all right. I was only in for a few days. Kate popped over from Norwich with a basket of plums."

"Did she? Nice of her." He scowled at his boots and then brightened, patting Derek on the arm. "Heck, we're wasting time. I'll take a quick wash and we'll head for Inverness."

Derek had a car and brought Colin up to date as he drove to the ferry. It was nearly nine o'clock, but the sun still lingered, sparkling off the Moray Firth. They got out of the car and stood by the rail and he told of how his squadron had been attached to another at Kentish Hill and that the nine pilots who were left, including himself, had been sent to Turnhouse near Edinburgh to qualify in Spitfires.

"You lucky bastard."

"I hate to rub it in, old boy, but it is one hell of a kite. Light as a feather and powerful as a train."

"I'm glad *you're* happy."

"The job that bad?"

Colin thought about it for a moment. "Not really. I like the guys, especially the skipper. And what we do is important,

I guess, but we don't kill Germans. I've dropped a tin can or two but never even damaged a sub as far as I know. One of our mob sank an E-boat off Bergen a few weeks ago. That's about the size of it. How many planes have you shot down?"

"Three confirmed. Two probables."

"You're an easy man to envy, Fat Chap. Say, how would you like to go out with me tomorrow? I'll show you the wide and empty spaces of the North Sea."

"I'd like nothing better, but I'll be flying down in the morning. I was on a training flight to Wick but ran into some mag problems on the way back and landed at Dingwell Field . . . just up the road."

"Convenient."

Derek grinned. "That's what I thought as I flew over it. A good place to have the electrical system checked out."

The pub was in a cobblestoned street near the river and was jammed with RAF and naval officers. A pretty redhead wearing too much makeup brushed up against Colin and gave him a wink as they squeezed their way to the bar.

"Well, hello, Colin," she said with a Scotch lilt. "Just lettin' you know I'm here."

"Who was that?" Derek asked.

"Local tart. I don't know her name."

"She knew yours, old man."

"Heck, yes. Everyone knows me."

They took their beers to the least crowded part of the pub and leaned against the wall to drink and talk—not that they had much to talk about, Derek was thinking. They lived in two different worlds and had no "shop" in common. And he seemed to wish to avoid talking about Kate.

"Do you remember Valerie A'Dean-Spender? You met her years ago at Burgate House . . . a thin, blond kid."

Colin frowned and shook his head. "Can't say that I do. Why?"

"Oh, just that she's still blond—and totally smashing. I want to marry her."

Colin's laugh was vaguely uncomfortable. "Marry? Helluva time for something like that."

"The more abnormal the times, the more normal one should act—or so it seems to me."

"To each his own." He took a swallow of beer. "Set a date yet?"

"Unfortunately, there's the slight problem of an existing husband. A Captain Raymond Monnier, currently in a Jerry POW camp."

"That's tough. Anything you can do about it?"

"Maybe. We have a solicitor working on the problem, a specialist in divorce and annulment cases. In the meantime, she's taking a little house in Watford so we can be together at least once in a while. I'll jot down the address for you in case they ever let you roam out of the Highlands."

"Not much chance of that. *Leave* isn't a word they use around here." He watched the redhead. She was talking with one of the navy fliers but glancing past the man at him. He looked away. "Marriage, huh? You sure must have a lot of faith in the future, Fat Chap."

THEY COORDINATED THEIR takeoffs the next morning. Colin had just cleared the firth, water streaming behind him, when the Spitfire came low over the hills, Derek waggling the wings in greeting. Colin had Sergeant Pilot O'Conner flash a message with the Aldis lamp as Derek throttled back and flew alongside . . . NOT . . . TOO . . . BAD . . . FOR . . . BEGINNER.

Derek waved, then boosted the throttle and roared ahead, climbing at full power. Colin watched the little fighter do a series of graceful barrel rolls and then turn south over Inverness and disappear from view in the haze.

They droned on, hour after hour. Mist across the sea as the cold polar waters met warmer currents. They flew seven hundred miles to the Arctic Circle and then turned slowly southwest a hundred miles off the Norwegian coast, flying low and at slow speed, hoping to catch a U-boat on the surface.

"U-boat to starboard . . . half a mile!" An excited shout over the intercom. Colin banked to the right, all nerves tense. The sub turned out to be a whale which sounded in fright as they flew over it.

"Sorry, Skip."

It didn't matter. It happened a hundred times—if not a whale, then a porpoise or a steel oil drum. The gunners looked forward to drums or barrels as they gave them a chance to shoot at something.

A gunner brought thermos jugs of tea from the tiny galley and packets of sandwiches—corned beef and cheese. The menu never varied. Colin munched, drank, yawned, turned the controls over to O'Conner, and walked aft to stretch his legs, thinking of Derek in his Spitfire . . . Derek and his "smashing blonde." A little house in Watford. Why not? Did anyone give a damn these days if people lived in sin? He thought with a sharp pang of regret of the stone house in Glen Garry. Kate in his arms and his breath catching in his throat. The girl wiser than he. The infinite wisdom of the heart.

"Object port . . . two . . . three miles!"

Colin hurried back to the cockpit and flipped on his intercom. "What have we got?"

"Can't tell, Skip. Something jutting up from the drink. Saw it in a break in the mist . . . gone now."

"Could have been a sub crash diving," O'Conner said.

"Or that whale's pals."

He banked sharply to the left and then leveled out a few feet above the sea, easing off on the throttles so that their airspeed dropped to less than eighty miles per hour. They seemed to be floating in the mist.

"On the button, Skip! Dead ahead!"

Colin could see it now even without the aid of binoculars. A submarine churning along on the surface at flank speed, diesel exhaust and water vapor rising from the stern. On its merry way from Trondheim to the North Atlantic via the Shetland Passage.

"Not this time, baby," he murmured. Four small depth charges under the wings. Not the most potent sting, but if they were lucky . . . if they fell just right . . . He jigged the plane left. They were coming up astern of the U-boat and he could see two men standing in the open well of the conning tower.

"Fire whenever you want, Burns," he called down to the front gunner.

The man opened up immediately, tracer skipping ahead of them, flicking across the long, dark hull of the submarine. No better than rifle bullets, Colin thought bitterly. Bounce right off the steel. They needed cannon, something with bite. They skimmed over the sub and O'Conner pulled the handle, sending two depth charges dropping ahead of the speeding boat. Colin shoved the throttles open and pulled back on the control column, turning hard right to come around for another pass. Glancing to the side he could see that the men were no longer on the bridge. Dead? Maybe, maybe not. The boat was turning sharply to avoid the depth charges ahead. The round cylinders sinking, set for fifteen feet. As they passed and began to turn again, one of the charges went off, humping the gray sea upward then exploding into a tower of foam and spray that caused the sub to lurch sideways and bring its sharp bow leaping out of the water like a hooked trout. The waist gun was firing now, tracer slapping all along the boat's gleaming black sides. Waste of ammunition . . . might as well shoot pellets at it from an air pistol.

"Turning in for another pass," he shouted.

"Only one charge went off," O'Conner said. "Goddamn dud!"

"Nobody's perfect, Billy. 'Try, try again.' "

By the time he had made the turn the U-boat was crash diving, the deck gun already underwater. Going down fast . . . flooding all tanks. The conning tower under now, only the aerial mast slicing the surface. O'Conner's hand tensed on the bomb release as they roared over it.

"Down your throat, buggers!"

"That's the spirit, Billy," Colin yelled, the plane lurching upward as the charges fell away.

Both exploded this time, twin towers of white water. They could feel the jolt at three hundred feet as they made a banking turn. As the fountains fell back to the sea, the boat rose ponderously between them and lay wallowing in the churning wake of the explosions, bleeding oil and compressed air.

"We ruptured some tanks, Skip!" Someone over the intercom.

"Down but not out, boys," Colin said. "Send our position, Sparks. Say we have a U-boat on the surface and in pain." He glanced at the taut, anxious face of O'Conner. "How long can we stick around, Billy?"

"No more than fifteen minutes, unless we want to row the ship home."

Men were coming on deck now from the front hatch and running for the gun. Other men were appearing on the conning tower and stripping the cover from the twenty-millimeter cannon.

"Get some of those guys, for chrissakes!"

The front and the starboard machine guns began firing, the noise pulsating through the plane, cordite fumes forming a thin haze in the cockpit. Tracer whipped the length of the sub as they swept past it and they could see two men stagger and fall on its wet deck.

"Keep sending, Sparks," Colin called to the radioman. "There must be a limey destroyer somewhere in this goddamn ocean."

He was a mile back of the U-boat and beginning another turn when the German gun crews began firing. They could see the blossom of flame as the powerful deck gun opened up and a split second later the shell exploded in the air a hundred yards to their right. Colin began to bore in, but the twenty-millimeter Oerlikon was firing now, balls of tracer rushing to meet them.

"Screw it," he said. "Leave 'em to the navy." He pushed the stick hard forward and dipped toward the sea, cannon shells cracking over them, and pulled up inches above the glassy swells. Full throttle, racing away, the prop wash spewing spray behind them. A brilliant, eye-searing flash of light to one side. The plane rocked, staggering in the blast of the flak shell. There was the hideous shriek of tearing metal.

"God*damn!*" Colin cried, gripping the wheel tightly.

Sergeant Pilot O'Conner bent forward, eyes scanning the instrument panel and its multitude of dials.

"Everything looks okay, Skip."

Another explosion, far behind them; a savage reflection of scarlet against the mist.

"Anyone . . . hurt?" Colin asked over the intercom.

The crew reported back. No injuries, but a dozen or more flak holes in the skin. "The old kite's whistlin' like a flute back here, Skip!"

"We did the best we could," O'Conner said. "Browning guns! Might as well've pissed on it for all the bloody good they did."

"Yeah," Colin said. He turned sideways in his seat. "You take over, Billy. Bring her to . . . ten thousand."

He stood up and walked slowly aft as O'Conner eased the stick back. The engines sounded out of sync to the sergeant and he adjusted the throttles. As he did so he noticed the jagged little hole in the side of the cockpit and a splattering of blood on Colin's seat. "Burns," he said over the intercom, ". . . Clark. Skip's caught one. Get the medical kit . . . fuckin' hurry!"

They found him braced in the galley opening, one hand

pressed to his side. Leading Aircraftman Clark lowered the canvas cot from its bracket along the bulkhead and Flight Sergeant Burns eased Colin onto it and began to unbutton his jacket.

"Heck," Colin said. "I'm okay, boys. Little . . . tired."

"Sure, Skip," Burns said. "Let's just get the old jacket off."

There was only a small hole between two ribs and not much bleeding. Sergeant Burns patched it thickly with gauze. "Be right as rain, Skip."

But he was already dead.

Teletypes

It is a summer of high, blue skies etched with the white traceries of vapor trails. Slowly moving arcs and loops so high above, viewed from summer gardens in Kent and Surrey, the South Downs and the Weald.

Death in the skies, in the cold, thin air. A line of smoke against the cirrus, trailing down. A black dot . . . a machine . . .

One of ours, you think?

A nineteen-year-old boy in the seat, dead, plunging to earth.

Or one of theirs?

RAF VERSUS LUFTWAFFE

BIG TEST MATCH

London (INA) 18 August 1940. In some of the heaviest air fighting so far over southern England . . .

Men in white flannels still play cricket in the long shadows of Saturday afternoons. There is tea and toast waiting at Kentish Hill when the Spitfires drop in one by one over the trees, low on fuel, out of ammunition, smoke staining the wings. Honey still for tea. And then up again before the sun sets. To the clouds. To the murderous sky.

TODAY'S SCORE
US 68 THEM 6

The newspapers deliberately exaggerate German losses so as to help British morale. The battle is not a lopsided rout of the many by the few. The losses mount day by endless day throughout August and into September. Fighter Command is not winning, but they are not losing either. They continue to exist. To the dismay of the German bomber crews there are always the slim, deadly little fighters slashing into their formations as soon as they cross the coast. There can be no invasion of England until they are total masters of the sky.

"The English are filled with curiosity and keep asking: 'Why doesn't he come?' Be calm. Be calm. He's coming! He's coming!" says Hitler in a speech in Berlin, in a rare moment of humorous sarcasm.

But he is not coming. There is no humor to be found in the attrition over England. In the fifty-six planes downed by the RAF on September 15 alone. No humor to be found in the French and Belgian channel ports where the invasion barges are being bombed every night. Hitler cancels all plans to land troops in England. He turns his eyes eastward and pores for hours over maps of the vast steppes of Russia. England he will punish by air—at night only. Bomb the cities. Burn the towns. *Gott strafe England.*

The Battle of Britain is over. The Blitz begins.

LONDON CAN TAKE IT!

The editorial room here at the *Daily Post* was bombed last night, gutted by incendiaries, but we are carrying on. Business as usual. We are like Archie Potts of Cheapside. Archie runs a little shop in Winders Lane. He sells men's boots and ladies' shoes. He, too, was bombed last night. On the frame of his blown-out shop window he attached a small sign this morning. "Archie's," it reads. "More Open than Usual."

Hello, America. This is Martin Rilke speaking to you from London. It is midnight here and an air raid that began at seven thirty this evening is still going on. There are Nazi bombers flying high over the city, over the great docks lining the Thames from Tilbury to Wapping, over East End slums and Mayfair mansions. I will bring the sounds of this raid to you in a moment, recorded with our wire recording machines a few hours ago from the roof of Broadcasting House, in Portland Place. You will hear the sharp bark of the anti-aircraft guns, the rolling thunder of the bombs. You will even hear, if you listen closely, the sound of a Nazi plane high over the city—a Heinkel one-eleven—my guest for this broadcast, RAF Squadron Leader Derek Ramsay, Distinguished Flying Cross, assures me. What you will not hear, what cannot be captured on magnetized wire, is the sound of the heart of a courageous people. A people living with the fear of death night after night. Never knowing when they go to the shelters if they will have a home to go back to when the raid is over. And the bombs spare no one. They fall just as readily on the crowded row houses of Stepney and Bethnal Green as they did on Buckingham Palace last week. The little man, the king, all going about their day-to-day business knowing they could well be dead that night. It is the mettle of a people, the spirit of a race. It is England.

A Day in October 1940

Charles Greville took the train up from Dorset and his father met him at Abingdon station. Charles was surprised at how well he looked, the bounce to his step, the strength in his handshake.

"Have you seen the place yet?" he asked.

Lord Stanmore nodded vigorously. "Drove down early. Been puttering about for hours, chatting with the fire brigade chaps and the staff. They had a frightening time—staff, I mean, not the fire brigade. *They* enjoyed themselves hugely."

The Pryory had been blitzed the night before. A stick of bombs had tumbled down in darkness and light rain and two had slammed into the east wing and one into the stables. The rest had fallen across the lawns and into the kitchen garden. No one had been injured and there had been no horses in the stalls.

"Jettisoned," the earl said as he hurried Charles to the car. "That's the opinion of the firemen, anyway. Some Hun in a blue funk let 'em drop before scooting for home."

"Doubt it," Charles said. "Probably aiming for the Blackworth plant."

"But that's eight miles away, dear boy."

"The type of error one could make on a dark night at twenty thousand feet."

"Perhaps so. Still, hardly matters, does it? The old house has been bombed. That's the main thing. Felt you should see it as well as me. Your ruddy house one day, you know."

"I doubt if I'd ever live in it."

"Who are you to break tradition? Been an earl of Stanmore living there since God knows when. You'll see. You, your lovely Marian, and my little grandson will reside there yet. And a better house it will be, too. I have some excellent ideas in my head. Never really liked that wing of the house too much. Gone now. Blown and burnt to rubble. Chance to start from scratch and build something really grand one day."

Charles smiled to himself as he got into the back of the car. Nearing eighty and still making plans. Hope springs eternal.

"Bought some flowers on the way. From that hothouse chap in Leatherhead. Always bring some when I come down with your mother. She would have come today, but I felt it would be too painful for her. Lord knows there are enough bombed-out houses for her to look at from our windows in London."

"You should move out of there, Father."

"William and Dulcie tell me the same. If the king doesn't see fit to run I don't see why I should."

The Rolls-Royce glided up the High Street and stopped opposite the church. The rain was gentle, a floating mist drifting through the branches of the leafless elms in the rectory garden. Charles helped his father from the car as the chauffeur opened an umbrella.

The earl waved it aside with contempt. "I don't need a bloody bumbershoot, man."

"Her ladyship . . ."

"Made you promise," he said in resignation, taking it from him. "If that woman has her way I'll live to Methuselah's age."

They walked along the gravel path, the earl holding the umbrella in one hand and a bunch of flowers wrapped in newspaper in the other. There were many old headstones rising from the lush grass, sheened with moss, the inscriptions weathered and worn. There were new stones, startlingly white against the vivid greens. They stopped by one of them.

COLIN MACKENDRIC ROSS

1920–1940

Per ardua ad astra

"He would have liked that, I believe," the earl said, unwrapping the flowers. "The motto of the RAF. He was proud being in it. Not a patriot as such. Not love of king and country, Lord knows."

"Just Colin," Charles said quietly, taking the flowers from his father and placing them on the mound of wet grass.

Derek Ramsay turned his battered motorbike into Fern Lane and pulled to a screeching halt in front of a whitewashed stone cottage. His usually neat uniform was wrinkled and black with rain after a furious drive from Kentish Hill. Valerie had heard the sound of his approach and opened the door before he could fish the latch key from his pocket.

"Bloody hell!" he said angrily as he stepped inside.

"Delightful greeting, I must say. My first forty-eight-hour leave in weeks and you arrive late and pleasant as a bear."

He bent to her, kissing her firmly on the lips. "Sorry. Not quite myself. The powers that be shot me a rocket and I'm just blowing off steam."

"Oh? What happened?"

Removing his sodden hat, he tossed it toward a peg on the wall, missing by a foot. "They bumped me up to wing commander. *Wing commander!* To a bloody *training* command! An inspiration to the new lads, they told me. Paterfamilias to the fledging brood of Fighter Command . . . a bloody scoutmaster!"

"Calm down," she said, holding him, feeling giddy with relief. Selfish of her she knew, but he had done so much during the desperate summer. Ribbons on his chest. Fifteen German planes shot down. But she knew the terror of his nights. The sudden cries and twitching limbs as he relived in his dreams each terrible fight. "I can't think of a better choice for the job, Derek."

"And something else. Hush-hush at the moment. I could be sent to America some time next year . . . to Arizona and Texas. The Yanks may lend us bases there to train our pilots. If that happens, what about us?"

She smiled into his troubled eyes and ran her fingers across his mouth. "I shall stay here, do my job—and keep on loving you. Exulting in the joy of being *Mrs.* D. Ramsay."

"You heard from Raymond through the Red Cross?"

"No, but I did hear *of* him. A chap on De Gaulle's staff phoned me from London. Raymond isn't a POW and never was. He's in Vichy, an aide to Laval. I knew his father's Fascist friends would take care of him."

Derek looked puzzled. "I don't see how that can be of any great use to us."

"I will write a letter, a very charming letter, and send it to Raymond via the Swiss chargé d'affaires in Vichy. In it I will tell him that I have no objection to *his* divorcing *me*, realizing as I do what an embarrassment it would be to him if it were known that his wife is a sergeant in the Royal Air Force! That should do it, don't you think? Deliciously uncomplicated."

"Clever little girl, aren't you?"

"Clever enough to have found you, Fat Chap."

"A mutual cleverness," he said, holding her tightly, breathing in her delicate perfume. Savor every second, he was thinking as he kissed her. Etch them into memory for the long days ahead.

VICTORIA CARRIED THE one suitcase they shared between them and held Jennifer by the hand as she pushed and shoved her way toward the ticket counter at Euston Station.

"Two first-class returns to Liverpool, please."

"Is this journey really necessary, miss?"

Victoria glared imperiously at the little man behind the

wicket. "Of course it's necessary. Would anyone go to Liverpool if it weren't?"

"Sorry, miss. Have to ask, you know."

The carriage was nearly filled, stuffy and dim.

"A seat by the corridor would be best for you," Victoria said.

Two naval officers occupied those seats. They both noticed Jennifer's drawn face and obvious pregnancy and gave them up gallantly. Victoria flashed them a devastating smile. "Knew the navy would come through."

"Think nothing of it," one of them said.

"My husband's in the navy . . . Lieutenant Commander Gerald Smith Blair. He's serving on *Rodney.* Perhaps you know him."

"Afraid not. But meeting his wife is pleasure enough."

"What a charming thing to say."

Jennifer gave her a poke in the ribs and whispered, "Stop flirting, for heaven's sake."

"It's quite harmless," Victoria whispered back. "And it helps pass the time."

Liverpool in the afternoon was dark and smoky. There had been a raid the night before and an oil tank still burned at Birkenhead, the black smoke rolling across the Mersey in the wind. The two naval officers, who had been laughing and joking with Victoria for the entire journey, made themselves useful by practically commandeering one of the few available taxis, and they rode with them as far as the Adelphi Hotel.

"You must come in for a drink," Victoria said. "You've been most kind, both of you."

"Sorry," one of them said wistfully, "but we have to get to our ship."

"Nice boys," Victoria said as they walked into the hotel.

Jennifer began to laugh. "Oh, Vicky, you'll never change."

"Good. You laughed. I thought you might be annoyed with me."

"That would be rather like being annoyed with one's cat because it doesn't bark."

They had adjoining rooms and Victoria unpacked, sorting out their things after insisting that Jennifer take off her shoes and lie on the bed. She ordered Bovril and toast to be sent up.

"You can be very motherly, Vicky."

"Your condition brings out my better instincts." She sat on the side of the bed and stroked her sister's brow. "I'm going to be a very proud aunt, Jenny. I hope it's a girl. All dark curls and ringlets."

"I don't much care what it is. I just wish it were here. Four months. God!"

"The time will pass, darling. And you'll enjoy staying with Dulcie. To be born in a stable. A peaceful thought."

Jennifer fell briefly asleep and awoke with Albert beside her, holding her hand.

"Hello, Thax."

"And to you, hello." He bent his head and kissed her. "Feel all right?"

"Never better. A bit tired. Crowded train."

"William will pick you up tomorrow in the car. Did you ship your things?"

"Sent them off last week. I cried when I locked up the flat. Just couldn't help it. Pregnancy makes one sentimental."

He lightly touched the soft swell of her belly. "It won't be forever." She sat up and he placed an arm around her waist.

"Plans have been changed, Jenny. I can't stay the night. The convoy's sailing before midnight."

She rested her head against his shoulder with a sigh. "Oh, dear, I was afraid something like that might happen."

"An admiral told me that it's imperative we sail now and not tomorrow. Wouldn't tell me why, of course, but they know what they're doing. It's the largest and most important convoy they've ever sent to Egypt, so they're being almost excessively cautious."

"They'd better be. With you on it." She pressed his hand tightly. "I have a feeling you're going to be covering events in the Middle East for a long time, Thax."

"You could be right."

"If you're still there in a year I'm coming out to join you . . . take a house in Cairo or Gezireh."

"Now, Jenny, please . . ."

"No," she said with surprising intensity. "I'll get there somehow. Go to Capetown . . . make my way from there. You'll see."

"I hate to remind you that there's a war on."

"All the more reason to be together. I married you for richer or poorer, sickness and health, war, famine, and pestilence."

He smiled at her and moved their interlocked hands to rest where life was growing, beating gently against their fingers.

"I'll not stop you," he said.

Squadron Leader Allison parked in Norham Gardens. The letter from Kate Wood-Lacy was in his pocket and he checked the address again before getting out of the car. It was the sixth letter he had received from her during the past few months, but the first from Oxford.

It was starting to rain again, quite hard, and he was glad he had remembered to bring his overcoat. He found her rooms after a bit of trouble. She had moved into an old warren of a building, and the pattern of numbering made little sense. She was on the top floor with a splendid view of University Parks and the River Cherwell. She was wearing slacks and an old sweater and looked very pretty with her hair tied severely back with a piece of ribbon.

"I didn't expect you until tomorrow," she said as she opened the door.

"I took my leave a day early. Couldn't telephone because you neglected to include your number."

"Telephoning is hopeless. There's only one phone and that's in a sort of common room buried in the depths someplace."

"This is very nice," he said, glancing around. It was plainly furnished but large and comfortable. Boxes of books lay everywhere. "Still moving in, I see."

"I think I'll still be moving in at the end of term. There's not nearly enough shelf space."

"Find a chap to build some for you. That's what I did when I entered Trinity." He toyed with the hat in his hands. "Look, if it's inconvenient today . . ."

"Not at all. I'm happy to see you. It's such a horrid afternoon. You've brightened it up."

"I thought we might have tea. I know an excellent place in St. Giles."

"Super. It'll only take me a minute to get dressed. Would you like a coffee? I can heat some up on my trusty hot plate."

"No, thanks. I'm fine."

"All right, then," she said, starting from the room. "Won't be a tick."

A girl of sense and sensibilities, he was thinking as he sat down to wait for her. He had only met her once before meeting again at the funeral. His impression of her in the Norwich pub had been one of admiration for Colin's taste in women. Lovely of face and charming of manner. No more than that. Their long walk together through the streets of Abingdon after Colin had been laid to rest had revealed far deeper qualities to him. She had been so calm and self-possessed, so perceptive of his own feelings of pain and loss which he had done his best to keep hidden. She had said something that afternoon that had touched him deeply. *"It must be so terribly hard on you . . . sending friends out every day . . . knowing they may never come back."*

He had felt the need to write her a week later and they had been corresponding ever since.

She wore a light wool dress in soft shades of heather blue, a little plaid tam on her head. Her hair was down now, hanging in brown folds to her shoulders. He wanted to tell her how beautiful she looked.

"You'll need a raincoat," he said.

It was a small and very old tea room. Countless generations of Oxford scholars had carved their initials in the heavy oak tables and into the wooden beams.

"Have you ever been here before?" he asked.

"No, but I've heard of it. I will certainly come again."

He ordered tea and fresh, hot scones. "Looking forward to your first classes?"

"Yes and no. Excited and depressed at the same time. Studying seems such a waste somehow."

"Does it? What if all the colleges closed and no one was working for the future?"

"If there can be such a thing as a future. I want to be a botanist. Flowers, trees, plants. To study them . . . learn how to protect them from disease . . . to grow newer, better strains. And while I'm doing that other people are bent on destroying the very earth. It's lunacy."

"It would be an even greater lunacy if you gave up in despair." He reached across the table and touched her hand. "There has to be a tomorrow or Colin's death and all the other deaths have been wasted. I can't accept that, Kate."

She studied his face for a moment, her expression somber and thoughtful; then she smiled in sad remembrance. "Neither can I. Not in my heart."

It had stopped raining when they left. Clouds scudded low in the brisk wind, wreathing the spires of Trinity. They walked down St. Aldates and into Christ Church Meadows toward the river. She suddenly took his hand and held it very tightly and they began to walk faster, not saying anything, striding along together as though something wondrous—magical—lay not too far ahead.

Insights, Interviews & More . . .

About the author

About the book

Read on

About the author

Phillip Rock

Born in Hollywood, California, in 1927, Phillip Rock was the son of Academy Award–winning silent film producer Joe Rock. Phillip moved to England with his family when he was seven, attending school there for six years until the blitz of 1940, when he returned to America. He served with the U.S. Navy toward the end of World War II. He spent most of his adult life in Los Angeles, and was the author of three previous novels before the Passing Bells series: *Flickers*, *The Dead in Guanajuato*, and *The Extraordinary Seaman*. He died in 2004.

Of *The Passing Bells*, Phillip Rock wrote, “The idea came to me when I was a boy and stood with my father in a London street at the hour of eleven on the eleventh day of November and first heard that awful minute of total silence as the entire nation stood with bowed heads remembering their dead. It took a long time to put it on paper.” ~

The Passing Bells Series

THE GUNS OF AUGUST are rumbling throughout Europe in the summer of 1914, but war has not yet touched Abingdon Pryory. Here, at the grand summer home of the Greville family, the parties, dances, and romances play on. Alexandra Greville embarks on her debutante season, while brother Charles remains hopelessly in love with the beautiful, untitled Lydia Foxe, knowing his father, the Earl of Stanmore, will never approve of the match. Downstairs, the new servant Ivy struggles to adjust to the routines of the well-oiled household staff while shrugging off unwelcome attentions, and the arrival of American cousin Martin Rilke, a Chicago newspaperman, threatens to disrupt the daily routine.

But ultimately, the Great War will not be denied, shattering the social season and household tranquility, crumbling class barriers, and bringing its myriad horrors home—when what begins for the high-bred Grevilles as a glorious adventure soon begins unraveling the very fabric of British high society. ▸

The Passing Bells Series ***(continued)***

He drove up to Flanders in the early summer of 1921 knowing that it would be for the last time. He had finally, after nearly four years, reconciled himself to the unalterable fact that she was dead.

So begins this haunting novel of war's aftermath and the search for love and hope in a world totally changed. A generation has been lost on the Western Front. The dead have been buried, a harsh peace forged, and the howl of shells replaced by the wail of saxophones as the Jazz Age begins. But ghosts linger—that long-ago golden summer of 1914 tugging at the memory of Martin Rilke and his British cousins, the Grevilles.

From the countess to the chauffeur, the inhabitants of Abingdon Pryory seek to forget the past and adjust their lives to a new era in which old values have been irretrievably swept away. Charles Greville suffers from acute shell shock and his friend Colonel Wood-Lacy is exiled to faraway army outposts, while Alexandra Greville finds new love with an unlikely suitor; and to overcome the loss of his wife, Martin Rilke throws himself into reporting, discovering unsettling currents in the German political scene. Their stories unfold against England's most gracious manor house, the steamy nightclubs of London's Soho, and the despair of Germany. Lives are renewed, new loves found, and a future of peace and happiness is glimpsed—for the moment.

The final installment of the saga of the Grevilles of Abingdon begins in the early 1930s, as the dizzy gaiety of the Jazz Age comes to a shattering end. What follows is a decade of change and uncertainty, as the younger generation, born during or just after "the war to end all wars," comes of age: the beautiful Wood-Lacy twins, Jennifer and Victoria, and their passionate younger sister, Kate; Derek Ramsey, born only weeks after his father fell in France; and the American writer Martin Rilke, who will overcome his questionable heritage with the worldwide fame that will soon come to him. In their heady youth and bittersweet growth to adulthood, they are the future—but the shadows that touched the lives of the generation before are destined to reach out to their own, as German bombers course toward England.

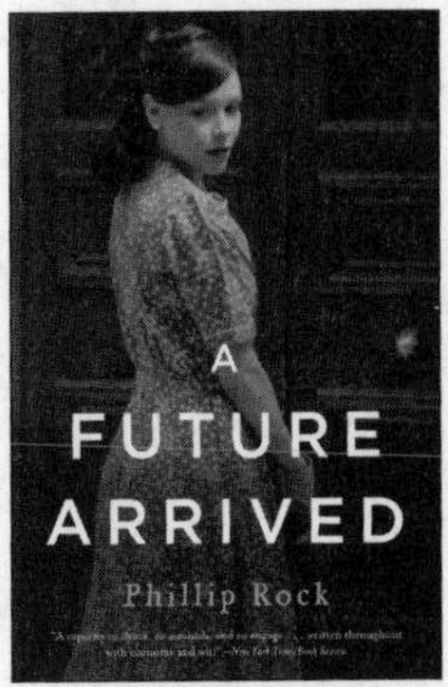

Discussion Questions

1. At the beginning of the novel, the earl suffers from a spell of severe chest pain. What stress seems to bring on this health scare?
2. "It's going to be a lousy decade," says Martin Rilke on air when civil war breaks out in Austria, giving hint to the arrived "future" of the book's title. First Martin, then Albert, witnessed the rise of the Nazi party and the chaos breaking loose in Europe. Do you think they have any idea of what is to come?
3. Charles Greville's path has not run as smoothly or to such noble heights as his parents once imagined, and the same applies to Alexandra's and William's occupations. Do you think the parents are disappointed with their children's choices?
4. Why do you think Albert Thaxton wants to pursue journalism when his way is paved to attend university?
5. In the novel, while some war-weary citizens would rather be distracted than think about another impending war, people like Martin and Albert gravitate toward the center of the action. Which reaction do you sympathize with more?
6. *All Quiet on the Western Front* by Erich Maria Remarque is a novel about the experiences of ordinary German soldiers during World War I. Published in 1928, it was

instantly an international success and is still known for its realistic portrayal of a soldier's experience. But in Berlin, in 1930, Albert Thaxton witnesses a riot caused by the release of the film version. Why are this antiwar book and film so unpopular in Germany?

7. Through Dulcie's activism we see a side of English society that the Grevilles are not privy to—unwed mothers, closed factories, lines of the unemployed, and protest marches. How does Colin's perspective change as a result of working with Dulcie?

8. Does Dulcie support the war? Why or why not? What insights do Jennifer Wood-Lacy's and Dulcie's efforts give into British society at this time?

9. After Neville Chamberlain signs the Munich Agreement, permitting Germany to annex Sudetenland in an attempt to avoid going to war, Albert Thaxton witnesses celebration in the streets of London. Demonstrating the appreciation of the peace movement, a woman sings the American antiwar song "I Didn't Raise My Boy to Be a Soldier," printed on the following page. Why does this political agreement inspire Jennifer to resign from the peace movement, while many of the activists are ecstatic?

10. What do you think compels some of the characters, like Colin and Derek, to enlist? What compels ►

Discussion Questions ***(continued)***

others, like Jennifer Wood-Lacy or Dulcie, to work for peace or social progress?

11. Why does Jennifer refuse Albert's proposal of marriage at first? Did you agree with her decision? How do the young couples in the novel—Jennifer and Albert, Derek and Valerie, Colin and Kate—find ways to reconcile the demands of a country at war with their personal lives?

12. How does Rock portray the technological and military innovations of the war, from Martin's radio broadcasts to the planes flown by Colin and Derek? How do those innovations affect the lives of the characters?

13. In what ways does the Passing Bells trilogy support or discredit romantic notions of war, honor, and patriotism?

The Wartime World of *A Future Arrived*

In Chapter 9 of *A Future Arrived*, Albert Thaxton witnesses celebration in the streets of London after Neville Chamberlain signs the Munich Agreement. A woman at a piano plays "I Didn't Raise My Boy to Be a Soldier," an American antiwar song that helped to strengthen the pacifist movement before the U.S. entered World War I.

"I Didn't Raise My Boy to Be a Soldier"

Ten million soldiers to the war have gone,
Who may never return again.
Ten million mothers' hearts must break,
For the ones who died in vain.
Head bowed down in sorrow in her lonely years,
I heard a mother murmur thro' her tears:

Chorus:
I didn't raise my boy to be a soldier,
I brought him up to be my pride and joy,
Who dares to put a musket on his shoulder,
To shoot some other mother's darling boy?
Let nations arbitrate their future troubles,
It's time to lay the sword and gun away,
There'd be no war today,
If mothers all would say,
I didn't raise my boy to be a soldier. ▸

What victory can cheer a mother's
heart,
When she looks at her blighted home?
What victory can bring her back,
All she cared to call her own?
Let each mother answer in the year
to be,
Remember that my boy belongs to me!

(Chorus)

Source: Al Pianadosi and Alfred Bryan, "I Didn't Raise My Boy to Be a Soldier," 1915. Recording: Edison Collection, Library of Congress.

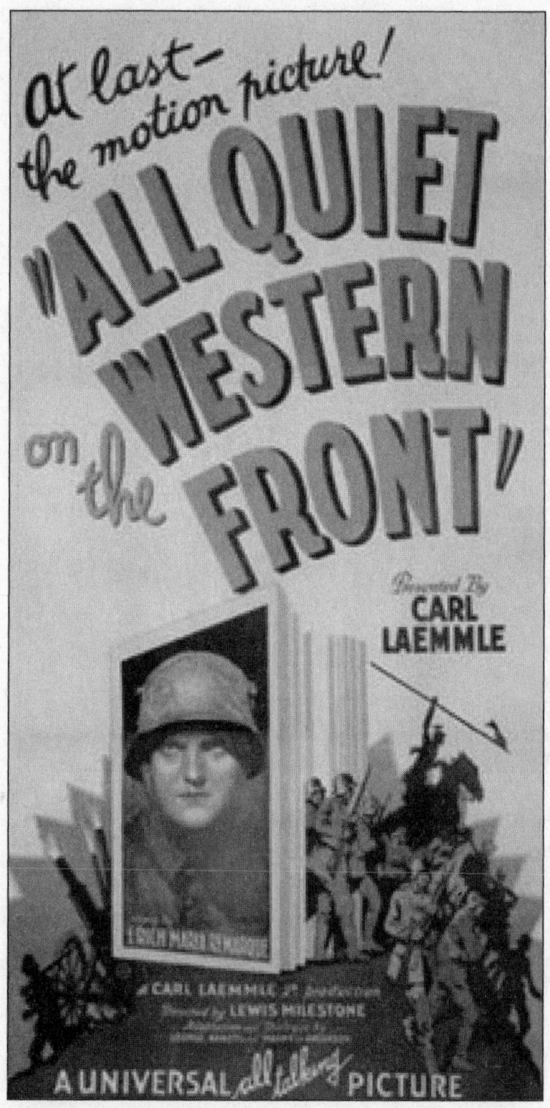

Poster for the movie All Quiet on the Western Front *(1930), featuring star Lew Ayres.*

World War II propaganda poster for the United States.

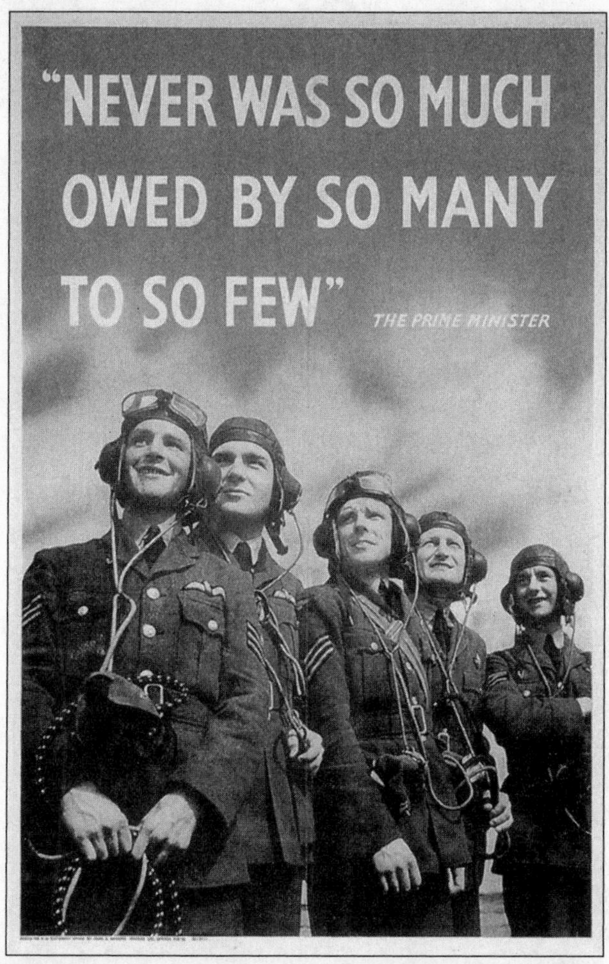

The line "Never in the field of human conflict was so much owed by so many to so few" is from a wartime speech made by British Prime Minister Winston Churchill on August 20, 1940. This line referred to the ongoing efforts of the Royal Air Force pilots who were fighting the Battle of Britain, the pivotal air battle with the German Luftwaffe. Britain expected a German invasion.

The RAF Supermarine Spitfire, used extensively during the Battle of Britain.

Shots from a Supermarine Spitfire Mark I hitting a Luftwaffe Heinkel He 111 (left) on its starboard quarter.